OXFORD WORLD'S CLA

THE BOOK OI
AND TRA

SIR JOHN MANDEVILLE'S *Book of Ma* was one of the most popular books in medieval Euro was composed in the 1350s, probably in northern France, and was soon translated into many languages. Mandeville's *Book* instructs the reader how to reach Jerusalem, and goes on to give an account of the wonders beyond the holy city. Mandeville tells us about the Sultan in Cairo, the Great Khan in China, and the mythical Christian prince Prester John. He also tells us about the many wonderful and monstrous peoples and animals living in the East: cannibals, Amazons, Pygmies, dog-headed semi-humans, and many more. We know almost nothing about the true identity of the *Book*'s author, although he says that he was from the English town of St Albans, and that he travelled the world for thirty-four years before returning home to write this account.

ANTHONY BALE is Professor of Medieval Studies at Birkbeck College, University of London. He is the author of *The Jew in the Medieval Book: English Antisemitisms 1350–1500* (2006) and *Feeling Persecuted: Christians, Jews and Images of Violence in the Middle Ages* (2010).

OXFORD WORLD'S CLASSICS

For over 100 years Oxford World's Classics have brought readers closer to the world's great literature. Now with over 700 titles—from the 4,000-year-old myths of Mesopotamia to the twentieth century's greatest novels—the series makes available lesser-known as well as celebrated writing.

The pocket-sized hardbacks of the early years contained introductions by Virginia Woolf, T. S. Eliot, Graham Greene, and other literary figures which enriched the experience of reading. Today the series is recognized for its fine scholarship and reliability in texts that span world literature, drama and poetry, religion, philosophy, and politics. Each edition includes perceptive commentary and essential background information to meet the changing needs of readers.

OXFORD WORLD'S CLASSICS

SIR JOHN MANDEVILLE

The Book of Marvels and Travels

Translated with an Introduction and Notes by
ANTHONY BALE

Great Clarendon Street, Oxford OX2 6DP
United Kingdom

Oxford University Press is a department of the University of Oxford.
It furthers the University's objective of excellence in research, scholarship, and education by publishing worldwide. Oxford is a registered trade mark of Oxford University Press in the UK and in certain other countries

First published as an Oxford World's Classics paperback 2012
Impression: 14

British Library Cataloguing in Publication Data
Data available

Library of Congress Cataloging in Publication Data
Data available

ISBN 978–0–19–960060–1

Printed in Great Britain by
Clays Ltd, Elcograf S.p.A.

ACKNOWLEDGEMENTS

I AM grateful to the many colleagues and friends who have responded to queries about various medieval languages, locales, and translation cruces, discussed Mandeville with me, and clarified points of information. Special thanks are due to John Bale, Ruth Bale, Rebecca Beasley, Alexandra Gillespie, Caroline Goodson, Mina Gorji, Iain Higgins, Elliot Kendall, Judith Luna, Megan McNamee, Jeff New, Timothy Phillips, Maryanne Rhett, Alan Stewart, Li Wei, and Jocelyn Wogan-Browne. Audiences at York and Munich provided much helpful feedback on drafts of this work. I am very grateful to The Queen's College, Oxford, for allowing me to work with its Mandeville manuscript. I am grateful to Matthew Francis and Faber & Faber Ltd for permission to quote from Matthew Francis's collection, *Mandeville* (London, 2007).

This book is for my dad John, the geographer.

CONTENTS

INTRODUCTION

> I, Sir John Mandeville, have travelled to here and here,
> seen this wonder and that, and returned home. Believe me.
> What I have said is true, or as good as, or was once.
>
> ...
>
> We have travelled across the world and received only
> sores, blisters, fever, wounds, chills, sunburn, hunger and thirst.
> We are tired. And this may be some spell or delusion.
>
> (Matthew Francis, *Mandeville*)

The Book of Marvels and Travels, supposedly written by a free-wheeling independent traveller, describes a perilous journey from Europe to Jerusalem and into Asia. It describes *jihadi* suicide-warriors in central Asia who believe in sacrificing themselves for the promise of heavenly virgins. It describes the dizzyingly rapid rise to power and wealth of the Chinese ruling class and free love, wife-swapping, and incest in south-east Asia. It describes the distinctive religious life of the people of Tibet, subject to the great ruler in Beijing. It describes the Jews' lack of a homeland, their national ambitions, their invention of a national language, and their difficult relations with their neighbours. The reader might be forgiven for thinking this book is a contemporary tabloid, a pulp chronicle of the early twenty-first century, but it is in fact a fourteenth-century text, and one of the 'bestsellers' of its day. *Plus ça change, plus c'est la même chose?*

Sir John Mandeville's *Book of Marvels and Travels* appeared in England and northern France in the second half of the fourteenth century and quickly became a key medieval European book, a widely read narrative of an Englishman's voyage to Constantinople, Jerusalem, and beyond. Mandeville's *Book* combines reports of foreign politics and non-Christian religions with stories, culled from geographies, natural histories, and romances, of extraordinary peoples and beasts. Mandeville includes accounts of the Sultan in Cairo, the Great Khan of Cathay and his vassals in Asia and Tartary, and the mythical Christian prince of the Far East, Prester John. These sit alongside descriptions of fantastical semi-human 'monstrous races' of Ethiopia, Armenia, India, and elsewhere.

The author-narrator, one John Mandeville, claims to be a knight from the southern English town of St Albans, Hertfordshire, travelling in the 1320s or 1330s, but it is clear that this persona is as fictional as some of the peoples he depicts. Meanwhile, his book, which became very popular in England and northern France from the 1360s, is a mixture of many kinds of learning: part travelogue, part fantasy, part scholarly treatise, part pilgrimage of both body and soul, part record of ethnographic desire, wit, and whimsy. Mandeville's *Book* was, quite simply, one of the most important books of later medieval and early modern Europe: it first circulated in French, Anglo-French, and English, but was translated into many languages, from Danish to Gaelic to Latin. A 'bestseller' in manuscript and print, Mandeville's *Book* reflects far more than medieval ideas of what lay beyond Europe on the eve of the Age of Discovery. Mandeville playfully but brilliantly explores and interrogates ideas of fantasy, good society, the human body, sexuality, magic, language, and belief.

In Search of John Mandeville

Our author says he is 'John Mandeville, knight . . . [who] was born in England in the town of St Albans' (p. 6). In later medieval St Albans, Canterbury, and Liège, if not elsewhere, John Mandeville was clearly believed to be a real person. The first fresco one sees upon entering the magnificent cathedral at St Albans is, in fact, an early modern epitaph to Mandeville, apparently copying a medieval tomb commemorating the writer. Thomas Walsingham (d. *c.*1422), a learned monk and historian who was master of the scriptorium and archives at St Albans, himself claimed Mandeville for St Albans,[1] and the abbey owned a copy of Mandeville's *Book*, in English, in the fifteenth century.[2] Around the year 1500 an imaginative monk from the Benedictine abbey in Canterbury wrote a Latin letter purporting to be from Mandeville.[3] Mandeville had at least two tombs (the one at St Albans

[1] London, British Library Cotton MS Claudius E.IV. f. 333r.

[2] Now London, British Library Egerton MS 1982. The abbey also owned an early Latin version, now London, British Library Royal MS 13.E.IX.

[3] Now Canterbury Cathedral Archives Add. MS 6. See M. C. Seymour, 'A Letter from Sir John Mandeville', *Notes and Queries*, 21 (1974), 326–8.

and one at Liège).[4] There were relics associated with him: a set of jewel-encrusted rings in St Albans, possibly an orb at Canterbury, and some pieces of reed (the *lignum aloes* described at p. 98) which were being peddled to the pious (or gullible) in the early fifteenth century and are mentioned in the Canterbury letter.[5] Other texts, including lapidaries and a herbal, were attributed to Mandeville.[6] The earliest surviving European globe, made in Nuremberg in 1492, mentions many of the real and mythical places 'visited' by Mandeville, and cites Mandeville as an authority, describing him as both 'knight' and 'physician'.[7]

There are three separate questions to consider here: first, did our author 'John Mandeville'—whoever he was—see what he claims to have seen? Secondly, who was 'John Mandeville'? And thirdly, where did the text come from?

The first issue is easily resolved: the *Book* comprises a wide range of material borrowed from elsewhere: Mandeville's *Book* is certainly not Mandeville's eyewitness account. This is not to say that its narrator did not undertake a journey to, say, the Mediterranean or the Holy Land, as medieval pilgrims, traders, soldiers, and mercenaries often did.[8] It is important to state, however, that Mandeville's *Book* was not a 'factual' account like a modern guidebook, but a more hybrid thing, mixing fact, error, and fantasy, mostly drawn from the reports of others (see below, 'Mandeville's Sources') and recounted by a narrator best described as playfully unreliable.

The second question, which Josephine Waters Bennett regarded as 'the problem of who wrote *Mandeville's Travels*', remains impossible to resolve conclusively but need not be regarded as a problem.[9] In what follows I shall offer only the briefest of summaries of the

[4] See M. C. Seymour's life of Mandeville in the *Oxford Dictionary of National Biography* (Oxford, 2004); Rosemary Tzanaki, *Mandeville's Medieval Audiences: A Study on the Reception of the* Book *of Sir John Mandeville (1371–1550)* (Aldershot, 2003), 66, 274.

[5] See Tzanaki, *Mandeville's Medieval Audiences*, 272–4; Seymour, 'A Letter'.

[6] See Tzanaki, *Mandeville's Medieval Audiences*, 273.

[7] See C. W. R. D. Moseley, 'Behaim's Globe and "Mandeville's Travels"', *Imago Mundi*, 33 (1981), 89–91.

[8] On medieval travel to the Holy Land see Nicole Chareyron, *Pilgrims to Jerusalem in the Middle Ages* (New York, 2000); Annabel Wharton, *Selling Jerusalem: Relics, Replicas, Theme Parks* (Chicago, 2006), 49–97.

[9] Josephine Waters Bennett, *The Rediscovery of Sir John Mandeville* (New York, 1954), p. i.

suggested identities of 'John Mandeville'; the notion that Mandeville was not the real name of our author is almost as old as his *Book*.

Since the Middle Ages the true identity of Mandeville has been associated with two men who lived in the city of Liège, the physician Jean de Bourgogne (a.k.a. Joannes ad Barbam, d. 1372) and Jean d'Outremeuse (1338–1400). Jean de Bourgogne, who wrote medical treatises and was named as patron, but not author, of Mandeville's *Book* by Outremeuse, cannot be convincingly identified as the *Book*'s author.[10] A story, which circulated widely from the fifteenth century, held that on his deathbed Bourgogne revealed himself to Outremeuse to be the real John Mandeville, an English knight who had been forced to flee England after killing a nobleman. This has led some scholars to suggest that Outremeuse was in fact the author. Outremeuse, a writer and historian of Liège, himself possibly wrote a later version of Mandeville's *Book* (the 'Liège' or 'interpolated' version), but certainly was not the original author.[11] Christiane Deluz, in her important recent work on Mandeville, agrees that the *Book* is connected to the city of Liège, arguing that the author was an Englishman living there in the 1350s.[12] Deluz posits that this Englishman took his book to both England and France, hence the ensuing complicated textual history in which various versions of Mandeville's *Book* developed in English, French, Anglo-French, and many other languages.

A third contender for the real Mandeville has been proposed by M. C. Seymour and John Larner as Jan de Langhe (Jean le Longue or Long John, d. 1388) of Ypres, a Franco-Flemish writer and monk. In the 1350s Langhe translated various writings (Marco Polo's account of the East, Odoric of Pordenone's account of missionizing in Asia, William of Boldensele's account of his pilgrimage to Palestine in the mid-1330s) into French, texts that were also used extensively by Mandeville.[13] But Langhe seems to have been a confident Latinist

[10] See Malcolm Letts, *Mandeville's Travels: Texts and Translations* (London, 1953), pp. xviii–xxiv; Bennett, *Rediscovery*, 147–58; Christiane Deluz, *Le Livre de Jehan de Mandeville: une géographie au XIVe siècle* (Leuven, 1998), 15–20; Iain Macleod Higgins, *Writing East: The Travels of Sir John Mandeville* (Philadelphia, 1997), 260–4.

[11] Bennett, *Rediscovery*, 158–69.

[12] Deluz, *Jehan de Mandeville*, 273–5.

[13] Seymour, 'Mandeville' in *ODNB*; John Larner, 'Plucking Hairs from the Great Cham's Beard', in Suzanne Akbari and Amilcare Iannucci (eds.), *Marco Polo and the Encounter of East and West* (Toronto, 2008), 133–55.

where Mandeville is tentative, and Langhe, based at the Benedictine monastery of St-Bertin near St-Omer in northern France, seems never to have travelled to England or anywhere far from his cloister. Nonetheless, Langhe certainly demonstrates that a mid-fourteenth-century monk could have extensive interests in those topics which preoccupied Mandeville: natural history, geography, marvels, and pilgrimage.

Whilst there were various Norman families living in medieval England with the name Mandeville—literally, *magna ville* ('large town')—Michael Bennett has recently identified one such aristocrat who fits the 'Anglo-French' royal moment from which Mandeville's *Book* emerged. Bennett has described a Hertfordshire man named John Mandeville who visited Isabelle of France, Edward II's widow, at Hertford Castle, near St Albans, with a brace of deer at Christmas 1357.[14] Bennett's evidence is intriguing, showing that this John Mandeville—apparently recently returned from France in 1356(ish), and attested to elsewhere as park-keeper of Enfield Chase, not far from St Albans—fits in terms of time, place, and social class (although this Mandeville was not a knight, he was of gentle birth). Whilst many have argued that the author of the *Book* must have been a monk in order to have access to such a diverse library, a well-educated and well-travelled reader (like Geoffrey Chaucer some twenty years later) could easily have developed the wide range of intellectual interests we see in the *Book*. Yet, as Bennett acknowledges, his identification of Mandeville is far from watertight and is at odds with earlier traditions of authorial attribution.

Mandeville's *Book* must have been composed, in the forms we now have it, after 1351 (the date of some of the translations by Jan de Langhe used by Mandeville) and probably after 1356 (the earliest date given in manuscript for the return of the narrator from his travels). Mandeville's description of the Jews' plans to harm Christendom (p. 105) might show some familiarity with accusations against the Jews as poisoners that developed with the European Black Death in 1348–50.[15] The earliest dated manuscript of the *Book* is from 1371, and was

[14] M. J. Bennett, 'Mandeville's Travels and the Anglo-French moment', *Medium Aevum*, 75 (2006), 273–92, at 273.

[15] See Séraphine Guerchberg, 'The Controversy over the Alleged Sowers of the Black Death in the Contemporary Treatises on Plague', in Sylvia Thrupp (ed.), *Change in Medieval Society: Europe North of the Alps 1050–1500* (New York, 1965), 208–24.

made in Paris.[16] Thus we can be sure that Mandeville's *Book*, for which no authorial or perfect manuscript survives, was first produced in the 1350s or 1360s. Michael Bennett's work on a recently rediscovered manuscript in private hands suggests that the *Book* originated in an Anglo-Norman, rather than French or Franco-Flemish, literary context, and was possibly circulating in England before it reached the Continent.[17] At this time French, or the dialect which might better be called the French of England or Anglo-French, remained the most prestigious literary and courtly language in England, even as English was replacing it as the language of administration and popular religion. Certainly, as Bennett has commented, '[t]he Channel was no cultural barrier' and 'the difficulty of assigning Mandeville to a literary culture conceived as *either* insular *or* continental testifies to the internationalism of francophone culture in England at this period'.[18]

A few words remain to be said about the mention of the English monastery of St Albans as the place of the author's origins. There is, throughout Mandeville's *Book*, a strong sense that our author/narrator was an Englishman, even if he was educated in France and/or writing in French. The perspective of the *Book* is largely (though often implicitly) an English or northern European one—for example, when the narrator demonstrates his awareness of the English letters 'thorn' and 'yogh' (p. 68). Ten manuscripts of the *Book* include an extravagant dedication to Edward III, King of England (r. 1327–77).[19] St Albans was a large and wealthy Benedictine abbey, a royal house closely connected to the English monarchy, and a centre of learning, undergoing a 'monastic renaissance' in the mid- to late fourteenth century.[20] The main feature of this environment was its commitment

[16] Now Paris, Bibliothèque Nationale MS nouv. acq. 4515, as edited and translated by Letts, *Mandeville's Travels*. This is a manuscript of the 'Continental' French version.

[17] Michael Bennett, 'France in England: Anglo-French Culture in the Reign of Edward III', in Jocelyn Wogan-Browne *et al.* (eds.), *Language and Culture in Medieval Britain: The French of England c. 1100–1500* (York, 2006), 320–3, at 325. London, British Library Microfilm RP3761. Bennett's article also usefully considers contacts between French and English soldiers, princes, and prisoners around the 1350s.

[18] Ibid. 321; see too Ardis Butterfield, *The Familiar Enemy: Chaucer, Language and Nation in the Hundred Years War* (Oxford, 2009).

[19] Although this is unlikely to be 'authorial'. See Jean de Mandeville, *Le Livre des Merveilles du Monde*, ed. Christiane Deluz, Sources d'Histoire Médiévale, 31 (Paris, 2000), 483.

[20] The term is from James Clark, *A Monastic Renaissance at St Albans: Thomas Walsingham and his Circle c.1350–1440* (Oxford, 2004).

to scholarship, including history, poetry, preaching, book production, and book decoration. St Albans had a well-known grammar school and the monastery would have supplied a monastic education, so it is certainly plausible that our author, whoever he was, was educated there.[21]

More specifically, St Albans was an appropriate place with which to *associate* a geographical text about the world, for it was the centre of mapping, in particular the mapping of the Holy Land; this was part of the legacy of the dazzling intellect of Matthew Paris (d. 1259), a monk of St Albans who made a major contribution to the development of cartography. Paris produced several maps at St Albans: a *mappa mundi* or world map (with Rome, rather than Jerusalem, near the centre), itineraries from London to Italy, maps of the Holy Land, and various maps of Britain. Paris was, like Mandeville, a dedicated collector and compiler of information, and his maps take the model of travel and pilgrimage as an organizing principle through which to understand time and place.[22] Paris's maps were hugely original, and demonstrate the intellectual vivacity of both Paris and his monastery at St Albans. In associating his *Book* with St Albans, Mandeville may have been recalling this famous place where the most modern knowledge about the world was ordered and disseminated. It would be in keeping with the spirit of Mandeville's playful sense of centre and periphery to be setting out from the edge of the world (England) and the centre of cartography (St Albans) to visit the centre of the world (Jerusalem) and the places evoked on the peripheries of world maps.

For all the attempts to pin Mandeville down to a time, place, and biography, it is worth recalling that it was not unusual for medieval writers to write anonymously or to insert cryptic and ludic references to themselves into their texts. For instance, Geoffrey Chaucer's narrative personae are famously unreliable, the moments when they seem most authentic being the moments at which they are most artificial or synthetic. The medieval author—that is, the person who wrote or composed a text—rarely felt the need to publicize his or her name at all.[23] Moreover, scribes often made changes during the

[21] See Bennett, *Rediscovery*, 192–3.

[22] See Daniel K. Connolly, *The Maps of Matthew Paris: Journeys through Space, Time and Liturgy* (Woodbridge, 2009).

[23] Indeed, Mandeville's very name may be based on an earlier French text, the *Roman de Mandevie*, an allegorical moral satire by Jean Dupin (*c.*1340).

copying process. Author-based criticism is no longer sovereign, and we are now able to consider things like Mandeville's *Book* through attention to sources, audiences, and interpretation rather than suppositions about authorial genius. John Mandeville is the narrator's persona with which we are invited to engage. Whilst the manuscripts of the *Book* disagree about even the most basic details of its author's life—his date of birth, the date of his voyage—this did not detract from the immense popularity and influence of his text.

Mandeville's Medieval Readers

Whatever the provenance of the text, several versions of Mandeville's *Book* quickly became extremely popular: by the 1360s the *Book* 'was part of the staple of the Parisian stationers', and was being read widely, by secular and religious audiences, in England, France, and the Low Countries.[24] Mandeville's *Book* was certainly widespread amongst the elite. For instance, an elegant copy of the book, dated 1371, was made for the French king Charles V, 'the Wise' (1338–80), whilst Jean, Duke of Berry (d. 1416), was given a magnificently illustrated copy by Jean 'the Fearless', Duke of Burgundy (1371–1419), in 1413 and Edward III of England's son, Thomas, Duke of Gloucester (1355–97), had a copy in his splendid and up-to-date library.[25] Yet non-elite and religious audiences also enjoyed Mandeville's *Book*: for example, John of Scardeburgh, a rector from Yorkshire, owned a copy in 1395, the Augustinians at Bolton in Yorkshire had a copy in the 1420s, and Richard Lee of the London Grocers' Guild signed his name in a copy around 1450.[26] By about 1415 the *Book* had been translated into further versions in English and French, into two German versions by Otto von Diemeringen (a monk, probably at

[24] M. C. Seymour, 'Mandeville in England: The Early Years', in Laden Niayesh (ed.), *A Knight's Legacy: Mandeville and Mandevillian Lore in Early Modern England* (Manchester, 2010), 15–27, at 15.

[25] Charles V's copy is now Paris, Bibliothèque Nationale MS nouv. acq. fr. 4515-4516. Jean of Berry's copy is now Paris, Bibliothèque Nationale MS fonds. fr. 2810, also including Marco Polo's travels and Jan de Langhe's texts about the East. On Thomas of Gloucester's copy see Bennett, *Rediscovery*, 208–9.

[26] On Scardeburgh see Bennett, *Rediscovery*, 209. Bolton Priory's copy is now London, British Library Harley MS 212. Richard Lee's copy is now London, British Library MS Harley 1739 (f. 77^v), a book featuring other owners' signatures including those of 'Alys Warwyk' and 'Alys Maynwaryng' (f. 77^v), revealing two of Mandeville's medieval female readers.

Metz) and Michel Velser (a Tyrolean nobleman), from German into Czech by Vavřinec of Březov (a courtier at Wenceslaus IV's Prague court), from French into Aragonese, and from English and French into Latin.[27]

Around 300 manuscripts and fragments survive, a huge number by medieval standards (in comparison, there are about eighty-three extant manuscripts of Chaucer's *Canterbury Tales*). In the print era Mandeville's *Book* became no less widely read, first printed around 1470 (in Dutch), illustrated in print in 1478 (in Germany), printed in eight languages before 1515, and in about sixty editions before 1600.[28] In English, following Richard Pynson's 1496 edition, the *Book* was printed at least twenty-two times before 1725. Such wide circulation and frequent translations produced huge variations in the texts: local additions and new legends were added, whilst dates, names, and places were altered, or often deleted. Mandeville's *Book* is itself a playful interrogation of 'right' and 'wrong' evidence, true and false reports, and, as Iain Higgins has persuasively suggested, 'there is every reason to argue that there is no necessarily "authoritative" text' of the *Book*.[29]

Some audiences responded to it as a straightforward pilgrimage guide, but others turned to it as a source of scientific and geographical information.[30] Some found romance and imaginative inspiration in the *Book*, whilst others understood its deeper theological significance as an examination of the many different places and various ways in which God makes Himself manifest on this planet. Mandeville's *Book* was known to Geoffrey Chaucer by the 1380s (Mandevillean lore appears in his 'Squire's Tale' and 'Knight's Tale') and one of Chaucer's contemporaries, the so-called *Gawain*-poet, probably writing in Cheshire or north Staffordshire, had almost certainly used Mandeville in his poem *Cleanness*.[31]

From early on, illustrations accompanied the *Book*. Mandeville's descriptions of unusual beings and strange beasts lend themselves to

[27] The versions of the *Book* are clearly and helpfully set out by Higgins, *Writing East*, 22–3.

[28] See Bennett, *Rediscovery*, 230, 335–405.

[29] Higgins, *Writing East*, 17.

[30] See Tzanaki, *Mandeville's Medieval Audiences*.

[31] J. W. Bennett, 'Chaucer and Mandeville's Travels', *Modern Language Notes* 68 (1953), 531–4; Carleton Brown, 'A Note on the Dependence of *Cleanness* on the *Book of Mandeville*', *Periodical of the Modern Language Association of America* 19 (1904), 150–3.

illustration, akin to the illustrated bestiaries and maps that were a staple of thirteenth- and fourteenth-century libraries. A magnificent 'textless' version was made, possibly in Prague in the early fifteenth century, in which Mandeville's written words disappear altogether in favour of beautiful *grisaille* scenes from the narrative.[32]

Mandeville's Sources

The Argentinian writer Jorge Luis Borges is famously reported as once having said 'I have always imagined that Paradise will be a kind of library'. Mandeville's world, from St Albans to Paradise, is likewise 'a kind of library': a library according to the medieval definition, as a storehouse of reading, an archive of memories, and the whole of history in written form. Mandeville's *Book* is entertaining and wide-ranging, but it is far from 'original' as that term is understood today: in fact, the majority of the material in it was taken from texts frequently read in monasteries and universities in fourteenth-century France and England. This is not to accuse Mandeville of plagiarism: rather, the *Book* is in keeping with medieval habits of *compilatio* (compiling) and *ordinatio* (arranging), reorganizing others' material in new ways. By taking the words of others and putting them into a new frame, Mandeville was merely doing what it took, in medieval literary culture, to gain *auctoritas*: the authority attributed to someone who has repeated the authoritative words of others.

What, then, is the 'originality' of Mandeville? He certainly took great pains to reorganize his material in new ways, moving between different registers and perspectives. His *Book* insists on the unstable quality of knowledge and the relative quality of a group's social, religious, and political values. He wittily juxtaposes marvels with facts, and contrasts 'true' faith with a wide range of non-Christians and semi-Christian peoples in order to explore the hypocrisy and failings of European, Christian society. The authorial asides, the narrator's 'I', the suasions of eyewitness ('I have seen . . .', 'We would never have believed it if we hadn't seen it') and the moments at which Mandeville describes what cannot be proved ('There are many

[32] Now London, British Library Add. MS 24189. See *The Travels of Sir John Mandeville: A Manuscript in the British Library*, ed. Josef Krása, trans. Peter Kussi (New York, 1983), with facsimiles of its images and a full introduction on the manuscript's art-historical background.

countries and marvels I have not seen, therefore I can't describe them correctly')—these all complicate the 'authoritative' reliability of the text.

Scholarship on Mandeville's sources has located the borrowings, innovations, and misunderstandings the author made in his translation and rewritings.[33] The two main sources used by Mandeville for the description of the Holy Land and the regions beyond are Odoric of Pordenone's *Relatio* (*The Account*, *c.*1330) and William of Boldensele's *Liber de quibusdam ultramarinis partibus* (*The Book of Certain Regions Overseas*, *c.*1336). Odoric, a Venetian Franciscan friar who was a missionary in Russia and Asia, described various Eastern places and *mirabilia* (wonders or marvels), basing much of his account on Marco Polo's famous journey of *c.*1298 from Venice via Palestine to the Mongol court. Odoric's narrative was followed by Mandeville for the account of Ararat (p. 70), the ox-worshippers of Lombe (p. 76), the idolaters of Ma'bar (p. 77), the naked cannibals of Lamuri (p. 78), the vegetable lamb of Caldilhe (p. 104), Prester John's kingdom of Pentoxoire (p. 106), and the original 'assassins', the murderers employed by Catolonabes (p. 110). From William, a German Dominican who undertook an unauthorized pilgrimage to the Holy Land in 1330, Mandeville took much of the material on Palestine and the holy sites of the Near and Middle East: the churches and relics of Constantinople (p. 12), the Bosphorus and Cyprus (pp. 16–17), the description of Cairo (p. 19), the routes over Sinai to Jerusalem (p. 35), the holy places of Jerusalem (pp. 39–49), and some of the sites at Saidnaya and in Lebanon (p. 18). Both Odoric's account of marvels and William's more pious journey had been translated into French by Jan de Langhe at St-Bertin, and it was Langhe's French versions with which Mandeville undoubtedly worked.

Mandeville, however, neither slavishly lifted material nor relied on these two texts alone. The *Book* is indebted to wide-ranging and cosmopolitan reading. Key Christian authorities were consulted—such as Isidore of Seville, Josephus, and Orosius—as were those encyclopedic texts which would have been held by almost any

[33] See in particular Albert Bovenschen, 'Untersuchungen über Johann von Mandeville und die Quellen seiner Reisebeschreibung', *Zeitschrift der Gesellschaft für Erdkunde zu Berlin*, 23 (1888), 177–306; Deluz, *Le Livre*, 429–91; Tamarah Kohanski and C. David Benson (eds.), *The Book of John Mandeville* (Kalamazoo, Mich., 2007), appendix (see http://www.lib.rochester.edu/camelot/teams/tkap1.htm).

monastery—in particular, Bartholomew the Englishman's *De proprietatibus rerum* (*c.*1240), Vincent of Beauvais' *Speculum historiale* and *Speculum naturale* (*c.*1250, from which Mandeville took, amongst other things, his accounts of Mount Athos, the legend of the Amazons, and the monstrous races of the East), and Brunetto Latini's *Livres dou Trésor* (*c.*1265). Mandeville's *Book* also often turns to the Bible (particularly in the account of the Holy Land, essentially a digest of biblical and quasi-biblical sites), to exemplary tales told by preachers, to Alexander romances, to historical works including *The Letter of Prester John* (*c.*1165), to saints' lives as given in Jacobus de Voragine's *Golden Legend* (*c.*1270), and, notably, to a scientific work, John of Holywood's *De sphaera* (*c.*1220), a university 'set-text' from which Mandeville gleaned his account of the firmament (pp. 79–82).[34]

Also integral to Mandeville's *Book* is the figure of Prester John, the mythical Christian prince of the East and one of Mandeville's most vivid characters. The myth of Prester John was widespread in medieval Europe, based on a series of twelfth-century letters supposedly sent from the Eastern Christian Prester John to the Emperor of Byzantium. The main letter describes the huge extent of Prester John's power and territory and the luxury and wealth of his palace's decoration.[35] Scholars now tend to explain the letters as rather clumsy fabrications designed to offer hope to increasingly disheartened Crusaders and the failing Latin Crusader state in the Middle East. The letter circulated widely in later medieval Europe, and Mandeville took from it his description of Prester John's kingdom, as well as some details such as the accounts of the Fountain of Youth (p. 76) and the sandy sea (pp. 107–8).

Thus Mandeville emerges as a well-read figure, interested in translation and compilation, immersed more in French texts than Latin, and adapting Latinate, clerical material to vernacular, 'romance' tastes (and vice versa). In placing such a wide and diverse range of sources together, Mandeville's *Book* articulates a kind of relativism (or 'proto-multiculturalism') about the world, its religions,

[34] For full accounts of Mandeville's sources and his use of them see Higgins, *Writing East*.

[35] On Prester John see Michael Uebel, *Ecstatic Transformation: On the Uses of Alterity in the Middle Ages* (Basingstoke, 2005), with a full English translation and discussion of the Latin *Letter of Prester John* (pp. 155–60).

and its various peoples, a world uniquely open to dozens of seductive, if morally ambiguous, versions of 'good' and 'true' faith.

Mandeville as Crusader, Pilgrim, and Armchair Traveller

Mandeville's voice is that of a didactic, quasi-factual 'guidebook' for the armchair traveller, sometimes scientific, sometimes moralizing, often indebted to the romantic and fantastical. His *Book* opens stridently with crusading, that most medieval of bloody pastimes. Yet the Holy Land sites visited by our narrator are often nothing more than memories of the Crusaders' glories—by the 1350s many of these churches and castles had become mosques or houses, or had been reduced to rubble. Mandeville insists that 'every decent Christian who is able and has the wherewithal should fortify himself to conquer our rightful heritage', and that 'we must demand the inheritance bequeathed to us by our Father and wrest it from the foreigners' hands' (p. 6). The Christian Latin Kingdom of Jerusalem had been established by European Crusaders after the First Crusade of 1096; most of the churches, monasteries, and castles described in Palestine by Mandeville date from this period, during which the Holy Land became a colonial territory run by European Christians. The Crusader Kingdom may have inspired fervour, and certainly moved many pilgrims to visit and many men to take up arms to protect it; but it did not endure. Jerusalem fell to the Muslim warrior Saladin in 1189, and the last mainland vestige of the Crusader kingdom, the magnificently fortified city of Acre, was taken by the Mameluk Arabs in 1291. The Crusader orders of Hospitaller and Templar knights were forced to reconstitute themselves in Cyprus and Rhodes. Yet despite its ultimate and relatively swift failure, crusading provided European Christians with an enduring imagery and militaristic vocabulary of sacred politics.[36]

Mandeville's *Book*, as a creative and spiritual endeavour, has as much to do with realms of the imagination as cities visited in commerce and conflict. It was one particularly widely translated version of the many travel narratives and geographical artefacts which described a marvellous and moralized version of the world. The *ur*-text of such

[36] On the development of this imagery and vocabulary of crusading see Geraldine Heng, *Empire of Magic: Medieval Romance and the Politics of Cultural Fantasy* (New York, 2003).

imaginative geography was the *Natural History* of Pliny the Elder (d. 79 CE), a remarkably influential catalogue of zoological and geographical observation and fantasy. Pliny's description of the 'human freaks' of Ethiopia—'races without noses and with completely flat faces', 'people [who] breathe through a single hole and similarly suck in drink by means of oat straws', 'a race of pygmies', and so on—takes its place in Mandeville's *Book* (pp. 86, 87, 89).[37] St Augustine had used Pliny, along with other classical authorities, in his *City of God* (*c.* 413), where he described pygmies, hermaphrodites, and others to launch an important discussion of God's design of mankind. Augustine argued that 'anyone who is born anywhere as a man (that is, as a rational and mortal animal), no matter how unusual he may be to our bodily senses in shape, colour, motion, sound, or in any natural power or part or quality, derives from the original and first-created man; and no believer will doubt this'.[38] Mandeville's insistence on the rationality of many of the monstrous peoples he describes can clearly be traced back to this attitude.

Mandeville's *Book* is also related to medieval travellers' itineraries, highly sequential lists of *loci* (places) to be visited in order to perform the correct kind of pilgrimage. Such pilgrimages could be 'real', undertaken on foot, or 'imagined', contemplated from home through books, images, maps, and liturgy. The precursor of the Stations of the Cross still venerated in many Christian traditions, these itineraries organized the spaces of a church, monastery, or city as a route through a sacred landscape. The ideal *itinerarium* was fixed on its *telos*, its sacred end-point—usually Jerusalem, Calvary, or a saint's shrine like that of St James (Santiago, Spain) or St Thomas Becket (Canterbury, England). This is certainly the model that Mandeville's *Book* imitates in its first dozen chapters, which are mostly concerned with the best ways of reaching Jerusalem, organizing the route as a kind of holy information (or *sapientia*). However, *sapientia* gives way to *curiositas*, literally 'curiosity' or, in Christian Zacher's words, a 'dangerous diversion for wayfaring Christians', 'a wandering, errant, and unstable frame of mind . . . best exemplified in metaphors of motion and in the act of travel'. As Zacher says, Mandeville 'advertises a pilgrimage and

[37] Pliny the Elder, *Natural History: A Selection*, ed. and trans. John F. Healy (London, 1991), 70–1.

[38] Augustine, *The City of God against the Pagans*, ed. and trans. R. W. Dyson (Cambridge, 1998), 708.

something more, but by the final chapter it is the curious journey and Mandeville's curious speculations that have dominated the book'.[39] Our pilgrim wanders past Jerusalem, into seductively dangerous, licentious, and fascinating Eastern realms. These have more in common with romances of Cockaigne, the medieval fantasy-land of plenty, than the landscapes of the Bible.[40] Mandeville's *Book* heads in the direction of the never-reached Earthly Paradise (pp. 119–21), and the realm of Prester John, whose kingdom is directly opposite England on the other side of the globe (p. 80). Travel, in Mandeville's *Book*, is not so much a way to see the world but an allegory of how people understand their place amongst others in this world. Likewise, the distinctive Egyptian, Hebrew, and Saracen alphabets included by Mandeville (pp. 29, 54, 68) may bear little relation to those they purport to represent, but they do reveal Mandeville's interest in cultural relativity and his respect for other kinds of learning.

Whilst Mandeville is not always polite about foreigners—describing some as unattractive or as having foul manners—his *Book* avoids, on the whole, damning people simply on the basis of their physical appearance. For instance, Mandeville describes Ethiopians who 'have only one foot and they get about so quickly on it that it's a wonder to behold; it's a large foot, which can provide shade and cover the entire body from the sun' (p. 72), here emphasizing the marvellous, rather than corrupt, possibilities of their bodies. Likewise, the southern Ethiopians are, says Mandeville, 'utterly black' (p. 72), but no further comment is made. People living near the Indus 'have a foul yellow-and-green complexion' and are sluggish (p. 74), but this is due to planetary disposition, rather than what we might now call ethnicity or biology. An emerging racial theory, articulated in Bartholomew the Englishman's thirteenth-century encyclopedia, held that black people were produced by the hot weather, saying, for example, that Ethiopians are blue because the sun 'roasts and toasts' them. He goes on to say that 'the colour of men sheweth the strengthe of the sterre', that is to say, human complexion is dictated by the sun. Conversely, Christ was believed to have been the whitest, 'fairest',

[39] Christian Zacher, *Curiosity and Pilgrimage: The Literature of Discovery in Fourteenth-Century England* (Baltimore, 1976), 21, 152.

[40] On Cockaigne romances, which feature some of the mythical lands and peoples described by Mandeville, see Hermann Pleij, *Dreaming of Cockaigne: Medieval Fantasies of the Perfect Life*, trans. Diana Webb (New York, 2001).

and 'cleanest' human who ever lived, as described in popular religious texts.[41] Mandeville reflects a characteristically medieval emphasis on racial taxonomy, of dividing peoples up according to their physical appearance and identifying the differences between them. Yet he makes little attempt to extend this categorization to biological or moral essentialism, usually letting the audience interpret these peoples' condition. Mandeville seems to take his cue from Isidore of Seville's fascinating account, in which physical difference is merely a way of distinguishing people from each other: 'so that we see the curls of the Germans, the mustaches and goatees of the Goths, the tattoos of the Britons. The Jews circumcise the foreskin, the Arabs pierce their ears, the Getae with their uncovered heads are blond, the Albanians shine with white hair. The Moors have bodies black as night, while the skin of the Gauls is white . . .'[42] It is a sign of our own prejudices if we are surprised that medieval people were not always as racist as we imagine, or that they did not think of 'race' as rigidly as we might. We might even see Mandeville as an early kind of cosmopolitan, his viewpoint privileging the East over Europe:[43] in structuring the *Book* through Jerusalem-bound itineraries and distant Eastern lands, Mandeville's Europe starts to appear provincial, unexciting, and even naive. As he says, 'people should not look down upon other people because of their different laws, because we don't know whom God loves or hates' (p. 117).

The main exception to Mandeville's perspective of tolerant curiosity is the Jews: they are, by his account, the tormentors and killers of Christ, concealers of the True Cross, and reside beyond the mountains of Gog and Magog, speaking their secret language and waiting for the 'era of Antichrist' when they will 'do much harm to Christians' (p. 105). The Jews in the *Book* are neither

[41] *On the Properties of Things: John Trevisa's Translation of Bartholomaeus Anglicus De Propretatibus Rerum*, ed. M. C. Seymour *et al.*, 3 vols. (Oxford, 1975), 2. 754. See further Linda Lomperis, 'Medieval Travel Writing and the Question of Race', *Journal of Medieval and Modern Studies*, 31 (2001), 149–64; Geraldine Heng, 'The Invention of Race in the European Middle Ages, I: Race Studies, Modernity and the Middle Ages', *Literature Compass*, 8 (2011), 315–31, who comments that 'Elite human beings of the 14th century have a hue, and it is white' (p. 317).

[42] *The Etymologies of Isidore of Seville*, ed. and trans. Stephen A. Barney *et al.* (Cambridge, 2006), 386.

[43] Karma Lochrie, 'Provincializing Medieval Europe: Mandeville's Cosmopolitan Utopia', *Periodical of the Modern Languages Association of America*, 124 (2009), 592–9.

monsters—through whom curious lessons can be taught—nor are they a parallel society, like the Saracens or Tartars. Jews and Judaism are singled out for special vilification because, to Mandeville's mind, whereas the Saracens and others do not yet have Christianity but do have some aspects of it, the Jews *rejected* Christ. For Mandeville, the Jews 'will not believe that Jesus Christ was sent from God' (p. 63), whereas other non-Christians are yet to receive, or be turned to, Christianity.

Mandeville's Intellectual and Cultural Influence

Some of the most fabulous travellers of the globe have read Mandeville in preparation for their voyages and discoveries: for instance, Christopher Columbus on Hispaniola, Walter Ralegh in Guiana, and Martin Frobisher on Baffin Island. Other kinds of travellers—travellers of the mind—have also turned to Mandeville for models of alternative ways of living: Leonardo da Vinci in Milan, Thomas More in Utopia, and Jonathan Swift in Lilliput. It is clear from Ralegh's account of the marvellous peoples he did (and did not) encounter in Guiana that he was unsure what to make of Mandeville, 'whose reports were holden for fables many yeeres, and yet since the East Indies were discovered, we find his relations true of such things as heretofore were held incredible'.[44] The 'Age of Discovery' held to have been inaugurated by Columbus's journey to the New World did not herald a break with older kinds of knowledge about travel, although it did make incredible things suddenly plausible. Stephen Greenblatt has eloquently described how the colonial cultures of sixteenth-century Europe remained captivated and guided by Mandeville, so much so that Samuel Purchas (d. 1626), the English editor of geographical texts, could call Mandeville 'the greatest *Asian* Traueller that euer the World had'.[45]

Many early visitors to the Americas represented cannibalism as both a horrifying and seductive feature of the New World, profoundly

[44] Sir Walter Ralegh, 'The Discoverie of the Large, Rich, and Beautifull Empire of Guiana', in Richard Hakluyt (ed.), *The Principal Navigations, Voyages, Traffiques and Discoveries of the English Nation*, 12 vols. (Glasgow, 1903), 10. 349–50.

[45] Stephen Greenblatt, *Marvelous Possessions: The Wonder of the New World* (Oxford, 1991), esp. 28–33; Samuel Purchas, *Purchas his Pilgrimes* (London, 1625), 3. 65.

reminiscent of Mandeville's fascination with this kind of eating (pp. 79, 113).[46] William Shakespeare, writing *c.*1603, has Othello reading something like Mandeville to Desdemona, captivating her with descriptions of 'the Cannibals that each other eat, | The Anthropophagi, and men whose heads | Do grow beneath their shoulder'.[47] Similarly, the New World did not disprove medieval fantasies, but rather was understood as physical, geographical evidence of these fictions: enduring examples include Patagonia, named after terrifying monsters in the Spanish romance *Primaleón* (1512); the Antilles, named after the legendary land of Antilia from medieval maps; and the River Amazon, which takes its name from the mythical female warriors. Legendary places, from Mandeville or similar texts, were thus made real in Europe's encounter with the Americas;[48] the only framework for narrating discovery was that provided by books like Mandeville's. The Spanish explorer Ponce de Leon (d. 1521), who in 1513 led the first European expedition to Florida, was searching for the Fountain of Youth (mentioned by Mandeville, p. 76). Likewise, the governor of Cuba sent the *conquistador* Hernán Cortés (d. 1547) in search of people with dog-heads (for Mandeville's comments on whom see p. 85). Such examples show how what may appear to us as romantic fantasies could motivate people to risk their all—and seek their fortunes—on gruelling journeys. The Portuguese missionary Francisco Álvares (d. 1541) wrote the first eyewitness account of Ethiopia and made a major contribution to European knowledge of Africa, but the title of his book, the *Verdadeira Informação das Terras do Preste João das Indias* (*The True Relation of the Lands of Prester John of the Indies*, 1526–7), harks back to an older 'medieval' view of what lay beyond Europe (see pp. 106–9).

[46] Mario Klarer, 'Cannibalism and Carnivalesque: Incorporation as Utopia in the Early Image of America', *New Literary History*, 30 (1999), 389–410; see also Lynn Tarte Ramey, 'Monstrous Alterity in Early Modern Travel Accounts: Lessons from the Ambiguous Medieval Discourse on Humanness', *L'Esprit Créateur*, 48 (2008), 81–95.

[47] *Othello*, I. iii. 143–4. Similarly, Shakespeare's *The Tempest* abounds in Mandevillian creatures, 'men | Whose heads stood in their breasts' and 'a most delicate monster' with 'four legs and two voices' (III. iii. 52, II. ii. 83). See further Gordon McMullan, 'Stage-Mandevilles: The Far East and the Limits of Representation in the Theatre, 1621–2002', in Niayesh (ed.), *A Knight's Legacy*, 173–94.

[48] See Nicholás Wey Gómez, *The Tropics of Empire: Why Columbus Travelled South to the Indies* (Cambridge, Mass., 2008), esp. 161–228; Michael Householder, *Inventing Americans in the Age of Discovery: Narratives of Encounter* (Farnham, 2011), esp. 21–48 on Mandeville.

Whilst not all such accounts are directly traceable to Mandeville's *Book*, they do show how the reality of European colonialism was accompanied by and predicated on earlier fantasies and reports: of Mandeville, Marco Polo, the *Bestiary* (the medieval book of animal lore), Pliny, and others. Those undertaking the famous voyages of discovery to the New World could only have expected to meet the marvellous peoples they had read so much about, and with whose doings they had become so familiar.[49] That said, doubts were raised about the authenticity and validity of Mandeville's *Book* by early readers. For example, Richard Hakluyt (d. 1616), the English geographer whose massive travel-writing compilation *The Principall Navigations* (1589) was reprinted many times, described Mandeville as *fabulosus*—that is, fabled—and he dropped Mandeville from the second, expanded edition of his collection (1598).[50] In Ben Jonson's *The New Inn* (1629), Mandeville is cited as the author of silly fantasies, 'Colonies of beggars, tumblers, ape-carriers . . . savages . . . odd discoveries', to which fools become 'addicted'.[51] Othello's reading of a text like Mandeville to Desdemona suggests not only the sixteenth-century currency of such books in the Age of Discovery but also the powerful pull of otherworldly romance.

How far, then, can we say that medieval and early modern people 'believed' in what they read in Mandeville's *Book*? We cannot be sure. However, monsters, prodigies, miracles, and wonders provided the backdrop (or, rather, the punctuation) to medieval life. In medieval Christianity, as in the Age of Discovery, the experience of the unexpected, whether a divine miracle or a new-found cannibal, fed an appetite for astonishment, for the sudden irruption of the marvellous into the everyday. At several places in his *Book* Mandeville draws our attention to the pleasures of wonder and novelty (pp. 6, 124), and it was a commonplace of medieval learning that what is strange, new, and shocking is what is most memorable, most instructive. The extravagant aestheticization of the marvellous peoples we meet in Mandeville's *Book* shows delight in unfamiliarity and

[49] See John Block Friedman, *The Monstrous Races in Medieval Art and Thought*, 2nd edn. (Syracuse, NY, 2007), 197–202.

[50] See C. W. R. D. Moseley, '"Whet-stone leasings of old *Maundeuile*": Reading the *Travels* in Early Modern England', in Niayesh (ed.), *A Knight's Legacy*, 28–50, at 33–5.

[51] McMullan, 'Stage-Mandevilles', 174.

strangeness, and such wonder profoundly informed the travellers to the New World. A French writer, Jean de Léry (d. 1613), visiting Brazil in the 1560s, found the term 'New World' most fitting, as it caused him to revise 'the opinion that I formerly had of Pliny and others when they describe foreign lands, because I have seen things as fantastic and prodigious as any of those—once thought impossible—that they mention'.[52] This rhetoric of fabulous surprise, and its implications of abundant possibility, shows how the early modern discovery of new lands held within it a kind of proof positive of Mandeville's marvellous world.

[52] Lorraine Daston and Katharine Park, *Wonders and the Order of Nature, 1150–1750* (New York, 1998), 147–8.

NOTE ON THE TEXT AND TRANSLATION

THIS new translation of Mandeville's *Book* is designed to provide non-specialist readers with an approachable, representative text of this fascinating medieval source. The emphasis of this translation is on accessibility and readability. I have sought to preserve the forceful, often opinionated narrative voice of the book, and to maintain the modulation (or inconsistency) of the narrator: instructive (sometimes bossy, never boring), omniscient, learned, but often subjective and playfully spurious. Place-names and other proper nouns are modernized where they are one step away from a clear contemporary reference (e.g. 'Beruth' becomes 'Beirut', 'Iherusalem' becomes 'Jerusalem'; where they exist, I have used the English form for place-names, so 'Trebizond' rather than contemporary Turkish 'Trabzon', 'Jerusalem' rather than modern Hebrew 'Yerushalayim'). However, more fantastical places have retained their medieval names, so 'Milstorak' remains 'Milstorak'—Mandeville's *Book* obliges its readers to move between the actual and the fantastical, never entirely sure where the former ends and the latter begins. Syntax of the translation is organized according to the modern idiom, but the distinctive paratactic style ('And . . . and . . . and . . .') has partly been retained, to give a sense of Mandeville's prose voice with its distinctive lists. The Middle English pronoun 'man' (and Anglo-French *homme*) is often used as the impersonal pronoun and has been translated in most places as 'one' or 'people', except where it is clear that Mandeville is talking specifically about men and not women.

Where the medieval text has biblical quotations, these are translated after the Douay–Rheims Bible, to give a sense of the difference in register between biblical quotation and reportage (where book names differ from those of the Revised Version the latter are supplied in brackets in the Notes), with the Latin quotation remaining as given in the Middle English text (Mandeville and his scribes were not always the most reliable Latinists!). References to the *Bestiary* are taken from the excellent Aberdeen Bestiary website (http://www.abdn.ac.uk/bestiary/).

The title I have given my version reflects the kind of titles, if given, used in the Middle Ages. Mandeville's *Book* is usually referred to as a 'book of marvels' (for example, *Sr John Maundeville de mervailles de mounde* in an Anglo-French manuscript, *tractato de la piu maravegliose cose* . . . in Italian printed editions, *de miraculis mundi* in a Latin manuscript) or by its author's name (*Ce livre est appelle Mandevill'*, 'a lytell treatyse or booke named Iohan Mandevyll').

Mandeville's *Book* is neither a consistent text nor, in Middle English and medieval Anglo-French, an easy read. On the contrary: the manuscript history of Mandeville's *Book* wanders almost as much as its narrator. I have by no means sought to present a critical edition in what follows. I have edited the medieval English and Anglo-French texts, focusing on readability and economy, whilst acknowledging that medieval readers not only accepted but also repeated 'mistakes': Mandeville's is a text in which omission, digression, divergence, and error generate meaning. All translations are in and of themselves new versions and I am unabashed about that here; my Explanatory Notes seek mostly to give indications of where further information can be found, to provide details of historical context, and to identify some of the notable variants in the text's manuscript traditions and translations. Of course, most medieval readers did not set their copies of Mandeville's *Book* side-by-side with others to compare them, as the modern scholar might.

The main source text for this translation is the 'Defective' Middle English version of the Insular text. The base manuscript I have consulted is Oxford, The Queen's College MS 383, probably dating from about 1400, read with related manuscripts.[1] There are slightly earlier versions of Mandeville's *Book*, but the 'Defective' version has been chosen simply because, based on surviving manuscripts, it was the most widely read version of Mandeville in Europe, it was the

[1] M. C. Seymour (ed.), *The Defective Version of Mandeville's Travels*, Early English Text Society OS 319 (Oxford, 2002). The 'Defective' version was certainly made after 1377, as it mentions the Pope being at Rome (p. 124), whereas before this date Pope Gregory XI had resided at Avignon. Seymour's edition is based on Queen's College MS 383, and I have largely followed Seymour's emendations. This small manuscript was written by a scribe named 'Edward Jenkyn'; accompanying Mandeville's text in this manuscript are a Sarum calendar, the *Spirit of Guy* (a religious prose text written in the same hand and attributed to Mandeville at f. 164v), three charms, and a recipe. However, the book evidently circulated for some time in booklets before being bound together in its present form. The manuscript is good quality, and has some decoration and illumination. The text of Mandeville was glossed twice, once by the medieval scribe (noting major sights and subjects) and again in the early modern period. Two marginal *nota bene!* marks are included in the text here.

dominant English-language version of the text from the fourteenth to the eighteenth centuries, and it was the source of Richard Pynson's later printed edition of the *Book* which was influential in the early modern period and was the base-text for subsequent English printed editions.[2] Some thirty-seven surviving manuscripts or extracts of manuscripts of the 'Defective' version survive.[3] Thus, this is the single most widespread version of Mandeville's *Book*, and represents Mandevillean lore known most widely; moreover, it is amongst the more economical and readable versions of Mandeville's *Book*.

The source of the 'Defective' version is the Insular text, written in the French of England, or 'Anglo-French'. In general, the 'Defective' version follows the Insular closely, compressing some information, tending to omit some of the more strident material on crusading and conversion, as well as 'defectively' omitting the account of Egypt. The 'Defective' version is also in places over-brief and occasionally confused, and so has been supplemented with its Anglo-French source (see Jean de Mandeville, *Le Livre des Merveilles du Monde*, ed. Christiane Deluz, Sources d'Histoire Médiévale, 31 (Paris, 2000), abbreviated henceforth as *Livre*). I have used my editorial judgement to decide where to add material from the Anglo-French version, and in a few places omissions by the Defective version's translator have been silently inserted in the text or noted in the endnotes. At other points I have left the text's inconsistencies intact, to retain the sometimes disorientating nature of Mandeville's narration. The original subject-headings of the 'Defective' version have been used.

The missing account of Egypt and Sicily of the 'Defective' version is almost certainly due to a missing quire (a constituent booklet of a book) in the scribe's exemplar. I have supplied this missing material, the account of Egypt and Sicily (pp. 20–34), using the 'Egerton' text, another early English version.[4] This was written *c.*1400 and is a

[2] See Ralph Hanna, 'Mandeville', in A. S. G. Edwards (ed.), *Middle English Prose: A Critical Guide* (New Brunswick, NJ, 1984), 121–32, commenting that the 'Defective' version was the most commonly known version of Mandeville but 'prevalent scholarly confusion about what a Mandeville text should be has denied the common version that central status it should hold in Middle English studies' (p. 123).

[3] A clear, simplified table of the English transmission of Mandeville manuscripts is given in M. C. Seymour, 'Mandeville in England: The Early Years', in Laden Niayesh (ed.), *A Knight's Legacy: Mandeville and Mandevillian Lore in Early Modern England* (Manchester, 2010), 15–27, at 23–7.

[4] So called because it survives in the manuscript British Library MS Egerton 1982. This has been edited as *The Egerton Version of Mandeville's Travels*, ed. M. C. Seymour,

conflation of the 'Defective' with another version of Mandeville's *Book*, apparently a Middle English translation of one of the Latin texts. This manuscript was owned by the Benedictines at St Albans, and made its way in 1490 from there to the printer William Caxton (d. *c.*1492). Although this section is missing from most English-language manuscripts and prints of the *Book*, it does appear in Continental versions. This is a particularly interesting section of Mandeville's narrative, in which the narrator claims to have been in the service of the Sultan. Mandeville's account gives the reader an idea of medieval knowledge of Egypt, Egyptian antiquities, and reports of the Crusades. It shows his approach to Islamic and Arab society, very much at odds with his comments on the Jews and the more aggressive crusading rhetoric elsewhere in the *Book*.

Early English Text Society OS 336 (Oxford, 2010); the 'Egypt Gap' corresponds to pp. 20–35 in Seymour's edition ('And ȝe schalle vnderstand . . .' to '...þe forsaid abbay synges oft tyme').

SELECT BIBLIOGRAPHY

Other Relevant Editions and Translations

Deluz, Christiane (ed.), *Le Livre des Merveilles du Monde* (Paris, 2000): a full scholarly edition of the Anglo-French ('Insular') text, with excellent notes on sources; cited here as *Livre*.

Higgins, Iain Macleod (ed. and trans.), *The Book of John Mandeville with Related Texts* (Indianapolis, 2011): a modern English translation of the Anglo-French version.

Kohanski, Tamarah, and Benson, C. David (eds.), *The Book of John Mandeville* (Kalamazoo, Mich., 2007, online at http://www.lib.rochester.edu/camelot/teams/tkfrm.htm): edition of London, British Library MS Royal 17 C. xxxviii, which in turn was used for Richard Pynson's printed edition.

Letts, Malcolm (ed.), *Mandeville's Travels: Texts and Translations*, Hakluyt Society, 101 (London, 1953): modernized editions of three versions (Egerton, Paris, and Bodleian) with full introductory material.

Seymour, M. C. (ed.), *The Defective Version of Mandeville's Travels*, Early English Text Society OS 319 (Oxford, 2002): edition of the Middle English base-text used for the current edition.

—— (ed.), *The Egerton Version of Mandeville's Travels*, Early English Text Society OS 336 (Oxford, 2010): edition of the Middle English text used for the account of Egypt and Sicily.

Warner, George F. (ed.), *The Buke of John Maundeuill, being the travels of Sir John Mandeville, knight, 1322–1356: A hitherto unpublished version, from the unique copy (Egerton MS 1982) in the British Museum* (London, 1889).

General Background

Campbell, Mary B., *The Witness and the Other World: Exotic European Travel Writing 400–1600* (Ithaca, NY, 1991).

Gómez, Nicholás Wey, *The Tropics of Empire: Why Columbus Travelled South to the Indies* (Cambridge, Mass., 2008).

Metlitzki, Dorothee, *The Matter of Araby in Mediaeval England* (New Haven, 1977).

Nebenzahl, Kenneth, *Mapping the Silk Road and Beyond: 2,000 Years of Exploring the East* (London, 2004).

Phillips, J. R. S., *The Medieval Expansion of Europe*, 2nd edn. (Oxford, 1998).

Zacher, Christian, *Curiosity and Pilgrimage: The Literature of Discovery in Fourteenth-Century England* (Baltimore, 1976).

Mandeville, his Book and his Biography

Bennett, Josephine Waters, *The Rediscovery of John Mandeville* (New York, 1954).

Bennett, Michael J., 'Mandeville's Travels and the Anglo-French Moment', *Medium Aevum*, 75 (2006), 273–92.

Bremer, Ernst, and Röhl, Susanne (eds.), *Jean de Mandeville in Europa* (Munich, 2007).

Deluz, Christiane, *Le Livre de Jehan de Mandeville: une géographie au XIVe siècle* (Leuven, 1998).

Higgins, Iain Macleod, *Writing East: The Travels of Sir John Mandeville* (Philadelphia, 1997).

Howard, Donald R., 'The World of Mandeville's Travels', *Yearbook of English Studies*, 1 (1971), 1–17.

Letts, Malcolm, *Sir John Mandeville: The Man and His Book* (London, 1949).

Moseley, C. W. R. D., 'Behaim's Globe and "Mandeville's Travels"', *Imago Mundi*, 33 (1981), 89–91.

Seymour, M. J., *Sir John Mandeville* (London, 1993).

Tzanaki, Rosemary, *Mandeville's Medieval Audiences: A Study on the Reception of the Book of Sir John Mandeville* (Aldershot, 2003).

Crusading and Jerusalem

Atiya, Aziz, *The Crusade in the Later Middle Ages*, 2nd edn. (New York, 1965).

Chareyron, Nicole, *Pilgrims to Jerusalem in the Middle Ages* (New York, 2005).

Housley, Norman, *The Later Crusades 1274–1580: From Lyons to Alcazar* (Oxford, 1992).

Riley-Smith, Jonathan, *The Crusades: A Short History* (New Haven, 1987).

Schein, Sylvia, *Fideles Crucis: The Papacy, the West and the Recovery of the Holy Land, 1274–1314* (Oxford, 1991).

—— *Gateway to the Heavenly City: Crusader Jerusalem and the Catholic West (1099–1187)* (Aldershot, 2005).

Tyerman, Christopher, *The Crusades: A Very Short Introduction* (Oxford, 2005).

Wharton, Annabel, *Selling Jerusalem: Relics, Replicas, Theme Parks* (Chicago, 2006).

Romance and Literary Culture

Akbari, Suzanne Conklin, *Idols in the East: European Representations of Islam and the Orient, 1100–1450* (Ithaca, NY, 2009).

Bennett, Josephine Waters, 'Chaucer and Mandeville's Travels', *Modern Language Notes*, 68 (1953), 531–4.

Grady, Frank, *Representing Righteous Heathens in Late Medieval England* (Basingstoke, 2005).

Heng, Geraldine, *Empire of Magic: Medieval Romance and the Politics of Cultural Fantasy* (New York, 2003).

McDonald, Nicola (ed.), *Pulp Fictions of Medieval England: Essays in Popular Romance* (Manchester, 2004).

Ramey, Lynn Tarte, *Christian, Saracen and Genre in Medieval French Literature: Imagination and Cultural Interaction in the French Middle Ages* (London, 2001).

Yaeger, Suzanne, *Jerusalem in Medieval Narrative* (Cambridge, 2008).

Monsters and Marvels

Bildhauer, Bettina, and Mills, Robert (eds.), *The Monstrous Middle Ages* (London, 2003).

Bovey, Alixe, *Monsters and Grotesques in Medieval Manuscripts* (London, 2002).

Cohen, Jeffrey Jerome, *Monster Theory: Reading Culture* (Minneapolis, 1996).

Daston, Lorraine, and Park, Katharine, *Wonders and the Order of Nature, 1150–1750* (New York, 1998).

Verner, Lisa, *The Epistemology of the Monstrous in the Middle Ages* (London, 2005).

Williams, David A., *Deformed Discourse: The Function of the Monster in Mediaeval Thought and Literature* (Montreal, 1999).

Geography and Postcolonialism

Cohen, Jeffrey Jerome (ed.), *The Postcolonial Middle Ages* (Basingstoke, 2001).

Connolly, Daniel K., *The Maps of Matthew Paris: Journeys through Space, Time and Liturgy* (Woodbridge, 2009).

Harvey, P. D. A., *The Hereford World Map: Medieval World Maps and Their Context* (London, 2006).

Lampert-Weissig, Lisa, *Medieval Literature and Postcolonial Studies* (Edinburgh, 2010).

Lavezzo, Kathy, *Angels on the Edge of the World: Geography, Literature, and English Community, 1000–1534* (London, 2006).

Lilley, Keith, *City and Cosmos: The Medieval World in Urban Form* (London, 2009).

MANDEVILLE'S MEASUREMENTS

In an era of salvation rather than of standardization, medieval measurements were loosely conceived, emphasizing the physical experience of measured time and space: as a number of footsteps, as the distance an arrow can be shot. Different regions had different norms, the English measurements given here differing from those of France and Italy used in Mandeville's sources. A brief guide is given below to the measurements Mandeville uses, but such measurements were local, inconsistent, and largely only standardized after the medieval period. See further Witold Kula, *Measures and Men* (Princeton, 1986); Ronald Edward Zupko, *British Weights and Measures: A History from Antiquity to the Seventeenth Century* (Madison, Wisc., 1977).

bowshot: a variable measure marking the distance to which an arrow can be shot from a bow or the time required for the flight of an arrow
cubit: the length of a man's forearm, from elbow to middle fingertip; about 18 inches
degree: 1/360th of a circle
English mile: 1,000 paces (8 furlongs), about 1,666 yards; only fixed at 1,760 yards by statute in 1592
foot/footstep: the length of a man's foot; in England, about 12 inches
furlong: the length of a furrow; 1/8th of a mile
hand: the breadth of a man's hand or four fingers; usually 3 or 4 inches
league: about 3 miles, but used without precision simply to mean a long distance by sea
Lombard mile: Mandeville uses this measurement for nautical miles, historically defined as a minute of arc along the Earth's meridian
mile: *see* English mile; Lombard mile
minute: the angular measurement (minute of arc), 1/60th of a degree
pace: a measurement of approximately 5 feet
shaftment: the breadth of an extended hand from thumb to little finger; usually 6 inches

CHRONOLOGY

1095	Pope Urban II launches the First Crusade.
1099	Capture of Jerusalem by the Crusaders.
1145	Launch of Second Crusade, following the fall of the Crusader County of Edessa to Zengi of Mosul.
*c.*1165	*The Letter of Prester John* starts to circulate in Europe.
1187	Capture of Crusader Jerusalem by Saladin.
1189	Launch of the Third Crusade, to retake Jerusalem.
1192	Richard I of England signs treaty with Saladin, allowing Jerusalem to remain under Islamic control with access for Christian pilgrims.
1204	Fourth Crusade, resulting in the plunder of Constantinople.
1213	Launch of the Fifth Crusade, which stalls at Damietta (Egypt) in 1218.
1227	Death of Genghis or Chingis Khan; at this point, the Mongol empire stretched from the Caspian Sea to the Sea of Japan.
1228	Launch of the Sixth Crusade, which stalls at Cyprus in 1229.
*c.*1260	Jacobus de Voragine compiles the *Legenda Aurea*, the pre-eminent medieval collection of saints' lives.
1271	Marco Polo sets off from Venice with his father and uncle for the East; later reported in his journal, *Il Milione.*
*c.*1290	The making of the Hereford *Mappa mundi.*
1291	Fall of Acre, the last mainland Crusader settlement in Palestine.
1307	Papal bull establishes the See of Khan-Baliq (Beijing), formalizing the Franciscan mission to China.
*c.*1317	Date of the beginning of Odoric of Pordenone's mission to Asia.
1333	William of Boldensele's journey to the Middle East.
1337	Beginning of the Hundred Years' War (to 1453) for the French throne.
1348–9	Great pandemic of the Black Death throughout Europe.
1356/66	The most common dates given for the return of Sir John Mandeville from Asia to England.
1371	Earliest dated manuscript of Mandeville's *Book.*
*c.*1380	Chaucer's *Canterbury Tales.*

1402	Greatest extent of the Timurid empire, led by Temür (Tamerlane), stretching from Damascus to Delhi.
1453	Fall of Byzantine empire to the Ottoman emperor, Mehmet II.
*c.*1470	First printed edition of Mandeville's *Book* appears, published in The Hague.
1492	Christopher Columbus lands at San Salvador (Guanahani) in the Bahamas.

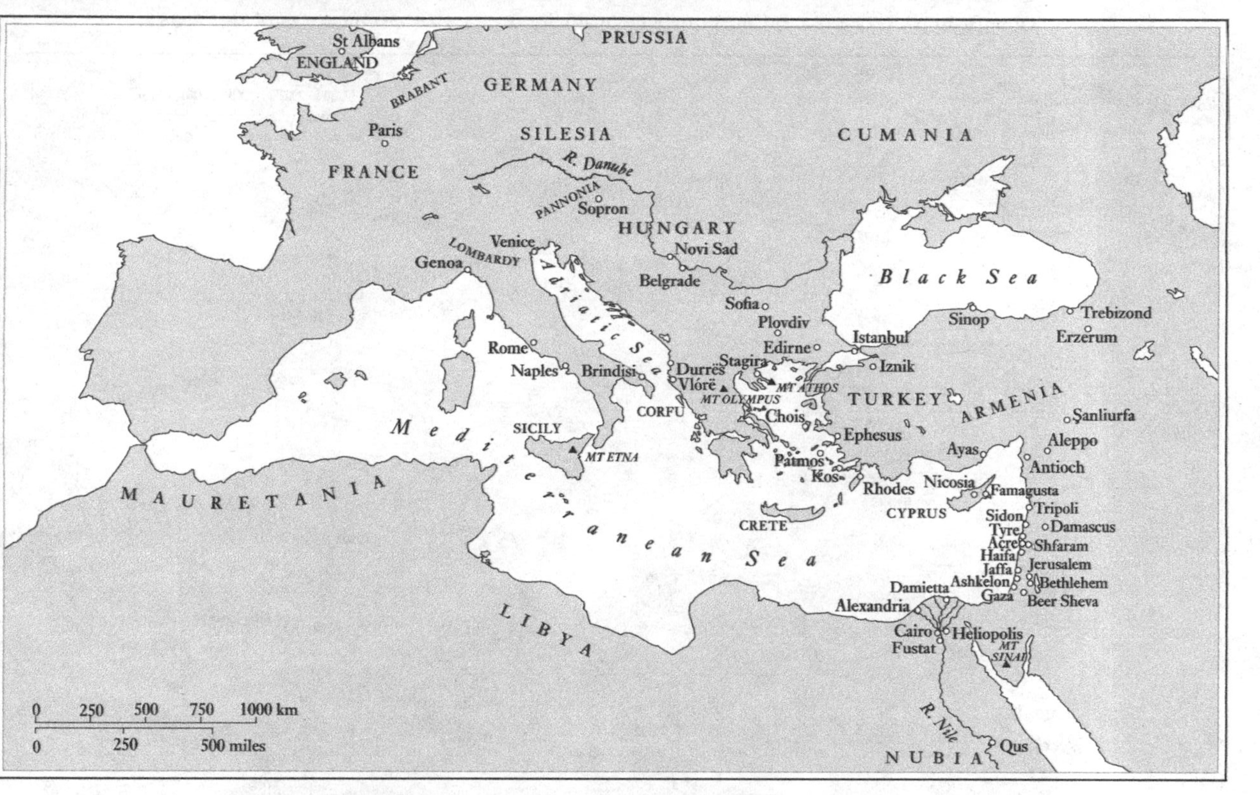

MAP 1. Sir John Mandeville's Europe, showing the main identifiable places mentioned by Mandeville.

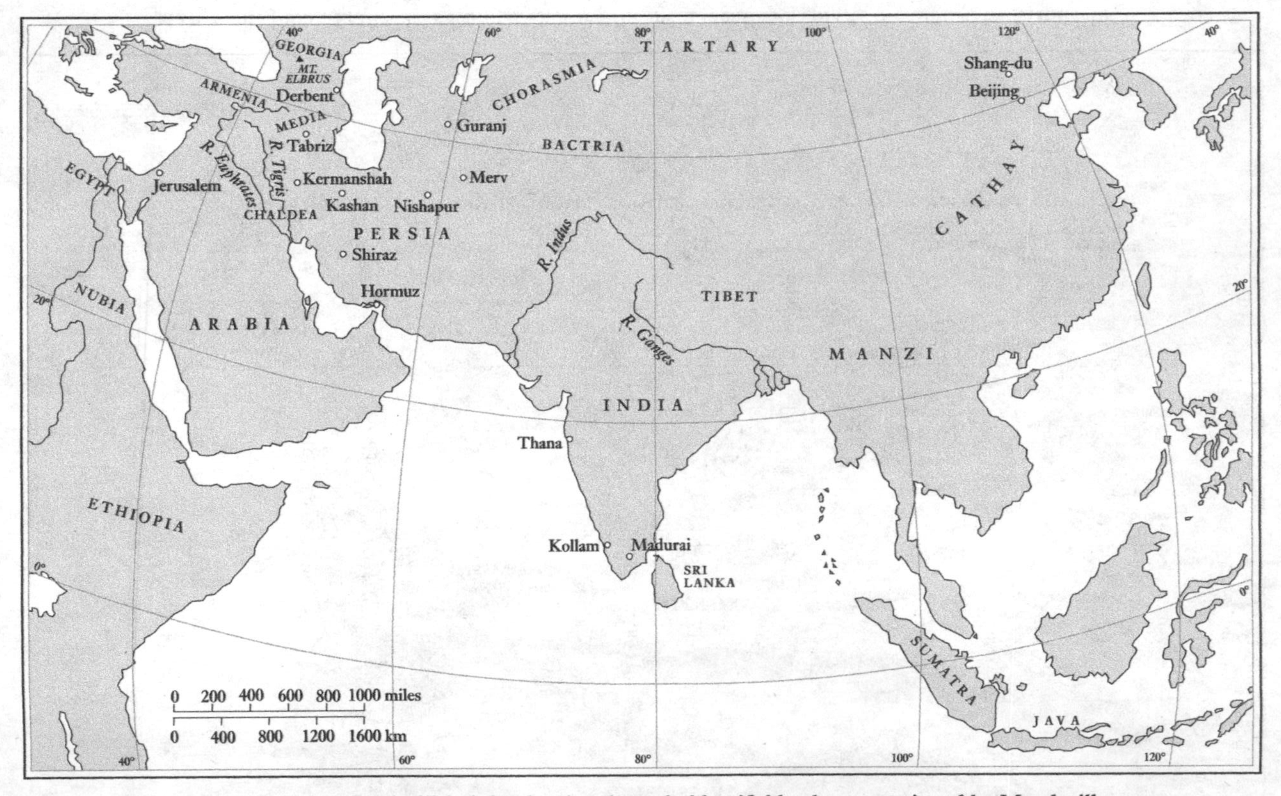

MAP 2. Sir John Mandeville's Asia, showing the main identifiable places mentioned by Mandeville.

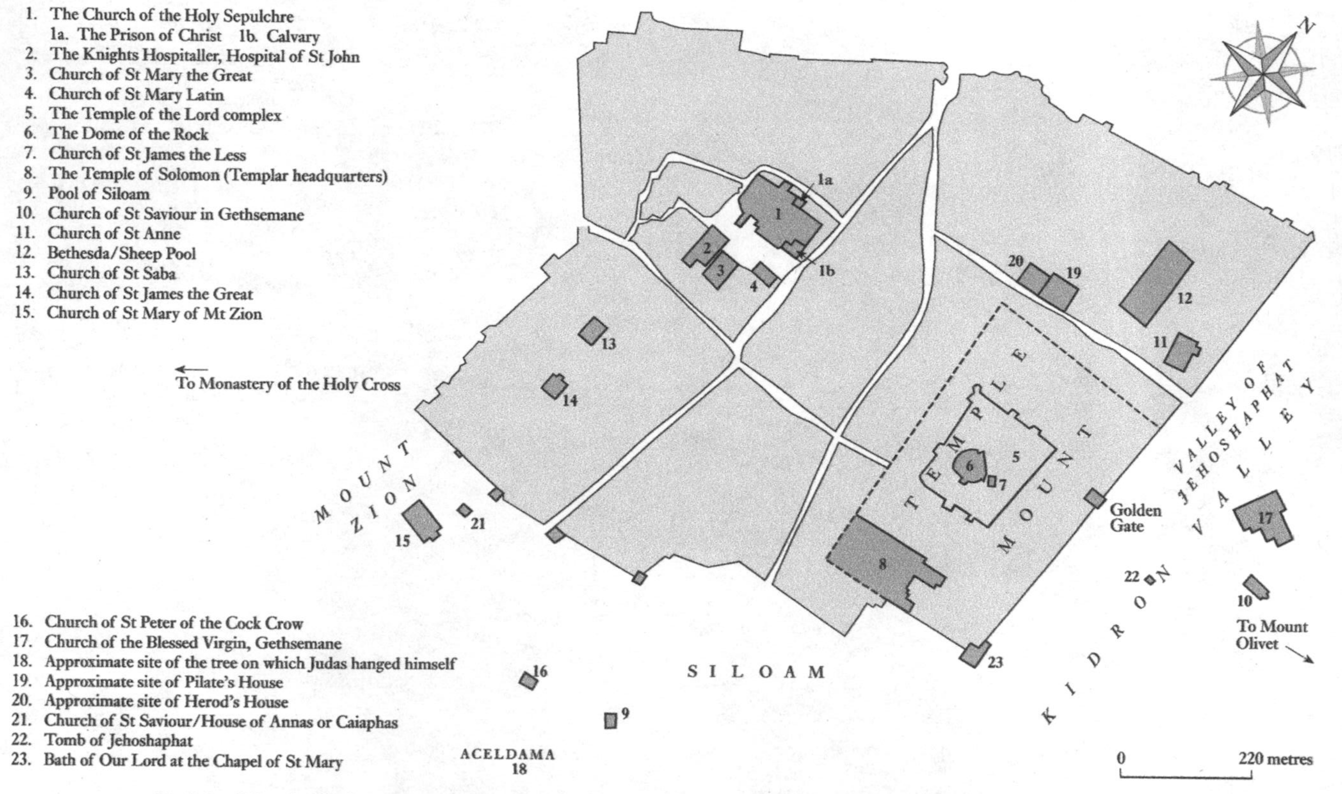

MAP 3. Sir John Mandeville's Jerusalem, showing the sites described by Mandeville and simplified Crusader-era street plan.

THE BOOK OF MARVELS AND TRAVELS

CONTENTS

1

PROLOGUE

BECAUSE the land overseas, that is to say the Holy Land which people call the Promised Land, is amongst all other lands like the most excellent lady and it is sovereign over all other lands, and it is blessed and hallowed and made sacred by the precious blood of Our Lord Jesus Christ;*

and because in this land it pleased Him to take flesh and blood, conceived of the Virgin Mary, and travel throughout that land by His blessed feet;

and because there He chose to perform many miracles, preaching and teaching the faith, our Christian law, as if to His children; and there He chose to suffer so much disgrace and mockery for us; He who was King of Heaven and of earth, of air, of sea, and all things contained in them, but would only be called king of that land when He said *Rex sum Iudeorum*, that is, 'I am the King of the Jews',* because at that time this land belonged to the Jews;

and because that land was chosen by Him as the best over all other lands, the most virtuous, the worthiest in the world: as the philosopher says, *Virtus rerum in medio consistit*, that is, 'The virtue of things is in their middle';*

and because in that land He wished to live His life and suffer His Passion and death at the Jews' hands for us, to redeem us and deliver us from the torments of Hell and from eternal death, which had been ordained for us because of the sin of Adam, our father, and also because of our own sins; and He did not deserve any evil treatment, because He had never either thought or done anything evil; and He who was the King of glory and joy chose that place as the best in which to suffer death: because if one wants something to be known by everybody one shouts out in the middle of a city or town, so that all parts of the city know what is happening;*

therefore He who was King of all the world chose to suffer death at Jerusalem,* because that is in the middle of the world, so it was known to everybody in all parts of the world at what price He redeemed mankind which He made in His own likeness out of His immense love for us; He could not have proffered any more precious property than His own blessed body and His own precious blood, the which He sacrificed for us.

Oh dear God, such love had He for His servants when He who was without sin suffered death for sinners! People should truly love and worship and fear and serve such a god and a ruler, and worship and praise this holy land that bore such fruit, through which each person is saved (unless it might be through their own fault). This is the land promised to us in hereditary succession, and in that land He chose to die and He was put in seisin, in actual possession, of this place to leave it to His children;* therefore, every decent Christian who is able and has the wherewithal should fortify himself to conquer our rightful heritage and chase out those of an evil creed. For we are called Christians on account of our Father Christ, and if we are the lawful children of Christ, we must demand the inheritance bequeathed to us by our Father and wrest it from foreigners' hands.

Nota bene! So now men's hearts are so aroused with pride, envy, and covetousness that they are busier making their neighbours destitute than demanding or conquering the aforementioned rightful inheritance. As for the common people, who might want to offer their bodies and their property to win back our inheritance, they cannot do so without noblemen. This is because an assembly of the people without a chief to govern them is like a flock of sheep without a shepherd: it becomes scattered and doesn't know which way it should go. If it pleases God that noblemen are in agreement with each other and have the backing of the common people to make a holy journey overseas, I really believe that within just a little time our rightful inheritance should be regained and placed into the hands of Jesus Christ's rightful heirs.

Because it has been a long time since there was a crusading expedition overseas, and because many men long to hear about that land and various countries nearby (and from that I take great pleasure and comfort), I, John Mandeville, knight, although I'm not worthy, who was born in England in the town of St Albans, set sail on Michaelmas Day in the year of Our Lord 1332* and have been abroad a long time since then. And I have seen and traversed so many kingdoms and lands and provinces and islands, and travelled through Turkey and Armenia the Lesser and the Greater, and Tartary, Persia, Syria, Arabia, Upper Egypt and Lower Egypt, Libya, Chaldea, and most of Ethiopia, Amazonia, Upper India and Lower India, and through lots of islands near India, where many kinds of people live, of different customs and shapes (of which territories and islands I will speak more fully). And I shall describe a part of what each one is, according to how I remember it, especially for those who wish and intend to visit the holy city of Jerusalem and the holy places thereabouts. And I will tell you the route to take to get there, because I have travelled and ridden this way many times with numerous noble companions.*

2

ONE WAY TO JERUSALEM

IN the name of Almighty God, whoever travels overseas can go from his country by many routes, both by land and by sea, but many of these routes lead to one destination. But don't believe that I will list all the towns and cities and castles that one passes by, for this would be too long-winded. I will give only some countries and the most important settlements through which one passes in order to go the right way.

First, if someone sets out from the western side of the world—that is, England, Ireland, Wales, Scotland, Norway—they may, if they like, go through Germany and through the kingdom of Hungary which borders the land of Poland and the lands of Pannonia* and of Silesia.*

Now, the King of Hungary is a very strong and powerful ruler, holding a great deal of fine land, because he rules over the territories of Hungary, Savoy, Cumania,* a significant part of Bulgaria which people call the Land of Buggers,* and a large part of the kingdom of Russia, all the way up to the region of Nevelond* and to the borders of Prussia. One travels through the territories of Hungary to a city called Sopron* and to Neiseburgh* castle and via the island-town* near the Hungarian border. Here one travels along the River Danube, a truly huge river which flows into Germany from beneath the hills of Lombardy, and it is fed by some forty other rivers and it runs through Hungary, Greece, and Thrace and enters the sea with such strength and in such a tumult that the sea-water there is fresh within twenty miles.

Next, one goes to Belgrade and enters into the lands of the Buggers, and there one crosses a stone bridge over the River Maritsa.* One passes through the land of the Pechenegs* and arrives in Greece, at the cities of Sternes and Philippopolis* and then to the city of Adrianople* and then to Constantinople that was once called Byzantium; the Emperor of Greece usually lives there.

The finest and most beautiful church in the world is in this place, and it is dedicated to St Sophie.* And in front of the church is a gilded figure of the Emperor Justinian crowned and on horseback.* He used to hold an apple in his hand, but the apple has fallen out of the effigy's hand.* People say this is a symbol that the Emperor has lost a large part of his empire. He was once Emperor of Romania, Greece, Asia Minor, Syria, the land of Judea in which Jerusalem is situated, the lands of Egypt, of Persia, and Arabia; but he has lost all of this except Greece, so now he only holds that land. People have tried many times to put the apple back into the statue's hand again, but it will not hold it; this apple signifies the lordship he once had over the world. As for the other hand, he holds it up towards the west as a symbol by which to threaten sinners. This statue at Constantinople stands on a marble pillar.

And in this place is the sponge and the reed the Jews gave Our Lord with which to drink when He was on the Cross.* There is also one of the nails with which Christ was nailed to the Cross. Some men believe that half of Christ's Cross is in Cyprus in an abbey of monks called The Hill of the Holy Cross;* but this isn't true, because the cross in Cyprus is the cross on which Dysmas,* the good thief, was suspended. But not everyone knows this, and by saying that this is the Cross of Our Lord Jesus Christ they commit an offence, for the purpose of gaining offerings.

You need to be aware that the Cross of Our Lord Jesus Christ was made from four kinds of wood, as it is described in this verse, which is written here thus: *In cruce sit palma, cedrus, cypressus, oliua*.* Thus the piece which went vertically from the ground to His head was made of cypress; the piece which went crosswise, to which His hands were nailed, was made of palm; and the stump that stood in the earth, out of which a mortice was made, was made of cedar; and the tablet above His head, on which the inscription was written in Hebrew, Greek, and Latin, was made of olive, and it was one-and-a-half feet long.

So the Jews made this Cross out of these four kinds of wood because they believed that Our Lord Jesus Christ should be suspended on that Cross for as long as the Cross could last. Therefore they made the foot out of cedar, because that does not rot in either earth or water, and they wanted it to last a long time. And because they believed that Christ's body would stink, they made the piece that went vertically up from the ground, on which His body was suspended, out of cypress, which has a good perfume, so that the smell of His body wouldn't offend passers-by. And the crossbeam, to which His hands were nailed, was made of palm, because in the Old Testament it was ordained that when any man was victorious over his enemy he should be crowned with palm, and because they believed that they had been victorious over Jesus Christ they made the crossbeam with palm. And the tablet on which the inscription was made out of olive is a sign of peace for, as the story of Noah bears witness, when the dove brought the olive branch this was a sign of peace between God and man;* and so the Jews believed they would have peace when Christ was dead, because they said that He caused strife amongst them.

And you must know that Our Lord was nailed to the Cross lying down, and through this He suffered all the more pain. Moreover, Greek and foreign Christians say that the wood used for the Cross which we say was cypress was actually from the tree of which Adam ate the apple, and this is backed up in their writings. Also they describe how their scriptures say that Adam was sick and told his son Seth to go to Paradise and request of the angel who guarded Paradise to send some oil from the tree of mercy* with which to anoint his limbs and so be healed. So Seth went, but the angel would not let him in and told him that he couldn't have the oil of the tree of mercy. But he took with him four seeds of that very tree from which his father ate the apple and requested, as soon as his father was dead, that he should put these seeds under his tongue and bury him thus. And this he did. Out of these four seeds sprang trees, as the angel had said, that would bear a fruit through which Adam might be saved. And when Seth returned he found his father almost dead, and did with the seeds as the angel had told him. From these sprang the four trees with which the Cross was made, which bore a good fruit, that is Jesus Christ, through which Adam and all those descended from him were saved and delivered from death without end (unless it is through their own sinfulness).

The Jews hid this holy Cross in the earth under the rocks of Mount Calvary, and it lay there for more than two hundred years until that time when St Helena* found it; this St Helena was the mother of Constantine, the Emperor of Rome, and she was the daughter of King Cole who was king of England (at that time it was called Great Britain), and the Emperor, during a visit to that country, took her as his wife on account of her beauty. You need to know that Our Lord Jesus Christ's Cross was eight cubits long, and crosswise three and a half cubits wide.

A piece of Our Lord's crown and one of the nails and the spear-head and lots of other relics are in France in the King's chapel.* The crown sits in a beautifully wrought, decorated crystal vessel, because a French king purchased these relics from the Jews,* to whom the Emperor had pawned them for a massive sum of gold. Whilst it's true that people say that the crown is made of thorns, you must understand that it is actually made of rushes, from the sea, what we might call 'sea-rushes', which were white and they pricked as sharply as thorns. I have seen and examined the crown at Paris and the one at Constantinople many times, and they were both one crown made of sea-rushes, but people have divided it into two pieces, and one piece is in Paris and the other piece is in Constantinople. And I've got a spine from it that is like a white thorn (and that was given to me out of great friendship) because many of them have broken off and fallen into the vessel in which the crown is stored, and they break when people move the vessel to show the fine gentlemen who visit there.

You should be aware that Our Lord, when He was arrested in the night, was led into a garden and He was brutally examined there. The Jews scorned Him, and made a crown for Him out of hawthorn* that grew in that garden, and they placed it on His head so tightly that the blood flowed all over His face and His neck and His shoulders; because of this, the hawthorn has many virtues, for if anyone carries a branch of it with him, neither thunder nor any other kind of storm will harm him, and no wicked spirits will come into a house or any other place where the branch is. Also, in that same garden St Peter three times forsook Our Lord.*

Then Our Lord was led in front of the bishop and constables into another garden, belonging to Annas,* and He was interrogated and scorned there too and crowned soon after with white thorns (which some call barberry)* that were growing there in the garden, and that too has many virtuous properties. Then afterwards He was led into a garden belonging to Caiaphas,* and there He was crowned with briar.*

Then He was taken into Pilate's room, and there He was examined and scorned. The Jews placed Him in a chair and dressed Him in a cloak, and they made the crown of sea-rushes, and they genuflected to Him and thereby mocked Him, saying *Aue rex Iudeorum*, that is 'Hail, King of the Jews.'* Now this crown, of which one half is in Paris and the other half in Constantinople, is the one Christ had on His head when He was placed on the Cross. Therefore people should worship it and value it above any of the other crowns. Also, the Emperor of Germany has the spear-shaft, but the head of it is in Paris. The Emperor in Constantinople has repeatedly said that he has the spear-head, and I've often seen that indeed he does have one, but it is bigger than the one in Paris.*

Also in Constantinople rests St Anne, Our Lady's mother, whom St Helena had brought from Jerusalem. There too rests the body of St John Chrysostom* who was the bishop of Constantinople. And St Luke the evangelist rests there too, as his bones were brought from Bethany* where he was buried. Lots of other relics are there, as well as stone vessels which look like marble, called *idriouns*,* which constantly drip water and fill themselves each year.

It is my task to make you know that Constantinople is a very beautiful and great city with strong walls and it is three-cornered. There is a strait of the sea that people call the Hellespont, and some call it Constantinople's Mouth, and some call it St George's Arm. This water surrounds two parts of the city. And further up the same coast is where the great city of Troy used to be, on a beautiful plain, but that city was destroyed by the Greeks.

There are many islands there too, which are called Chalcis, Calastre, Ceytige, Tesbiria, Armona, Faxton, Milos, Karpathos, Lemnos.* On this last island is Mount Athos, higher than the clouds. There are also many languages spoken and nations obedient to the Emperor, to wit Turcopoles,* Pechenegs and Cumans, and Thrace and Macedonia (of which Alexander was king), and many others.

Aristotle* was born in this region, in a city called Stagira, a short distance from Thrace, and Aristotle's body rests at Stagira. There is an altar on his tomb, and here each year a giant feast is made, as if he were a saint. Great councils and assemblies are held upon his altar, people believing that through the inspiration of God and Aristotle their judgements should be better.

In this region there are three huge mountains, and towards the border of Macedonia there is a massive mountain which people call Olympus; it divides Macedonia and Thrace and it goes as high as the clouds. Another mountain there is called Athos, which is so high that its shadow stretches to Olympus, even though they are seventy-seven miles apart! At the top of this mountain the air is so pure that you can't even feel the wind, and because the air is so dry no animals can live there. And it is said by locals that philosophers once dwelt in these mountains and they held moist sponges to their noses so they could breathe, the air is so dry there. In the dust at the top of the mountain they wrote letters with their fingers, and a year later they returned and found the same letters, written a year earlier, without a single flaw. Therefore it seems that these mountains go beyond the clouds to the pure air.

Also, at Constantinople the Emperor's palace is really lovely and beautifully adorned. Within, there's a pretty court* for jousting, and there are tiered seats in which one can sit and watch and not impede other people's views. Under the rows of seats are vaulted stables for the Emperor's horse, and all the pillars are made of marble.

One Emperor wanted to lay the body of his dead father inside the church of St Sophie. As they were making the grave they found a body in the ground, and on the body was a great sheet of gold and upon it was written in Hebrew, Greek, and Latin letters the following: *Ihesu Cristus nascetur de uirgine Maria et ego credo in eum*, that is, 'Jesus Christ shall be born of the Virgin Mary and I believe in Him.' Now, the date when this was written and buried in the ground was two thousand years before Our Lord was born.* This sheet is now in the treasury of the church, and it is said to have been written by the sage Hermes Trismegistus.*

Even though it is true that all people in the land of Greece are Christian, it's a very different faith from ours; for they say the Holy Ghost doesn't proceed from the Son but only from the Father; they are not obedient either to the church of Rome or to the Pope; they say that their patriarch has as much power abroad as the Pope does in his territories. Therefore Pope John XXII* sent documents to them, saying that the Christian faith should be united and that they should obey the Pope who is Christ's vicar on earth, to whom God gave full power both to obligate and to absolve and therefore they should obey him. They sent back many answers, amongst which they said: *Potenciam tuam circa tuos subiectos firmiter credimus. Superbiam tuam summam* *tollerare non possumus. Auariciam tuam summan saciare non intendimus. Dominus tecum sit quia Dominus nobiscum est. Vale.* That is, 'We confidently believe that you have great power over your subjects. We will not tolerate your great arrogance. We do not propose to satisfy your avarice. May the Lord be with you, because the Lord is with us. Goodbye.'* And the Pope never got any further answer from them.

They make the sacrament of the altar with unleavened bread because Our Lord made it with unleavened bread when He made the Last Supper. And on Maundy Thursday they make unleavened bread as a sign of the Last Supper and dry it in the sun and keep it all year and give it to ill men instead of God's body. They only perform the rite of unction when they christen children; they don't anoint sick men. They say there isn't a Purgatory and that souls shall have neither pleasure nor pain on the Day of Judgement. They say that fornication isn't a deadly sin but a natural thing, and that men and women should only be married once, and if any were to marry more than once their children are bastards and conceived in sin. Their priests are also married. They say that usury isn't a deadly sin. Just as people do elsewhere, they sell the benefices of Holy Church because simony is now crowned king in Holy Church, and that is an immense scandal. God can correct it when He wills it.

Also the Greeks say that during Lent one should not sing mass except on Saturday and Sunday. And they don't fast on Saturday at any time of the year unless it is Christmas Eve or Easter Saturday. And they will not permit anybody who comes from this side of the Mediterranean* to worship at their altars. If this chances somehow to happen, they quickly wash their altars with holy water. And they say that there should be only one mass said at an altar each day. Over and above that they say that Our Lord never ate food, He just made the gesture of eating. And they also say that we commit a mortal sin in shaving our beards, for the beard is the physical sign of humanity. And they say that we sin in eating the beasts which were banned in the Old Testament and the Old Law, such as pigs and hares and other creatures; also that we sin in eating meat on the days before Ash Wednesday and eating meat on Wednesdays and when we eat cheese or eggs on Fridays, and they curse all those who don't eat meat on a Saturday. Moreover, the Emperor of Constantinople creates the patriarch, archbishops, and bishops, and he bestows all church offices and livings, and he removes from office those who deserve it.

And if all these things are not relevant to the journey, they are nevertheless relevant in so far as I have undertaken to show some of the customs and manners and differences of these countries. And because this is the nearest country that varies from, and conflicts with, our faith and religious texts, I have written it here so that you can see the differences between our faith and theirs, for many people take great pleasure and comfort to hear talk of unfamiliar things.

3

RETURN TO THE ROUTE VIA CONSTANTINOPLE

Now I return to the route via Constantinople. If one wishes to go through Turkey, one travels towards the city of Nicaea and passes through the gate of Civetot, which is extremely high up in the mountains and a mile and a half from Nicaea. Those who wish to travel via St George's Arm and via the Mediterranean, past the resting place of St Nicholas and various other places, first arrive at Chios.* Mastic grows on that island on little trees, like plum-trees or cherry-trees. Then one travels through the island of Patmos, where St John the Evangelist wrote the Apocalypse. And I make it known to you that when Our Lord died St John was thirty-two years old, and he lived another sixty-two years after the Passion of Christ.

From Patmos one travels to Ephesus, a lovely city near the coast, and that is where St John died and was buried in a tomb behind the altar. There is an attractive church, because Christians once held this place. However, in St John's tomb there is nothing but manna, because his body was translated into Paradise. Turks now hold that city and that church and all of Asia Minor, and so Asia Minor is called Turkey. You should be aware that St John arranged his grave there when he was alive and laid himself in it still very much alive. Therefore some people say that he did not die but that he is resting there until the Day of Judgement. Truly, it is a really astonishing thing, for people say the earth around the tomb has stirred many times and moved as though there's a living thing underneath.

From Ephesus one travels through many islands in the sea all the way to the city of Patara where St Nicholas was born, and then on to Myra where he was elected bishop (by the grace of God). Rich, strong wine comes from there, people call it 'Myra wine'. From here one can see the Greek isles that the Emperor granted to the Genoese* some time ago. Then one passes through the islands of Kos and Lango, of which islands Hippocrates* was ruler.

Some people say that on this island of Lango is Hippocrates' daughter in the form of a dragon a hundred feet long (or so it is said, as I haven't seen it). The local people call her the local lady-of-the-manor.* She resides in an old castle and reveals herself three times a year, and she does not harm anyone unless someone harms her. She was transformed from a pretty damsel into a dragon by the goddess called Diana. It's said that she is lingering there until a knight comes along who is brave enough to go down there to her and kiss her on the mouth, and then she'll be transformed back into her natural state and become a woman again, and after that she'll not live for long.

It's not long since one doughty, bold knight, a hospitaller from Rhodes,* declared that he wished to kiss her. Mounted on his stallion, he went into the castle and entered into the cave. Then the dragon began to lift up its head towards him, and when the knight beheld such a hideous sight he fled. So the dragon followed after him and grasped the knight and carried him, despite his resistance, to a rock, and threw him from that rock into the sea, and so the knight perished.

Also, a young man who didn't know about the dragon got off a ship and strolled around the island until he reached that castle, and he went into the cave and continued through it until he found a bedroom. And there he saw a maiden combing her hair and gazing into a mirror, with treasures all about her, and he believed that she was a prostitute who lived there to ensnare men. And he waited until the maiden saw his reflection in her mirror, and then she turned around towards him and asked him what he wanted. So he said that he wished to be her sweetheart or her lover. She asked him if he was a knight, and he said 'no', so she said he couldn't be her lover. But she commanded him to go back to his shipmates and become a knight and return in the morning, and she would come out of the cave, and then request him to kiss her on the lips. She told him not to be afraid, because she'd do him no harm; she added that even if he thought she was very hideous to look at this was just done through magic, as she said that she was really just like he saw her then. She added that if he kissed her, he would own all the treasure and have lordship over her and over those islands.

So he left her and went to his shipmates and he was knighted and returned the next morning to kiss her. And when he saw her coming out of the cave in the form of a dragon he was so terrified that he fled to the ship. She followed him, and when she saw that he wouldn't come back, she began to weep like a thing that has suffered some great sadness, and she turned back. And the knight died at once.

Since then no knight has been able to lay eyes on her without dying very soon after. However, when a knight does come who is bold enough to kiss her, he shall not die but shall transform that damsel into her proper form, and he shall be her master and the ruler of the aforementioned islands.

From there one arrives at the island of Rhodes, held and governed by the Knights Hospitaller who took it some time ago from the Emperor.* That island used to be called Collosus, as the Turks still call it. Likewise St Paul, in his epistles, wrote to these islanders *Ad Collosenses*.* This island is nearly eight hundred miles from Constantinople.

Now, from this island of Rhodes one travels to Cyprus, where there are many grapes which are at first red and then, after a year, become white. The whitest of these grapes are utterly translucent and have the best scent. One travelling this way passes by a site where there used to be a huge city called Satalia.*

All this territory was lost through the folly of one young man, as there was a beautiful damsel he truly loved, and she suddenly died and was put into a marble tomb. Because of the immense love he had for her, one night he went to her tomb and opened it and entered in and had sex with her, and then he went on his way. After nine months, a voice came to him one evening and said 'Go to that woman's tomb and open it and see what you have begotten on her, and if you don't go you shall be seriously harmed.' So he went and opened the grave and a dreadfully hideous-looking head flew out, which then flew all around the city and the region, and at once the whole city was submerged. Now the sea-crossings there are really dangerous.*

It is nearly five hundred miles from Rhodes to Cyprus, but you can go to Cyprus without going to Rhodes. Cyprus is a pleasant and large island, with many fine cities. There is an archbishop at Nicosia, and four other bishops in that region. At Famagusta is one of the best harbours to be seen in the world, and Christians, Saracens,* and people of all nations live there. In Cyprus is the Hill of the Holy

Cross of the good thief Dysmas, as I've described earlier. Some believe that half of Our Lord's Cross is there, but it's not true and they sin by having people believe in this.

In Cyprus rests St Sozomenos,* in whose honour the locals hold splendid festivals. At the castle of Dieu d'Amour rests the body of St Hilarion,* and people tend it with great devotion. St Bernard* was born near Famagusta. The Cypriots hunt with *papiouns*,* which are like leopards. They are somewhat larger than lions and they are truly excellent at capturing wild animals, which they do better and more savagely than hounds.

In Cyprus it is the custom that gentlemen and everybody else eat on the ground; they make ditches in the earth all around the hall, as deep as one's knees, and they pave it. When they want to eat they get in there and sit down; they do this because it makes things fresher, because that region is hotter than it is here. At great feasts and when foreigners visit they set up tables and benches as people do in this country, but they would rather sit on the ground.

From Cyprus one travels by land to Jerusalem and also by sea. In one day and one night, with a good wind, one can arrive at the harbour of Tyre, which is now called Sur,* and it's the entry-point for Syria. A beautiful Christian city once stood here, but the Saracens have destroyed a large part of it and they watch over the harbour really closely because they are so afraid of Christians. One can travel straight to that port without stopping at Cyprus, but many people happily go via Cyprus to rest there or maybe to buy the provisions they need for sustenance.

There, on the seashore, one can find many rubies. There's also a well, described in Holy Writ thus: *Fons ortorum et puteus aquarum uiuencium*, that is, 'The fountain of gardens and the well of living waters'.* And a woman said to Our Lord in the city of Tyre, *Beatus uenter qui te portauit et ubera que succisti*, that is, 'Blessed is the womb that bore thee, and the paps that gave thee suck.'* Our Lord forgave the Canaanite woman her sins there.* At Tyre there used to be the rock on which Our Lord sat and preached, and at that rock the church of St Saviour* was founded. On this coast is the city of Sarafend or Sarepta, where the prophet Elijah used to live and raised from the dead the prophet Jonah,* the widow's son, there.

Also, five miles from Sarafend is the city of Sidon, where Dido, who was Aeneas' wife after the destruction of Troy, came from.

Also, she founded the African city of Carthage, which is now called Sidonsayto. And Agenor, Dido's father, once reigned over the city of Tyre.* Eighteen miles from Tyre is Beirut, and from Beirut to Saidnaya is three days' travel, and from Saidnaya it is five miles by land to Damascus.

4

A LONGER WAY, BY SEA, TO JERUSALEM

IF one wants to travel more by sea on the approach to Jerusalem, one can go from Cyprus to the port of Jaffa by sea, as that's the nearest harbour to Jerusalem and from there it's only a day and a half's travel to Jerusalem. The port is named Jaffa and the town is named Yaffa after one of Noah's sons, called Japheth,* who founded it and now it's called Joppa. You should know that it's the oldest town in the world, as it was constructed before Noah's flood.

Whoever travels overland via the port of Tyre or via Syria can continue by land, if he wants, to Jerusalem, and it will take a day to get to the city of Acre (which was once called Ptolemais). This was once a city of Christians, but it's now destroyed. From Venice to Acre is 2,080 Lombard miles. From Calabria or Sicily to Acre is 1,300 Lombard miles, and Crete is exactly midway.

Near Acre, one hundred and twenty furlongs southwards on the coast, is Mount Carmel, where the prophet Elijah lived, and where the Carmelite Order of friars* was first founded. This mountain is not really very big or high. At the foot of this mountain was once a fair Christian city which was called Haifa, because Caiaphas* founded it, but it's now all laid waste. At the left side of the hill is a town called Shfaram,* which is set on another hill. St James and St John were born there, and there's an attractive church made in honour of them.

Now, it is one hundred furlongs from Acre to a high mountain called the Ladder of Tyre.* Next to the city of Acre runs a little river, called the Belus. Nearby is the circular Fosse of Mennon, which is nearly a hundred hands in size, and is full of shiny sand from which people make fine, clear glass. People come from afar with ships and by land with carts to get some of this sand. Although ever so much of it is taken in one day, the next day it is as full as ever, and that truly is a miracle. There is always a strong wind in that ditch churning the sand and making it swirl. If someone puts metal into it, it turns immediately into glass. If glass that was made here is placed back into the sand, it turns into sand again, as it was at first. Some say that it is a chasm of the sandy sea.*

From the aforementioned city of Acre one travels for three days to the Philistine city now called Gaza, that is to say, 'the rich city';* it is exceptionally pretty and full of people and is near the seaside. Samson the Strong destroyed the gates of this city when he was captured here and he killed the King in his palace and many thousands with him, by causing a house to fall down on top of them.* From here one travels to Caesarea* and then to Chastiau Pélèrin* and then to Ashkelon and then to Jaffa and thus to Jerusalem.

5

THE WAY FROM GAZA TO BABYLON

WHOSOEVER wishes to travel overland to Babylon, where the Sultan lives, should obtain, by request from him, permission to travel in safety through the country, in order to go to Mount Sinai before reaching Jerusalem and then returning again via Jerusalem, going from Gaza to Castle Dair.* After that, one leaves Syria and enters into the desert, where the route becomes really sandy, and to travel across the desert takes eight days, but one finds all one needs to survive. People call this wilderness the Achellek desert. When one leaves this desert one enters Egypt; they call Egypt 'Canopat', and in another language 'Misrin'. The first decent town one encounters is called Bilbeis, and it's at the edge of the kingdom of Aleppo, and from Aleppo one arrives at Babylon and Cairo.*

In Babylon there's a beautiful church of Our Lady, where she lived for seven years when she fled from the land of Judea in fear of King Herod.* The body of St Barbara* the virgin rests there. Joseph lived there when he was sold by his brothers.* Nebuchadnezzar put three children in the furnace there because they were entirely holy: these children are called Hananiah, Azariah, Mishael as the psalm called 'Benedicite' says, but Nebuchadnezzar called them Shadrach, Meshach, and Abednego, meaning 'God glorious, God victorious,

God over all kingdoms';* and it was through a miracle, as he said, that the Son of God accompanies these children through the fire.

The Sultan lives at Babylon, because there is a handsome, strong castle there, well placed on a rock. In that castle, to protect it and to serve the Sultan, there are always some eight thousand men who are provided with all the necessaries by the Sultan's court. I should know because I lived with him as a mercenary for a long time, in his wars against the Bedouins. He wanted me to marry a local noble prince's daughter, so that I would have abjured my faith.*

You really should know that the Sultan rules over five kingdoms, which he has conquered and gained by force; these are: Canopat, that is, Egypt; the kingdom of Jerusalem, of which David and Solomon were kings; the kingdom of Syria, of which the city of Damascus was the capital; the kingdom of Aleppo in the land of Damietta; and the kingdom of Arabia, of which one of the three kings who presented a gift to our newborn Lord was king. The Sultan also exercises his authority over many other lands, and he holds the Caliphate, which is a great thing for the Sultan: it's like them saying that he is *le roi*.* You should know that there used to be five sultans in keeping with the kingdoms, which are five in number, and they now belong to the Sultan. There is now only one Sultan, who is called the Sultan of Babylon.

The first Sultan of Egypt was called Yaracon, and he was the father of Saladin,* who was Sultan after Yaracon at the same time that King Richard* was in their country with his army of Christians. After Saladin his son Boradyn reigned, and after him his nephew reigned.

When he was dead, the Egyptian commoners realized they had been excessively enthralled and in awe of him, and they saw that they were strong because there were so many of them, and they went and chose one of their own as Sultan, and he was called Melechsala. In these days Louis, King of France,* travelled to the Holy Land and fought with the Sultan, and the King was captured and imprisoned there. This same Sultan was afterwards murdered by his own servants and another was chosen in his place, who was called Tympieman. He ransomed King Louis and freed him from prison.

Afterwards, a commoner called Cothas killed Tympieman and was made Sultan in his place, and he called himself Melechomethos,* who soon afterwards was murdered by another commoner, named Bendochdaer, who reigned in his place, and he called himself Melechdaer. During his reign good King Edward* travelled to Syria and did much harm to the Saracens. This same Sultan was poisoned at Damascus, and died there.

Now, after him his son would have reigned as the next in line and he had called himself Melechsayt. However, there soon came another person, called Elphy, with many followers, and he drove Melechsayt into exile and made himself Sultan. He captured the city of Tripoli and killed many Christian people there, in the year of Our Lord 1279. Afterwards, he, this Elphy, was poisoned by somebody else who coveted the Sultanate, and he himself was murdered shortly thereafter.

So then they chose Elphy's son as their Sultan and called him Melechesserak. He captured the city of Acre and exiled all the Christians there. Afterwards he died from poisoning, and his brother reigned in his place and was called Melechinasser. Soon afterwards a man called Guytoga seized this Sultan and had him imprisoned in the castle of Montreal,* and he reigned in his place and was named Melechadelle.

Because this Melechadelle was a foreigner, that is a Tartar, he was forced into exile and another person, called Bathyn, was made Sultan and named Melechynanser. One day, while this Melechynanser was playing chess with someone else, with his sword standing drawn beside him, he got into an argument with this other person and this other person grasped his own sword and killed him with it.

Afterwards, the election of a new Sultan caused an enormous amount of discord amongst them. In the end they all agreed that the aforementioned Melechinasser, the one imprisoned by Guytoga at Montreal, should be their Sultan. This Melechinasser reigned for a long time, and governed with such great wisdom that when he died his eldest son was elected Sultan, and he was named Melchinadere, whom his brother had secretly killed and reigned in his place, and he was called Melechimandabron. He was Sultan when I left this country.

The Sultan can lead more than twenty thousand soldiers out of Egypt, and more than fifty thousand soldiers out of Syria, Turkey, and other realms subject to him. Every single one of them is paid his wages and supplied with all his needs by the Sultan; that is to say, each one of them is paid one hundred and twenty florins* a year, but each is required to keep three horses and a camel.

In the different towns and cities there are people amongst them who are appointed, called admirals.* Each individual admiral has at his command four, five, or six soldiers, and some have more. Each individual admiral takes as much in wages for himself as those serving under him. Therefore when the Sultan wishes to promote any excellent man he makes him an admiral. If there is any kind of shortage then the knights and the soldiers sell their armour and weapons out of poverty.

The Sultan has three wives, of which one is always a Christian woman and the other two are Saracens. One of his wives must live in Jerusalem, another in Damascus, and the third at Ashkelon. He visits them whenever he wants to and he sometimes travels around with them. Nevertheless he has as many lovers as he wishes. When he arrives at any city or town he has all the noblest and prettiest virgins of the region brought before him, and he has them detained there respectfully and with dignity. When he wants to have any of them he has them brought before him and he sends or throws his ring to the one who is to his liking. Then she is led away and washed and sprinkled with fragrance and nicely dressed and then a meal will be brought to his bedroom. And he does this whenever he wishes.

No foreigners are allowed to present themselves before the Sultan unless they are dressed in the kind of clothing the Saracens wear: cloth-of-gold or tars* or camlet.* As soon as anyone glimpses the Sultan, even if it's at a window or elsewhere, he is required to kneel down and kiss the ground, as this is the way those who wish to speak with the Sultan show their reverence for him. When any foreigners visit with an embassy from distant lands, his people stand around the Sultan with their swords drawn and one hand aloft ready to slap down the foreigner if he says anything that displeases the Sultan. No foreigners present themselves before the Sultan to request things unless they are reasonable and not contrary to his law. This is just the same for other princes and noblemen in that country, as they say that nobody should approach a prince without being happier on leaving his presence than he was when coming there.

You ought to know that this Babylon of which I am now speaking, where the Sultan lives, is not the Great Babylon where the confusion of tongues was made, when the Tower of Babel* existed, the walls of which were sixty-four furlongs high; this is in the Arabian desert as one travels towards the kingdom of Chaldea. It has been a long time since anybody dared to go near that wretched place, as it is now desolate and absolutely full of dragons and snakes and other venomous beasts that nobody would dare even to approach. The circumference of the Tower encompassing the city was some twenty-five miles, as they report in that region. Although it is called the Tower, there were actually many fine buildings within, which are now destroyed and there is nothing but wilderness. You should be aware that it was built in the pattern of four squares, and each square was at least six square miles. This Tower was established by Nimrod,* who was king of that land, and people say that he was the first earthly king that ever was. He also had an effigy made in his father's memory and ordered all his subjects to worship that effigy. All the powerful lords thereabouts did the same things, and so idolatry first began.

That city of Great Babylon was located in a pleasant plain, which was called the field of Shinar,* on the banks of the River Euphrates which then ran through that city. The city walls were two hundred cubits high and fifty cubits thick. Afterwards Cyrus,* the Persian king, caused the water to be cut off and the city and all the surrounding area destroyed. He split the River Euphrates and had it run in three hundred and forty different ways. He had sworn a great oath and sworn so seriously that he would have it in such a state that women would be able to wade through it without getting their knees wet, and this he did. This was all because often so many of his finest soldiers had drowned in that river.

Travelling north-east from the Babylon where the Sultan lives to the Great Babylon is forty days' travel through the desert. The latter Babylon is not subject to the Sultan but under the lordship of the King of Persia. It is held by the Great Khan, who is a great emperor, indeed the greatest in the world, as he is lord of the great isle of Cathay* and many other countries and of a large part of India. His land borders Prester John's land. He is lord of so many territories that he doesn't know where it ends. He is incomparably greater and stronger than the Sultan. I will describe his impressive circumstances and his grandeur afterwards, when I get to it.

In the great deserts of Arabia is the city of Mecca, and the body of Muhammad rests there, most nobly, in a temple the Saracens call 'Mosque'. This city is thirty-two days' travel from Babylon where the Sultan lives. You need to be aware that the realm of Arabia is very large but it has many deserts within it and these are not easily habitable because they are lacking in water and the deserts are so dry and sandy that nothing may grow in them. However, where the land is inhabited there are very many people.

Arabia stretches from the ends of Chaldea to the far end of Arabia, and it borders Idumea near Botron.* The main city of Chaldea is Baghdad. The main city of Africa is Carthage, which was founded by Dido, the wife of Aeneas,* the first King of Troy and then of Italy. Mesopotamia borders the Arabian Desert and is a large country, in which is the city of Haran* where the patriarch Abraham once lived. The great scholar Ephrem* was from this city, as was Theophilus, whom Our Lady freed from enslavement to the Devil,* as one can find written in the book *The Miracles of the Virgin*. Mesopotamia extends from the River Euphrates to the River Tigris, for the realm lies between the two.

Beyond the Tigris is the kingdom of Chaldea, which is a great and large country. In that country, as I said before, is the city of Baghdad in which the Caliph was accustomed to live, he who was pope and emperor of those people, that is to say, both the spiritual and temporal lord. He was the successor to Muhammad and his lineage. The city of Baghdad was once called Susa, and Nebuchadnezzar established it. The prophet Daniel lived there and many times had visions of God, and he interpreted the King's dreams there. Since the Sultan Saladin the Caliph has been called Sultan.

Babylon the Lesser, where the Sultan lives, and the nearby city of Cairo, are both great, pleasant cities. The former is situated on the River Gehon that is also called the Nile, and it comes out at the Earthly Paradise.* Every year, when the sun enters the sign of Cancer, this river begins to rise and it continues to rise as long as the sun is in that sign and in the sign of Leo. Sometimes it rises so much that it is twenty cubits deep, and then it floods all the land and does great damage to the places situated by the river. Nobody can get to work at tilling the land during those times, and so it often happens that there is a great shortage of corn in that country due to the excessive wetness. Likewise, there are great shortages when this river only rises a little because of the excessive dryness. When the sun enters the sign of Virgo then the Nile begins to fall until the sun enters the sign of Libra, and then it contains itself within the riverbanks. This river, as I said before, flows out of Paradise and runs through the deserts of India, and then it runs down into the ground and thus flows underground through a large region and it comes up again under a mountain called Alloche, which is between India and Ethiopia, some five months' travel from the Ethiopian border. Then it flows around

Ethiopia and Mauretania and all the way through Egypt to the city of Alexandria, and there it enters the sea at the edge of Egypt. Along this river there are very many fowl called, in Latin, *ciconie* or *ibices*.*

The land of Egypt is long but narrow, as people cannot inhabit it widely because of the deserts where there is a lack of water, and so it is inhabited along the length of this aforementioned river. They have no source of water apart from that supplied by this river, as it does not rain there, and the land is flooded by this river at certain times of the year, as I said before. Moreover, because there is no turbulence in the air from rain, the air is always fine and clear, without clouds, and so the best astronomers in the world were customarily found there. The aforementioned city of Cairo, in which the Sultan dwells, is next to the city of Babylon, as I said before, and is only a little way from the aforementioned River Nile towards the Syrian desert.

Egypt is divided into two parts. The first part is between the Nile and Ethiopia, and the other is between the Nile and Arabia. The land of Rameses* is in Egypt, and so is the land of Goshen where the patriarch Jacob and his offspring* lived. Egypt is a very formidable country, for there are many dangerous ports there on account of the numerous stark crags lying in the entrance to each harbour. On the east side, Egypt has the Red Sea that runs as far as the city of Qus. On the west side is the land of Libya, which is barren because of the excessive heat and it bears no kind of fruit. On the south side is Ethiopia, and at the north are the great deserts lasting all the way to Syria. So the country is formidable on every side. The land of Egypt is fifteen days' travel in length and only three days' travel in breadth, not counting the deserts.

It is twelve days' travel through the desert between Egypt and the land called Nubia. The tribe who live in that region are called Nubians and they are christened. However, they are black in colour, and they believe that to be very beautiful, and indeed the blacker they are the fairer they think themselves. They say that if they were to paint an angel and a devil, they would paint the angel black and the devil white. If they feel that they are not black enough when they are born they use certain medicines to make themselves thoroughly black. This country is spectacularly hot and that's what makes the people there so black.

There are five provinces in Egypt. One is called Sa'id, another Damanhur, the third Rashid (which is an island in the River Nile), the fourth is Alexandria, the fifth is Damietta. The city of Damietta was once exceptionally formidable, but it was captured twice by

Christians and then the Saracens destroyed its walls and all the castles in the region. So they made another city on the coast called New Damietta. This city of Damietta is one of the ports of Egypt, and there is another one at Alexandria, which is a formidable and well-walled city. However, it would have no water but for that which comes from conduits from the River Nile, and so if people cut off their water they could not endure for long. In Egypt there are only a few castles because the country is strong enough by itself.

Once upon a time, in the Egyptian desert, a holy hermit met a deformed beast, for it had the form of a human from the navel down and from there upwards the form of a goat, with two horns standing on the head. The hermit asked him what in God's name he was, and the beast answered, saying, 'I am a mortal creature as God created me and I live in this desert and seek out my sustenance. Therefore I beg of you, hermit, that you will pray to God for me, that He who came from Heaven to Earth for the salvation of man's soul and was born of a Virgin and suffered His painful Passion through which we all live, and move, and have existence, that He will have mercy on me.' The head of that beast with the horns is still kept and looked after at Alexandria, as a miracle.*

In Egypt there is also a city called Heliopolis, which is as if to call it 'the city of the sun'. In this city there is a circular temple, in the manner of the Temple of Jerusalem. The temple priest has a book in which is written the dates relating to a bird called the phoenix.* There is only one in the world, and this bird lives for five hundred years and at the end of the five-hundredth year he comes to the aforementioned temple and, on the altar, burns itself to ash. The priest knows, from his book, when the bird will come, and prepares the altar, and lays thereupon various spices and live sulphur and twigs of juniper wood and other things that will readily burn. Then the bird comes and descends on the altar and beats its wings until the said things set on fire, and he burns himself there until all is ash. The next day they find, in the ashes, a kind of worm. On the second day that worm has turned into a perfectly formed bird. Then on the third day it flies from that place to the place where it ordinarily lives. There is only a single one of these. This very bird is a token of Our Lord Jesus Christ just as there is only one God who rose on the third day from death to life. This aforesaid bird is often seen flying about when the weather is fine and clear. Local people say that when they see that bird soaring through the air they will afterwards have good, happy years, as they say it is a bird of heaven. This bird is no bigger than an eagle in its body. He has a crest, like a peacock's, on his head, although it is much bigger than a peacock's. His neck is yellow and his back is indigo. His wings are red and his tail is striped across in green and yellow and red. In sunlight he is wonderfully pretty, as there the colours are shown best.

In Egypt there are places where the land bears fruit eight times per year. There they find, in the ground, the prettiest emeralds available anywhere, and this is why they are cheaper there than anywhere else. Also, if it should happen to rain once in the summer the whole of Egypt is full of mice. In the city of Cairo foreign men and women are frequently brought to the market and sold as people might sell animals in other countries. Moreover, in Cairo a public building has been designed and made full of hollows like hens' nests, and the local women bring eggs—of hen, goose, or duck—and place them in the nests. Certain people are appointed to look after that house and to cover the eggs with warm horse-dung. Through the heat of the horse-dung the eggs hatch birds without needing a setting hen or any other bird. After three or four weeks the women come who brought the eggs and they take away the birds and rear them as local custom dictates. In this way the whole country replenishes its stock of birds, and they do this in winter as well as summer.

At a certain time of the year in that country people sell long apples, which the local people call 'paradise apples',* and they are sweet and delicious to taste. If one should slice them in different places across the middle one finds the sign of the Cross. However, they rot within eight days, and so they cannot be taken far abroad. The trees that bear them have leaves a foot and a half wide and often one can find a hundred of these apples in a bunch. There are other apples there called 'Adam's apples',* and each of them has teeth-marks on one side just like they've been bitten by a person's teeth. There are also fig trees that never have leaves but bear fruit on bare branches, and they are called 'Pharaoh figs'.*

A little way from the city of Cairo is a field in which balm grows on small bushes, about a foot high, like wild vines. In this field there are also seven wells where, in His youth, Christ liked to play with other children, and He demonstrated various miracles there.* This field is not so well fenced-off that one cannot enter when one wishes, except at the time the balm is growing and then the field is guarded very rigorously, as the balm grows nowhere else, not in that region or elsewhere. Even if people take plants or grafts from them and plant them in other places, they might grow but they will never fruit. The leaves of the balm do not smell as good as the balm itself does. They cut away the dead branches with a specially designed instrument, not made out of iron, and this instrument is called *gaylounagon*. If that instrument were to be made out of iron it would corrupt the good properties and the healthy nature of these trees, as experience has often proved. When the time comes for it to be cultivated, local people get Christians to cultivate it and harvest it, otherwise the trees would not bear fruit, as the Saracens themselves say and as has often been proved. The Saracens call the trees that bear this balm *enochbalse*, and the fruits, which are like wild berries, are called *abedbissam*. However, the sap that is exuded from the branches is called *oxbalse*, that it to say 'opobalsamum'.* Some people say that this balm grows in the deserts of Upper India, there where the Trees of the Sun and the Moon spoke to Alexander the Great.* But I haven't seen that place, because of the dangerous routes leading there, and so I cannot tell you the truth of it.

You should be aware that people are easily deceived when buying balm unless they have superior knowledge about it. This is because some people sell a kind of gum called turpentine and add a little balm to it to make it smell nice. Some people also add oil from the tree or berries from the balm and then say that it is good balm. Some people distil cloves, valerian, and other sweet-smelling spices and they sell the sap distilled from them instead of balm, and in this way many people, both aristocrats and commoners, are deceived. Because, to be sure, the Saracens perform such tricky adulterations in order to deceive Christians, as I have often found out from experience. Merchants and apothecaries perform similar deceptions to it afterwards too, and then it is of even less value.

So, if you would like, I will show you how to test and prove which is the real balm and so not be deceived. You should be aware that the good, natural balm is absolutely clear and golden and has a strong, pleasant scent. If it's thick, red, or black then it is adulterated. Also, you can take a little balm and lay it in the palm of your hand and hold it to the sun, and if you cannot bear holding it because of the heat then it is real balm. Also, take a little balm on the tip of your knife and place it in a flame, and if it burns it is real balm. Then take a drop of balm and put it in a dish or a cup and add goat's milk to it, and if it is real balm the milk will curdle at once. Also, add a drop of it to pure water in a goblet or in a clean basin and mix the water and the balm together; the stirred water will be clear if the balm is real, and if it is cloudy and muddy then it is adulterated balm. The real balm is much stronger than that which has been adulterated.

Now I have said something about balm, I will tell you about Joseph's barns, which are in Egypt, beyond the Nile, towards the desert between Egypt and Africa. Joseph's barns are here, made for storing corn during the seven barren years which were signified by the seven dead ears of corn which King Pharaoh dreamt of, as described in the first book of the Bible.* They are extraordinarily ingeniously made, cut from splendidly hewn stone. Two of them are astonishingly high and also very wide, and the others are not so high. Each one them has a porch at the entrance. Each barn is now totally full of snakes, and people can still see written on them inscriptions in different languages. Some say that these are the graves of great people of olden times, but the general opinion is that they are Joseph's barns, and they find that in their chronicles. Indeed, truthfully, it is not likely that they are tombs in as much as they are empty inside and they have porches and gates in front of them, and also tombs should not, rationally, be so high.

In Egypt there are different languages and different letters and these are of a different shape than in other places. Therefore I will set down both the letters and their sounds and names here, so you can know the difference between these letters and the letters of other languages:* *Athomanus*, *Binchi*, *Chinok*, *Dynam*, *Em*, *Fiu*, *Gomor*, *Heket*, *Ianiu*, *Karacta*, *Linzamin*, *Miche*, *Narme*, *Oldach*, *Pilon*, *Qyny*, *Rou*, *Sichen*, *Thela*, *Vr*, *Xyron*, *Ypha*, *Zarum*, *Thou*.

Athomanus	*Binchi*	*Chinok*	*Dynam*	*Em*	*Fiu*
Gomor	*Heket*	*Ianiu*	*Karacta*	*Linzamin*	*Miche*
Narme	*Oldach*	*Pilon*	*Qyny*	*Rou*	*Sichen*
Thela	*Vr*	*Xyron*	*Ypha*	*Zarum*	*Thou*

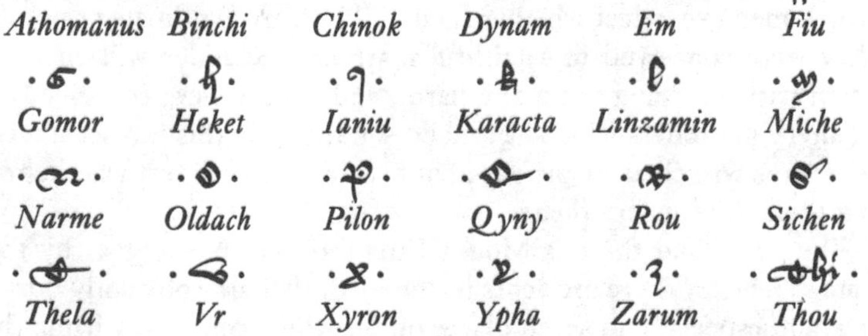

Before I go any further I would like to go back and describe other routes by which one may travel to Babylon where the Sultan lives, which is at the entrance to Egypt; because many pilgrims travel there first and then to Mount Sinai and then return via Jerusalem, as I described before. So they make the furthest pilgrimage first and then come back via the holy places, which are closer (even though these places are not as important as Jerusalem which is without compare in terms of pilgrimage). It is only to make their journeys as safe as possible and with the least difficulty that some people go to the furthest places first and then to the nearer places.

Now whoever wants to go to Babylon first by a shorter route from this country or another one nearby, as I have already described, can go through France and through Burgundy. It is not necessary to give all the names of the cities and towns through which one must go, as the route is familiar and widely known to everybody who engages in travelling. However, there are many ports at which to embark. Some embark at Genoa, some at Venice and sail through the Adriatic Sea, which is called the Gulf of Venice and divides Italy and Greece on that side, and some travel to Naples, some to Rome and then to Brindisi and embark there, or otherwise some go to other places where they find a port and available boats.

Indeed, some travel through Tuscany and Campania and Calabria and Apulia and the Italian islands via Corsica, Sardinia, and Sicily, which is a pretty and large island. On that island there is a garden with many different kinds of fruit, and that garden is always green and full of flowers in both winter and summer. This island is three hundred and fifty leagues in circumference. Between Italy and Sicily there is just a tiny strait of the sea called Faro.* The island of Sicily is between the Adriatic Sea and the Lombardy Sea. From Sicily to Calabria it is eight Lombard miles. In Sicily there is a kind of adder which men use to test whether their children are legitimate or not. If they were conceived in a faithful marriage the adder will encircle them without doing them any harm, and if they were conceived in adultery the adders will sting and poison them. In this way local men who have wretched suspicions about their wives can test whether or not their children are theirs.

On this island there is Mount Etna too, which also goes by the name Gebel.* There are vents in the earth that are constantly burning, and especially in seven places out of which come fiery flames in different colours. From the variation of the colour local people know and predict whether there will be a shortage of corn or a good market, whether the weather will be hot or cold, rainy or fair. They prognosticate and divine many other things by the colour of the flames. From Italy to the vents is only twenty-five miles, and they say there that these are the entrances and gates of Hell.

Some people travel via the city of Pisa, where there is an inlet of the sea and two ports, and those embarking at sea there will travel via the island of Corfu, which belongs to the Genoese. Once one disembarks in Greece at Port Myroch or at the city of Vlorë or Durrës, which belongs to the dukes of Durazzo, or at some other ports on the coast, one continues thus to Constantinople by sea to the Greek islands and to the islands of Rhodes and Cyprus. So to take the correct route by sea from Venice to Constantinople is 1,880 Lombard miles.

From the kingdom of Cyprus one may travel by sea to the port of Jaffa and onwards, leaving all that region on the left-hand side, until the town of Alexandria, which stands on that side of the coast. St Catherine's head* was slashed off in that city. Also St Mark was martyred and buried in that city, but later the Emperor Leo had his bones brought and transported to Venice and they continue to rest there.* At Alexandria there is still a pretty church entirely whitewashed, and this is like all the other Christian churches there, as the pagans and the Saracens had them whitewashed to remove the paintings and the images that were portrayed on the walls. This city of Alexandria is thirty furlongs in length and ten wide, and it is a truly fine and gracious city. The River Nile enters the sea at this city, as I described before. In that river one often finds many precious gems and wood that is called 'aloe',* which comes from Paradise. It is a medicinal substance for many illnesses and it is sold at incredibly high prices. From Alexandria one travels to Babylon where the Sultan lives, and it stands on the River Nile. This is the most direct and short way one may travel to Babylon.

Now I will describe the route one should follow from Babylon to Mount Sinai, where the body of St Catherine rests. It is necessary to pass through the Arabian deserts where Moses and Aaron led the people of Israel.* On that route there is a well to which Moses led them and gave them a drink when the people murmured against him because of their thirst. Further on this route there is another well, called Mara,* where they found bitter water when they wanted to drink, and Moses put a kind of wood in there and the bitterness was immediately removed. From there one travels through this desert to the Elim Valley,* where there are twelve wells and sixty-two date-bearing palm trees, where Moses and the Children of Israel camped. From this valley to Mount Sinai is only one day's travel.

Whoever wishes to go some other way from Babylon to Mount Sinai might well travel by the Red Sea, which is an inlet of the Western Sea, through which the Children of Israel went with dry feet when King Pharaoh pursued them, in which he and all his army was drowned.* It is about six miles across. The waters of that sea are no redder than seawater elsewhere, except for the very red sand on the seashore, and that is why people call it the Red Sea. It runs to the borders of Arabia and Palestine. One can travel for four days by this sea and then you will reach the said Elim Valley and so on to Mount Sinai.

You should be aware that the desert is impassable with horses because there are no stables or provender for the horses to eat and drink. So people make this pilgrimage with camels, for they can always find edible boughs of trees on the route, as they greatly love that food, and they can do without drink for two or three days, which a horse may not.

From Babylon to Mount Sinai is twelve days' travel. Nevertheless some people hurry so fast on their journey that they travel in less time. It is necessary on this journey to have people who can speak Latin until one has picked up the local language, and this is also necessary for people coming from other countries to this area. It is necessary also for them to pack up all their provisions that they need to survive and carry them through the desert.

Mount Sinai is called the Desert of Sin,* which is to call it Burning Bush, for Moses saw Our Lord God there speaking to him in a burning bush.* At the foot of Mount Sinai a monastic abbey has been established, firmly surrounded by high walls and iron gates out of fear for the cruel and wicked wild animals living in the desert. The monks living within are Arabs and Greeks and they dress like hermits and there is a large community of them. They survive on dates and roots and herbs. They don't usually drink wine, except on high holidays. They are devout men and they lead a chaste life and live in great abstinence and great penance.

The church of St Catherine is there, with many burning lamps. They use olive oil both for food and for burning lamps. That oil comes to them as if miraculously. Rooks and crows and other birds come flying there each year, in a great swarm all together as if they are making their own kind of pilgrimage, and each one of them brings in its beak an olive branch in place of an offering and leaves it there. For this reason there is a great abundance of olives left to sustain the monastery. Since birds, which have no reason, can perform such reverence to the glorious virgin, well ought Christians visit that holy place with great piety.

Behind the altar of that church is the place where Moses saw Our Lord in the burning bush. Now when the monks come to that place they take off their stockings and their shoes, because God said to Moses, 'put off the shoes from thy feet: for the place whereon thou standest is holy ground'.* That place is called the Shadow of God.

Next to the high altar are four steps to go up to the alabaster tomb where the body of the holy virgin St Catherine rests. The monks' prelate displays the relics of this virgin to pilgrims, and with a silver instrument he moves the virgin's bones about on an altar. Then a little bit of oil is exuded, like sweat, but it is neither oil nor balm, as it is blacker. He gives this liquid in little quantities to the pilgrims, as only a tiny amount comes out. Then they display the head of St Catherine and the cloth it was wrapped in when the angels brought the body up Mount Sinai. They buried it there with that very cloth, and it is still bloodied and always will be. They also display that bush which Moses saw burning when Our Lord spoke to him. They display many other relics too.

Each monk at this monastery constantly has a lamp burning. I was told that when an abbot dies his lamp is extinguished. To elect another abbot a lamp lights itself, which, by the grace of God, belongs to the one who is most worthy of being the next abbot. As I said, each of them has his own lamp and when one of them is about to die they know by his lamp, for the light of the lamp will weaken close to the time he is to die.

I was also told that when a prelate is dead and is to be buried, he who sings the high mass will find on a scroll placed in front of him on the altar the name of the one who shall be chosen to be their prelate. I asked the monks if this was so, but they would not tell me, other than to say that formerly it happened like this. They still would not say very much, so I told them that it was not for them to keep secrets or to hide God's grace and miracles but rather to publish and display them openly to prompt people to devotion. Moreover, I told them that it seemed to me that they really sinned by hiding this, for the miracles that God displays are testimony to His great power, as David says in the psalter.* When I had said these words to them, they immediately said what I told you before, and they would not answer any more of the questions I asked them.

Through a miracle of God, His mother St Mary, and the holy virgin St Catherine, in that abbey there are never any fleas or flies or any other kind of noxious pests. Once there was great swarm of such dirty bugs and the monks of the abbey were so tormented by them that they left that place and fled elsewhere, up into the mountains. And the Blessed Virgin arrived just so, and met with them and requested that they return to their abbey, and they would never more have such irritation and discomfort. They did as she requested and returned. Never again after that day did they see a flea or a fly or any kind of noxious thing to harass them. In front of the gate of that abbey is the well where Moses struck the stone with his rod and it ran with water, and it shall do so eternally.*

From this abbey one climbs up many stairs to Mount Moses and there is a church of Our Lady where she met the monks, as I described before. Further up the mountain is Moses' chapel and the rock he fled to when he saw Our Lord, in which rock is imprinted the outline and shape of his body, because, fleeing, he threw his body so strenuously against it that through a divine miracle the shape of his body was left in it. Very close to this place is the place where Our Lord gave Moses the Ten Commandments* of the Law written on two tablets of stone by God's own hands. Under a rock there is the cave where Moses lived when he fasted for forty days and forty nights.* However, he died in the Holy Land and nobody knows where he was buried.

From this mountain one goes through a large valley to another mountain, where the angels buried the body of St Catherine. In that valley there is a church of forty martyrs where the monks from the aforementioned abbey often sing. This valley is so cold. One can go up St Catherine's Mountain, and it's much higher than Mount Moses.* There, where St Catherine was buried, is no church or chapel or any other dwelling, but just a pile of stones gathered together on the spot where she was buried by angels. There used to be a chapel here, but it has been destroyed and the stones are still lying there. And according to the prayers specific to the veneration of St Catherine,* this is the very place where Our Lord gave the Law to Moses and where St Catherine was buried, but by this it is understood that one name is given to the whole region and the specific places, as they are both called Mount Sinai, but it is actually a long way between them.

6

THE WAY TO JERUSALEM

AFTER visiting St Catherine's holy place, if you wish to turn towards Jerusalem, you should first take leave of the monks and recommend yourself specially to their prayers. These monks generously provide provisions to pilgrims in order to pass through the desert to Syria, deserts which last more than thirteen days' travel.

Lots of Arabs live in that desert, one calls them Bedouins and Ascopards.* These peoples live in wretched conditions: instead of houses they have tents which they sleep in, made out of the skins of animals like camels and others which they also eat. They live in places where they can get water, such as the Red Sea, because in that desert there's a serious lack of water. It often happens in this region that where you find water in one season it's not there in another season, and so people don't build houses in that region. These people of whom I speak don't cultivate the land, because they eat no bread unless they live near a large town. They roast all their fish and their meat on hot stones in the sun. They are strong folk, good at fighting, and they do nothing for sustenance apart from hunt wild animals. They don't value their lives, and so they are not afraid of the Sultan or any other prince in the world. They are often at war with the Sultan. That same time I was with the Sultan, I saw them bear nothing but a shield and spear in order to defend their bodies. They had no other armour, except that they wound a large white linen cloth around their heads and their necks. They truly are stinking, perfidious people of a very wretched disposition.

Once one has crossed this desert on the way to Jerusalem, one arrives at Beer Sheva, which used to be a pretty and delightful city of

Christians, and some of their churches are still there. Abraham the patriarch used to live in this town. This town of Beer Sheva was founded by the wife of Uriah, on whom David begot Solomon the Wise, who was King of Jerusalem and of the Twelve Tribes of Israel, and who reigned for forty years.*

From here one travels to the Vale of Hebron, which is twelve miles away. Some call it the Vale of Mambre,* and it's also called the Vale of Tears as in this valley Adam lamented for one hundred years for the murder of his son Abel by Cain.* Hebron was once the Philistines' main city, and giants lived there, and it was the priestly city of the Tribe of Judah. It used to be so exempt from external control that they took in all the criminals and fugitives from other places. In Hebron, Joshua and Caleb and their retinue scouted out how they could win the Promised Land.* In Hebron, King David reigned first for seven and a half years, and in Jerusalem he reigned thirty-three and a half years.* Right there in Hebron are the graves of the patriarchs: Adam, Abraham, Jacob, and their wives, Eve, Sarah, and Rebecca, and they are on the slope of the hillside. Below them is a very beautiful church,* crenellated in the form of a castle, which the Saracens guard very vigilantly, and they hold that place in great reverence because of the patriarchs buried there. They won't let any Christian or the Jews enter in there unless they have the Sultan's special permission, because they believe Christians and Jews are like dogs and should enter no holy place. They call that place Spelunk or Double Cave or Double Tomb, because one lies on top of another. And, in their language, the Saracens call it Kiryat-Arba, that is, the Place of the Patriarchs. And Jews call it Arbee.*

Abraham's house was in that same place, and it's here that he sat at his door and saw three persons and worshipped one:* as Holy Writ bears witness, *Tres uidit et unum adorauit*, that is, 'He saw three and he worshipped one'.* And Abraham received him into his house.

Very close to that place is a cave in the rock where Adam and Eve were living when they were driven out of Paradise. It was here that they begot their children. In that same place Adam was made, as some say, for once people called that place the Field of Damascus because it was under the sovereignty of Damascus; it was from here that he was translated into Paradise, as they say, and afterwards he was driven out of Paradise and put in that place again, because on the same day that he was put into Paradise he was driven out, as he sinned so quickly.

The Vale of Hebron begins here, and continues nearly all the way to Jerusalem. The angel ordered Adam to have intercourse with his wife, and there Seth was conceived,* from whose descendants Jesus Christ was born.

In that valley there's a field where people extract a thing called *chambille** from the ground, and they eat it instead of spices. They take it away to sell at the market. One cannot dig deep and wide enough that, by the end of the year, the field isn't full up again, by the grace of God.

Also, two miles from Hebron is that grave of Lot, who was Abraham's brother. A little distance from Hebron is Mount Mamre,* from which that valley took its name. There is an oak tree dating from Abraham's time which the Saracens call *dirpe*, or one might call it the Dry Tree.* They say that it has been there since the beginning of the world, and that once it was green and bore leaves until the time when Our Lord died, and then it dried up. All the trees in the world did likewise, or else they withered in their core or some others wilted, and many of these trees are still there and can be seen. Some prophecies say that a leader, a prince from the western side of the world, shall gain the Promised Land (that is, the Holy Land) with the assistance of Christians, and he will perform a sung mass under the Dry Tree and then the tree will turn green, bear fruit, and grow leaves. So many Saracens and Jews will be converted to the Christian faith through that miracle. Therefore the locals are very devoted to this tree and they tend it very diligently; even though it's totally dry, it has tremendous qualities for, to be sure, one who carries just a little bit can be healed of epilepsy, and it also has lots of other benefits and therefore it is considered to be very precious.

From Hebron one can go to Bethlehem in just half a day, as it's only five miles, and it's a perilous journey through very pleasant woods.* Moreover, Bethlehem is a little city, long and narrow and handsomely walled and enclosed by a fine moat. It used to be called Effrata, as it says in Holy Writ, *Ecce audiuimus eum in Effrata,* that is, 'Behold we have heard of it in Ephrata'.* At the eastern city-limits is a pretty church and it has many finely wrought towers, pinnacles, and crenellations. Within that church there are forty-four strong and beautiful marble pillars.*

Between this church and the city is a flowery field, and it's called *Campus floridus* or the Flowery Field* on account of a beautiful virgin who was wrongly accused of fornication, for which she was sentenced to be burnt in that place. She was led there, and, as the faggots began to burn, she prayed to Our Lord that He would help her make it known to everyone that she was not guilty. When she had said her prayer thus, she entered the flames, and immediately the fire was extinguished. The burning branches became red rose-bushes, and the branches that were not burning became white rose-bushes full of flowers. These were the first roses and rose-bushes that any person ever saw. And so the virgin was saved through the grace of God, and that's why the field, full of blooming roses, is called Flowery Field.

Also, to the right of that church,* next to the choir, descending seventeen steps, is the place where Our Lord was born, which is now very beautifully decorated in marble and painted richly with gold, silver, azure, and other colours. Three paces from there is the Crib of the Ox and the Ass.* Beside this is the place where the star appeared that led the three kings: Jasper, Melchior, Balthazar (but the Greeks call them Galgath, Galgalath, Saraphy).* These three kings offered Our Lord frankincense, gold, and myrrh. They travelled together through a divine miracle, for they met in an Indian city called Kashan which is fifty-three days' travel from Bethlehem, and they arrived in Bethlehem on the fourth day after they had seen the star.

Eighteen steps under the church's cloister, to the right-hand side, is the charnel-house where the bones of the Holy Innocents* lie. In front of the place where Christ was born is that tomb of the sometime cardinal and priest, St Jerome,* who translated the Bible and the psalter from Hebrew into Latin. Adjacent to that church is a church of St Nicholas where Our Lady rested when she had delivered her child.* She had so much milk in her breasts that it hurt her, so she expressed it onto the red marble stones so that even now one may see white stains on these stones.

You should be aware that everyone who lives in Bethlehem is a Christian. There are excellent vineyards around the city and plenty of wine made by the Christians, as the Saracens neither cultivate vines nor drink wine. This is on account of the scriptures delivered to them by Muhammad (which they call *al-Koran* and some call it *Massap*, and some call it *Harme*)* that forbid them to drink wine, as in that book Muhammad curses all those who drink wine and all who sell it. Some people have said that in his drunkenness Muhammad murdered a good hermit, whom he loved very much, and therefore he cursed the wine and those who drink wine. But he turned his malediction upon himself, as it says in the Holy Scriptures, *Et in uerticem ipsius iniquitas eius descendet*, that is, 'and his iniquity shall come down upon his crown'.*

Also, the Saracens eat neither suckling pigs nor any other kind of swine flesh, because they say it is mankind's brother and it was forbidden in the Old Law.* And in both the land of Palestine and the land of Egypt they hardly eat veal and beef unless the animal is so ancient that it can't labour or work any longer, not because it's forbidden but because they use these beasts for cultivating the land.

King David was born in this city, Bethlehem. He had sixty wives (of which the foremost was named Michal) and three hundred lovers.* From Bethlehem to Jerusalem is not even two miles, and a mile and a half on the way to Jerusalem from Bethlehem is a church where the angel told the shepherds about the nativity of Christ.* On that road is Rachel's Tomb,* who was the mother of Joseph the patriarch, and she died straight after she had given birth to Benjamin, and she was buried there. Her husband Jacob placed twelve large stones there as a token that she had borne twelve children.* On this road to Jerusalem one passes many churches, by which many people go to Jerusalem.

7

JERUSALEM

NEXT, to speak of Jerusalem: you need to know that it is well situated amongst hills, and there are neither rivers nor wells, the only water comes by conduit from Hebron. And I should tell you that it was first called Jebus, and then it was called Salem until the time that David was king; and he put these two names together and called it Jebusalem.* And then Solomon came and called it Jerusalem, as it is still called.

Around Jerusalem is the kingdom of Syria, while nearby are the lands of Palestine and Ashkelon, but Jerusalem is in the land of Judea. It is called the land of Judea because Judas Maccabeus* was king of this land. It borders to the east with the kingdom of Arabia, to the south with the land of Egypt, to the west with the Mediterranean, and to the north with the kingdom of Syria and the Cyprus Sea.

There used to be a patriarch in Jerusalem and there were archbishops and bishops throughout the country.* Around Jerusalem there are these cities: Hebron, seven miles away; Jericho, six miles away; Beer Sheva, eight miles away; Ashkelon, eighteen miles away; Jaffa, twenty-seven miles away; Ramatha-in-Ephraim,* three miles away; and Bethlehem, two miles away. And two miles to the south is a church of St Chariton who was the abbot there, for whom much lamenting was made when time came for him to die. And a painting is still there, showing the manner in which the people grieved when he died, and it is an affecting thing to see.*

The province of Jerusalem has been in the hands of many different nations, such as Jews, Canaanites, Assyrians, Persians, Medians,* and Macedonians, Greeks, Romans, Christians and Saracens, Barbarians, Turks, Tartars, and many other peoples; for Christ does not desire that it should be in the hands of traitors and sinners, whether they are Christians or not. Yet the sinful ones have held that land in their hands for more than a hundred and fifty years,* but they shall not hold it for much longer, if God so wills it.

Now, you should be aware that when people go to Jerusalem, they make their first pilgrimage to the church of the Holy Sepulchre;* this was outside the city on the northern side but is now enclosed within the town's walls. This is a really handsome circular church, finely roofed with lead and with an open ceiling. On the western side is an attractive and sturdy bell-tower; and in the middle of the church is a tabernacle like a little house,* beautifully crafted in the manner of a semicircle and richly decorated with gold, azure, and other colours; and to the right is the sepulchre of Our Lord; and the tabernacle is eight feet long and five feet wide and eleven feet high.

It is not long since the sepulchre was entirely open so one was able to kiss it and touch it. However, because people came along and attempted to break the stone in pieces or into dust to take away with them, the Sultan has had a wall made around the grave so nobody can touch it except on the left side. This tabernacle has no windows, but inside there are many lamps burning. Also, there is a burning lamp hanging in front of the sepulchre and, on Good Friday, it extinguishes itself, and lights itself again on Easter Sunday at that time at which Our Lord rose from death to life.*

Also, to the right, inside that church, is Mount Calvary where Our Lord was placed on the Cross. And the Cross was set in a cleft in the rock, which is white in colour with a little red mixed in; blood dropped onto that rock from the wounds of Our Lord when He was tortured on the Cross, and it is now called Golgotha. And one goes up onto this Golgotha by a staircase. In that cleft Adam's head was unearthed after Noah's flood, signifying that Adam's sins should be redeemed in this same place. Above that rock Abraham made a sacrifice to Our Lord, and there is an altar and in front of it lie Godfrey of Boulogne, Baldwin, and others who were Christian and kings of Jerusalem.*

So, there, just as Our Lord was placed on the Cross, it says written in Greek letters thus: *Otheos basilio ysmon presemas ergaste sothias oys*, that is to say in Latin, *Hic deus rex noster ante secula operates est salute in medio terre*, that is to say, 'But God is our king before ages: he hath wrought salvation in the midst of the earth'.* And also at the rock on which the Cross was set up it is written thus: *Gros ginst rasis thou pestes thoy thesmoysy*: that is to say in Latin, *Quod uides est fundamentum tocius mundi et huius fidei*, that is to say, 'What you see is the foundation of the entire world and of this faith'.*

You should know that when He died Our Lord was aged thirty-three years and three months. And David's prophecy states that He should be forty years old before He died when he said, *Quadraginta annis proxima fui generacioni huic*, that is to say, 'Forty years long was I neighbour to that generation'.* Thus it might seem that the prophecy is not true. Each is true, for in olden days people made a year from ten months, of which the month of March was the first and December the last. But Gaius Caesar,* who was Emperor of Rome, decided to create these two months, January and February, and ordered that the year have twelve months, that is to say, comprising 365 days without a leap year in keeping with the sun's correct movement. Therefore by calculating using ten months to the year He died in the fortieth year whilst according to our years of twelve months He was aged thirty-three years and three months when He died.

Also near Mount Calvary, to the right, is an altar where the pillar lies to which Our Lord was bound when He was scourged. And nearby there are four stone columns always dripping water, and some say that these stones weep for Our Lord's death. And near to this altar, in a place forty-two steps down, was found the True Cross, as endorsed by St Helena, under a rock where the Jews had hidden it.

And it was tested because they found three crosses, one of Our Lord and two of the two thieves; so St Helena tested them on a dead body, that revived as soon as the True Cross was laid upon it.

And nearby in the wall is the place where the four nails of Our Lord were hidden, for he had two nails in his hands and two in his feet. And one of these nails was made, by the Emperor of Constantinople, into a bridle for his warhorse; for by the power of this bridle he overcame his enemies and won all these lands:* Asia, Turkey, Armenia the Greater and the Lesser, Syria, Jerusalem, Arabia, Persia, Mesopotamia, the kingdom of Aleppo, Egypt both Upper and Lower, and many other kingdoms deep into Ethiopia and to Lesser India, which was then Christian.

Now, there were, in those days, many good holy men and holy hermits in these regions, of whom the book *The Lives of the Fathers** speaks. But all these regions are now in pagan and Saracen hands. Yet when God wishes, just as these regions were lost through the sinfulness of Christians, so shall they be won again by means of God's aid through Christian folk.

In the middle of this church is a circular area in which Joseph of Arimathea* laid the body of Our Lord when he had taken Him down from the Cross. And people say that this circle is the middle of the world. In the church of the Holy Sepulchre on the north side is a place where Our Lord was put in prison, though He was nevertheless imprisoned in many other places.* There's also a piece of the chains with which He was bound. And there He first appeared to Mary Magdalene when He was resurrected, and she thought that He was a gardener.* Canons of the Benedictine order dwelt in the church of the Holy Sepulchre, and they had a prior there, but the Patriarch was their leader.*

Outside the church doors, to the right, as one climbs thirty-eight stairs, Our Lord said to His mother thus: *Mulier ecce filius tuus*, that is to say, 'Woman, behold thy son'.* And then He said thus: *Deinde dicit discipulo, ecce mater tua*, that is to say, 'After that, he saith to the disciple: Behold thy mother'.* These words He said also on the Cross. Our Lord went by these stairs when He carried the Cross upon his shoulders.

Underneath this staircase is a chapel where priests sing, not according to our rite but according to their own rite. They always perform the sacrament of the holy bread as well as the prayers with which the bread is consecrated by saying the *Paternoster* and little else, because they don't know the additions that many popes have made; but they do sing with sincere devotion. Nearby is the place where Our Lord rested when He was weary from carrying the Cross.

You should know that in front of the church of the Holy Sepulchre the city is most vulnerable to attack, because of the large plain between the city and the church on the eastern side. Outside the city walls is the Valley of Jehoshaphat, which reaches all the way to the walls. In this Valley of Jehoshaphat outside the city is the church of St Stephen, where he was stoned to death.* Nearby is the Golden Gate that cannot be opened.* Our Lord entered through that gate on Palm Sunday, riding on an ass, and the gate opened for Him when He wished to go to the Temple. And the ass's hoof-prints can still be seen in the hard stones of the pavement in three places.

Two hundred paces in front of the church of the Holy Sepulchre is a great Hospital of St John, where the Knights Hospitaller have their institution.* And if one goes east from the Hospital there is an exceedingly pretty church which people call *Nostre Dame le Graunt*. Then nearby is another church, which they call *Nostre Dame de Vatyns*.* Mary Cleophas and Mary Magdalene stood there tearing their hair when Our Lord was put to death.*

And one hundred and sixty steps from the church of the Holy Sepulchre to the east is the Temple of Our Lord,* and it is a very beautiful building. It's completely circular and exceptionally tall and roofed with lead and handsomely paved with white marble. But the Saracens will allow neither Christians nor Jews to enter, because they say that wicked people shouldn't go into such holy places. But I went in there and into sundry other places as I desired, because I had letters of introduction from the Sultan bearing his chief seal, whereas others usually only have his seal.*

People carry his letters and seal in front of them on a spear, they revere it enormously and genuflect to it as we might in front of God's body.* People who are shown this seal bow their head towards it before they receive it and then they take it and lay it on their heads, and then they read the letters all bent double in great reverence, and then they offer to do all that the bearer wishes.

In this Temple of Our Lord, or *Templum Domini*, there used to be Canons Regular and they had an abbot to whom they were obedient.* Charlemagne was in this Temple when an angel brought him the

Holy Foreskin,* the prepuce of Our Lord from His circumcision, and afterwards King Charles had it taken to Paris.

Also, you need to understand that this is not the Temple which Solomon built, for that temple only stood for 1,102 years—Titus, Vespasian's son, who was the Roman Emperor, besieged Jerusalem in order to defeat the Jews, because they had killed Christ without the Emperor's consent. When Titus had taken the city, he burned down the Temple and gathered all the Jews and killed 110,000 of them. He put the rest in prison and sold them thirty a penny, just as they said that they had bought Jesus Christ for thirty pence.*

Yet afterwards Julian the Apostate* was emperor and gave the Jews permission to build the Temple in Jerusalem, because he hated Christians (even though he was Christian and forsook his faith). When the Jews had finished building the Temple there was an earthquake, as God ordained, which cast down everything they had constructed.

After that the Emperor Hadrian* (who came from Troy) rebuilt Jerusalem, including the Temple in the same manner as Solomon had. He permitted no Jew to live there, only Christians, because even though he himself wasn't christened he loved Christians above any other people except those of his own faith. This emperor had the church of the Holy Sepulchre enclosed within the city walls (as before it had been outside the city), and he wanted to change the name of Jerusalem to Helyam.* However, that name didn't last long.

Also, I think you should know that the Saracens really revere the Temple of Our Lord, and they say that this place is extremely holy. When they enter it, they go in barefoot and kneel repeatedly. When my friends and I went in there, we took off our shoes and entered barefoot, and aimed to worship in an equal or superior way to the unbelievers.

This Temple is 64 shaftments wide and the same in length, and 125 shaftments high. Inside, it's all marble pillars, and in the middle of the Temple is a kind of stage, 88 steps high, ringed with pillars. This is the place the Jews call *sancta sanctorum*, that is, the Holy of Holies.* Nobody approaches this place except their priest who makes a sacrifice, and the people stand all around placed according to their different ranks of nobility and piety.

There are four entrances to this Temple, and the doors are finely turned in cypress wood. Inside the east door Our Lord said 'This is Jerusalem'.* Inside the north door is a pool but it doesn't run with water, of which Holy Writ states, *Vidi aquam egredientem de templo*, that is, 'I saw water coming out of the Temple'.* On the other side is a rock that was once called Moriah,* but was later called Bethel,* or the Ark of God containing Jewish relics.* Titus had this Ark taken to Rome once he had vanquished the Jews.

In this Ark were the Ten Commandments and Aaron's Rod and Moses' Staff (with which he parted the Red Sea so the people of Israel passed through dry-footed). With this staff he struck the rocks and water flowed from them, and with this staff he performed many miracles.* There was also a golden vessel filled with manna, and garments and ornaments and the Tabernacle of Aaron.* There was a square table made of gold with twelve precious stones, and a green jasper chest with four figures and eight names of Our Lord inside, and seven gold candlesticks, and twelve gold pots, and four gold censers, and a gold altar, and four gold lions upon which they had put a gold cherub twelve spans in length, and a gold tabernacle, and twelve silver trumpets, and a silver table, and seven barley loaves, and all the other relics there were before Christ was born.

Also, it was on this rock that Jacob slept when he saw the angel go up and down by a ladder and said, *Vere locus iste sanctus est et ego ignorabam*, that is, 'Indeed the Lord is in this place, and I knew it not'.* And there an angel detained Jacob, and changed his name and called him Israel.* And in that place David saw the angel who killed the people with a sword and put it all bloodied into the sheath.* And it was at this rock that St Simeon presented Our Lord to the Temple.*

Also, Our Lord set Himself on this rock when the Jews wanted to stone Him, and the rock was cleft in two and He hid Himself in that cleft and a star descended and provided Him with light.* It was on this rock that Our Lady sat and learned her psalter.* And there on this rock Christ was circumcised;* and there the angel first revealed the nativity of St John the Baptist;* and there Melchizedek first made an offering of bread, wine, and water to Our Lord as a prefiguration of the sacrament.*

And it was there, on this rock, that David fell in prayer to Our Lord, to have mercy on him and on his people, and Our Lord heard his prayer. He wanted to build the Temple there, but Our Lord forbade him through an angel, because of the treason he had committed when he murdered Uriah, a good knight, in order to take his wife.

Therefore everything he had designed for the construction of the Temple he handed over to Solomon, his son, and Solomon made it. Also, Solomon requested of Our Lord that he should hear and grant the rightful prayers of all those who prayed devoutly in that place and did so with a pure heart; and Our Lord granted it. Therefore Solomon called this 'the Temple of Counsel and the Help of God'.* Outside the doors of the Temple is an altar where Zacharias* was slain. And from the spire the Jews hurled St James,* the first bishop of Jerusalem, to the ground.

A little way from this Temple, on the right-hand side, is a church roofed with lead, called the School of Solomon.* Towards the south is the Temple of Solomon,* a truly beautiful and impressive place. Knights, called Templars, live in this place, and the Templars and their order were founded here. Moreover, canons live in that Temple of Our Lord.

From this Temple to the east, some hundred and twenty paces, in a corner of the city, is the Bath of Our Lord, and this bath used to flow with waters from Paradise (and Our Lady's Bed is adjacent).* Nearby is the tomb of St Simeon. Outside the Temple cloister, to the north, is a very pretty church dedicated to St Anne, Our Lady's mother, and Our Lady was conceived there. In front of that church is an enormous tree that began to grow that same night.

As one descends from that church, there, after twenty-two steps, rests Joachim, Our Lady's father, in a stone tomb.* St Anne also used to lie there, but St Helena had her translated to Constantinople.* In this church is a well in the form of a cistern, called *Probatica Pissina*,* which had five entrances. In that cistern, an angel used to descend and stir the water. Whoever first bathed in the water after it had been stirred was healed of any illness he had. And there the man from the palace who had been ill for thirty-eight years was healed, and Our Lord said to him there, *Tolle grabatum tuum et uade*, that is, 'Arise, take up thy bed, and walk'.* Pilate's house was next to this place.*

A little way from here stood the house of King Herod,* who had the Innocents slain. This Herod was a wholly wicked and treacherous man, for he also had his beloved wife killed. Because of the great love he felt for her once she was dead, he thought about her and went out of his mind. Then he commanded the children to be slain, those he had begotten with her, and then he had another of his wives slain and a son he had begotten with her. And he committed all the evil deeds that he could.*

When he realized that he was going to die, he sent for his sister and for all the noblemen of his kingdom. When they had all arrived he imprisoned all the noblemen in a tower and told his sister that he knew all too well that the local men would not mourn his death. Therefore he forced her to swear that she would chop off all of the noblemen's heads as soon as he died, and then all the country would be filled with sorrow because otherwise no one would mourn him at all. Thus he made his last testament. However, his sister didn't fulfil his wishes, for as soon as he was dead she released the noblemen from the tower and told them about her brother's will and she let each of them go where he wished.

You should understand that there were three very well-known Herods, and the one of whom I spoke was called Herod the Ashkelonite.* He who had St John the Baptist's head cut off was Herod Antipas.* And it was Herod Agrippa* who had St James killed.

Furthermore, there is the church of St Saviour in this city, and the arm of St John Chrysostom is there, and the main part of St Stephen's head is there too.* And on the other side, towards the south, as you go to Mount Zion, is a beautiful church dedicated to St James* where his head was cut off, and then there is Mount Zion. There's a pretty church dedicated to God and Our Lady where she lived and where she died; there was once an Augustinian abbey there.* From this place her body was carried with the apostles to the Valley of Jehoshaphat. Also the stone the angel carried to Our Lady from Mount Sinai is there, and it's the colour of the rock at St Catherine's monastery.* Nearby also is the gate* through which Our Lady went when she was pregnant and on the way to Bethlehem.

At the entrance to Mount Zion is a chapel, and in that chapel is the great big stone with which the sepulchre was covered when Christ was laid in it, the which stone the three Marys saw turned aside when they came to the sepulchre. They found an angel there who told them how Christ had risen from death to life.* There is also a little piece of the pillar to which Our Lord was bound and scourged. The house of Annas* was here too; he was the Jews' bishop in those days. It was in this place that St Peter committed his betrayal three times before the cock crowed.* There is also a piece of the table on which God took part in the Last Supper with His disciples (and the drinking-vessels for water are still there). Nearby here is the place where St Stephen was buried. There's also the altar where Our Lady heard the angels singing a mass. And in this place Christ appeared to His disciples after His resurrection at the locked doors and said to them, *Pax uobis*, that is, 'Peace to you'.* Here, on Mount Zion, Christ appeared to St Thomas and asked him to test His wounds, and he first believed in Him and said, *Dominus meus et deus meus*, that is, 'My lord and my God'.*

In this same chapel, behind the high altar, is where the apostles gathered on Whitsun, when the Holy Ghost descended to them in the form of a flame,* and God made His paschal sacrifice with His disciples there. St John the Evangelist slept on Our Lord's knee,* and as he slept he had many visions of the secrets of Heaven.

Mount Zion is within the city, and it's a little bit higher than the other side of the city. The city is stronger on this side than on the other because, at the foot of Mount Zion, there's a strong and elegant fortress. King David and Solomon and many other kings were buried on Mount Zion.* This is where St Peter wept very tenderly when he had denied Christ.* A stone's throw from that chapel is another chapel, where Our Lord was sentenced, for in those days this was Caiaphas' house. Between the Temple of Solomon and Mount Zion is the place where Christ resurrected the young virgin from death to life.*

South of Mount Zion towards the Valley of Jehoshaphat is a well which is called *Natatoire Siloam*.* Our Lord was washed there after He was baptized. Nearby the tree on which Judas hanged himself in despair after he had sold and betrayed Christ is still there.* Then there's the synagogue where the Jews and the Pharisees gather together to hold their councils. In this place Judas cast the thirty pieces of silver before them and said, *Peccaui tradens sanguine iustum*, that is, 'I have sinned in betraying innocent blood'.*

On the other side of Mount Zion, a stone's throw away to the south, is Aceldama, which means the Field of Blood, which was bought for thirty pence when Our Lord was sold. There are many Christian tombs here, where many pilgrims are buried. To the west of Jerusalem is a pretty church where the tree grew of which the Cross was made for Our Lord.* There is also a fine church where Our Lady met St Elizabeth when they were both pregnant, and

St John stirred in his mother's womb in worship of his creator, Our Lord.* Under that church's altar is a place where St John was born, and nearby is the castle of Emmaus,* where Our Lord appeared to His disciples after His resurrection.

Two miles from Jerusalem is Mount Joy,* a pretty and delightful place. The prophet Samuel is buried there in a fine tomb. It is called Mount Joy because it is from there that pilgrims first see Jerusalem, a cause of great joy after their exertions. And in the middle of the aforementioned Valley of Jehoshaphat is a little river called *torrens Cedron*, or Kidron. Over this stream there once lay a tree, out of which the Cross was made, over which people passed. Also in that valley is a church of Our Lady,* and there is the tomb of Our Lady. When Our Lady died she was seventy-two years old.*

Nearby is the place where Our Lord forgave St Peter of all his sins. Also near is the chapel where Judas kissed Our Lord, and people call this Gethsemane, and He was arrested by the Jews here.* In that place Christ took leave of His disciples before His Passion, when He went to pray and said *Pater si fieri potest transeat a me calyx iste*, that is, 'My Father, if it be possible, let this chalice pass from me'.* Very close too is a chapel where Our Lord sweated blood and water.*

Nearby there is the tomb of King Jehoshaphat,* after whom the valley takes its name. On one side of that valley is Mount Olivet, so called because so many olives grow there. It is higher than Jerusalem, and therefore from it one can see into the streets of Jerusalem. Between the hill and the city is nothing but the Valley of Jehoshaphat, and it's not very wide. Our Lord stood on that hill when He ascended to Heaven, and His left foot appears still to be imprinted in the rock.*

There used to be an Augustinian abbey there, but it's now a church. Also nearby, about twenty-eight feet away, is a chapel, and there one can see the stone on which Our Lord sat and preached to the people, saying *Beati pauperes spiritu quoniam ipsorum est regnum celorum*, that is, 'Blessed are the poor in spirit: for theirs is the kingdom of Heaven'.* Here He taught his disciples the entire *Paternoster*.* The church of St Mary the Egyptian* is adjacent and she's buried there; three bow-shots away is Bethphage, where Our Lord sent St Peter to fetch an ass on Palm Sunday.* Towards the east is a chapel called Bethany.* Simon the Leper lived there: he gave shelter to Our Lord and afterwards he was baptized as His disciple and called Julian.* He is the patron saint of hospitality, and he was made a bishop.

In that place Our Lord forgave Mary Magdalene her sins, and she washed His feet there with tears from her eyes and dried them with her hair.* There too Lazarus* was raised from death to life, even though he had been dead in his stinking grave for four days. There too is the place where Our Lady appeared to St Thomas and handed him her girdle after her Assumption.* Just nearby is a stone on which Our Lord often sat and preached, and it is upon this stone that He shall sit on the Day of Judgement, as He himself said. Near there is Mount Galilee, where the apostles gathered when Mary Magdalene told them about Christ's resurrection.* Between Mount Olivet and Galilee is a church where the angel told Our Lady about her death.*

So, from Bethany to Jericho is about five miles. Jericho was once a decent city, but it is desolate and now there is only a small town. Joshua seized that town through a divine miracle and on the angel's command, and he destroyed it and cursed all those who rebuilt it. Rahab the harlot* came from this city, she sheltered the spies of Israel and protected them from many dangers and from death. For this she was rewarded, as Holy Writ says, *Qui accipit prophetam in nomine meo mercedem prophete accipiet*, that is, 'He that receiveth a prophet in the name of a prophet, shall receive the reward of a prophet'.*

Then from Bethany one travels to the River Jordan through the desert, and it's nearly a day's travel between the two. To the east is a great mountain, where Our Lord fasted for forty days. The diabolical fiend took Christ there and said this to Him: *Dic ut lapides isti panes fiant*, that is, 'command that these stones be made bread'.* There's a hermitage where a kind of Christian men live, called Georgians, because St George converted them.* Abraham once lived on that mountain for a very long time. Moreover, as one travels to Jericho the blind men sat in the road crying, *Ihesu fili Dauid Miserere mei*, that is, 'Jesus, Son of David, have mercy on me!'* It is two miles from Jericho to the River Jordan.

You need to be aware that the Dead Sea flows from the lands of Judea and Arabia, and goes all the way from Zoar* to Arabia. The water in this sea is very bitter, and it produces a thing called 'asphalt'* in pieces as big as a horse. Jerusalem is two hundred furlongs from this sea. It's called the Dead Sea because it doesn't flow. Neither man nor living beast is able to die in it, and that has often been tested: they throw men in who have been condemned to death, and it spits them out again. Nobody can live near it or drink water from it. If one throws in a piece of iron it comes up again, and if one throws in a feather, it sinks to the bottom: and that is against nature. This is like the cities that were destroyed for their sins against nature. These five cities were submerged because of their crimes against nature: Sodom, Gomorrah, Adama, Seboim, and Zoar.* But, due to the prayers of Lot, Zoar was saved for a long time, as it was situated on a hill, and some of it still appears about the water and one can see the walls in fine weather. Some call that sea Lake Alsiled,* some call it Devil's River, and some call it Stinking River, because the water there stinks.

Trees grow thereabouts bearing a prettily coloured fruit which appear to be ripe, but when one splits them or cuts them open one finds nothing but cinders and ashes; this is a token of God's vengeance through which these cities were burned with hell-fire.

Lot stayed in this place for a long time, and got drunk with his daughters and slept with them, because they believed that God was going to destroy the entire world (as He had with Noah's flood). So they slept with their father so that they could bring people into the world. If he hadn't been drunk, he wouldn't have slept with them. Lot's wife lingers on at the right-hand side of this sea in the form of a salt stone, because she looked back when these cities were submerged.*

You should be aware that Abraham had a son called Isaac, and he was circumcised when he was eight days old. He had another son, called Ishmael, and he was circumcised at fourteen years old. They were both circumcised on the same day.* Therefore, the Jews began to circumcise at eight days, and the Saracens circumcise at fourteen years.

The River Jordan runs into the Dead Sea and it terminates there. This river is by no means a great, broad river, but there are many fine fish in it. It flows from Mount Lebanon from two springs called Jor and Dan, and it takes it name from them.* On one side of this river is Mount Gilboa and there's a pretty plain there. On the other side one passes the mountains of Lebanon all the way to the Desert of Pharaoh. These mountains separate the kingdom of Syria from the land of Phoenicia. On this hill there are cedar trees bearing long fruit as big as a man's head.

This River Jordan separates Galilee from the region of Idumea and the region of Botron,* and it runs into a plain called, in the Saracen language, Maidan.* Job's Temple is in that plain.* Christ was baptized in this river, and the voice of the Father was heard there, saying *Hic est filius meus dilectus in quo michi bene complacuit. Ipsum audite*, that is, 'This is my beloved Son, in whom I am well pleased: hear ye Him.'* The Holy Ghost descended there to Him in the form of a dove, and so at this baptism the entire Trinity was there.

The children of Israel passed through the River Jordan without getting wet, and they placed stones in the water as a sign of that miracle. Also Naaman of Syria* bathed in that river when he was a leper, and he was healed there. A little distance from there is the city of Hai, which Joshua attacked and took.* Also, at the mouth of the River Jordan is the Vale of Mambre, a pleasant and fertile valley.

8

THE CASTLE OF KRAK DE MONTREAL, AND ELSEWHERE

YOU need to know that as you travel east from the Dead Sea from the border of the Promised Land is a sturdy castle called, in the Saracen language, *Krak*, that is, in French, *Réal-Mont*. A French king, called Baldwin,* had this castle built for him, for he had won all this land and placed it in Christian hands for safekeeping. Below the castle is a fair town called Gabaon.* Christians live around here under obligation to pay tribute.

Then one travels to Nazareth, from which Our Lord took his surname. From Nazareth to Jerusalem is three days' travel. One travels through the province of Galilee, through Ramatha, through Sophim,* and via the high mountain of Ephraim where Hannah, the mother of the prophet Samuel, once lived, and it's here that the prophet was born.* After his death he was buried at Mount Joy, as I've already said.

Then one reaches Sybola where the Ark of God was kept under the prophet Eli.* There the people of Hebron made sacrifices to Our Lord, and also there Our Lord first spoke to Samuel, and there God administered the sacrament.* Nearby, to the left, is Sabon and Rama Benjamin, about which Holy Writ speaks.*

Then one reaches Shechem, which some people call Sichare. This is the Samaritan region, and there used to be a church but it was knocked down. It's a pretty, fertile valley and there's a fine city called Nablus. It's one day's travel to Jerusalem from there, and in this place is the well where Our Lord spoke to the Samaritan woman.*

The city of Shechem is ten miles from Jerusalem, and is called Nablus (that is to say, Neapolis, New City).* Nearby is the temple of Joseph, who was Jacob's son who governed Egypt, and his bones were brought from there and placed in this temple. Jews often come on pilgrimage to Nablus with great devotion. Jacob's daughter was raped in that city, for which her brothers slew many men.* Nearby is the city of Garrison,* where the Samaritans make their sacrifices. On this mountain Abraham wished to sacrifice his son Isaac. Nearby is the Valley of Dothan,* and the pit is there in which Joseph was thrown by his brothers before they sold him.* It is two miles from Sichar.*

From there one goes into Samaria and to Sebastiya, the main city in that region. The twelve tribes of Israel came from that city, but it's not as big as it once was. St John the Baptist is buried there, between the two prophets Elisha and Obadiah, but he was beheaded in the fortress of Machaerus beside the Dead Sea.* He was translated by his disciples and entombed in Samaria, but Julian the Apostate, who was emperor at that time, had his bones moved and burnt. However, the finger with which St John called attention to Our Lord, saying *Ecce, agnus dei*, that is, 'Behold the Lamb of God',* couldn't be burnt, and St Thecla the Virgin had it taken into the mountains and great reverence was made to it.*

The head of St John the Baptist was shut up in a wall there, but the Emperor Theodosius had it taken out; he found it wrapped in bloodied cloth and so he had it taken to Constantinople. One half of the head is still there, and the other half is in Rome at the church of St Sylvester. The vessel in which his head had been placed after it was chopped off is at Genoa, and the Genoese greatly revere it. Some people say that St John the Baptist's head is at Amiens in Picardy, and some say that it's the head of St John the Bishop.* I don't know, but God knows.*

From Sebastiya to Jerusalem is twelve miles. Amongst the mountains of this region is a well that is called *fons Jacob*, that is, Jacob's Well.* It changes its colour four times a year, sometimes being red, sometimes clear, sometimes opaque.

The people dwelling there are called Samaritans, and they were converted by the apostles. Their law is different from Christian law,

Saracen law, Jewish law, and pagan law. They fully believe in a god who shall judge everybody, and they believe in the Bible by the letter. They wrap their heads in red linen to distinguish themselves from others, because Saracens wrap their heads in white cloth, and local Christians in blue cloth, and Jews in yellow cloth, for many Jews live there, paying tribute as the Christians do.

If you want to know the Jews' letters,* these are the names of them: *aleph*, *beth*, *gimel*, *he*, *vav*, *zayin*, *ex*, *yod*, *kaph*, *lamed*, *men*, *nun*, *samech*, *ey*, *phe*, *lad*, *koph*, *fir*, *soun*, *thau*, *lours*. Now you shall see the shapes of the Jews' letters:

From this region I have described one travels through the plain of Galilee and leaves the adjacent mountains. Galilee is in the province of the Promised Land. In that province is the region of Naim and Capernaum and Corozain and Bethsaida. St Peter and also St Andrew were born at Bethsaida. The Antichrist will be born at Corozain, but some say he shall be born in Babylon. Thus the prophet says, *De Babilonia exiet coluber que totum mundum deuorabit*, that is, 'A serpent shall come out of Babylon that will devour the whole world'.* This Antichrist will be raised in Bethsaida and he shall reign in Corozain. Therefore Holy Writ says of them, *Ve tibi Corosayme, Ve tibi Bethsayda, Ve tibi Capharnaum*, that is, 'Woe to thee Corozain, Woe to thee Bethsaida, Woe to thee Capharnaum'.* Also nearby is Cana in Galilee, four miles from Nazareth. The Canaanite woman* of whom the gospel speaks was from that city. Our Lord performed His first miracle there, at the chief steward's wedding, when He turned water into wine.*

One goes from there to Nazareth, which used to be a huge city but is now just a little town and it has no walls. Our Lady was born there, but she was conceived in Jerusalem. Our Lord took His surname from Nazareth. Joseph married Our Lady there, when she was fourteen years old.* It was here that the angel Gabriel greeted Our Lady, Mary, saying to her, *Aue Marie gracia plena dominus tecum*, that is, 'Hail, Mary, full of grace, the Lord is with thee'.* There used to be a grand church there, but now there is just a little booth to receive the pilgrims' offerings. In this place is Gabriel's well where Our Lord used to bathe when He was little. Our Lord was raised in Nazareth. Nazareth means 'flower of the garden',* and this is particularly fitting because the flower of life that was Christ was raised there.

Half a mile from Nazareth is Our Lord's Blood,* for the Jews led Him up to a high peak to throw Him off to kill Him, but He escaped from them and leapt up onto a rock where His footsteps can still be seen. Therefore some people, when they are afraid of thieves or enemies, say this verse written here: *Ihesus autem transiens per medium illorum ibat*, that is, 'He passing through the midst of them, went His way'.* One might also say these verses from the psalter, *Irruat super eos formido et pauor in magnitudine brachii tui, domine. Fiant inmobiles quasi lapis donec pertranseat populus tuus domine et populus iste quem redemisti*, that is, 'Let fear and dread fall upon them, in the greatness of thy arm: let them become unmoveable as a stone, until thy people, O Lord, pass by: until this thy people pass by, which thou hast possessed.'* When this is said, one may proceed without any hindrance.

You need to be aware that Our Lady had a child when she was fifteen years old, and she lived with Him for thirty-three years and three months and, after His Passion, she lived for twenty-four years.*

It is three miles from Nazareth to Mount Tabor, and Our Lord was transfigured there in front of St Peter, St John and St James, and there they saw Our Lord spiritually with Moses and the prophet Elijah beside Him. Therefore St Peter said, *Bonum hic esse faciamus tria tabernacula*, that is, 'it is good for us to be here: and let us make three tabernacles'.* Christ requested that they tell no man of this until that time He was resurrected from death to life. On that very mountain on the Day of Judgement four angels shall blow their trumpets and raise all dead men to life, and they shall appear body and soul. But the Day of Judgement shall be in the Valley of Jehoshaphat on Easter Sunday at that time of Our Lord's resurrection.

A mile from Mount Tabor is Mount Hermon, where the city of Naim was. At the gates of that city Our Lord revived the widow's only son.* From there one travels to a city called Tiberias, sited on the Sea of Galilee. Even though it's called the Sea of Galilee, it is neither an ocean nor an estuary but just a lake of fresh water. It is nearly one hundred furlongs in length and forty furlongs wide, and there are many fine fish in it. On that same sea (even though it changes its name depending on the cities on its coast) Our Lord walked with dry feet.* In this place He said to St Peter, who had gone into the water and was nearly drowned, *Modice fidei quare dubitasti?*, that is, 'O thou of little faith, why didst thou doubt?'*

In this city of Tiberias there is the table at which Christ ate with his disciples after His resurrection, and they knew Him through the breaking of bread, thus Holy Writ says, *Et cognouerunt eum in fractione panis*, that is, 'and they knew Him in the breaking of the bread'.*

You should be aware that the River Jordan rises in the foothills of Lebanon, and that's where the Promised Land begins which goes all the way to Beer Sheva, to the north and to the south. It is nearly one hundred and eighty miles in length, and in width it stretches from Jericho to Jaffa, and that is some forty miles. You should know that the Promised Land is in the kingdom of Syria and it goes all the way to the Arabian Desert.*

You should also be aware that in many places Christians live amongst the Saracens, paying tribute to them. They have various customs, and there are many different kinds of monks, and though they are all Christians and have a range of laws yet they all really believe in God the Father and in the Son and in the Holy Ghost. However, they still want for the articles of our faith. They are called Jacobites,* because St James converted them. St John baptized them, and they say that they will only confess to God and not to man, as they declare that God did not command that men should confess to one another. So David says in the psalter, *Confitebor tibi domine in toto corde meo*, that is, 'I will give praise to thee, O Lord, with my whole heart'.* In another place he says *Delictum meum tibi cognitum feci*, that is, 'I have acknowledged my sin to thee'.* And in another place he says *Deus meus es tu et confitebor tibi*, that is, 'Thou art my God, and I will praise thee'.* And in yet another place he says *Quoniam cogitacio hominis confitebitur tibi*, that is, 'For the thought of man shall give praise to thee'.*

They know the Bible and the psalter well, but they cite it in their own language and not in Latin, and say that David and the other prophets say this. St Augustine and St Gregory say, *Qui scelera sua cogitate et conuersus fuerit ueniam sibi credat*, that is, 'Whosoever acknowledges his sins and will change may believe himself to be forgiven'.* St Gregory says *Dominus pocius mentem quam uerba considerat*, that is, 'Our Lord pays more heed to thoughts than to words'.*

And St Hilary says *Longorum temporum criminal in ictu oculi perient si corde nata fuerit contempcio*, that is, 'Sins that were done a long time ago will vanish in the winking of an eye if remorse for them is conceived in the heart'.*

So these authorities say that men shall confess only to God and not to man. This was the confession of olden times, but St Peter and other apostles and popes since then have ordained that one can confess oneself to priests, men though they are. And this is their reasoning: they say that you cannot provide good medicine to a sick man unless you know the nature of the sickness, and so they say that you cannot provide a suitable penance unless you know the sin; one kind of sin is more serious to one man than another, and in some places more than in another, and in some times more than in another, and therefore it is necessary that one understands the nature of the sin.

There is another people and they are called Syrians.* They keep the Greek faith, and they have long beards. There are other people, who are called Georgians, who were converted by St George. They worship the saints in Heaven more than others do, and they have shaved tonsures: the clerics have round tonsures and the laymen have square tonsures. They keep the Greek faith. There are other men, called Girdling Christians,* because they wear girdles down below. There are also some others called Nestorians, some called Arians, some called Nubians, some called Gregorians, some called Indians, who come from the land of Prester John.* Each of these has some of the articles of our faith, but each one varies somewhat from the others. It would be too much to describe the differences between them.

9

THE WAY FROM GALILEE TO JERUSALEM VIA DAMASCUS

So, since I've told you of many kinds of people living in the aforementioned countries, now I'll return to my route. Whoever wants to return from the region of Galilee that I described shall go to the gracious city of Damascus,* that is full of excellent goods and wares. It's three days' travel from the sea and five from Jerusalem. However, they carry goods upon camels, mules, dromedaries, horses, and other beasts. Eliezar of Damascus (who was Abraham's servant before Isaac was born) founded this city;* he believed himself to be Abraham's heir so he called the city after his surname: Damas. In this place Cain slew his brother Abel.*

Adjacent to Damascus is Mount Seir.* There are many physicians in that city. St Paul was a physician too, keeping people's bodies healthy, before he was converted, and after that he was a physician of souls. St Luke was his disciple, and many others too, in order to learn medicine.

From Damascus one arrives at a place called *Nostre Dame de Gardemarche*,* five miles from Damascus; it's situated on top of a rock and has a pretty church, and Christian monks and nuns live there. In that church, in the wall behind the high altar, is a wooden panel on which an image of Our Lady is painted, which has many times turned into flesh and blood. However, that image can now rarely be seen, but through the grace of God the panel perpetually drips oil like that from an olive tree, and there is a marble pot under the panel to catch the oil. They give this to pilgrims, as it heals many ailments, and if it's kept unpolluted all through the year at the end of the year it turns into flesh and blood.

Between the cities of Arqa* and Rafineh there is a river called the Sabbatory, because on Saturdays it flows quickly and for the following week it stands still and doesn't flow (or flows hardly at all). There is another river that freezes solid at night but in the daytime no ice can be seen on it.

So one travels on to a city called Beirut, where those wishing to can embark on the sea for Cyprus. One disembarks at the port of Sur or Tyre and then goes on to Cyprus; otherwise one can go from the port of Tyre not to Cyprus but to some port in Greece, and then enter into Jerusalem by the routes I have already described.

10

THE SHORTEST WAY TO JERUSALEM

I HAVE now described to you the longest and shortest routes by which one travels to Jerusalem, that is via Babylon and Mount Sinai and many other places from which one turns back to the Promised Land. Now I'll describe the correct route, and the shortest one to

Jerusalem, as some people do not wish to go by a longer route: some because they have no funding, some because they have no companions, and because of other good reasons. Therefore I will briefly describe to you how one can travel at little expense and in a short time.

One travelling from the West goes through France, Burgundy, Lombardy, and so on to Venice or Genoa or some other port, and one embarks on a ship there and goes to the island of Corfu,* and thus disembarks in Greece at Port Myroch or Vlorë or Durrës* or at another port, and rests there for a while. One then puts to sea and lands at Cyprus, leaving aside the island of Rhodes, and disembarks at Famagusta, which is the best harbour in Cyprus (or else at Limassol). Then one puts to sea again (passing by the port of Tyre) and does not disembark until one reaches the port of Jaffa, the nearest harbour to Jerusalem (as it is only twenty-seven miles between them).

From Jaffa one travels a short distance to Ramleh, a beautiful city. Near that city is a fair church dedicated to Our Lady, where Our Lord revealed Himself to her in three shadows signifying the Trinity. Also nearby is a church dedicated to St George, where his head was chopped off, and then on to the castle of Emmaus, and then on to Mount Joy, from which many pilgrims first see Jerusalem, and then to Mount Modein, and then into Jerusalem. At Mount Modein rests the Machabee prophet.* Beyond Ramleh is the town of Tekoa where the prophet Amos came from.*

11

ANOTHER ROUTE TO JERUSALEM

I JUST told you about the shortest route to Jerusalem. But because many people will not endure the stench of the sea and would rather go by land, even though it's a longer distance and more difficult, one can go to one of the Lombard ports, such as Venice or Genoa or somewhere else. One then goes by sea to Greece, to Port Myroch or somewhere similar, and then on to Constantinople.* One travels by the waterway which is called St George's Arm,* which is a sea-strait. Then one goes by land to Pulverale then to the castle at Sinop,* and from there to Cappadocia, which is a large region where there are many high mountains. One then travels through Turkey and to the city of Iznik, which the Turks won from the Emperor of Constantinople, and it's a pleasant city with good walls, and it has a river called the Lake.* From there one travels via the Mornaunt Alps* and the Malabrun Valley and the Ernay Valley and so on to Greater Antioch, which is in the region of Edessa.* Thereabouts are many fine and pretty mountains and attractive forests and wild animals.

Whoever wants to go another way should go via the Roman Plain on the coast of the Roman Sea.* On that coastline there's a beautiful castle called Florache. Once one has emerged from the mountains and the crags, one travels through the city of Maraş and Artah,* where there is a great bridge over the River Ferne, which is also called Pharphar,* and it is a grand river which carries ships, and it runs ever so quickly towards the city of Damascus.

Next to the city of Damascus is another river, which comes from the Lebanon hills, called the Abana.* When crossing this river St Eustace (sometimes called Placidus)* lost his two children after he had lost his wife. It runs through the Arachite Plain and then to the Red Sea. From there one reaches the city of Phenne where there are hot springs and thermal baths. And from there one goes to the city of Ferne, and between Phenne and Ferne are many pleasant forests.

Then one reaches Antioch,* which is ten miles away. The city of Antioch is a beautiful city, with excellent walls and many fine towers, and it is two miles long and half a mile wide, and the walls used to have three hundred and fifty towers. The River Ferne or Fassar flows through that city, and there was a bridge and at each pier of the bridge was a tower. This is the finest city in the kingdom of Syria. Ten miles from the city is the port of St Symeon, where the River Ferne flows into the sea.*

From Antioch one travels to a city which is called Latakia, and then to Jabala, and then to Tartus. This is the region of Cambre, where there is a sturdy fortress called Baalbek.* From there one travels to Tripoli and then to Acre. Then there are two ways to Jerusalem. On the left-hand side one travels to Damascus by the River Jordan. On the right-hand side one travels to the region of Flagame and to the city of Haifa, of which Caiaphas was the ruler, and some call it Pilgrim Castle.* From there it is four days' travel to Jerusalem, on through Caesarea and then on to Jaffa and Ramleh and the castle at Emmaus and then one goes on to Jerusalem.

12

A WAY TO JERUSALEM ENTIRELY OVERLAND

Now I've told you some of the ways by land and by sea by which one can go to Jerusalem. Even though there are many other routes by which people can travel from whichever countries they come from, they all reach the same place. There is even a way from France and Flanders by land to Jerusalem without travelling by sea, but that route is extremely long and dangerous and so full of hardships and therefore few people take that route. If one wishes to go that way one travels through Germany, Prussia, and on to Tartary.

This land of Tartary* answers to the Great Khan of Cathay, of whom I shall speak later, for his power extends this far and the Tartar rulers pay tribute to him. This is a truly wretched region: sandy, hardly fertile at all, little corn grows there, no wine, no beans, no pulses; there are, however, plenty of animals. So they eat meat without bread, and they eat the broth as a meal. They drink the milk of all kinds of beasts. They eat cats and other wild animals and rats and mice. They have only a little wood, so they prepare their meat with horse-dung dried in the sun. Princes and other gentlemen eat only once each day, and a very small amount at that. They are extremely wretched people and have a wicked nature.

In summer there are many gales and thunderstorms, which kill a large number of people and many animals. Suddenly it becomes extremely cold, and then just as suddenly it gets exceedingly hot. The prince of this region is called Batu, and he lives in a city called Orda.* Truly, no decent person would linger in that region, for I've heard that hemlock and nettles and similar weeds thrive there, although I've not been there.

I have, however, been in other bordering regions, such as Russia and Nevelond and the kingdoms of Krakow and Lithuania,* and in the kingdom of Gasten* and many other places. But I never went that way to Jerusalem, and so I won't describe it. For, as I understand it, one may not travel easily that way except in winter because of the water and seas there, which cannot be crossed until they are frozen utterly solid and it is very snowy and so, if there were no snow, nobody could travel there.

From Prussia one should travel for three days until one reaches the habitable lands of the Saracens. Even though Christians travel this way every year, they carry their provisions with them because they won't be able to get any there. They go on the ice in carriages on sleds and carts without wheels called 'sleighs'. They can only dwell in one place for as long as their provisions last, but no longer. When the local spies see Christian men coming, they run to their towns and they shout out as loud as they can '*Kera! Kera! Kera!*',* and they prepare at once to take them captive.

You need to understand that the frost and ice are harder there than here. Therefore everyone has a stove in their house where they eat and do everything that they can. For this is at the northern side of the world, where it is usually very cold and where the sun hardly shines and some places in that region are too cold for anybody to live there. On the south side of the world it is too hot in some places for anybody to live there, because the sun gives so great a heat in these regions.

13

THE SARACENS' FAITH

BECAUSE I have mentioned the Saracens and their lands, if you like I will now tell you about parts of their law and their faith, according to what their book, called *al-Koran*, says. Some people call that book *Massap*, some people call it *Harme*,* according to the languages of the different regions, and this book was given to them by Muhammad. Amongst other things, he wrote (as I have many times read and seen) the following: that those who are good shall go to Paradise when they die, and the wicked shall go to Hell; that's what all the Saracens believe. If one enquires about what kind of Paradise they envisage, they say that it's a place of sensuous pleasures, where one can find all kinds of fruit at all times and rivers flowing with wine, milk, honey, and fresh water. There they shall have such fine houses and goods as they have deserved, and these houses will be made of precious stones, gold, and silver. Every man shall have ten wives, all virgins, and he'll have sex with them each day and they'll still remain virgins.*

They also frequently describe and discuss the Virgin Mary, and they describe the Incarnation which Mary was informed of by angels and was announced to her by Gabriel, that she was chosen since the world began before all others, and this is fully witnessed in their book *al-Koran*; and that Gabriel announced to her the Incarnation of Jesus Christ, and that she would conceive and bear a child and still remain a virgin; and they say that Jesus Christ spoke as soon as He was born, and that He was a true and holy prophet in word and deed, meek, righteous to all, and without vice.

They say too that when the angel told her of the Incarnation she was terribly afraid because she was young. There was a local man who dealt in sorcery, he was called Takina,* and through magic he could make himself appear like an angel, and thus many times he slept with virgins. Therefore Mary was afraid of the angel Gabriel, and she thought he was this Takina, and she demanded to know whether he was Takina or not. The angel told her not to be afraid, as he was a genuine messenger of God.

Their book also says that she conceived and had a child beneath a palm tree, and then she was ashamed, and she cried, and said that she wished she were dead. But straightaway the child spoke, comforting her, and said to her, *Ne timeas Maria*, that is, 'Don't be afraid, Mary'.* In many other places this *al-Koran* book of theirs says that Jesus Christ spoke as soon as He was born. This book says that Jesus Christ was sent from Almighty God to be an example to all people, and that God shall judge all men: the good to Heaven, the wicked to Hell. It also says that Jesus Christ is the finest prophet above all others, and the nearest to God, and that He was a genuine prophet who gave sight to the blind, healed lepers, resurrected dead men, and ascended to Heaven still completely alive; and they greatly revere books which have the gospels written in them, especially the gospel *Missus est angelus Gabriel*,* which the educated amongst them say often in their prayers with great devotion.

They fast for one entire month* a year and during that month they eat nothing except at night and they abstain from their wives. However, those who are sick are not obliged to keep this fast.

This *al-Koran* book describes the Jews and says that they are wicked, because they will not believe that Jesus Christ was sent from God. They say that Jews speak falsely of Mary and her son Jesus when they say that they crucified Jesus, Mary's son: Saracens say that Jesus did not die crucified, for Jesus was God's son and ascended to Heaven very much alive and He never died. However, the Saracens say that Jesus transformed His appearance into he who was called Judas Iscariot, and it was he the Jews crucified, but the Jews say it was Jesus. The Saracens say that Jesus ascended to Heaven alive, and so He will come and judge the entire world. Therefore they say that all Christians are not of good faith when they believe that Jesus Christ was crucified, because they say that if He had been crucified then God would have transgressed his own righteousness by making Jesus suffer, who was not guilty to be sentenced to death and was without any sin. In this doctrine they say that Christians are erroneous, because the immense justice of God will not permit any wrong to be done.

They very much accept the works of Jesus Christ as good and true, and the same goes for His words and His interpretations and His gospels and His miracles; and also that the Virgin Mary is a true virgin and was holy both before and after bearing Jesus Christ; and that those who believe entirely in God shall be saved.

Because their beliefs are close to our faith, they are easily converted to our religion when people preach our law to them and reveal the prophecies to them. Also they say that they are well aware that, according to their prophecies, Muhammad's law will fail just as the Jews' law has proved a failure, and the Christian law will endure until the end of the world.

If someone asks them in whom they believe and in what they believe, they say 'We believe in God who created Heaven and Earth and all other things that have been made, and nothing is done except by Him, and we believe in the Day of Judgement in which every man shall get what he deserves, and we believe that everything God said through the mouths of His prophets is true'.

Also, Muhammad entreated in his *al-Koran* that every man should have two wives, or three, or four, but now they take nine, plus as many lovers as they wish. If any of their wives stray from their husband, he can eject her from his house and take another one, but he is obliged to give her a fraction of his property.

Moreover, when one speaks to them about the Father, the Son, and the Holy Ghost they say that there are three persons but not one god, for their *al-Koran* book does not mention the Trinity. But they say that God spoke, because otherwise He would be dumb, and that God had a spirit, because otherwise He would not be alive.

They say that Abraham and Moses were close to God because they spoke with Him, and they say Muhammad was the lawful messenger of God.

When they describe the Incarnation, how wisdom was sent to earth by the word of the God-sent angel and alighted in the Virgin Mary, and that through the word of God those who are dead shall be resurrected, they say that it is true and that the word of God is truly virtuous. So says their *al-Koran* when it says the angel spoke to Mary and said 'Mary, God shall send word to you by His mouth, and His name shall be Jesus Christ'. And they say that Jesus Christ was the word and the spirit of God.

So they have a lot of good principles of our faith, and all those who comprehend the prophecies and scriptures are easily converted, because they have all the prophecies and gospels and the Bible written in their language, and therefore they know a good deal of Holy Writ. But they only understand it according to the letter, just like the Jews, who do not understand the spiritual meaning. Thus St Paul says *Littera occidit spiritus autem uiuificat*, that is, 'For the letter killeth, but the spirit quickeneth'.*

The Saracens also say that the Jews are wicked people because they do not adhere to the law Moses delivered to them. They say that Christians are wicked as they do not adhere to the commandments of the gospels received through Jesus Christ for them.

So I'll tell you what the Sultan said to me one day in his private apartment. He had all his gentlemen, the nobles, and everyone else sent out of the room, because he wanted to speak to me in private. He asked me about how Christians govern in our countries, and I said, 'They govern well, thank God'.

So he said, 'Surely not, because service to God doesn't matter to your priests. They should be giving a good example to people to behave well and instead they provide a wicked example. So when the people should be at church on holy days in order to serve God, instead they go to the tavern to be gluttonous all day, and all night they eat and drink like beasts that don't know when they've had enough. Also, all Christians seem compelled to fight each other or cheat each other over everything. And they are so proud that they can't decide how to get dressed, now in long clothes, then short, now wide, then straight, and cut in all sorts of other ways.

'You should', he said, 'be simple, meek, and steadfast, and be charitable like Christ, in whom you believe. Christian men', he continued, 'are so covetous that they will sell their daughters or sisters, or their own wives to let men sleep with them, for just a few silver coins. Men have sex with one another's wives and no one is faithful to each other. So they disregard and transgress the law, which Jesus gave to them for their salvation. Therefore,' he said, 'it is for your sins that you have lost all this land that we hold: because of your vile way of life and your sinfulness God has placed all this land into our hands. We didn't gain this land through our own strength but because of your sins, as we know full well that whenever you come to serve your God properly then He will help you so nobody will be against you. And we also know, by our own prophecies, that Christians shall regain this land when they serve their God properly. But while they live as disgustingly as they do, we're not afraid of them, because their God won't help them.'

Then I asked him how he knew all this about the state of the Christians. He said he knew all about it, concerning both noblemen and commoners, from his scouts who he had sent throughout all the countries pretending to be merchants with precious gems in order to find out the customs of all nations. Then he had all his lords called back into his private apartment, and he showed me four of them who were great noblemen in that country, who described my own country to me and all the other countries of Christendom as if they were themselves from those countries. They spoke French really well, and so did the Sultan.*

After that I was truly astounded by this egregious slander of our faith, as they who should be converted by our *good* example to the faith of Jesus Christ were being drawn away by our *evil* manner of living. So it's no wonder that they call us wicked. Yet the Saracens are faithful: they uphold the commandments of their *al-Koran*, which God sent to them through His messenger Muhammad, to whom they say the angel St Gabriel spoke many times and told him about God's will.

You should know that Muhammad was born in Arabia, and at first he was a poor servant-boy, looking after horses and travelling alongside merchants; and so he once went to Egypt with merchants, and Egypt was, at that time, Christian. In the Arabian desert he went into a chapel where there was a hermit, and when he entered this very tiny chapel the entrance became as wide and high as the gates of a huge palace. The Saracens say this was the first miracle he performed in his youth.

After that Muhammad became rich and wise, and he was an accomplished astronomer. He was made land bailiff for the Prince of Khorasan, and he administered the land very prudently, to such an extent that when the prince died he married the princess, called Khadija.*

Muhammad had epilepsy and often collapsed, and the princess really began to regret that she had taken him as her husband. But he made her aware that each time he collapsed like this the angel Gabriel spoke to him, and it was because of the great radiance of the angel Gabriel that he collapsed. Therefore the Saracens say that the angel Gabriel often spoke to him.

This Muhammad reigned in Arabia in the year of Our Lord 620.* He was from the tribe of Ishmael (who was Abraham's son, begotten of his handmaiden Hagar).* Therefore some Saracens are called Ishmaelites, some are called Hagarians after Hagar, some are called Moabites and some Ammonites after the two sons of Lot, which he begot on his daughters. And some are correctly called Saracens, after Sarah.*

Anyway, Muhammad truly loved one good man, a hermit, and this hermit lived in the desert, a mile from Mount Sinai on the route as one travels from Arabia to Chaldea in the direction of India (a day's travel from the coast where Venetian merchants often come to buy goods). Muhammad went so often to this hermit to listen to him delivering a sermon that his retinue became angry with him, as he would rather hear this hermit preaching and keep his men awake all night. His men thought that they would prefer to see this hermit dead. So one evening it happened that Muhammad had plenty of fine wine to drink so he was drunk and fell asleep. While he was sleeping, his men drew a sword from his own sheath and with that sword they killed this hermit. Then they replaced the bloodied sword in the sheath.

The next day, when Muhammad found the dead hermit, he was extremely angry and he wanted to have his men executed, as he said that they had killed the hermit. But, in total agreement and in unison, they said that he himself had killed the sleeping hermit when he was drunk. Then they showed him his bloodied sword, and so he believed that they had told him the truth. Then he cursed wine and all those who drink it.

For this reason devout Saracens drink no wine, although some Saracens happily drink wine in private but not publicly. If they drink wine in public, they will be criticized for it. However, they do drink a tasty, sweet, and nutritious beverage made from sweet lemon-grass, and tasty sugar can be made from it.

It happens sometimes that Christians become Saracens either because of poverty, or out of stupidity, or out of their own wickedness. The chief imam,* when he receives them to their law, says *La esses ella Macomet rozes alla*, that is, 'There is no God but one alone and Muhammad is his messenger'.*

Given that I've told you something of their law and of their customs and traditions, now I'll describe their letters, with their names and the manner of shapes they have: *almoy*, *bethath*, *cachi*, *delplox*, *ophoty*, *fothi*, *hechim*, *iocchi*, *kaithi*, *iothim*, *malachi*, *nahaloth*, *orthi*, *choziri*, *zoth*, *rutholat*, *routhi*, *salathi*, *thatimus*, *yrthom*, *azazoth*, *aroithi*, *zotipin*, *ichetus*. They are names of the letters. Now these are the shapes:

Another difference in their language, because they speak so gutturally, is that they have four extra letters, as we have in England in our speech two letters more than they have in their ABC, that is, þ and ȝ, which are called thorn and yogh.*

14

VARIETIES OF PEOPLES AND COUNTRIES

SINCE I have given a description of the Holy Land and the countries thereabouts and the many routes by which to get there, and to Mount Sinai, to Babylon, and other places, now I'll narrate and describe to you islands and various people and animals, because there are many different people and countries which are separated by the four rivers, which come from the Earthly Paradise.*

Thus Mesopotamia and the kingdom of Chaldea and Arabia are between the two rivers Tigris and Euphrates. The kingdom of Media and Persia is between the two rivers Tigris and Nile. The kingdoms of Syria and Palestine and Phoenecia are between the Euphrates and the Mediterranean Sea, and that goes all the way from Morocco (on the Spanish Sea) to the Black Sea (so it goes 3,040 Lombard miles beyond Constantinople). Towards the sea called the Indian Ocean is the kingdom of Scythia, which is entirely surrounded by mountains.

You should be aware that in these countries there are many islands and territories that would take a great deal to describe. But later I'll tell you about some of them more fully.

If one wishes to go into Tartary or Persia or Chaldea or India, one embarks at sea at Genoa or Venice or some other port. Then one travels by sea and arrives at Trebizond, which is a good city and used to be called *le Port de Pounce*.* The ports of the Persians and Medians are there, and those to other frontiers.

The body of St Athanasius, the former bishop of Alexandria, rests in this city and he devised the psalm *Quicumque uult*.* This man was a great doctor of divinity, and because he spoke so profoundly about theology and about the Godhead he was accused, to the Pope in Rome, of being a heretic. So the Pope sent for him and put him in prison, and there, while he was in prison, he composed that psalm, sent it to the Pope, and said if this was heresy then a heretic was he, for that was his faith. When the Pope read this, he said that it contained all our faith within it and had him released from prison. The Pope commanded that the psalm be said every day first thing in the morning, and he believed Athanasius to be a good Christian man. But Athanasius refused to go to his bishopric ever again because they had accused him of heresy.

Trebizond was once held by the Emperor of Constantinople, but a rich man whom he sent to guard it against the Turks took it for himself and dubbed himself the Emperor of Trebizond.*

From there one travels through Lesser Armenia. In this country there's an old castle, on a crag, called *Le Castel d'Épervier*,* between the cities of Ayas and Parcipia, of which the Lord of Korikos is the ruler and he's a rich man. In that castle a hawk can be found sitting on a finely wrought perch with a beautiful lady from Fairyland keeping it. Whoever keeps watch over this hawk for seven days and seven nights (some say three days and three nights) all alone will be visited by this pretty lady at the end of the seventh day (or the third day) and she'll grant him the first material thing he requests. This has been attempted many times.

So it happened one day that an Armenian king, a courageous man, kept watch over this hawk and, after seven days, the lady came to him and asked him what he wanted, as he had performed his duty very well. So the King replied that he was a great enough lord and totally contented and wealthy, so he wanted to request nothing but the body of the pretty lady with which to do as he desired. She said that he was a fool, for he knew not what he was asking for; he could not have her because she was not an object, and she asked him to request a material thing. The King said he wished for nothing else. So she said to him that, since he wouldn't ask, she would grant something to him and all his descendants, and she said, 'Your highness, you'll have war without peace for nine generations and you'll be in subjection to your enemies and you'll lack provisions and income'. And ever since that time all the kings of Armenia have been at war, in need of help, and under tribute to the Saracens.

Another time a poor man's son kept watch over the hawk and then asked the lady if he could be rich and prosperous in business. So the lady granted him this wish, and he became the richest and most famous merchant who ever lived on earth or sailed the sea. He was so rich that he barely knew the thousandth of what he had, and he was wiser in his wishes than the king was. Another time a Templar knight kept watch there and wished for a purse which would always be full of gold and the lady granted him this. But she said that he had wished for his own undoing because of his great pride. So he who guards this hawk needs to keep him awake because if it sleeps he'll be lost and never seen again. However, this castle isn't on the correct route, other than for the marvel.

From Trebizond people go to Greater Armenia to a city called Erzerum,* which used to be a large city but the Turks have almost totally destroyed it, and no wine or fruit grows there.

From there one travels to a mountain called Mount Sabissa, and there's another mountain called Ararat; the Jews call this Thano,* where Noah's ship rested, and it is still there. One can glimpse it from afar in clear weather, and the mountain is seven miles high. Some people say they have visited there and stuck their fingers in the hole where the Devil came out when Noah said *Benedicite*,* but they're not telling the truth, because nobody can climb that mountain due to the constant snow, come winter and summer. Actually nobody has been there since Noah, except one monk who, through the grace of God, went there and brought back a plank that is at the abbey at the mountain's foot. He truly wanted to climb that mountain, and so he set out to do so. When he had reached the top third of the hill, he found he was so tired that he could go no further, so he rested there and slept. But when he woke up, he was down at the foot of the mountain! So then he fervently prayed to God to allow him to climb, and an angel said to him that he should climb, so he did. Since then nobody has been there, so anyone who says they have is lying.

Then one travels to a city called Tabriz, a fine, handsome city. Near that city is a mountain of salt and each person can take whatever he wants from it. Many Christians live there under tribute to the Saracens. From there one can travel to many cities, towns, castles, and towards India, and reach a city called Kashan, also a fine city. The three kings met there when they went to make their offerings to Christ in Bethlehem. From that city one can travel to a place called Cardabago,* and the pagans say that Christians can't live here because they die really quickly, and they do not know the cause.

From there one can travel for many days, via many towns and cities, until one reaches a city called Kenarah,* which used to be so huge that the walls around it were twenty-five miles in circumference. The walls are still evident, but people don't live there. This is the limit of the Persian Emperor's land. On the other side of Kenarah one enters the land of Job, a fine district with an abundance of fruit, and people call it the land of Swere.

The city of Thomar is in this region. Job, Zara's son, was a pagan,* and he ruled over this region as prince. He was so rich that he hardly knew the hundredth of his wealth. After Job fell into poverty, God made him richer than he was before, as he then became King of Idumea after King Esau, and when he was king he was called Jobab. He lived for a hundred and seventy years in that kingdom, and he was two hundred and forty-eight years old when he died. This region of Job lacks nothing that the human body needs.

There is a mountain in this region where one can find manna.* Manna is called the bread of angels: it's extremely sweet, white stuff, much sweeter than any sugar or honey, and it comes from heavenly dew that falls on the grass, where it solidifies and becomes white. It is put in medicines for rich people.

The land of Job borders on the land of Chaldea, which is a vast nation with attractive, well-dressed men. The women are really repulsive and hideously dressed, and they go about barefoot, and wear ugly big, wide coats, cut short at the knee but with long sleeves going all the way to the feet. They have extremely long hair hanging all around their shoulders.

Then one reaches the land of Amazonia,* in which there are no men, only women. People say they will not allow any man either to live amongst them or to have dominion over them. This is because there was once a king in that land, and men lived there and had wives as they did in other countries, and it happened that the King, who was called Scolopitus, went to war against the Scythians. He was slain in battle and all his country's noblemen of good blood died with him. When the Queen and the other ladies of that land heard that the King and the noblemen had been killed, they gathered together and armed themselves and they killed all the men left in their country.* Since that time no man has lived amongst them.

When they want a man to sleep with them they send for him from a nearby country, and the men stay for up to eight days or as long as the women want and then go away again. If they have little boys they send them to their fathers when they have been weaned. If they have little girls they look after them properly. If they come from aristocratic stock, they cauterize the left breast so they can carry a shield. If they are of normal stock, they cauterize the right breast, so they can shoot a bow-and-arrow. The women there are terrific warriors, and are often mercenaries for other rulers. The Queen rules the country well.

This country is surrounded by water. Next to Amazonia is the land of Turmagut, a good, profitable country, thanks to King Alexander who founded a city there called Alexandria.*

On the other side of Chaldea, to the south, is Ethiopia, a vast country. The people in the south of this country are utterly black. In the south is a spring from which, during the day, the water is so cold that nobody can drink it, whilst at night it is so hot that nobody can bear to touch it. In this country there are rivers and all the water is murky and a bit salty, because of the intense heat. People from that country get drunk easily, and have little appetite for food. They often have dysentery and they don't live long.

In Ethiopia there are people who have only one foot and they get about so quickly on it that it's a wonder to behold; it's a large foot, which can provide shade and cover the entire body from the sun.*

Also in Ethiopia is the city of Saba, and one of the three kings who made an offering to Our Lord at Bethlehem reigned there.*

15

THE LAND OF INDIA

I'VE described Ethiopia to you, from which one travels to India through many different countries. One calls it Greater India, and it is divided into three parts: that is, Greater India, an exceedingly hot region; Lesser India, a temperate region; and a third, to the north. In this part it is cold indeed and, on account of the frost and ice, water there becomes crystal, and then murky, yellowy coloured diamonds grow on it. These diamonds are so hard that nobody can break or smooth them. There are other diamonds that can be found in Arabia; they're not as fine, they are darker and softer. There are also some in Cyprus and some in Macedonia, but the best and most precious are in India. They have often been discovered within a mass of minerals extracted when one refines gold from a mine, when one breaks the mass into many pieces. Sometimes one finds some the size of a bean, some are even smaller, and these are as hard as the Indian ones.

Even though one can find excellent diamonds in India on the icy, crystalline rock, good, hard diamonds can also be found on adamantine rock in the sea, and also on the mountains, like hazelnuts. They are all angular and pointed in their own way, and they grow together, male and female. They are fed by heavenly dew, and they conceive and engender little children that multiply and grow through the years.* I've put it to the test many times: if one looks after them, together with a little bit of rock, and waters them often with May-dew,* they'll grow each year and the small ones will grow large.

If a man carries the diamond on his left side it is more efficacious than on his right; this is because the strength of their birth comes from the north, which is on the left side of the world, and on the left side of a man when he turns his face to the east.

If you want to know what the efficacy of the diamond is, I'll tell you what foreigners say. The diamond gives courage to one who carries it, and it keeps one's limbs healthy. It gives a man grace to defeat his enemies, if he is in the right, both in battle and in litigation.

Whoever carries it is kept sound of mind, it protects one from quarrels, arguments, civil unrest, and from nightmares and apparitions and evil spirits. If one who dabbles in sorcery or magic wishes to hurt someone who is carrying a diamond, he won't be able to do so. Also, no wild animal can attack anyone who is carrying a diamond.

Moreover, diamonds should be given, not coveted; they should be free, not bought; then they are more beneficial and make one more stalwart against one's enemies. A diamond heals lunatics, and those tormented by the Devil. If venom or poison is brought to the same place as a diamond, it immediately becomes damp and begins to sweat. Even though some people believe diamonds cannot be polished, one certainly can polish them, but many craftsmen maliciously refuse to polish them.

One can test a diamond in the following way. First, one cuts sapphire or some other precious stone with them, or cuts them with crystal or something else. Then one takes the adamant, which is the sailors' lodestone that attracts the needle, and one lays the diamond on the adamant and lays the needle in front of the adamant. If the diamond is pure and efficacious, the adamant will not pull the needle towards it while the diamond is there. This is the test foreigners use. Sometimes it happens that a pure diamond loses its efficacy because of the sinfulness of the person carrying it, so it's necessary to make it efficacious again or else it's of little value. There are many other kinds of precious gems besides.

This country is called India because of a river running through it, called the Indus. In that river one finds eels thirty feet long. The people living near that river have a foul yellow-and-green complexion. In India there are more than five thousand pleasant and large inhabitable islands, not to mention others on which people don't live. On every one of these there are many cities and towns and lots of people, as Indians are of such a disposition that they don't often leave their country. They live under a planet called Saturn, and this planet takes twenty years to make its circuit through the twelve signs, whilst the moon takes a month to pass through all the twelve signs. Saturn being so sluggish in his movements, those people who live under him and in his climate have little desire to move about very much. In our country it's the absolute opposite, because we live under the moon's climate and its nimble movements, for the moon is the planet of travel. Therefore it gives us the desire to move about a lot and to travel to lots of different countries around the world, because it orbits the earth more swiftly than other planets.

So, people travel through India to many countries up to the Great Ocean and then they reach the island named Hormuz,* which Venetian and Genoese and other merchants visit in order to buy merchandise. It's so hot there that men's bollocks hang down to their shins due to their considerable physical degeneracy.* Local people know how to bind them up tightly and smear them with a special ointment to hold them up, or else these men could not survive.

In this country, and in many others besides, men and women together lie stark naked in rivers and pools from mid-morning until gone noon. They immerse themselves in the water except for their faces because of the intense heat there. On this island there are ships without nails or other ironware, because the adamantine rocks in the sea would pull the ships towards them.*

From this island one travels by sea to the isle of Thana,* where there is abundant wine and corn. The king of this island used to be so powerful that he went to war against King Alexander. People on this island have different beliefs, because some worship the sun and some worship fire, some worship trees, some worship the first thing that they encounter in the morning, some worship effigies, some worship idols. There's a great difference between an effigy and an idol:* an effigy is an image made to resemble something someone knows, whereas some idols have three heads and are therefore against nature: one of a man, another of a horse, and another of an ox or some other beast nobody has ever seen.

You should be aware that those who worship effigies worship them because of ancient estimable men like Hercules and others, who performed many marvels in their day. They say they know full well these effigies are not God, who made all things; but they are godly because of the miracles that they perform, and therefore they worship them. This is what they say of the sun, as it changes throughout the year many times and provides heat to nourish all the things on earth. Because it is of such great benefit, they say they know full well that it is not actually God but that it is godly and God loves it above other things, and so they worship it. They say that fire likewise yields so many benefits. Thus they invent reasons to worship planets and things.

They say that, amongst idols, the ox is the holiest beast on earth and the most useful, because he does many good things and no wicked things. They know full well that this comes about through the special grace of God; so they make a god who is half man and half ox, because man is the best and most beautiful creature God made and the ox is the holiest.

Also, they worship adders and other beasts they encounter first thing in the morning, and especially those beasts that have good fortune and help them thrive for the rest of that day on which they meet them, and they have a great deal of experience of this. And so they say these fortunate encounters come from God. Therefore they make effigies like those animals they keep in their houses and they worship them first thing in the morning before they encounter anything else.

However, there are even some Christians who say that some animals are better to meet than others, like hares and swine that are said to be the most unfortunate to meet with.

On this island, Thana, there are many wild animals, and the local rats are as big as dogs, and they have to use mastiffs to catch them because the cats there are too small. From there one travels to the land of Lombe, where the city of Kollam* is, and besides that city is a mountain called Kollam, from which the city takes its name. At the foot of the mountain is a pretty well with water sweet with the flavours and fragrances of all kinds of spices, and it changes its flavour every hour of the day. Whoever drinks from this well three times a day is healed of any sickness they might have. I once drank from that well and I do believe that I'm still the better for it. Some people call this the Fountain of Youth, because those who drink from it seem to be eternally young and live without serious illness. They say that this well flows from the Earthly Paradise, as it's so wholesome. Ginger grows in this country, and many excellent merchants travel there for the spices.

People in this country worship the ox, on account of his innocence and his meekness and the many uses he has. They get the ox to work for six or seven years and then they eat him. The local king always has an ox with him. The person who looks after this ox is paid a fee each day for his care, and each day he gathers the ox's urine and dung in a gold vessel and carries it to their high-priest, who's called Archiprotapapaton.* This high priest carries it to the king and confers a great blessing on it. Then the king puts his hand into it, and it is called 'gall',* and he smears his forehead and chest with it. They greatly worship this and they say the king will be filled with the virtues of this ox and he shall be sanctified through the power of this holy thing, or so they say. When the king has done this, then the aristocrats take it and then other people according to their rank, when they can get a bit of the remainder.

In this country their idols—that is, their false gods—are in the form of half man and half ox, and the Devil speaks to them in these false gods, answering whatever they ask. In the presence of these false gods they often slay their children, sprinkling their blood on the false gods, and thus they make sacrifices to them.

In this country they burn anyone who dies, as a sign of penance, so he will suffer no torment if he were to be laid in the earth and eaten by worms. If his wife has no children, they burn his wife alive with him and say that it's for a good reason: she will keep him company in the other world, just as she did in this one. If she has children, she may live with them if she wishes. If the wife dies first, men burn her and her husband, if he wants. Good wine is grown in this country, and women drink wine and men do not, and women shave their beards and men do not.

From this country one travels for ten days to another land, which is called Ma'bar.* This is a grand kingdom, with many fine cities and towns. The corpse of St Thomas is buried in this land, in a beautiful tomb in the city of Calamy.* That arm with its hand, which he put in Our Lord's body when He had been resurrected and Our Lord said to him *Noli esse incredulous sed fidelis*, that is, 'be not faithless, but believing',* that very hand is still placed uncovered outside the tomb: with this hand the local people make judgements and decisions to ascertain who is in the right. If there's any dispute between two parties, they have them set out their cause in two documents, and these documents are placed in St Thomas's hand. The hand immediately casts aside the document of the wrong party and keeps hold of the document in the right. For this reason people come from afar to have judgements made about undetermined legal cases.

In the church of St Thomas there is a massive representation, finely and expensively crafted with precious gems and with pearls, of a false god; people travel with great reverence to that effigy on pilgrimages from afar, like Christians who visit St James.* Some pilgrims visit there carrying sharp knives in their hands, with which they cut at their shins and thighs as they travel, so that they bleed out of love for their god. Moreover, they say that one who is willing to die for this god's sake is blessed. There are some who travel there who kneel on the ground, from the time they leave their house until the time they reach this place, at every third step. They bring incense or some other sweet substance to waft smoke around their idol, just as we like to do with God's body.

In front of the church there is a fishpond full of water in which pilgrims throw gold and silver, and any number of gems and pearls, in place of making an offering. So when the church is in need of assistance, they take what they need from that pond and it provides what is needed to furnish the church.

You should be aware that when there are great celebrations on account of that false god, such as the dedication of the church or the enthronement of that god, the entire country is assembled there; people place this false god or a smaller idol in a beautifully made chariot, decorated with elegant cloth-of-gold, and they lead it with great sacredness around the city. All the local virgins go in front of the chariot at the head of the procession, in pairs; then all the pilgrims follow, some of whom fall down in front of the chariot and let it ride over them, and so some die and others have their arms or legs broken, and they do this out of love for their idol. They believe that the more pain they suffer for their idol's sake, the more pleasure they'll have in the next world. One can find few Christians who are willing to suffer so great a penance for Our Lord's sake as these people do for their idol.

Immediately in front of the chariot are countless local minstrels, making many different melodies. When they return to the church they set up this idol in his throne, and in reverence to the idol two or three men kill themselves, through their own choice, with sharp knives. It's similar to how in our country a person would consider it a great honour to have a holy man in one's kin, someone who is called a saint after his death and is written about in books and litanies; here, friends of the dead burn their bodies and take the ashes and keep them as relics, and they say that this is a holy thing. They have no anxieties while they carry these ashes with them.

One travels from this country via many lands and islands, about which it would be too prolix to describe, and after fifty-two days' travel one reaches the land called Lamuri.* This is a very hot country and it is normal there for men and women to go about naked, and they are scornful of people who wear clothes; they say that God created

Adam and Eve naked and that people shouldn't be ashamed of that which God made, because nothing God made is repulsive. They believe in God who made Adam and Eve and the entire world.

There are no married women there, but all women are shared in common and they reject no man. They say that God commanded it of Adam and Eve and all that are descended from them, saying *Crescite et multiplicamini et replete terram*, that is, 'Increase and multiply, and fill the earth'.* Thus no man there says 'this is my wife', and no woman says 'this is my husband'. When the women have children, they give them to whosoever they like or to the man who had sex with them.

The land is held in shared ownership, in that one man has it one year, another man another year. Also, all the crops and corn are held in common because nothing is kept locked away, and each man is as rich as another. They do, however, have one wicked habit: they eat human flesh more enthusiastically than anything else. Merchants bring them their children to sell, and if they are fat they are eaten straightaway, and they keep the others and feed them until they're fat too and then they are eaten, because they say it is the best and sweetest meat in the world.

In this country and in many others thereabouts one cannot see the star called the Tramontana,* because it is not seen in the south. This is the star by which sailors are led and which stands due north and never moves. There is another star there which is called Antarctic,* and that is directly opposite (that is, due south) to that other star, the one by which sailors are led; therefore it is not seen in the north. By this one can easily perceive that the earth and the sea are circular in form, because parts of the firmament that appear in one place do not appear in another. From this one can prove that, if one might find a sea-crossing and if one wished to go to see the world, one might circumnavigate it, above and below.* I can prove this through what I've seen:* because I've been to Brabant and seen with the astrolabe that the Tramontana is fifty-four degrees north in Germany, and near Bohemia it is fifty-eight degrees north, and further north it goes to sixty-two degrees north and several minutes.*

You should understand that directly opposite to the Tramontana star is the Antarctic star. These two stars never ever move, and the firmament rotates around them like a wheel on an axle so that these two stars divide the entire firmament in two parts.

After this, I went to the south and I found that one first sees the Antarctic star in Libya. As I went further, I found that in Upper Libya it is eighteen degrees north and some minutes (by which sixty minutes make a degree). So having travelled by land and by sea to the countries which I have described before and other lands and islands opposite to them, I found this Antarctic star at thirty-three degrees north and many minutes.

If I had a retinue and a fleet that could go further, I truly believe that we would have seen the entire circumference of the firmament. Because, as I've already told you, half the firmament is between these two stars, the which half I have seen, because each half of the firmament has no more than one hundred and eighty degrees, of which I've seen sixty-two degrees and ten minutes under the Tramontana, and under the Antarctic star in the south I've seen thirty-three degrees and sixteen minutes. And so, apart from eighty-four degrees and about half a degree, I have seen the entire firmament.

Therefore I say with certainty that a person who has a ship is able to go all around the world, above and beneath, and return to his own country. He'll always find people, nations, islands in these regions, because you know full well that people who live under the Antarctic star are totally in step with those of us who live under the Tramontana. Those people who live opposite to us are in step with us, because all parts of the earth and sea have their opposites facing them.*

You should know that the region of Prester John, Emperor of India, is underneath us, for one travelling from Scotland or England towards Jerusalem keeps climbing,* for our lands are in the lowest part of the west and the region of Prester John is in the lowest part of the east, and they have daytime when we have night, and night when we have day. Just as one climbs out of our countries towards Jerusalem, one goes down towards the region of Prester John from Jerusalem, and that's because the entire earth is round.

Now, you've heard how Jerusalem is in the middle of the world, and that can easily be demonstrated thus: if one takes a spear there and sets it straight in the earth at midday (when night and day are of equal length) it creates no shadow. And David bears witness to this when he says, *Deus operatus est salute in medio terre*, that is, 'God hath wrought salvation in the midst of the earth'.*

Therefore whoever leaves our western countries for Jerusalem, as much as they travel upwards to get there, they'll travel the same amount downwards from Jerusalem into the region of Prester John. And then thanks to the roundness of the earth and sea one can travel on to these surrounding islands until one comes directly beneath us.

On this subject, I've had cause many times to think about a story I heard when I was young, about a courageous man from our country who went away for a time to see the world. He passed India and more than five thousand islands beyond India and he went so far in his travels by land and by sea that he found an island where he heard people speaking his own language and herding cows using exactly the same words as did people in his own country. He was truly astonished, he really couldn't understand how that could be. But actually he had travelled so far on land and by sea around the world that he had come to the borders of his own country! Because he could travel no further, he turned around the way he had come and so he had to make a very long journey. It happened that afterwards he went towards Norway, and a sea-storm steered him so that he arrived at an island. When he disembarked at this island, he thought that it was the island he had visited before* where he heard his own language spoken as the ploughmen spoke to their beasts.

This is absolutely possible, even though uneducated people do not believe that one may go to the earth's underside, for just as we think that these men are underneath us, so they think that we are underneath them!* So if a person could topple off the earth into the firmament, then the earth and the sea, which are so heavy, would be even more able to fall into the firmament. But that can't happen, and of this God said, *Non timeas me suspendi terram ex nichilo*, that is, 'Do not be afraid of me, who hung the earth from nothing'.*

Even though it's possible for one to travel all around the world, nevertheless not one in a thousand men would choose the way which leads directly back to his country; there are so many routes and territories that one is likely to take an incorrect way unless it is by the grace of God. For the earth is massive and long, and its circumference—around, above, and beneath—is 20,425 miles, according to the opinions of ancient wise men.* I will not find fault with this, but, according to my slight wisdom, I think, with all due respect, that it is actually bigger.

To illustrate what I'd like to say rather better, I imagine a huge compass, and around the point of that compass, which is called the centre, there's another smaller compass divided by lines into many parts, and all these lines meet together in the centre: so that as many parts or lines as has the larger compass are on the small compass, although the spaces will be smaller. Now, if the larger compass is positioned in place of the firmament, which is divided by astronomers into twelve signs, and each sign is divided into thirty degrees, this is three hundred and sixty degrees around. Now, if the earth (represented by the smaller compass) is divided in as many parts as the firmament, and each of these is equal to a degree of the firmament, this totals seven hundred and twenty. So, if all this is multiplied by three hundred and sixty, it comes to a total of 31,500 miles, each mile being seven furlongs as miles are in our countries. According to my opinion and my understanding, this is what the earth's circumference is and what it encompasses all around.

You'll be aware that, according to the learning of ancient, wise philosophers and astronomers, England, Scotland, Wales, and Ireland are not factored in the height of the Earth, as it appears according to all the books of astronomy, for the surface of the Earth is divided by the seven planets into seven parts called 'climates'.* The countries I spoke of before are not in these climates, as they descend towards the west. Moreover, the Indian isles directly opposite us are not factored in the climates, as they are so low in the east.* These climates extend all around the world.

Near this island of Lamuri, of which I have spoken, is another island, called Sumatra,* and this is a fine island. People from this island, both men and women, consider it extremely refined to mark themselves on the face with a hot iron, to distinguish themselves from others as they regard themselves as the most courageous people in the world. They are forever in conflict with the naked people about whom I spoke before.

There are many other countries and islands and different kinds of people, about which there is a great deal to say. But if one travels on a little by sea, one discovers a large island called Java.* The king of this country has seven other kings under him, as he is incredibly powerful. All kinds of spices grow in that island more bountifully than elsewhere, such as ginger, cloves, cinnamon, nutmeg, mace, and others. You should be aware that nutmeg yields mace.* There is plenty of everything, except wine.

The king of this land has a lovely, extravagant palace, in which there are steps into his hall and chambers made alternately from gold and silver, and all the walls are covered and plated in gold and silver, and on these plates are written stories of knights and battles. The flooring of the hall and chambers is made of gold and silver, and nobody could believe the luxury of this place unless one has seen it. The king of this island is so powerful that he has many times defeated in battle the Great Khan of Cathay,* who is the most powerful emperor in the world (as there is often conflict between them because the Great Khan wants to take his land off him).

If one continues by sea, one discovers another island called Salamasse (called Paten by some), a great kingdom with many delightful cities. In this land there are trees bearing a kind of flour, similar to wheat, with which one can make fine, white, tasty bread. There are other trees there which bear a poison for which there is no medicine but one: this is to take leaves* from that same tree, mash them and mix with water, then drink this, or else one will die quickly as no antidote or medicine can help.*

If you'd like to know how a tree can bear flour, I'll tell you. One cuts it with a hatchet all around the base of the trunk, near the soil, so that the bark is pierced in many places, and a thick liquid runs out which they collect in a pot and then place in the sun to dry. When it's dry they take it to the mill to grind it, and then it becomes beautiful, white flour. Also, wine, honey, and poison are drawn in the same way from other trees and are kept in pots.

There is a dead sea on that island, a body of water without a bottom; if anything falls in this lake it will never be found. Enormous canes grow next to that lake and under their roots one can find precious gems with excellent qualities, for anyone who carries these stones cannot be injured by any kind of iron or steel blade, or wounded or have blood drawn. So people from this country fight truly fiercely, because they cannot be injured by weapons. However, those who know this go into combat with them by shooting arrows without metal blades, and thereby they can kill these men.

Then there's another island, called Calonach, a large land with an abundance of goods. The king of this land has as many wives as he wants, indeed he has a thousand or more, and he sleeps with each of them but once, and therefore he has many children. He maintains four hundred tame elephants,* in case he goes to war; then he would make his men go in a castle placed on the elephants to fight against his enemies, for that is how warriors fight in battle in this land.*

In this land there's another wondrous thing that can be found nowhere else, which is that, at a certain time of year, all kinds of salt-water fish come, each kind after another, and lie down near and on the land. One kind of fish lies there for three days, and local people come there and take as many of them as they like, and then these fish go on their way. Then another kind of fish comes along and lies there for three days, and people take them. Every kind of fish does this, until they have all been there and the people have taken what they want. Nobody knows what causes this, but the locals say that the fish come to worship their king, who is the most noble in the whole world in that he has so many wives and has so many children by them. I do think that this is the greatest marvel I have seen, that fish have as much sea as they like to live in but, from their own good will, they go there to present themselves for death.

There are also snails there so large that people could be accommodated in some of their shells like in a little house. If a local man dies, they bury his wife alive and say that it is only appropriate that she should be as good company for him in the next world as she was in this one.

From this land one travels by the Great Ocean to another island people call Gaffolos. When people from this island have friends who are unwell and they believe are near to death, they hang them, still alive, from a tree and say that it's better for the birds, who are angels of God, to eat them than the worms in the earth.

From there, one travels to another island where the people have a totally wicked nature: they foster hounds to attack people. When their friends are unwell and they believe they are going to die, they let their hounds throttle them, because they don't believe they should die naturally for they say that then they would have to endure too much pain. When a person has been strangled in this way, they eat their flesh instead of venison.

From there one travels via many islands to another island called Milk. The people there are very evil, they like nothing other than fighting and killing people, indeed they happily drink human blood, and they give this blood the name 'god'. He who can kill the most people has the highest reputation amongst them. If two people are fighting each other and they make up, they are obliged to drink each other's blood, or else it's not considered to be true reconciliation.

From this island one travels to another island, which is called

Tracota,* where the people are like beasts and they are not capable of reason, and they live in caves because they haven't the intelligence to build houses. They eat snakes and they don't speak except to make a snake-like noise when they hiss at each other. Also, they regard worldly wealth as utterly unimportant, except for one mineral containing forty colours called traconite, after the island. They don't know the properties of this stone, but they covet it on account of its prettiness.

From that island one travels to another island called Natumeran, a large and pleasant island. Men and women from this island have dogs' heads* and they are intelligent. They worship the ox as their god. They go about stark naked except for a little cloth in front of their private parts. They are good at fighting, and they carry a large shield with which to cover their bodies and a spear in their hand.

If they capture a man during battle they send him to their king,* who is very powerful and devout in his religion, in that he has a necklace with three hundred giant, shiny pearls like an amber *Paternoster*.* Just like we say our *Paternoster* and *aue Maria*, the king says three hundred prayers every day to his god before he eats. He also carries around his neck an excellent and gracious shining ruby, which is almost a foot and five fingers long. When they elected him king they gave him that ruby to carry in his hand, and in this way he rides around the city. He also carries this ruby around his neck, because if he didn't carry it he would no longer be regarded as king. The Great Khan of Cathay has long coveted that ruby, but he still can't have it, either through waging war or for the exchange of goods. This king is a very faithful and righteous man, as people can travel safely and securely throughout his land, carrying anything they wish, and no one would be so insolent as to menace or rob another.

Then one reaches an island that is called Ceylon,* which is almost eight hundred miles in circumference. In this land there is much wilderness, because people do not dare to live there as there are so many snakes and dragons and crocodiles. These crocodiles are yellow snakes, with striped backs, and they have four feet and short legs and great, incredible claws. When they move over a sandy path it looks like someone has pulled a bush through the sand. There are many other kinds of wild beasts there, especially elephants.

There is a mountain in this land and in the middle of this mountain there is a plain with a great pool with a large quantity of water in it. Local people say that Adam and Eve wept on that mountain one hundred years after their expulsion from Paradise, and they say that the water is their tears. In this water there are many crocodiles and other serpents.

Once a year the local king allows poor men to get into that pool, out of their love of Adam, in order to gather precious stones, for there are many. But because of the vermin in the water these men smear their arms and legs with a special ointment,* and then they are not scared of crocodiles or serpents. Local people say that the region's snakes and wild beasts never harm outsiders who go there, but only harm the natives.

In this land and many others nearby there are wild geese with two heads, and there are lions, totally white, as big as oxen, and there are many other birds and beasts. You need to be aware that the sea is so high there that it seems to go up to the clouds and looks like it should envelop all the land. And therefore David says, *Mirabiles elaciones maris*, that is, 'Wonderful are the surges of the sea'.*

From this island one travels to another island, a large island called Dodim. In this land there are many different kinds of people and they have horrible customs, for the fathers eat the sons and the sons the fathers, the husbands their wives or the wives their husbands. If someone's father or mother or some friend is sick, the son goes at once to a priest of their law and asks him to request of their god, which is an idol, whether or not the father will die or not of their illness. So the priest and the son kneel in front of the idol and ask him, and he answers them. If the idol says that the father will live, they look after him very well. If the idol says that he will die, the priest goes with the son to the father (or with the wife or whichever friend of the sick person it is) and they lay their hands on his mouth and suffocate him and thus kill him. Then they cut all the body into pieces and invite all his friends to come and eat the dead man, and they make a great celebratory feast and have many minstrels at it. When they've eaten the flesh they bury the bones. Anyone who was his friend but was not there to eat him is humiliated and censured so he is no longer considered a friend. And all friends behave like this to each other.

The king of this land is a powerful ruler and he has over fifty-four islands* subject to him and he is the king of every single one of them. In one of them there are people with only one eye, and that's in the middle of their forehead. They don't eat anything but raw meat and fish.

There is another island where people have no heads and their eyes are in their shoulders and their mouths are on their chests.

On another island there are people who have neither heads nor eyes and their mouths are behind, between their shoulders.

On another island there are people who have a flat face without a nose or eyes, but they have two small holes instead of eyes and they have flat mouths without lips.

On another island there are disgusting people who have a lip above the mouth that is so big that when they sleep in the sun they cover up their whole face with that huge lip.

On another island there are people who are both male and female and have the genitals of both. They can use both whenever they want, one at one time, the other at another time. When they use the male member they produce children, and when they use the female member they bear children.

There are many other kinds of people on these islands, it would take too long a time to describe them. In order to continue, one travels to an island where the people are exceedingly small. They have a small hole in place of a mouth, and they cannot eat, except everything that they need to sustain themselves which they take through the tube of a feather or some similar thing.

16

THE KINGDOM OF MANZI

ONE who travels from this land eastwards by the Indian Ocean must voyage for many days until they arrive at the kingdom of Manzi;* this is the best region in India, the most pleasing and most bountiful in all things within man's power. Christians and Saracens live in this land, for it is large. There are two thousand cities in it and many other towns. In this land no one goes begging because it has no poor people in it. Also, the men have wispy beards like a cat's whiskers.

There are fair-complexioned women in this region, and therefore some people call it Albania on account of its white people. There is a city there which people call Latorim and it's larger even than Paris. That city has a fine waterway navigable by ship. There are birds in that land that are twice as big as in other places in the world.

There is plenty of food and also great snakes, which they use in lavish feasts and they eat them during great rituals. If someone held a banquet and provided all the best meat they could get but gave their guests no snake-meat, they would have no thanks for the entire banquet.

In this country there are white hens with no feathers but rather white wool, like sheep in our country. Married women there wear crowns* on their heads so that they can be recognized as such. In this land they take a beast called a *loires** and they teach it to go into fish-ponds and without delay it retrieves nice big fish. And so they take as much fish until they have all that they want.

From there one travels for many days to a city called Cassay, the biggest city in the whole world. This city is fifty miles in circumference. There are more than twelve gates to this city, and at each gate there is a fine tower in which men live to protect the town against the Great Khan, for it shares a border with his land. A great river runs on one side of the city, and fine wine is cultivated there which they call *bygoun*.* Christians and others live there, and the King of Manzi was accustomed to live there too. Religious men, Christian friars, devout men, live there.*

People travel by that river until they reach a monastic abbey, a little way from the city. In this abbey there's a large, pretty garden, and there are many trees with different fruits. In this garden there are many different animals, such as baboons, little monkeys, apes, and others. Then, when the convent community has eaten, a monk takes the remainder of the meal into the garden, and he strikes once a little silver bell he holds in his hand. Then all the animals, some three or four thousand of them, come out from their burrows and line up in a row. He gives them this remainder of food in a fine silver vessel and they eat it. When they've eaten, he strikes the little bell once again and they go back to where they came from. The monk said that these animals are the souls of dead men, the gentle and attractive animals being the souls of aristocrats and gentlemen, and those that are ugly being the souls of commoners. I asked him if it would not be better to give these leftovers to poor men than to these animals. He replied that there are no poor men in that country, and, even if there were people who needed alms, it would be better to give it to these souls which suffer their penance there and may not go to seek out food, unlike people who have the knowledge to find food and the capacity to work.

From there one travels for nearly six days and finds a city which is called Chibence. The walls are nearly twenty miles in circumference. In this city there are sixty fine, strong bridges. The original throne of the King of Manzi, who is a great ruler, as I have described previously, was in this city.

17

THE LANDS OF THE GREAT KHAN OF CATHAY

FROM the city of Chibence one crosses a large river, flowing with fresh water, which is nearly four miles across, and that leads to the lands of the Great Khan. The river goes through Pygmieland,* where the men are small of stature, being only three spans high, and they are truly very attractive. They get married when they are six months old, and they only live for eight years, and one who lives for eight years is considered to be really old. These little people don't work but they keep big people like us amongst them to work for them and they hold these people in such scorn as we would if we had giants amongst us.

From this land one travels through many countries, cities, and towns until one reaches a city called Menke. In that city there are many ships, and they are as white as snow due to the nature of the wood from which they're made, and they are constructed like large houses with halls, rooms, and other accommodation.

From there one travels by a river called the Caromosan. This river runs through Cathay and does great damage when it is in spate. Cathay is a large country: pretty, fine, wealthy, and abundant in good merchandise. Merchants visit there each year to collect spices and other goods more frequently than they go to other countries. You need to be aware that merchants who come from Venice or Genoa or other places in Lombardy or Rome travel by sea or by land for eleven months or more before they reach Cathay.

Eastwards there is an ancient city, in the province of Cathay, and near this city the Tartars have constructed another city, called Cadom.* This city has twelve gates and from one gate to another is always a long mile, so that these two cities, the old and the new one, are more than twenty miles in circumference.

In this city there is the Great Khan's throne, at a very beautiful palace with walls around it nearly two miles high, and within those walls are many other attractive palaces. There's a fine mountain in the garden of the palace and it's the prettiest to be found anywhere. All around the mountain are many trees bearing different fruits. Also, a great moat and other ponds surround the mountain, where there are many different fowl that the Great Khan can take so he can go hunting without leaving his palace.

The palace hall is richly decorated, as within the hall there are twenty-four golden pillars. All the walls are covered with red pelts from animals called panthers. These are pretty animals and they smell pleasant, and because of the scent of the pelt there are never foul smells there. These pelts are as red as blood, and they shimmer so much in the sun that one can hardly look at them. People value these pelts as if they were the finest gold.

In the middle of this palace there is a place laid out which they call the dais for the Great Khan, finely made with precious gems and large pearls hanging all round it. At the four corners of this dais are four golden serpents. Above and below the dais there are fountains for the beverages they drink at the Emperor's court. So the palace hall is finely and nicely decorated.

At the top end of the hall is the Emperor's throne, in a lofty position, where he sits to dine. The table from which he eats is prettily edged with gold, and this edging is full of precious stone and large pearls. The stairs upon which he ascends to the dais are made of different precious gems edged with gold.

At the left-hand side of his throne is his wife's seat, at a lower height than his, and this is made of jasper edged with gold. The seat of his second wife is at a lower height than the first one. This is also made of jasper and edged with gold. Next, the seat of the third wife is at a lower height than the second, for he always has three wives with him wherever he is. Next to the wives, on the same side, sit other ladies from the Emperor's kin, each one at a lower height than the other, according to their status.

The local married women have an image, a shaftment long, in the likeness of a man's foot on their heads, beautifully made out of precious gems and shining peacock feathers, betokening that they are under man's subjection (*nota bene!*). Those who are not married do not have such a thing.

On the right-hand side of his throne sits the Great Khan's eldest son, who shall follow him as emperor; he sits at a lower height than the Emperor on the same kind of throne as that of the Empress. Then other kinsmen of his sit there, each one at a lower height than the next, according to their rank.

The Emperor's table at which he himself sits is made of fine gold and precious gems, or of white or yellow crystal, edged with gold. Each of his wives has a table to herself. Under the Emperor's table sit four clerks, at his feet, to write down everything he says at table, both good and bad.

At great feasts a huge vine is made of the finest gold above the Emperor's table and all around the hall, and it has many bunches of grapes just like the grapes on vines, of which some are white, some yellow, some red, some black, some green. And those that are red are made of ruby or crimson or alabaster; the white ones are made of crystal or beryl; the yellow ones of topaz; the green ones of emerald or chrysolite; and the black ones are of onyx or irachite.* This vine is fashioned from precious stones so accurately that it seems to be an actual living vine.

The noble aristocrats stand in front of the Emperor's table and none is so bold as to speak to him unless he has first spoken to them, unless they are minstrels employed to entertain the Emperor. Moreover, all the vessels he has in his hall and in his chambers are made of precious gems: specifically, at the tables where the noblemen sit they are made of jasper, crystal, amethyst, others of fine gold. The cups are made of emerald, sapphires, topaz, chrysolites, and many other kinds of gems. They make no silver vessels, as they hold silver in too little regard to make vessels from it. However, they do use it to make their staircases, pillars, and the pavements in the halls and chambers.

You should know that my companions and I had a treaty with the Great Khan for sixteen months against the King of Manzi with whom he was at war.* This was because we had heard a great deal of gossip about him and we wanted to see the grandeur of his court, and if it was like people had said. To be sure we found it more magnificent and splendid that we had ever heard. We would never have believed it if we hadn't seen it.

You should also be aware that the taking of food and beverages is more dignified in our country than in theirs, for the commoners eat none of the meat that we do but all kinds of animals. When they have eaten it they wipe their hands on their skirts, and they only eat once a day. They drink milk from all sorts of animals.

18

WHY HE IS CALLED THE GREAT KHAN

As to why he is called the Great Khan, some say as follows. You know very well how the entire world was destroyed by Noah's flood, except Noah and his wife and their children, and that Noah had three sons, Shem, Ham, and Japheth. Ham was the one who saw his father asleep stark naked and he mocked him, and therefore he was cursed; and Japheth covered his father up again.* These three brothers possessed all the land in the world. Ham took the finest eastward part, which is called Asia. Shem took Africa. Japheth took Europe. Ham was the strongest and the richest of these brothers, and the pagan peoples come from him and different island peoples, some of them headless, some disfigured, and some with deformed limbs. On account of this Ham, the Emperor calls himself Khan,* because he possesses that land, and he calls himself ruler over the whole world.

However, you should be aware that the Emperor of Cathay is not called Ham but Khan, for this reason: only eight years ago* all of Tartary was in subjection and bondage to its neighbours, and they were forced into being herders to keep animals. Amongst them were seven peoples or tribes, of whom the first was called Tartary, the second was called Tangut, the third Oirat Eurasians, the fourth Chelair, the fifth Sunit, the sixth Merkit, the seventh Tibet.* These all owed allegiance to the Great Khan.

Now, it happened that amongst the first people there was an old man, he was not rich, and people called him Chaungwise.* One night this man was lying in his bed and a knight in white on a white steed came to him and said, 'Khan, are you asleep? Almighty God has sent me to you, and it's his will that you tell the seven tribes that you shall be their emperor, because you're going to conquer all the lands around you and they shall be subject to you as you have been to them.'

The next day Chaungwise said this to the seven tribes, and they scorned him and thought he was a fool. That next night the same knight came to the seven tribes and told them, on God's behalf, to make Chaungwise their emperor so they could be free from subjection and they would subject other countries to them. The next day they made Chaungwise their emperor, and honoured him in every way they could, and called him Khan as that white knight had previously called him. And they said that they would do anything he asked of them.

He made statutes and laws for them, which are called *Isakan*.* The first statute was that they should be obedient to Almighty God and believe that he would deliver them from their servitude, and that they should call on him in times of need. Another statute was that all men allowed to bear arms should be counted, and an officer in charge appointed to each group of ten of them, and an officer in charge of each hundred, and an officer in charge of each thousand.

He commanded too that all the most rich and noble of the seven tribes should abandon whatever they had in inheritance and governance, and consider themselves paid from whatever he would give them out of his grace, and they did so. He also requested that each man should bring his eldest son to him and murder his own son by his own hands and cut off the son's head, and they did so immediately. When he saw that they made no opposition to whatever he asked them to do, he requested them to serve under his banner. And then he conquered all the regions around him.

It happened one day that the Khan rode with a small retinue to see the lands he had conquered, and he encountered a great multitude of his enemies, and he was thrown from his horse and his horse slain. So when his men saw him on the ground they believed that he was dead, so they fled, and their enemies followed them.

When the Khan saw his enemies had gone far away, he crept into a bush in the dense woodland there. When the enemies returned from their pursuit, they went to the woods to see if anybody had hidden there, and indeed they found many of them. They reached the place where the Khan was, and they saw a bird—known as an owl—sitting on a tree. They said that there must be no man there, for the bird was sitting there, and so they went away and thus he was saved from death. He crept away at night and reached his own men, who were very glad to see him. Since then people of that country have piously worshipped that bird, and they worship that bird above any other kind of bird. So, the Khan then assembled all his men and rode up to his enemies and obliterated them. When he had conquered all the lands around him he held them in subjection.

Once he had gained all the surrounding regions up to Mount Belyan, the knight in white came to him in a vision and said, 'Khan, the will of God is that you shall go beyond Mount Belyan and then gain many lands. Because you shall not find a route, you shall go to the coastal side of Mount Belyan and you shall kneel there nine times, facing the east, in worship of God, and He will show you a way through so you'll be able to pass.'

The Khan did just so, and at once the sea lapping at the mountain's edge withdrew, and showed him a fine path, nine feet wide, between the mountain and the sea. And so he passed through with all his people. In this way he conquered the entire land of Cathay, which is the biggest country in the world. Because of these nine genuflections and the nine-foot pathway, the Khan and the Tartars hold the number nine in great reverence.

After he had won the land of Cathay he died, and then his eldest son, Chito Khan,* reigned after him. His brother went on to gain other lands for them, and then won the lands of Prussia and Russia. They called him Khan, but the Great Khan is of Cathay. The kingdom of Cathay is the biggest in the world and has the greatest Khan, for he is the greatest ruler in the world. He calls himself the ruler of the entire world in the letters he sends, in which he describes himself as *Chan filius excelsi uniuersam terram colencium summus imperator et dominus dominancium*, that is, 'Chan, God's son, emperor over all those who work the land and ruler of all rulers'. Also, the words around his great seal that he sends say *Deus in celo Chan super terram, eius fortitudo omnium hominum imperatoris sigillum*, that is, 'God in Heaven, Khan on earth, the strength of his seal, the Emperor of all men'. And the writing around his privy seal is *Dei fortitude omnium hominum imperatoris sigillum*, that is, 'Strength of God, seal of the Emperor of all men'. Even though they are not Christian men, nevertheless the Emperor and the Tartars believe in God Almighty.

19

THE ARRANGEMENT OF THE COURT OF THE GREAT KHAN OF CATHAY

I'VE now told you why he is called the Great Khan. Next I will describe for you the arrangement and the governance of his court when they make their special feasts—that is, principally, four times a year. This first is at his birthday; the second is at his circumcision; the third is at the time when their idol first spoke; and the fourth is at the time when their idol first began to perform miracles.

On these occasions the Great Khan has thousands of men neatly marshalled into hundreds and thousands, and each knows well what he shall do: first, four thousand wealthy, powerful barons are commanded to organize the feast and serve the Emperor. All these barons have golden crowns on their heads, beautifully decorated with precious gems and pearls. They are dressed in cloth-of-gold and camacas* and similar fabrics as fine as can be made. They can easily have these kinds of clothes because they are cheaper there than woollen clothes are here.

These four thousand barons are divided into four companies and each company is dressed in a suit of a different colour. When the first thousand have passed by for inspection and served the Great Khan, they stand aside and then the second thousand come forward, then the third, and so forth. Nobody speaks a single word, and in this way they move around the hall.

Many philosophers of various sciences sit beside the Emperor's table, some of astronomy, some of necromancy, and some of geometry, and some of pyromancy, and other sciences too. They also have golden or bejewelled astrolabes or vessels full of sand or of burning coals. Some have beautifully made, expensive clocks and many other instruments of their scientific pursuits.

At certain times, when it seems to them that the right time has come, they say to their assistants, 'Be quiet now!' Then these assistants say with loud voices to the entire hall, 'Be quiet now, and be still a while!' Then one of the philosophers says, 'Now every man shall show respect and bow to the Emperor, he who is God's son and ruler of entire world, for the time has now come'. Then everybody bows their heads towards the ground and then one philosopher says to them, 'Get up now!' At another time a different philosopher says, 'Everybody put their little fingers in their ears!', and they do it. At another time a different philosopher says 'Every man put their hand in front of their mouth!', and they do it. Then he tells them to put their hands on their heads, and they do it, and he tells them to take their hands off their heads, and they do it. So every hour they tell them different things, and they say these things have profound concealed meanings.

I discreetly asked what these things might mean, and one of the philosophers said that the bowing of the head signified that all those who bow their heads are forever obedient and faithful to the Emperor, and they would never be a false traitor to him for either incentives or promises. The putting of the fingers into the ear signifies that they shall neither say nor hear wicked things about the Emperor or a member of his council.

You should be aware that nobody makes or does anything for the Emperor, like clothes, bread, beverages, or other things, apart from at specific times dictated by the philosophers. If anybody in any country starts a war against the Emperor, the philosophers know about it immediately and inform the Emperor or his council, and he sends troops there.

After the minstrels have performed their tunes there in the hall for a long time, one of the Emperor's officers gets up on an elaborate, expensively wrought platform and loudly declaims, 'Be quiet!', and all the people are silent. In the meantime, all those of the Emperor's kin have gone away and dressed themselves up smartly in expensive cloth-of-gold and similar fabrics. Then the court steward says, 'X and Y, each come forward and worship the Emperor, the ruler of everything.' Then the Emperor's kinsmen each bring a white steed or a white horse and present it to the Emperor, each after the other. Then all the other barons and noblemen present him with some other gift or some gem. When they've all made an offering to the Emperor then the most senior priests there give a wonderful blessing, saying a prayer according to their law. Then the minstrels perform their tunes again.

After the minstrels have played for a while they are asked to be quiet. Then people bring lions, leopards, and other kinds of animals and birds and fish and serpents before the Emperor, because they say that all living things will worship the Emperor and be obedient to him. Then entertainers come in and perform many spectacles, as they seem to make the sun and the moon appear in the air in honour of him, and these shine so brightly that nobody can look at them. Then they command young maidens to enter, bringing golden cups full of mare's milk that they give to the lords and ladies to drink. Then they command knights in fine armour to joust through the air and their spears crash together so hard that the splinters fly all around the tables in the hall, and these jousts continue until everyone gets down from the dining-table.

This Emperor, the Great Khan, employs many gamekeepers to look after the birds, namely gerfalcons, sparrow-hawks, peregrine falcons, well-bred lanner falcons, saker falcons, chattering popinjays, and many other singing birds. He has ten thousand wild animals, like elephants, baboons, little monkeys, and others.

He's got many physicians, of whom two hundred are Christians and two hundred are Saracens, but he trusts the Christians most. There are many barons and others in his court who are Christian, converted to the Christian faith through the preaching of Christians who lived there. However, there are many who will not let on that they have been christened. And even though the Emperor and his men are not christened, they do indeed believe in God Almighty.

He's a really mighty ruler because he can spend whatever he likes. In his chamber he has a fine golden pillar, upon which there's a ruby garnet a foot long which illuminates the whole chamber at night. He has many other precious gems and rubies, but this is the largest and the finest and is more precious than any other.

In the summer this Emperor lives in the north in a city called Xanadu, and it's pretty cold there. In the winter he lives in a city called Khan-Balic* in an exceptionally hot region, and he lives there for the most part.

When this Great Khan rides from one region to another he has four large legions of his people drawn up; of which one legion travels a day in front of him (as this legion spends the evening where the Emperor will rest on the following evening), and they are well provided for. Another legion is at his right side, and another at his left, and in each legion are a great many people, and the fourth company follows the distance of a bowshot behind. In that company there are more men than in any of the other three.

You should know that the Emperor never rides on a horse unless he rides secretly with a household retinue. He only rides in a chariot with four wheels, and upon it there is a chamber made of a wood called *lignum aloes** that comes from the Earthly Paradise. This chamber is all covered inside with gold panels and precious stones and enormous pearls. Four elephants and four stallions go inside.* Five other powerful noblemen ride beside the chariot so that no other man can approach the Khan unless he beckons him.

The Empress rides in the same kind of chariot and with similar legions by another route, and his eldest son in the same arrangement, and they have so many people with them that it's a marvel to describe it.

The Great Khan's land is divided into twelve provinces with a king in each province, and in each kingdom more than two thousand cities and many other great towns. When the Emperor rides through the land and passes through towns and cities everyone sets a fire in front of his or her house, and they throw incense into it or other things that produce a pleasant fragrance for the Emperor.

If Christian religious live near the Emperor's route they approach him with a crucifix and holy water, loudly singing *Veni creator spiritus*.* When he sees them he commands his lords, riding close to him, to make way so that these religious may approach. As soon as he sees the crucifix he doffs his hat, so finely decorated with pearls and precious gems it's a wonder to describe. Then he inclines his head to the cross and the chief priest of these religious men says prayers in front of him and blesses him with the cross, and he bows with great devotion to the blessing. Then that same priest gives him nine fruits of some sort, and a golden platter, as the custom is that no foreigner should approach the Emperor unless he gives him something, as according to the Old Law, *Nemo accedat in conspectus meo uacuus*, that is, 'neither shalt thou appear before me empty'.* Then they go straight home again, so that men from the Khan's company cannot abuse them.

Religious who live where the Empress and the Emperor's son live do likewise, for this Great Khan is the most powerful ruler in the world, as neither Prester John nor the Sultan of Babylon nor the Emperor of Persia is as powerful as he.

In the Great Khan's land a man takes one hundred wives, some have forty, some more, some fewer. They marry their own kin, except mothers and daughters. All women (and men) have a way of dressing which means they cannot be identified, except that married women have signs on their heads, which I have already described. They don't live in houses with their husbands, and the husband can sleep with whosoever he wants. They have plenty of every kind of animal, except pigs, which they don't want.

This Emperor, the Great Khan, has three wives, and the principal wife is the daughter of Prester John. His people truly believe in God who created everything, though they still have gold and silver idols to whom they offer the first milk from their animals. The local people begin everything they have to do at the new moon, and they genuinely worship the sun and the moon. These men usually go riding without spurs.

Whatever name the Emperor has, they add Khan to it. When I was there the Emperor's name was Kuyuk and they called him Kuyuk Khan. The first of the wives was called Seroch Khan, the second Baruch Khan, and the third Charauk Khan.*

People of this region believe that it's a terrible sin to break a bone with another bone, and to throw milk or any other beverage on the ground. The greatest sin they may commit is to piss in the houses where they live, and anyone who pisses there will certainly be put to death. Wherever someone has pissed warrants purification or nobody can live there.

They give silver to their priests to make confession for all their sins. When they've done their penance they walk through fire in order to cleanse themselves of their sins. When a messenger brings a gift to the Emperor he passes through a fire to purify the object, in order that he brings neither poison nor anything else that might be dangerous to the Emperor.

They happily eat dogs, lions, rats, and all other animals, both big and small, except pigs and those beasts prohibited in the Old Testament. They scarcely eat bread, unless they are the most important noblemen. After they have eaten they wipe their hands on their laps, as they don't have table-linen unless they are important noblemen. After they have eaten they put the unwashed vessel, complete with remnants of meat they left, into the cooking-pot or cauldron until the next time they wish to eat. Rich men drink mare's milk, or asses' milk, or milk from similar animals. They also have another kind of drink which is made from honey and water, for in this land they have neither wine nor ale.

When they wage war they do so very cleverly; each one of them has two or three bows and plenty of arrows and also a large axe. Noblemen have short daggers with a single-edged blade, and they have plate-armour and helmets and caparisons made out of cuir-bouilli.* They execute anyone who flees in battle. They are always trying to bring all regions under their control, as they say that their prophecies predict that they will be overcome by people using archery and that they will be converted to these people's religion, but they don't know which people or which religion will conquer them. It's really very dangerous to pursue the Tartars when they flee, as in fleeing they can shoot behind them, as well as killing the people in front of them.

The Tartars believe olive oil to be an effective medicine. They have small eyes and little beards.* They are usually dishonest, as they don't keep any promises whatsoever. When someone amongst them is going to die they stick a spear in the ground next to him. When he approaches his death everyone leaves the dying man's house. When he has died they carry him into the fields and they place him in the ground.

When the Emperor, the one who is called the Great Khan, is dead they place him in a throne in the centre of a tent, and they arrange a table and a tablecloth in front of him with meat and other foods and a cup full of mares' milk. They place a mare with her foal and a saddled, bridled horse in front of him and they place gold and silver on the horse. They make a large grave all around the tent, and then they bury him and the tent and all these other goods with him in the ground. They say that when he arrives at the next world he won't be without a house, a horse, gold, and silver, and the mare will provide him with refreshment and produce more horses until he is well established in that other world. Indeed, they believe that when they are dead, in the next world, they eat and drink and make love to their wives, just as they do here. From the moment at which he is buried, nobody would be so insolent as to mention him in front of his friends.

After the Emperor has died, the seven tribes assemble and they elect his son or the next one in his line to be Emperor.

Next they say, 'We wish and we pray and we proclaim that you shall be our lord and our Emperor'. He answers, 'If you wish that I should reign over you, each of you must do as I say'.* Then, if he commands that someone should be executed, they'll be executed at once. So they all answer in unison, 'Everything that you ask shall be done'. Then the Emperor says, 'From this moment forth know that my word shall be as sharp as my sword'.

Then they place him in a throne and crown him. Then all the rich towns send him gifts, so that very same day he has more than a cartful of gold and silver and many other jewels from the noblemen, innumerable precious gems and gold and horses and rich fabrics like camaca and Tartary silks and the like.

This land of Cathay is in deepest Asia, and it borders to the west with the kingdom of Tars,* which once belonged to one of the three kings who went to visit Our Lord in Bethlehem. These Tartar men do not drink any wine. In the land of Chorasmia, to the north of Cathay, is a great abundance of everything, but there is no wine. To the east there is an enormous desert that goes on for more than one hundred days' travel. The finest city in the land is called Chorasmia,* and the region is named after this city. People from this region are fine, brave warriors.

Nearby is the kingdom of Cumania;* this is a great kingdom, but not all of it is inhabited, as the land here can be so cold that nobody is able to live there and in other places it is so hot that nobody can live there. There are so many flies there that a man doesn't know which way to turn. In this region there are only a few fruit-bearing trees. The local people go to bed in tents. They burn animal dung there because they are lacking in wood. This land stretches towards Prussia and Russia. The River Ethel* runs through this land, and it's one of the greatest rivers in the world. Sometimes it is frozen so solid that men fight huge battles on it with horses and on foot, sometimes more than a hundred thousand men all at the same time.

A short distance from that river is the great watery ocean that is called Maure, that is, the Black Sea.* Between the Maure and the Caspian is a very narrow passage to India. Therefore King Alexander had a city built to guard that passage, so nobody could pass through it unless he had his permission, and now that city is called Port de Fer.* The main city of Cumania is called Sarai.*

This is one of the three ways by which to reach India, but not many people can travel this way unless it's winter. This is called the Derbent Passage. Another way is from the land of Turkestan to Persia, which involves spending many days travelling in the desert.

The third way from Cumania is to go via the Black Sea and through the kingdom of Abkhazia. You should be aware that all these lands and kingdoms until Persia, and others besides, are owned by the Great Khan of Cathay, and therefore he truly is a great ruler of people and of many lands.

20

THE LAND OF PERSIA

So I have described for you the lands and kingdoms stretching from the land of Cathay to the land of Prussia and Russia, where Christian people live. Now I'll describe other lands stretching from Cathay to the Greek Sea, where Christians live. I shall describe the Emperor of Persia first, in so far as he is the greatest lord after the Great Khan of Cathay.

You should be aware that he has two kingdoms: one begins in the east at the kingdom of Turkestan and goes all the way west along the Caspian Sea and south to India. This land is good and flat and well populated; it has many cities, the largest cities in this kingdom being Bukhara and Samarkand.* The other Persian kingdom goes from the River Phison until Greater Armenia and northwards to the Caspian Sea and south to the land of India. This is a very fertile and good land, and there are three principal cities in this kingdom: Nishapur, Isfahan, and Sarmasse.*

Then there's the land of Armenia, which used to be four kingdoms. This is abundant, fine land. It starts at Persia and goes in length westwards to Turkey, and goes from Alexander's city, now called Port de Fer, until the land of Media. In Armenia there are many lovely cities, but Tabriz* is the most well known.

Then there's the land of Media, that is very long but narrow, which begins in the east at Persia and Lesser India and goes all the way until the kingdom of Chaldea and north to Lesser Armenia. In this land of Media are many high mountains and few plains, and Saracens live there together with another people, called Kurds. The finest cities in this land are called Sarai and Karmanâ.*

Then there's the kingdom of Georgia, which begins in the east at a huge mountain called Elbrus. This region goes from Turkey to the

Black Sea and the land of Media and Greater Armenia. There are two kings in this land, one of Abkhazia and another of Georgia, but the Georgian one is under the Great Khan. The Abkhaz one has a strong country and he defends himself well against all comers.

In the land of Abkhazia there is something truly marvellous, for there's a region which would take nearly three days to traverse and it's called Hemşin. This region is entirely covered in darkness so that it has no light by which one can see, and nobody dare go into this region because of the darkness. Nevertheless, people from near that region say that they can sometimes hear men talking, horses whinnying, and cocks crowing, and they know well that people are living there, but they don't know what kind of people.

They say this darkness is provided through a miracle of God that He showed the Christian men there, and they found this in old stories written in books (amongst other texts and marvels). Indeed, there was once a wicked Emperor from the land of Persia and he was called Shapur.* This Emperor persecuted all Christians then living in his land, and he wanted to destroy them or else have them sacrificed to his idols; many Christian men lived there, who forsook all their wealth and possessions and property and decided to leave for Greece.

When the Christians were all gathered together on a vast plain called Moghan, the Emperor and his men came to slay them. The Christians all got down onto their knees and prayed to God for help. Immediately, a dense cloud came and enveloped the Emperor and all his men so they couldn't move. Thus they live in darkness and shall do so forever. And the Christian men went wherever they wished. Therefore they say with David thus: *A domino factum est istud et est mirabile in oculis nostris*, that is, 'This is the Lord's doing: and it is wonderful in our eyes'.* A river flows from this dark region in which one can discern true signs indicating that people live there, although nobody dare enter therein.

Next comes the land of Turkey, which shares its borders with Greater Armenia, and it contains many nations such as Cappadocia, Isauria, Bryke, Question, Pytan, and Seneth. In each of these there are fine cities. It is a flat region with few hills and few rivers.

The kingdom of Mesopotamia is there, and that begins eastwards of the River Tigris at a city called Mosul and lasts westwards to the River Euphrates to a city called Edessa, and from northern Armenia to the desert in Lesser India. It's a fine, flat region with few rivers and only two mountains, of which one is called Sindjar and the other Lyson, and it borders on the land of Chaldea.

You should be aware that the land of Ethiopia borders to the east with the Great Desert, west to the land of Nubia, south to the kingdom of Mauretania,* and north to the Red Sea. That Mauretania goes from the mountains of Ethiopia to northern Libya, and it borders with Nubia, where there are Christian people, and then there's northern and southern Libya, which stretches to the great Spanish sea.

21

THE LAND OF CALDILHE

NOW, I've described and mentioned many countries on this side of the kingdom of Cathay, many of which are obedient to the Great Khan. Now I shall describe regions, countries, and islands that are beyond the land of Cathay. Therefore, should one go from Cathay to northern or southern India, one will go through a kingdom called Caldilhe. This is a very large country, where a kind of fruit grows like a gourd. When it is ripe people cut it open and they find inside an animal, a thing of flesh and blood and bone, it's like a little lamb without wool. People eat the animal and the fruit too, and that is marvellous indeed.

However, I told them that I really did not consider it much of a wonder, as I described how in my country we have trees which bear a fruit which turns into flying birds, called barnacles.* They are tasty, and those that fall in water live and those that land on earth die. They thought this was marvellous indeed. In this region and in many neighbouring ones there are trees bearing cloves, nutmegs, cinnamon, and other spices. There are vines bearing such enormous grapes that a strong man will be fully burdened by a bunch of these grapes.

In this same land are the Caspian Mountains, which some people call Uber.* Jews from the Ten Tribes are locked in these mountains, and people call them Gog and Magog,* and these Jews cannot leave on any side. Twenty-two kings were locked in there with the people who previously lived between the Scythian mountains. King Alexander chased them there because he thought he could lock them in through his men's labour.* When he saw that he was not able, he prayed to God that he might fulfil that which he had begun. God heard his prayer and locked together the mountains, which are so high and massive that nobody can cross them, so the Jews live there as if locked or fastened within. There are mountains all around them, except at one side, where the Caspian Sea is. One may well ask, 'Since there's a sea on one side, why do they not leave by this sea?' To this I would answer that, even though it's called a sea, it is actually no more than a lake standing amongst the mountains, the biggest lake in the world. If they were to leave by that sea, they wouldn't know where to disembark as they understand no language except their own.

You should be aware that the Jews have no land of their own in which to live, except amongst these mountains, and even for this they pay tribute to the Queen of Armenia.* Sometimes it has happened that a few of the Jews have made it over the hills, but a large number of people could not travel over these mountains, they are so huge and high.

People of the neighbouring region say that in the era of Antichrist these Jews will do much harm to Christians. Therefore all the Jews who live in other parts of the world have learned to speak Hebrew, because they believe that the Jews living amongst the mountains will emerge and speak nothing but Hebrew. Then the other Jews will speak Hebrew to them and lead them into Christendom in order to ravage the Christians; these Jews says that they know through their prophecies that the Jews who are within these Caspian Mountains will emerge and Christians will be subject to them as they have been subject to Christians.

If you want to know how they're going to find a way out, I'll tell you as far as I understand it. In the era of Antichrist a fox will make himself a den in the same place where King Alexander had the gates made to these hills. He will burrow into the earth so far until he surfaces amongst these Jews. When they see this fox they'll be very astonished by him, because they've never seen such an animal, although they do have many other animals amongst them. They'll chase him and pursue him until he has run again into the foxhole he came from. So then they'll dig after him so deeply until they reach those sturdily made gates which Alexander had made with great bricks and mortar, and they'll break these gates down and so they'll have found a passage out.

From this land one should travel to the land of Bactria,* where there are many wicked and treacherous people. There are trees here that bear wool as if it came from sheep, from which they make textiles.* In this land there are many hippopotami that sometimes live on the land, sometimes in the water, and they are half man, half horse, and they like to eat nothing more than men when they can get some.

In this land there are more griffins than elsewhere. Some people say they have the body at the front of an eagle and the back of a lion, and they speak the truth. But the griffin's body is larger than eight lions and bigger and stronger than one hundred eagles, for, to be sure, he could carry a large horse, or a man, or two oxen yoked together as if at the plough, whilst flying to his nest; for on his feet the griffin has long, large talons like ox-horns, and they are very sharp. From these talons people make drinking-cups, like we make bugles from horns, and from his ribs they make bows for archery.

22

THE LAND OF PRESTER JOHN

THERE are many kingdoms within the land of Prester John, from Bactria to which it is many days' travel. This Prester John is the Emperor of India, and people call his land the isle of Pentoxoire. The Emperor Prester John possesses huge estates and many large cities and fine towns, and in his kingdom are many great, fine islands, for this land of India is separated into islands because of the great floods flowing from Paradise. So in the sea there are many islands. The greatest city on the island of Pentoxoire is called Nisa,* a noble, rich city.

Prester John has many kings and many different peoples subject to him. His land is fine and fecund but not as rich as the land of the Great Khan of Cathay, for fewer merchants come to this land than to that of the Great Khan; it's a long way and, besides, they find all they need in the isles of Cathay, such as spices, cloth-of-gold, and other luxurious things. Also, even if there were better goods to purchase in the land of Prester John, they hesitate in going there because of the long distance and the dangers at sea. In many places there are great rocks of what is called adamantine, which pulls iron towards it, so no ship should pass with iron nails because the adamantine stone would pull it towards him;* therefore people dare not travel into that region by ship for dread of the adamantine. Local ships are made entirely from wood and no iron.

I was once travelling on that sea and I saw something like a kind of long island with many trees and branches and tree-trunks growing from it. The sailors there told me that it was all the big ships that the adamantine had caused to be left there, and all the things that had spilt from these ships. Because of these and other dangers, and because of the long route, people go to Cathay, which is nearer to them. Yet Cathay isn't so near for those travellers from Venice, Genoa, or other Lombard ports who still need to sail for some eleven or twelve months to reach Cathay.

Prester John's land is remote. Merchants reach it via the land of Persia and arrive at a city called Hormuz (because a philosopher called Hermes founded it).* They pass a peninsula and reach another city, called Soboth, and there they find all wares, and parrots in such abundance like larks are in our country. There's a scarcity of wheat and barley in this region, and so they eat millet and rice and cheese and different fruits.

The Emperor Prester John always marries the Great Khan's daughter, and the Great Khan marries his. In the land of Prester John there are many different things, many precious stones, including some so large and huge that they make vessels, platters, and cups and other things from them. However, I will tell you something about his faith and piety.

Prester John is a Christian, and so is the majority of his country too, but they don't have all the articles of our faith. However, they truly believe in the Father and the Son and the Holy Ghost, and they are extremely devout and loyal to each other and they set no store by material possessions. Prester John has seventy-two provinces or countries subject to him and in every one of these there is a king, and these kings have other kings under them.

In this land there are many marvels, for here there is a sandy sea made of sand and shingle and not a drop of water. It ebbs and flows with great waves, just like other seas, never still or resting. Nobody can traverse this sea by a ship or in any other way and therefore people don't know what land is beyond it. Even though there is no water in that sea, people still find good fish, a different shape from the fish in other seas, and they have a lovely, sweet taste and are good to eat.

There are massive mountains three days' travel from that sea through which flows a great torrent, full of precious stones and not a drop of water, coming from Paradise. It flows with great waves into that sandy sea. This torrent runs so fast for three days in each week and stirs up the boulders within it so it makes a great din, and the moment they reach the sandy sea these rocks can no longer be seen. In those three days when it flows like this nobody dares to come near, but on all other days people can go into it whenever they like and take the stones.

Beyond this torrent, towards the desert, there is a vast, sandy and stony plain amongst the mountains; in which plain there are trees upon which a fruit begins to ripen at sunrise every day. It grows like this until midday and then it shrivels, so that when the sun goes down there is nothing to see. Nobody dares eat this fruit because it's a kind of magical illusion. It does this each day.

In that desert there are many wild men with horns on their heads like animals and they are utterly hideous. They don't speak, they only grunt like pigs.

This Emperor has many parrots in his land, which, in their language, they call *pistake*.* These parrots speak entirely naturally as properly as does a man, and the speaking ones have large, long tongues and five toes on each foot, but some parrots have only three toes and they speak only a little or not at all.

This Emperor Prester John, when he goes into battle, doesn't have a banner carried before him; instead he has three crosses, made of fine gold, large and long and decorated with precious gems, carried before him. One thousand men-at-arms and a hundred thousand foot-soldiers are tasked with looking after each cross and more than a hundred thousand foot-soldiers guard the standard during battle in other places. He's got innumerable men when he goes into battle against other rulers.

When he rides with his household retinue and not in battle, then he carries before him a wooden cross, unpainted and without gold and gems but totally plain as a sign that Our Lord suffered death on a wooden cross. Also, he has carried in front of him a golden plate full of earth, signifying that his nobility and his power shall become nothing and his flesh will return to the earth. They also carry in front of him another vessel, full of gold and jewels, gems like rubies, diamonds, sapphires, emeralds, topaz, irachite,* chrysolites, and various other gems, signifying his lordship and his power.

23

THE ARRANGEMENT OF THE COURT OF PRESTER JOHN

NOW I shall describe the arrangement of Prester John in his palace, which is in the city of Shush* where he usually resides. And this palace is so magnificent that it's a wonder to describe, because above the main tower are two round gold finials, and each of these has two huge, brilliant gems that shine brightly in the night. And the main gates of the palace are made out of a precious stone called sardonyx,* and the edges of the bars of the gates are made of ivory. And the windows of the halls and chambers are made of crystal and some of the tables at which he eats are made of amethyst, some are of emerald, and others are of gold and precious gems. And the pillars supporting the tables are made of such gems too.

Moreover one of the steps by which the Emperor approaches his throne where he sits to dine is made of mastic wood, another of crystal, another of green jasper, another of amethyst, another of sardonyx, another of cornelian, another of calque. And his footrest is made of chrysolite. The steps are edged with pure gold, beautifully crafted with large pearls and precious gems, and the sides of his throne are embroidered with emeralds, gold, and precious gems.

The pillars in his chamber are made of pure gold with many gems and other precious stones that shine brightly through the night. And though these gems provide plenty of light during the night, nevertheless in his chamber twelve great crystal vessels full of balsam are lit, in order to provide an agreeable sweet fragrance and to take away foul air.

His bed is fashioned out of sapphires neatly fixed with gold, so that he may sleep well and refrain from debauchery, for he does not like to sleep with his wives except at four times each year according to the four seasons, and then that is only to conceive children.*

Furthermore, he has a lovely palace in the city of Nisa where he lives whenever he wishes, but the climate is not as temperate as it is in the city of Shush. And every day he has more than thirty thousand people at his court, not counting visitors and guests; but these thirty thousand people, either there or in the Great Khan's court, consume not nearly as much as would twelve thousand in our country. This emperor Prester John always has seven kings at his court to serve him, and each of these serves for a month in turn. With these kings there are always seventy-two dukes, and thirty earls, and many other nobles and knights; every day twelve archbishops and twenty bishops eat at his court.

The Patriarch of St Thomas is similar to a pope. In this country archbishops and bishops and abbots are all 'kings'. Some are Masters of the Hall, others are chamberlains, some are stewards, some marshalls, and some have other offices, and therefore he is very lavishly attended to.

And to travel across the breadth of his land is a four-month journey, and the length of his land cannot be measured. In this province of Prester John everything is abundant, with so much wealth, and many pearls and precious gems.

Nearby Prester John's island of Pentoxoire there is a long and well-favoured island called Milstorak, and this is under the lordship of Prester John. This island has a great plenty of good things.*

There, not long ago, once lived a rich man, called Catolonabes.* He was very wealthy and had a massive amount of property and a sumptuous, well-fortified castle on a mountain. He had very sturdy walls built around it, and within these walls he had the prettiest garden, where there were as many trees as he could get bearing different kinds of fruit. He had all kinds of sweet-smelling herbs and lovely flowers planted there. There were many fine fountains and also many pleasant halls and chambers decorated with gold and azure; he had contrived there various entertainments and beasts and birds that sang and moved by clockwork machinery as if they were alive. And in his garden he had every kind of bird and animal he could find that are pleasurable and relaxing for people to watch.

And in his garden he also had three virgins not yet fifteen years of age, the most beautiful he could get, and young lads of the same age. And they were dressed in golden clothes, and he said that they were angels. Then he had three pleasant, fine fountains made, all decorated with precious gems, jasper, and crystal, and fretted with gold and pearls and other kinds of gemstones. He then had an underground conduit made so that whenever he wished one fountain ran with wine, another with milk, another with honey. And he called this place Paradise.

Now, when any local young bachelor, some knight or squire, came to see him, Catolonabes took him into his Paradise and showed him all the various things and the different birdsongs and his damsels and his beautiful fountains. And, up in a high tower, he had various minstrels with musical instruments who couldn't be seen from the garden, and had different kinds of music played. Then he said that this was a Paradise that God granted to those that he loved, citing *Dabo uobis terram fluentem lac et mel*, that is to say 'I will give you . . . a land flowing with milk and honey'.*

And then this rich man gave to these visitors a kind of drink that made them drunk.* Then he told them that if they would die for the rich man's sake, once they were dead they should enter into his Paradise and should be the same age as these virgins; they should be able to live forever with them and have their way with them, and they would forever remain virgins, and then he could show them an even fairer Paradise where they should glimpse God in His glory and His majesty.

So they agreed to do everything he wished. And then he asked them to go and murder a nobleman or some enemy in his country, and they weren't afraid because they should enter that Paradise if they were to die. So he had many men from that country killed, slain by those who hoped to reach this Paradise. And through this deceit he avenged himself on his enemies.

Now, when the local nobles and rich men perceived the malicious ruse of this Catolonabes, they gathered together and attacked his castle and killed him and destroyed all his valuable possessions and the elegant site of his Paradise. The location of the fountains can still be seen along with a few other remains, but there is nothing left of value. It was destroyed not so long ago.

A short distance from that place, on the left-hand side near the River Phison,* is something very marvellous. There's a valley, four miles long, between two mountains. Some people call it the Enchanted Vale, some the Valley of Devils, some the Vale Perilous. In this valley are many storms and terrifying noises every day and every night, sometimes like the noise of drums, kettledrums, and horns like at a great party. This valley is full of devils and always has been, and people have said that an entrance to Hell is there.

In this valley there is a great deal of gold and silver, on account of which Christians and others who have travelled there out of covetousness are strangled by devils, and so few return. In the middle of that valley, on a rock, is the physical face and head of a devil, utterly repellent and horrible to see, and only the head is visible down to the shoulders. There is nobody in the world, Christian or otherwise, brave enough not to be terribly afraid should they see it. He looks at everybody so piercingly and so wickedly, and his eyes are so fast-moving, and flickering like fire, and he changes his countenance so often, that nobody dares for all the world to approach. Also, lots of flames of different colours come out of his mouth and nose and sometimes the fire stinks so much that nobody can bear it. However, good Christians who are secure in their faith can go into that valley without harm and, as long as they confess properly and they bless themselves with the sign of the Cross, devils will not injure them.

You should be aware that when my companions and I went into that valley we were really worried about hazarding our bodies to pass through it.* Some of my companions agreed and some did not. In our party there were two Franciscan friars from Lombardy, and they said that if any of us wanted to proceed, then they would too. When they had said this, we agreed that we would go because we trusted in them, and we had them sing a mass and we confessed our sins and took Communion. Fourteen of us went in, and when we came out there were only ten. We didn't know whether our comrades were lost there or whether they had turned back, but we saw no more of them. The other members of our party, who would not enter the valley with us, went around by another route to get there quicker than us, and so they were.

We went through this valley and we saw many wonderful things: gold, silver, precious gems, there seemed to us to be a great plenty of jewels on every side. Whether or not it was exactly as it seemed I'm not sure, because I didn't touch them, because devils are so clever and cunning that they often make things seem to be something that they're not, in order to beguile people. So I wouldn't touch any of it out of fear both of the devils I saw in many different forms and of the dead bodies I saw in that valley. But I dare not say that they were all dead bodies, but they *seemed* to be bodies, and many of them appeared to be wearing the clothing of Christians, and there seemed to be so many of them, as if two powerful kings had fought a battle and their armies had been slain there.

You should know that many times we were thrown down to the ground by the force of the wind, the thunder, and the storms, but God always assisted us and so we made it through that valley without jeopardy or harm, thanks be to God Almighty who looked after us well.

Beyond that valley* there is a large island where the people are as big as giants, twenty-eight or thirty feet tall. They have no clothing, only animal pelts hanging from them, and they eat no bread, only raw meat; and they drink milk. They have no houses and they would prefer to eat human flesh above any other.

People say that beyond that island there is another island where there are giants some of whom are seventy feet tall, others are fifty shaftments tall, but I have never seen them. Amongst these giants there are huge sheep like oxen, and they provide excellent wool. I have often seen these sheep.

Another island in the Great Ocean has many sinful and malevolent women, who have precious gems in their eyes. They have a way of looking at any man in anger and slaying him with their sight, as does the basilisk.*

There's another island with attractive, excellent people where it is customary, on the first night after a couple are wedded, to take a certain appointed man and have him sleep with the wife to take her virginity. They reimburse him very handsomely for this enterprise, and these men are called *gadlibiriens*,* because people in that region believe it is a major, and dangerous, thing to take a woman's virginity. If it happens that the husband discovers the next night that his wife is still a virgin (say, perhaps, the man who was with her was drunk or there was some other reason), the husband shall go to law and say that this man has not performed his duty, and he will be seriously punished. However, after that first night they look after their wives properly, and they never speak again with these men.

I asked them why they did this, and they said that some husbands had slept with their wives before any other man had, and some of these wives had serpents in their bodies that stung their husbands on the penis when inside the women's bodies, and in this way many men were killed. Therefore it was their custom to make other men test the passage before they should endanger themselves.

There's another island where the women are extremely sad when their children are born and they are very happy when their children are dead, and they throw them in a large fire and burn them. Those who truly love their husbands throw them in a fire when they are dead to burn them too, as they say that the fire will cleanse them of all filth and vice so they will be clean in the next world. They say that the reason why they weep and are sorrowful when their children are born and why they celebrate at their death is that they are born into this world of labour and grief and burdens, and when they are dead they go to Paradise, where there are rivers flowing with milk and honey, and there is life, joy, and abundant goods without work or sadness.

On this island they appoint their king through an election, and they don't choose him on account of his wealth or his nobility but rather they choose he who is morally superior and most righteous and just to every man, rich and poor, and the king judges each man according to the crime he has committed. The king cannot condemn a man to death without the advice from, and the assent of, the barons. If it happens that the king commits some major sin, such as murdering a man or suchlike, he will be killed but he won't be slain: they shall forbid that any man be allowed to come and keep him company, to talk to him, or give him food and drink, and thus he shall die. They spare nobody who has committed a crime, not for love or power, nor wealth or nobility, so that people face justice according to whatever they have done.

There is another island in that sea where there are many people, and they no longer eat the meat of hares, poultry, or geese, even though there are many of them around. They happily eat the meat of other animals and they drink milk.

The people of this region marry their sons and daughters and others of their kin to each other, as they please. If ten or twelve men live in a house there, each of their wives will be shared amongst them, and one night one man will have one of the wives and another night he'll have another one. Should any of these wives have children, she can give it to whichever of these men she likes, so nobody knows whose child is whose. If someone says that this means the men end up fathering other men's children, they respond that other men do the same with theirs.

In this region* and in sundry other places around India are many crocodiles, which are a sort of long serpent. They live in the water at night and they live on land and on the rocks during the day, and they don't eat during the winter. This serpentine beast kills men and eats them whole, and it has no tongue.

In this region and in many others there are trees bearing cotton, the seeds of which people sow annually and then little trees grow, bearing cotton.

In Arabia there are enormous beasts called *girsant*.* It's a pretty animal, higher than a large horse, and its neck is nearly twenty shaftments long. Its tail and rump are like those of a hart and it can see over a high house.

There are also many chameleons, a little animal which never eats or drinks. It often changes its colour—sometimes it has one colour, sometimes another—and it can change into all colours except red and white.

There are also many wild pigs, of different colours and the size of oxen, and they are spotted all over like little fawns. There are lions that are entirely white. There are other beasts the size of horses called *lonhorans* and some people call them *tontes*, and its head is black and it has three long horns in its forelock as sharp as a sword, and it chases and kills the elephants. There are many other kinds of animals, which it would be prolix to describe.

Then there's another fine, large and fertile island, with good, honest men who follow a fine faith and lifestyle. Even though they are not Christian, by natural law they are full of excellent qualities. They eschew all sinfulness, all vice, and all malice, as they are not jealous, proud, or covetous, and they are not lecherous or gluttonous, and they only do unto other men as they would have done unto them. They comply with the Ten Commandments, and they place no value in wealth or possessions, and they do not swear oaths—they only say 'yes' and 'no', as they say that one who swears betrays his neighbour. Some people call this island the Island of Brahmins and some call it The Land of Faith.* A great river runs through it which people call Thebe. Generally all people in that island and others nearby are more faithful and righteous than in other countries.

On this island there are neither thieves nor murderers, neither prostitutes nor beggars. Because they are such pious and good people there are no storms, no thunder, no war, no hunger, no other kind of tribulation, and so it seems that God indeed loves them and very much approves of their way of life and their faith. They truly believe in God who created all things and they worship Him. They eat and drink in such a sensible manner that they live for a very long time, and many of them die without sickness, it's just that nature fails them in old age.

Once upon a time King Alexander sent his men there, to conquer that region. So the people sent a letter to him saying, 'What is sufficient power for a man for whom the world is not enough? You'll find nothing here for which it is worth waging war against us, because we've got no wealth, and all the goods and chattels in our land are owned communally. The food we eat is our wealth; in place of wealth in gold and silver we make riches out of peace and love and harmony. We have nothing but rags on our bodies. Our wives are not finely dressed-up to please men, as we believe it is very silly for a person to decorate their body to make it seem prettier than God made it. We've always enjoyed peace until now, of which you will deprive us. We have our king not to judge anybody, as there are no sinners amongst us, but to teach us to be obedient to him. So the only thing you can take from us is our good peace.'

When King Alexander read this letter he thought it would be harmful to disturb them. He replied to them that they should diligently observe their virtuous customs and not be afraid of him, for he would not molest them.

There's another island nearby called Synophe,* where there are also good, pious, and religious people. They are very similar to the people just described, but they go about stark naked. King Alexander went to this island. When he observed their good piety and faith he said that he would do them no harm and requested them to ask of him any wealth or anything else they wished to have. They answered that they had sufficient wealth when they had enough food and drink to sustain their bodies. They said that worldly possessions have no worth, and they would only worship him if he could grant them eternal life. Alexander said that he wasn't able to do this, for he was mortal and would die just as would they. So they said, 'Why then are you so haughty, why do you want to conquer the whole world and make it subject to you as if you are a god? You do not have unlimited life and you want all the riches in the world, which will forsake you or you will forsake it. It shall all vanish and you will take nothing with you, and just as you were born naked so shall you be buried in the earth.' Alexander was utterly astonished by this answer.

Even though these people don't have the articles of our faith, I do nevertheless believe that God indeed loves them because of their good intentions and He regards their service as of the same order as that of Job, a pagan whom God accepted, along with many others, as His faithful servant. I believe that God truly loves all those who meekly and piously love Him and despise worldly vanities as do these men, and as Job did. Therefore Our Lord says through the mouth of His prophet Isaiah: *Ponam eis multiplices leges meas*, that is, 'I shall write to him my manifold laws'.* Moreover, the gospels say, *Alias oues habeo quae non sunt ex hoc ouili*, that is, 'And other sheep I have, that are not of this fold'.* A vision St Peter had at Jaffa accords with this, of the angel coming from Heaven bringing with him all kinds of beasts and snakes and birds, and he said to St Peter, 'Take and eat!' St Peter answered, 'I shall never eat unclean animals'. So the angel then said to him, *Non dicas immunda quae deus mundauit*, that is, 'That which God hath cleansed, do not thou call common.'* This was done in order to signify that people should not look down upon other people because of their different laws, because we don't know whom God loves or hates.

Then there's another island where the people are feathered all over except on their faces and the palms of their hands. These people can move across water just as well as across land, and they eat raw meat and fish. On this island there's a massive river, two and a half miles wide, which people call the Renemare. People say that there's a great desert beyond that river, and those who have been there say that in this desert are the Tree of the Sun and the Tree of the Moon which spoke to King Alexander and described his death to him.* People say that those who tend these trees and eat the fruit from them live for four hundred or five hundred years, because of the fruit's properties.

We would really have liked to travel there but I believe a hundred thousand soldiers couldn't get through that desert, because there's a large number of wild animals, such as dragons and snakes, which kill people when they get the chance to. There are innumerable blue-and-white elephants in this region, and unicorns, and many kinds of lion.

Then there's another island called Pytan. The local people don't cultivate the land, so they don't eat. The people are little (but not as small as Pygmies). They live on the scent of wild apples and when they go abroad they carry apples with them, and they die as soon as they are deprived of the scent of these apples. They're not really rational, but more like animals.

There are many other islands in the land of Prester John, and great wealth and precious gems, which would be too laborious to describe.

24

WHY HE IS CALLED PRESTER JOHN

I'M sure you've heard why this Emperor is called Prester John, but for those who don't know I shall tell you why. There was once an Indian Emperor who was a noble and valiant prince, and he had as many Christian knights in his retinue as has the current Emperor. This Emperor decided that he'd like to observe the rites of Christian churches, and so visited Christendom, in Turkey, Syria, Tartary, Jerusalem, Palestine, Arabia, Aleppo, and the entire land of Egypt. One Saturday, the Saturday after Pentecost, when the bishop was ordaining priests, this Emperor entered an Egyptian church with a Christian knight. He watched the service and he asked the knight what kind of people were standing in front of the bishop. The knight answered that they were going to be priests. Then the Emperor said that he no longer wanted to be called king or emperor but priest, and he would take the name of the first priest who came out of the church. The first priest to come out was called John, and so that Emperor and those following him since have been called Prester John:* that is, John Priest.

There are many faithful and pious Christians in Prester John's land, and they have priests who sing masses. They perform the sacrament in the same way as do Greeks, but they don't say as much as our priests, because when they sing the mass and say the *Paternoster* they say nothing except what the apostles said, like St Peter and St Thomas and other apostles, from whose words the sacrament is made. We have many new additions which popes have since ratified, additions of which the people of these regions know absolutely nothing.

In the east of Prester John's country is a fine island called Tabrobane,* which is very fertile. It has a strong, wealthy king, who holds this land directly from Prester John, and this king is always chosen by election. On this island they have two winters and two summers, so they reap corn twice a year and their gardens are in bloom all year round. Good, sensible people live there, amongst them many rich Christians. The water between this island and the land of Prester John isn't very deep, in fact one can see the seabed in many places.

Further to the east are two other islands, of which one is called Orelle and the other is called Argete;* throughout these lands gold and silver is mined. From these islands one can see no stars except a star called Canopus.* One cannot see the moon from here except in its last quarter.

On the island of Orelle is a huge golden hill maintained by ants, which sort the pure gold from the impure. These ants are as big as dogs, so nobody goes near this mountain out of fear of being attacked by these ants, and so nobody can obtain that gold except by cunning. Therefore, when the weather is hot these ants secrete themselves in the earth from mid-morning until noon; then local people take camels, dromedaries, and other animals and they go there and load up with gold and hurry off before the ants emerge from the earth, because the people are scared they'll be killed by them.

At other times of the year, when the weather isn't so hot that the ants hide away, people take mares with young foals; they put two empty vessels like barrels with the mouth open upwards upon these mares, and they take them to the mountain and keep the foals at home. When the ants see these vessels, because it's in their nature not to be able to bear to see anything empty, they fill these vessels with gold. When the people believe the vessels to be full, they fetch the foals and bring them as close as they dare. The foals neigh and the mares hear them and quickly run to their foals, and so the people get the gold; this is because the ants will tolerate animals amongst them but not humans.

Far to the east, beyond these islands and the land of Prester John (and the deserts over which he rules), one will find only mountains and great rocks and dark lands where one cannot discern day or night, according to local people. This desert and land of darkness lasts all the way to the Earthly Paradise, where Adam and Eve were placed; they were only there a little while. It is to the east, at the very beginning of the world. However, it's not our east, the one where the sun rises for us, because when the sun rises in this region it's actually midnight in our country, on account of the roundness of the earth.

Indeed, Our Lord made the earth entirely spherical in the middle of the firmament, as I've previously explained.

I can't really describe Paradise properly* because I haven't been there, and that grieves me. However, I'll describe what I've heard from wise men. People say that the Earthly Paradise is the highest region in the whole world, and it is so high that it nearly touches the sphere of the moon,* so high that Noah's flood, which covered all the surrounding land, couldn't touch it. Paradise is entirely enclosed by a wall. People don't know what this wall is made from. The whole wall is overgrown with something like moss, so people can't see the stone or whatever else it is made from.

The highest place in Paradise, in the very middle, is a spring discharging four rivers that run through different lands. The first river is called the Phison or Ganges, and that runs through India. There are many precious gems in that river, plenty of wood from the tree called *lignum aloes*, and much gold sand. Another river is called the Nile or Gehon, and that runs through Ethiopia and Egypt. The third river is called the Tigris, and that runs through Asia and Greater Armenia. The fourth river is called the Euphrates, and that runs through Media, Armenia, and Persia. Local people say that all the sweet, fresh waters of the world flow from this spring.

The first river is called Phison, which means 'gathering',* for many rivers are gathered together flowing into that river. Some call it the Ganges, because there was an Indian king called Gangeras, since it flowed through his land. The river is still in some places, turbulent in others, hot in some places, cold in others.

The second river is called the Nile or Gyon, and it is always turbulent, indeed Gyon means 'turbulent'.* The third river is called the Tigris, which means 'quick-running' (because it's always quick-running) and there is an animal called a tiger* that runs quickly after people. The fourth is called Euphrates, which means 'growing well',* as there are many good things growing along that river.

You should be aware that no mortal human can go to this Paradise; this is because, travelling by land, of the wild animals in the desert and the mountains and rocks which nobody can cross. Travelling by rivers, nobody can get through because of the great currents and huge waves that no ship can navigate or sail against. Many fine gentlemen have tried many times to travel by these rivers to Paradise but they cannot accomplish the journey, as some died of exhaustion from rowing, some became blind, some became deaf because of the din of the water, so nobody can get there unless by the special grace of God.

Because I can't tell you any more about that place, I shall describe what I have seen in the islands and country of Prester John, which are under the earth relative to us. Should somebody wish to go around the world, there are other islands around here. Whoever can proceed on this route through the grace of God might arrive back at the same country they came from, and so circumnavigate the earth as I have described beforehand. Because it's a long journey and a dangerous one, few people try to go that way, even though it still actually could be done.

Therefore people shun these islands for other shores under Prester John's rule, and they reach an island called Cassan. This territory is nearly sixty days' travel in length and more than ten days' travel wide, and it's the best land in the region apart from Cathay. If merchants were to visit as often as they do Cathay, it would be finer than Cathay, as it's so densely populated with towns and cities that when one leaves a city one immediately sees another in every direction. They have plenty of spices and other goods, and there are enormous trees like chestnut trees. The king of this island is very rich and powerful and he holds his land from the Great Khan of Cathay, as this is one of the twelve provinces that the Great Khan holds in subjection (not counting his own land).

From this island people should go to another great kingdom that is called Tibet, which is also under the Great Khan's control. This is a fine and fecund region, replete with wine, corn, and everything else. People from this land don't have houses, but they live in tents made of timber. The main city of that land is exceedingly black, constructed in black-and-white bricks, and all the streets are paved with this kind of brick. In that city nobody is so bold as to spill the blood of either man or beast on account of the love of an idol that they worship there. Their religion's pope, whom they call *Lobassy*, lives in this city, and he distributes all the honours and profits that pertain to the idol. Religious clerics and churchmen in that region are entirely obedient to him as we are to the Pope.

On this island, throughout the region, there is the following custom: when a person's father dies and they want to honour him respectfully, they send for all his friends, priests, monks, and many others. They carry the body to a mountain with much joy and merrymaking.

When they get there, the most senior priest cuts off the body's head and lays it on a great gold or silver platter, and he gives it to the son. The son takes it to his other friends whilst singing and saying many holy chants. Then the priest and the religious hack the flesh off the body in pieces and say chants. Local birds, such as eagles and other carrion birds, come there because they know the custom and they fly all about. The priests then throw the corpse's flesh to the birds, which carry it off a little way and eat it. Just as our priests in our country sing *Subuenite sancti dei* for souls, that is, 'Come to aid, saints of God',* so priests sing aloud there in their language, 'Look how good this man was, that the angels of God come to fetch him and carry him off to Paradise'. Thus the son thinks he is very blessed when the birds have eaten his father in this way. So then the son goes home with all his friends and they have a splendid feast. The son has his father's head cleaned, and he trims the flesh from the skull and gives it to his most treasured friends, a titbit and a memento of the holy man eaten by birds for each person. The son has a cup made from the skull and he drinks from it for the rest of his life, in memory of his father.

From here one travels for ten days through the land of the Great Khan to another fine island and a large kingdom. The king here is extremely powerful, and he receives as income three hundred horses loaded with rice and other payments each year. He lives a very fine, luxurious life according to the customs over there, as he has fifty damsels who serve each day at his meal, at his bed, and do whatsoever he wishes. When he sits down at the dining-table they bring him his food, and every time five of them chant together and sing the food in with a superb tune. They carve his meat for him and place it in his mouth, because he won't carve but rather holds his hands in front of himself on the table, for he has such long fingernails that he can't hold anything.

In that region it is thought to be most excellent to have long finger-nails, and so they let their nails grow as long as they like. Some people let theirs grow so long until they curl all around their hand, and they think it's really elegant and extremely fashionable. The custom for women is to have tiny feet, and so as soon as they are born they have their feet bound so tightly that they don't grow as large as they should.

This king has a very lovely, luxurious palace, around which is a wall two miles long. Inside there are lots of pretty gardens, and the hall and chambers are paved with gold and silver. In the middle of one of the gardens is a little hillock upon which is a little palace with golden towers and pinnacles. He often sits here, taking the air and relaxing, for it's made for no other purpose.

From this region one can travel through the Great Khan's land. You should be aware that all these people and nations I have described have reason, in as much as they have some of the articles of our faith. Even though they have different laws and various beliefs, they do have some of the good points of our faith. They believe in a natural god who made the whole world, and they call him God of Nature as their prophecies say, *Et metuent eum omnes fines terre*, that is, 'and all the ends of the earth fear him';* and, elsewhere, *Omnes gentes seruient ei*, that is, 'all nations shall serve him'.*

However, they cannot speak of God correctly, only as their natural intelligence teaches them; they speak of neither the Son nor the Holy Ghost as they should do. They can speak well enough about the Bible and especially about Genesis and the book of Moses.* They say that the things they worship aren't gods but rather they worship them because of the immense good powers residing in them, which may not be without the grace of God.

They say that their effigies and idols are like the effigies and idols all people have, as they point out that Christians have images of Our Lady and others. But they are not aware that we don't worship these stone or wooden images in themselves but rather for the saints in whose name they are made. For as the text teaches clerks how they shall believe, so images and paintings instruct unlettered people how to worship the saints in whose name they are made.

They also say that God's angel speaks to them through their idols and that they perform miracles. They speak the truth, for there is an angel within. But there are two kinds of angel, good and evil, like the Greeks call them Chaco and Calo.* Chaco is evil and Calo is good. It is not the good angel but the evil one who is in the idols, to delude them and to support them in their idolatry.

There are many countries and marvels I have not seen, therefore I can't describe them correctly. Moreover, in countries which I have visited there are marvels that I haven't described, as it would take too long, and so consider yourself sated now with what I have said. Also, I wish to say no more about such marvels as are there, so other people might travel there and find new things to describe, things I haven't mentioned or described, because many people very much like and desire to hear new things.

So I, John Mandeville, knight, who left my country and traversed the sea in the year of Our Lord 1332 and have passed through many lands, regions, countries, and islands, have now come to rest;* I have compiled this book and had it written in the year of Our Lord 1366, that is thirty-four years after my departure from my country, for I was travelling for thirty-four years.*

Because many people only believe that which they've seen with their own eyes and that which they can conceive of with their own human reason, I travelled homewards on a route via Rome. This was in order to show my book to the Holy Father the Pope,* and describe to him the marvels I had seen in different countries, so with his wise council he might examine it with different people in Rome, because there are always people living there from all kinds of nations around the world. A little later, when he and his wise council had thoroughly examined my book, he told me that, for certain, everything therein was true. Indeed, he said that he owned a Latin book containing all this and much more, according to which the book *Mappa mundi** is made, a copy of which book he showed to me. Therefore the Holy Father the Pope has ratified and confirmed my book in all topics.

I beseech all those who read this book, or hear it being read, that they pray for me, and I shall pray for them. All those who say a *Paternoster* and an *aue* for me, requesting that God forgive my sins, I will make them partners and grant them a part of all my good pilgrimages and all the other good deeds I have done or will do until the end of my life. I pray to God, from whom all grace flows, that He will fill all this book's readers and listeners with His grace and save them in their bodies and souls, and bring them to His everlasting joy, He that is in the Trinity: Father, Son, and Holy Ghost, God who lives and reigns without end. Amen.

HERE ENDS JOHN MANDEVILLE

EXPLANATORY NOTES

ABBREVIATIONS

CCKJ	Denys Pringle, *Crusader Churches of the Latin Kingdom of Jerusalem*, 4 vols. (Cambridge, 1993–2009)
Etymologies	*The Etymologies of Isidore of Seville*, ed. and trans. Stephen A. Barney, W. J. Lewis, J. A. Beach, and Oliver Berghof (Cambridge, 2006)
GL	Jacobus de Voragine, *The Golden Legend: Readings on the Saints*, ed. and trans. William Granger Ryan, 2 vols. (Princeton, 1993)
IE	Fredric C. Tubach, *Index Exemplorum: A Handbook of Medieval Religious Tales* (Helsinki, 1969)
Livre	Jean de Mandeville, *Le Livre des Merveilles du Monde*, ed. Christiane Deluz, Sources d'Histoire Médiévale, 31 (Paris, 2000)
ODNB	*Oxford Dictionary of National Biography* (via http://www.odnb.com)
OED	*Oxford English Dictionary* (via http://www.oed.com/)
Otia	Gervase of Tilbury, *Otia Imperialia*, ed. S. E. Banks and J. W. Binns (Oxford, 2002)
Properties	*On the Properties of Things: John Trevisa's Translation of Bartholomaeus Anglicus De Propretatibus Rerum*, ed. M. C. Seymour *et al.*, 3 vols. (Oxford, 1975)
Qur'an	The Qur'an, trans. M. A. S. Abdel Haleem (Oxford, 2004)
SBCKJ	Denys Pringle, *The Secular Buildings of the Crusader Kingdom of Jerusalem: An Archaeological Gazetteer* (Cambridge, 1997)

5 *Because the land . . . Jesus Christ*: the opening clauses may seem to be missing some crucial parts of speech but were accepted and repeated by medieval readers. I have read them as one very long preamble, akin to a preacher's exordium or a call-to-arms, put into separate paragraphs here to make reading easier. 'Therefore' in the sixth paragraph leads to the end of this sentence. For different views of the opening sentence see *Livre*, 94 n. 1; Josephine Waters Bennett, *The Rediscovery of Sir John Mandeville* (New York, 1954), 69–70; Iain Macleod Higgins, *Writing East: The Travels of Sir John Mandeville* (Philadelphia, 1997), 31–2.

'I am the King of the Jews': John 19: 21.

'The virtue of things is in their middle': a declaration of the 'Middle Way' or 'golden mean', a twelfth- and thirteenth-century commonplace of the preference for the middle over two extremes, here citing Aristotle, *Nicomachean Ethics*, ed. and trans. H. Rackham (London, 1926), 2. 6. 9

(pp. 92–3): 'virtue aims of hitting the mean', being 'a point equally distant from either extreme'.

5 *if one wants something . . . what is happening*: reflecting the Norman *Clameur de Haro* and English hue and cry, i.e. the use of a public cry to apprehend a criminal.

Jerusalem: a holy city in Christianity, Islam, and Judaism. The centrality of the city to Mandeville's world-view structures much of his *Book*. During the time Mandeville was writing, in the early fourteenth century, Jerusalem was controlled by the Mamluk dynasty, having fallen to Saladin in 1187. Whilst the Crusaders' Christian buildings were often converted to Islamic use or became derelict, there was a Christian community in Jerusalem throughout the Middle Ages and it was very frequently visited by Christian pilgrims. The *idea* of Jerusalem, and its recapture by Christendom, remained absolutely central to Christian self-identity in the Latin West. See Sylvia Schein, *Fideles Crucis: The Papacy, the West and the Recovery of the Holy Land, 1274–1314* (Oxford, 1991).

6 *He chose to die . . . His children*: throughout this passage the diction becomes notably legalistic, giving a sense of the transfer of property through hereditary rights.

1332: the English manuscripts mostly give the date of 1332, whereas the French texts tend to give 1322 (although some manuscripts give 1332); other manuscripts give 1312 and 1422! Almost all versions give the day of the start of the journey as Michaelmas (29 September), the Feast of St Michael, which celebrates the banishment of Satan from Heaven, the beginning of the shortening of the days, and was, in the Middle Ages, a Holy Day of Obligation. See *Livre*, 92; Bennett, *Rediscovery*, 149–53.

7 *numerous noble companions*: the Anglo-French prologue includes a paragraph here on the book's textual history and Latin origins. This states that the book was not written in Latin but in *romancz* (i.e. the vernacular) so that everybody may understand it. It goes on to give a conventional statement of the author's modesty and fallibility, that if there are mistakes in the author's memory it is because 'things long since passed out of view become forgotten and human memory can neither retain nor grasp everything' (*Livre*, 93).

Pannonia: a Roman province covering what is now western Hungary.

Silesia: a Central European province, covering what is now south-western Poland; in the Middle Ages it moved between Germanic and Slavic/Polish spheres of influence, and in the fourteenth century was part of the Bohemian empire.

Cumania: a Central European province, in present-day eastern Hungary and Ukraine; the kingdom of Cumania fell to the Mongols in the thirteenth century, but remained a diocese until the 1520s. See Nora Berend, *At the Gate of Christendom: Jews, Muslims and 'Pagans' in Medieval Hungary, c. 1000–c. 1300* (Cambridge, 2001), 87–93, on the Cumans.

Buggers: the Middle English text describes 'Bulgarie' as 'the lond of Bugers'; by 1340 to be called a 'buger' or 'bougre' (*OED*) connoted both unclean fornication (hence 'buggery') and heresy (from the eleventh-century Bulgarian heresies). The extent of the difference in meaning between 'Bulgar' and 'bugger' is unclear in Middle English.

Nevelond: referring to Livonia (present-day Latvia and Estonia), a partly Christian kingdom conquered by German and Danish Crusaders in the thirteenth century and established as a province of the Holy Roman Empire. The name may refer to the River Neva. See further Marek Tamm, 'The Eastern Baltic Region', in Alan V. Murray (ed.), *The Clash of Cultures on the Medieval Baltic Frontier* (Farnham, 2009), 11–35 (at 13–20).

Sopron: an important town at the western frontier of Hungary.

Neiseburgh: the fortress at Neiseburgh (Újvidék), refounded in the seventeenth century as Novi Sad (Serbia).

island-town: one of the many cases where Mandeville's place-names become so garbled in translation that they no longer refer to an identifiable place. In the Anglo-French sources the town is named *Maleville* (*Livre*, 96), designating Zemun (Serbia).

8 *Maritsa*: the long Balkan river, flowing from western Bulgaria to the Aegean Sea. Mandeville calls it 'Marrok', a version of its Turkish name, Meriç.

Pechenegs: the Pechenegs, or Patzinaks, were a Turkic nation who migrated into Byzantine lands in the ninth century. They were conquered by Byzantium in 1091 and 1122 and absorbed into Balkan and Hungarian (Magyar) communities.

Sternes and Philippopolis: Mandeville is referring to the two largest Bulgarian cities, now Sofia and Plovdiv; 'Sternes' is from 'Esternit', a Latinized version of Sofia's medieval Slavonic name Sredets; 'Affympayne' is a rendering of Philippopolis, now Plovdiv.

Adrianople: now Edirne (Turkey).

St Sophie: the Haggia Sophia in Constantinople (the Orthodox basilica, dedicated in 360) was dedicated to Wisdom (Greek Σοφία, Latin *sophia*); there are, however, two martyrs, named St Sophia (d. 137) and St Sophie of Rome (d. *c*.300) whose cults were sometimes confused with the Constantinople church.

Emperor Justinian . . . on horseback: Justinian I, Emperor of Byzantium (527–65). Descriptions of this equestrian statue, demolished in the sixteenth century, are common in medieval travel literature; see J. P. A. van der Vin, 'The Statue of Justinian I on Horseback', in *Travellers to Greece and Constantinople: Ancient Monuments and Old Traditions in Medieval Travellers' Tales*, 2 vols. (Istanbul, 1980), I. 271–8. The apple is described elsewhere as a globe or an orb, and indeed in Middle English 'apple' can mean orb.

He used to hold . . . effigy's hand: in both the Anglo-French and Middle

English versions the narrator moves between describing the statue as a thing ('image') and a person ('he').

8 *on the Cross*: Matthew 27: 48; Mark 15: 36; John 19: 29.

The Hill of the Holy Cross: the monastery at Stavrovouni (Cyprus) had a relic of the Holy Cross and claimed to have been established by St Helena.

Dysmas: St Dysmas, the Good Thief (Luke 23); the name and the details of Dysmas' life stem from the *Gospel of Nicodemus*, the early medieval apocryphal Passion narrative that became hugely popular in medieval Europe.

In cruce . . . cypressus, oliua: 'In this cross are palm, cedar, cypress, olive', quoting *GL* 1. 278. *The Golden Legend*, compiled *c.*1260, was the template for much medieval religious imagery and iconography.

9 *as the story of Noah . . . God and man*: Genesis 8: 12.

tree of mercy: the tree of life is described in Genesis, but the story about the angel and the oil of mercy comes from the apocryphal *Life of Adam and Eve*, composed in the third to fifth centuries. Mandeville could have read the story in the *Golden Legend*; see *GL* 1. 276.

10 *St Helena*: St Helena of Constantinople (d. 330), finder of the True Cross and mother of the Emperor Constantine; *GL* 1. 277–81.

King's chapel: the Sainte-Chappelle in Paris, consecrated in 1248, was built for Louis IX (1214–70) to house these relics although a separate *capella regis* (king's chapel) at Paris continued to function. Mandeville could be referring to either chapel. See Robert Branner, 'The Sainte-Chappelle and the Capella Regis in the Thirteenth Century', *Gesta*, 10 (1971), 19–22.

Jews: the manuscript records 'Iewis' ('Jews'), but all but one manuscript of the Anglo-French source states that the relics were obtained from the Genoese (*Livre*, 103). Louis IX of France (r. 1226–70) purchased these relics from his cousin, Baldwin II of Constantinople; the relics were actually transported via Venice and obtained through Venetian brokers. See H. A. Klein, 'Eastern Objects and Western Desires: Relics and Reliquaries between Byzantium and the West', *Dumbarton Oaks Papers*, 58 (2004), 283–314, at 307.

hawthorn: the white hawthorn (*crataegus*) was used in medieval medicine as a diuretic, for the heart, to relieve cramps, and improve circulation.

St Peter . . . forsook Our Lord: Matthew 26: 36–44.

Annas: high-priest of Judea and a judge at the trial of Jesus (John 18: 13–24).

barberry: the common barberry (*Barbarea vulgaris*). In the Middle Ages it was used medicinally for the liver.

Caiaphas: the counterpart of Annas, high-priest and judge at the trial of Jesus (Matthew 26: 3; John 18: 24–8).

briar: the eglantine (sweetbriar, *Rosa rubiginosa*), its name deriving from the Old French *aiglent*, prickly; Mandeville therefore, and unusually, suggests four crowns of thorn, one of sea-rushes, one of hawthorn, one of barberry, and one of briar.

11 *'Hail, King of the Jews'*: Matthew 27: 29.

The Emperor in Constantinople . . . the one in Paris: the Spear of Destiny or Holy Lance, with which Longinus pierced Christ's side (John 19: 34). The point of the lance was conveyed to Louis IX by two Franciscans in 1242; see Klein, 'Eastern Objects and Western Desires', 307. The lance owned by the 'Emperor of Germany'—the Holy Roman Emperor—likely refers to the Hofburg spear, now in the Vienna Schatzkammer (the Imperial Treasury of the Habsburgs). Various spears were venerated in Christendom as the Spear of Destiny. See H. L. Adelson, 'The Holy Lance and Hereditary German Monarchy', *Art Bulletin*, 48 (1966), 177–92.

St John Chrysostom: John Chrysostom (d. 407), Archbishop of Constantinople and Church Father.

Bethany: Bethany, near Jerusalem, is described later (p. 49) but is here elided with Bithynia (Asia Minor, present-day northern central Turkey), which was given as the location of Luke's death in early Greek writings.

idriouns: from the Latin *idria*, simply referring to a water vessel. Mandeville's description suggests knowledge of Constantinople's cisterns and possibly the Great Basilica Cistern (Yerebatan Sarayı), a subterranean 'palace' of dripping columns. See Van der Vin, *Travellers to Greece*, 1. 288, on medieval travellers' accounts of Constantinople's water-supply.

Chalcis . . . Lemnos: Deluz (*Livre*, 113) notes how this list of islands is confused, based on an equally unclear account given in Brunetto Latini's *Livres dou Trésor* (*c.*1260). The *Livres dou Trésor* is an early encyclopedia, consulted by Mandeville for many details. Mount Athos is not on Lemnos.

Turcopoles: mercenary Turkish archers in Byzantine armies. The name, according to the *OED*, indicates children born to a Turkish father and a Greek mother (*Turco*, Turk + *pullus*, foal).

Aristotle: Aristotle (384–322 BCE), Greek philosopher. On his medieval 'rediscovery' and reputation see Steven P. Marrone, 'Medieval Philosophy in Context', in A. S. McGrade (ed.), *The Cambridge Companion to Medieval* Philosophy (Cambridge, 2003), 10–50, at 32–6.

12 *court*: the Anglo-French *place* (square or courtyard) is rendered into the less likely 'paleys' (palace) in Middle English.

One Emperor wanted . . . Our Lord was born: a version of this story appears in the *Golden Legend* and its account of St Pelagius. See *GL* 2. 181.

Hermes Trismegistus: 'Hermes the thrice-great', held in the Middle Ages to be a great pagan prophet of Christianity and the author of various 'Hermetic' texts, including alchemical, magical, and syncretic wisdom literature. See Brian Copenhaver, *Hermetica: The Greek Corpus Hermeticum and the Latin Asclepius*, in a new English translation, with notes and introduction (Cambridge, 1995).

12 *Pope John XXII*: 1249–1334, pope 1316–34.

13 *'We confidently believe . . . Goodbye'*: while there is no evidence of this document, it is noteworthy that, in the Latin, Mandeville's Greeks address the Pope with the intimate, disrespectful *tu*.

from this side of the Mediterranean: Latin, or western, Christians.

14 *Chios*: under Genoese administration from 1346 and then known as Scio.

15 *Genoese*: under the Treaty of Nymphaeum (1261) several islands, including Samos and Chios, came under Genoese administration.

Kos and Lango . . . Hippocrates: these were not separate islands; Lango was the Venetian and Genoese name for the island of Kos. The Venetians ruled the island from 1204 to 1304, the Genoese from 1304 to 1523. Hippocrates of Kos (*c.*460–370 BCE) was the ancient physician, founder of medical knowledge in the West, but also the subject of various legends, like the one which follows.

lady-of-the-manor: the Anglo-French word is 'Dame', the Middle English 'Lady', so the sense is of her being a local aristocrat. The story is a version of what would become the legend of Melusine; see Christiane Deluz, *Le Livre de Jehan de Mandeville: une géographie au XIV*[e] *siècle* (Leuven, 1998), 215–20.

a hospitaller from Rhodes: the Knights Hospitaller evolved in pre-Crusader Jerusalem, providing care for pilgrims at their Hospital, the Muristan near the church of the Holy Sepulchre (see p. 43). During the Crusades they became a knightly, martial order and, following the collapse of the Crusader presence in the Holy Land, operated from Rhodes and later Malta. See Helen Nicholson, *The Knights Hospitaller* (Woodbridge, 2009).

16 *the Emperor*: by 'the Emperor' Mandeville means the Byzantine Emperor.

Ad Collosenses: Paul's epistle to the Colossians was written for the people of Colosae in Asia Minor; the mix-up comes from a memory of the famous statue, the Colossus of Rhodes. The Turkish name for Rhodes is the same as its Greek name, *Rodos*.

Satalia: a corruption of the ancient Greek name Attaleia (Αττάλεια), now Antalya (Turkey). Far from being ruined, it was a major city of both the Byzantine and Seljuk periods.

All this territory . . . dangerous: this necrophilia narrative is a condensed version of a story from the *Otia Imperialia* of Gervase of Tilbury (*c.*1150–*c.*1228), also set at Satalia (*Otia*, 330–31; for similar stories, see *IE* 2481, 2482, 2478, 2475). At this point in his *Book* Mandeville moves between 'exemplary' narratives like this and 'practical' information for the Jerusalem-bound traveller.

Saracens: used in the *Book* to describe both Arabs and Muslims.

17 *St Sozomenos*: Sozomenos or Sozomen (fl. *c.*400), early historian of the Christian Church, he was not a Latin saint although his *Historia ecclesiastica* was known in the West as part of the widely read *Historia tripartita* (the histories of Theodoret, Sozomen, and Socrates, translated by Cassiodorus).

Dieu d'Amour . . . St Hilarion: Dieu d'Amour is the Frankish name for the castle at Kyrenia (Cyprus); Hilarion was a Palestinian hermit (291–371) who died in Cyprus.

St Bernard: St Barnabas the Apostle (d. 61). His story is given in Acts 14; he is traditionally named as the founder of the Cypriot Church.

papiouns: the Middle English word 'papioun' cannot be identified with a specific animal, but Mandeville suggests a carnivorous, cat-like, beast. Medieval animal lore classed all big cats, foxes, and wolves together as 'beasts', 'animals which vent their rage with tooth or claw' (see http://www.abdn.ac.uk/bestiary/translat/7r.hti). On the medieval use of cheetahs and other large felines in hunting see Marco Masseti, 'Pictorial Evidence from Medieval Italy of Cheetahs and Caracals, and their Use in Hunting', *Archives of Natural History*, 36 (2009), 37–47.

Tyre . . . Sur: Tyre (Lebanon) was one of the major cities of the Crusader settlement. Sur is the city's Arabic name.

'The fountain of gardens and the well of living waters': Canticles [Song of Songs] 4: 15.

'Blessed is the womb . . . the paps that gave thee suck': Luke 11: 27.

Our Lord forgave . . . her sins there: Matthew 15: 21–8.

church of St Saviour: *CCKJ* 4. 220–7. The church was built by the Englishman and first Archbishop of Tyre, William of Malines (d. *c.*1146).

Elijah . . . Jonah: a confused version of the story of Elias healing the unnamed widow's son (3 Kings [1 Kings] 17: 13–24). This is one of several places where scribes of Mandeville's *Book* demonstrate a casual infidelity to biblical detail, here amalgamating the widow's son with the prophet Jonah.

18 *Dido . . . Tyre*: this passage reflects the story, as given in Virgil's *Aeneid* (1. 338 ff.), that Carthage was founded by colonists from Tyre under the leadership of Dido; some manuscripts give the current name as 'Dydonsayto', to suggest 'Dido's town'. Agenor is a misreading of Achilles, as given in the Anglo-French text. Either way, Dido's father is named Belus in Virgil's *Aeneid*, but Carthage is 'the town of Agenor' (1. 339). It is unusual for Mandeville to refer to secular literature.

Japheth: Genesis 5: 32, 9: 18; this etymology, here taken from Boldensele, is given frequently in medieval Christian sources.

Carmelite Order of friars: the Carmelite rule was first given papal approval in 1226; the order's first foundation, on Mount Carmel at Haifa, probably dated to the 1190s.

18 *Caiaphas*: the Jewish high-priest implicated in the trial of Jesus (Matthew 26). The etymological connection between Haifa and Caiaphas is a medieval invention, dating from the Crusader period.

Shfaram: now Shefa-'Amr or Shfaram (Israel), the Christian town and fortress passed between Crusader and Mameluk control in the thirteenth century. There were two churches visited by medieval pilgrims there, the church of St James and St John the Evangelist mentioned by Mandeville and the church of St Phocas. See *CCKJ* 2. 301–4.

Ladder of Tyre: a reference to the town now known as Rosh Ha-Nikra (Israel); Jewish sages referred to the cliffs here as the 'Ladder of Tyre' or 'Ladder of Flint' (*sullam Tzor*). Mandeville takes the story that follows, on the generation of glass, from an ancient legend, referred to by Pliny the Elder (*Natural History: A Selection*, ed. and trans. John Healy (Harmondsworth, 1991), 361–2), and Isidore (*Etymologies*, 328), who all locate this swamp at the base of Mount Carmel. See *Livre*, 131 n. 20.

19 *sandy sea*: see pp. 107–8.

'the rich city': another medieval etymological invention (the Hebrew-Canaanite etymology is 'the strong city' or 'stronghold'), from Isidore, *Etymologies*, 302 (which says that *gaza* is the Persian for 'treasury').

Samson the Strong . . . them: paraphrasing Judges 16: 28–30. The 'house' is described clearly in the Bible as the Temple of Dagon.

Caesarea: the Roman port city of Caesarea Palaestina, refortified by the Crusaders. Now Qisarya (Israel). See *SBCKJ* 44–5.

Chastiau Pélèrin: literally 'Pilgrim Castle', a coastal Crusader citadel south of Haifa, it was one of the last Crusader possessions to fall to the Muslims in 1291; now 'Atlit (Israel). See *SBCKJ* 22–6.

Castle Dair: the Crusader castle of Darum/Dair al-Balah (Gaza). See *SBCKJ* 46.

they call Egypt . . . Cairo: by 'Babylon' Mandeville refers to Fustat, now a suburb of Cairo but once the early medieval Arab capital of Egypt, its name here taken from the ancient Greek and Roman fortress at nearby Babylon (Βαβυλών) on the Nile Delta. The geography and nomenclature used here is jumbled, and represents various bits of knowledge about the Levant. 'Canopat' refers to an ancient Egyptian coastal town (Latin *Canopus*) on the Nile Delta, whilst 'Misrin' refers to Egypt (Hebrew *Misrayim*, Arabic *Misr*). Mandeville clarifies the difference between the Egyptian Babylon and the ancient Babylon in Chaldea, p. 22.

when she fled . . . King Herod: Matthew 2: 13–33.

St Barbara: virgin martyr. The early medieval Coptic church of St Barbara is located in Cairo's Babylon fortress area.

Joseph lived there . . . his brothers: Genesis 37: 27–8.

20 *Nebuchadnezzar called them . . . kingdoms*: giving the Hebrew and Vulgate names of the children in Daniel 3. The 'Benedicite' is not a psalm but rather a prayer, sung as part of the divine office at Lauds (early morning), also derived from Daniel 3.

I would have abjured my faith: historically, there were many examples of western Christian mercenaries in the employ of Arab sultans; see Robert Burns, 'Christian–Islamic Confrontation in the West: The Thirteenth-Century Dream of Conversion', *American Historical Review*, 76 (1971), 1386–1434.

le roi: the king. At this point the Middle English text departs from the Anglo-French source, omitting the account of Egypt (the so-called 'Egypt Gap' which gives the 'Defective' version its name); thus the first clause of the next paragraph in the Middle English text, 'This valley is so cold', seems to make no sense as it doesn't refer to any valley which has been mentioned. Readers of the Middle English version seemed to accept the sudden leap to the unnamed valley but I have supplied the account of Egypt and Sicily from the Egerton version here.

Saladin: Salah ad-Din Yusuf ibn Ayyub (d. 1193), first Sultan of Egypt and Syria, founder of the Ayyubid dynasty and warrior against the Crusaders.

King Richard: Richard I of England (1157–99), the 'Lionheart'. Richard was one of the leaders of the Third Crusade, which failed to recover Jerusalem from Saladin. By the fourteenth century Richard was the subject of popular verse romances.

Louis, King of France: Louis IX (1214–70), Crusader king; Louis was captured and ransomed in Egypt in 1250.

Melechomethos: the sultans' names are garbled, but the prefix *Melech-* derives from the Arabic *malik*, Hebrew *melech*, king.

King Edward: Edward I of England (1239–1307), Crusader prince.

21 *Montreal*: a Crusader castle, built by Baldwin I in 1115, the ruins of which can still be seen, near Shoubak (Jordan). See p. 52.

florins: the first florin (literally, 'coin of Florence') was struck in the mid-thirteenth century but was introduced in England in 1344. As an actual English unit of currency it was very short-lived, but it was a standard measure of Mediterranean trade.

admirals: the English word is formed from the Arabic *al-amir*, a commander; the word only took on its present maritime connotations in the sixteenth century.

22 *tars*: a luxurious Turkish fabric, possibly silk, from Tartary or perhaps Tarsus (Turkey).

camlet: a fine wool, possibly camel.

Tower of Babel: Genesis 11: 9.

23 *Nimrod*: Genesis 10: 9. The stories here associated with Nimrod are post-biblical, and developed out of Talmudic material.

23 *Shinar*: Genesis 10: 10.

Cyrus: Cyrus the Great (*fl.* *c.*600 BCE), Persian king who conquered a vast area of Asia Minor and Central Asia.

Cathay: in Latin Europe this name denoted the whole of China, with Manzi used to denote southern China (map 2). The name derives from the Khitan or Khitai, nomads who occupied northern China from the tenth century. See Peter Jackson, *Mongols and the West 1221–1410* (London, 2005), 331.

24 *Idumea near Botron*: see p. 51.

Dido . . . Aeneas: see also pp. 17–18, for other elements of their story.

Haran: Genesis 11: 31. Now identified with the ruined city of Harran (Turkey).

Ephrem: Syriac-language theologian (*c.*306–73).

Theophilus . . . Devil: a popular medieval story; see Adrienne Williams Boyarin, *Miracles of the Virgin in Medieval England: Law and Jewishness in the Marian Legends* (Woodbridge, 2010), 42–74.

Gehon . . . Paradise: see p. 120.

25 *ciconie or ibices*: storks or ibises.

Rameses: i.e. the pharaoh(s). See Exodus 1: 11, 12: 37 for the biblical city of Rameses, built by the Jews for Pharaoh.

Goshen . . . Jacob and his offspring: Genesis 47: 1–6.

26 *as a miracle*: this story is extracted from the miracles of St Antony, and was probably taken from Gervase of Tilbury's excursus on fauns and satyrs (*Otia*, 99). Here St Antony meets a 'hippocentaur', 'half man and half horse', and has a similar interview with him. Gervase adds that 'a man of this kind was brought alive to Alexandria and provided a great spectacle for the people'.

phoenix: a standard version of the parable from the *Bestiary* (see, for example, http://www.abdn.ac.uk/bestiary/translat/55r.hti).

27 *'paradise apples'*: the Old French *poume de paradis* was a name for the banana or plantain.

'Adam's apples': this name was later given to citrus fruits, such as the lime and shaddock (*OED*), but this description has been understood to be of a melon.

'Pharaoh figs': the Old French *figue de Pharaon* and Italian *fico di Faraone* are names for the 'sycamore fig', although this tree does have leaves and these names may themselves have been derived from Mandeville's *Book*.

In this field . . . various miracles there: a reference to a popular apocryphal story about the childhood of Jesus; the garden of al-Matariyya/Matarea was the resulting medieval pilgrimage site, near Heliopolis.

28 *opobalsamum*: see Elly R. Truitt, 'The Virtues of Balm in Late Medieval Literature', *Early Science and Medicine*, 14 (2009), 711–36, on the origins

and symbolism of balm or balsam. The names Mandeville uses are distorted versions of those given by Isidore (and repeated by Mandeville's ultimate source, Vincent of Beauvais); see *Etymologies*, 349.

Trees . . . Alexander the Great: see note to p. 117.

29 *Joseph's barns are here . . . the Bible*: Genesis 41: 5–35. This explanation of the Pyramids as Joseph's granaries can be traced back at least to the sixth century. Mandeville refutes one of his sources—William of Boldensele—who identified the Pyramids as tombs. See Higgins, *Writing East*, 96–100.

languages: Mandeville's 'Egyptian' language, reflecting an awareness of Coptic as the language of the Egyptian Christians, has nothing in common with the Coptic alphabet, and one will note that it follows the sounds of the Latin alphabet. The actual Coptic alphabet renders the Coptic language (derived from ancient Egyptian) in Greek characters, with a few extra letters derived from ancient Egyptian. See too the Hebrew and Saracen alphabets (pp. 54, 68). Other versions of Mandeville's *Book* included Greek, Persian, Chaldean, Cathayan, Pentexoirean, Armenian, Georgian, and Russian alphabets. See Marcia Kupfer, ' "letres . . . plus vrayes": Hebrew Script and Jewish Witness in the *Mandeville* Manuscript of Charles V', *Speculum*, 83 (2008), 58–111.

30 *Faro*: Greek φάρος, Italian *faro*, lighthouse. The ancient town of Punta del Faro is on the north-eastern tip of the Sicilian coast.

Gebel: from the Arabic *jebel*, mountain, the Italian name for Etna is *Mongibello* (literally 'Mount Mountain').

31 *St Catherine's head*: St Catherine of Alexandria, martyr. She was said to have been martyred on a wheel, but the wheel broke and so she was beheaded. *GL* 2. 334–41.

St Mark was martyred . . . to rest there: the foundation story of St Mark's, Venice. *GL* 1. 245.

'aloe': a medieval wonder-drug, recommended in medieval herbals for phlegm, choler, melancholy, headaches, wind, muscle pains, viscosity in the stomach, dropsy, tape-worms, gout, itching, lesions, mouth ulcers, and digestion; *Properties* 2. 907.

Moses and Aaron led the people of Israel: this, and the following information on wells, is from Exodus 15.

32 *Mara*: Exodus 15: 23.

Elim Valley: mirroring the biblical route described in Exodus 15: 27, Numbers 33: 9.

Children of Israel . . . army was drowned: Exodus 14: 22–8.

Desert of Sin: Exodus 16: 1, Numbers 13: 22.

burning bush: Exodus 3: 2.

33 *'put off the shoes . . . is holy ground'*: Exodus 3: 5. The quotation is given in the vernacular, not Latin.

34 *David says in the psalter*: e.g. Psalms 39[40]: 6, 106[107]: 8, 106[107]: 15, 106[107]: 21, 106[107]: 31, 110[111]: 4.

Moses struck the stone . . . do so eternally: Exodus 17: 6.

Ten Commandments: Exodus 24: 12.

Under a rock . . . forty days and forty nights: Exodus 24: 18.

St Catherine's Mountain . . . Mount Moses: Jebel Katarina and Jebel Mousa, or Mount Sinai (Egypt); Mandeville goes on to say that one name, Mount Sinai, is given to the whole area.

35 *prayers specific to the veneration of St Catherine*: i.e. the Collect of St Catherine, a standard prayer to the saint found in many medieval books of hours.

Ascopards: a term variously used to refer to Arabians (as, apparently, here), black Africans (Albert of Aix), or a ferocious giant (as in the Middle English romance *Bevis of Hamtoun*) (see *Middle English Dictionary* (via http://quod.lib.umich.edu/m/med), s.v. 'Ascopardes').

36 *This town of Beer Sheva . . . forty years*: the reference is to Bathsheba, wife of Uriah the Hittite (2 Kings [= 2 Samuel]); on Solomon 2 Paralipomenon [2 Chronicles] 9: 30. Whilst the origins of the place-name Beer Sheva (literally 'Well of Seven' or 'Well of the Oath') are distinct from Bathsheba (literally 'Daughter of the Oath'), the conflation was frequently made in medieval writing. Beer Sheva was an important Crusader city.

Mambre: Genesis 13: 18 locates the vale of Mambre at Hebron.

murder of his son Abel by Cain: Genesis 4: 8. The tradition connecting Cain and Abel with Hebron is another element of medieval apocrypha.

Joshua and Caleb . . . win the Promised Land: Joshua 14, 2: 1–24.

thirty-three and a half years: 2 Kings [2 Samuel] 5: 4–5.

graves of the patriarchs . . . beautiful church: the cathedral of St Abraham, the supposed bodies of the patriarchs being discovered there in 1119. See *CCKJ* 1. 225.

Spelunk or Double Cave . . . Jews call it Arbee: 'spelunk' is a Middle English word for cave (from Latin *spelunca*, French *spelonque*). The Hebrew name for the Cave of the Patriarchs (*Me'arat ha-Machpela*, literally 'the double cave') does, as Mandeville suggests, refer to the 'paired' or double burials there. Mandeville repeats two biblical Hebrew synonyms for Hebron: Kiryat-Arba (Joshua 14: 13–15) and Arbee (Genesis 23: 2, 35: 27).

Abraham's house was . . . three persons and worshipped one: Genesis 18: 1.

'He saw three and worshipped one': this quotation does not, in fact, come from Holy Writ but rather from the Church Office and *Glossa Ordinaria*, via Mandeville's source, Odoric.

37 *The angel ordered Adam . . . Seth was conceived*: Genesis 4: 25.

chambille: the *Defective Version of Mandeville's Travels*, Early English Text Society OS 319 (Oxford, 2002), ed. M. C. Seymour (pp. 143–4), shows how this is a report of the kamala spice (Arabic *kinbil*), an orange powder used for yellow dye and as an intestinal medicine.

Mount Mamre: see Genesis 13: 18 for the story of Abraham's Oak of Mamre.

an oak tree . . . the Dry Tree: this legendary Eastern tree (the *arbor sicca*) is mentioned in various texts as the tree on which the phoenix perches in a beautiful garden. It is based on the vision in Ezekiel 17: 24: 'And all the trees of the country shall know that I the Lord have brought down the high tree, and exalted the low tree: and have dried up the green tree, and have caused the dry tree to flourish. I the Lord have spoken and have done it.' See Roger Lancelyn Green, 'The Phoenix and the Tree', *English*, 7 (1948), 11–15. The Dry Tree was also understood, in the later Middle Ages, as an image of the Virgin (see Hugo van der Velden, 'Petrus Christus's *Our Lady of the Dry Tree*', *Journal of the Warburg and Courtauld Institutes*, 60 (1997), 89–110). Several early accounts, by Josephus and Jerome, as well as the Hereford *mappa mundi* mention the tree and later travellers' accounts, including those of Arculf and Marco Polo, also link it with Abraham's Oak of Mamre.

a perilous journey through very pleasant woods: the pairing of the 'perilous' journey with the 'pleasant' woods is a Middle English misreading, retained here to show how different versions of the text can utterly transform their sources. In the Anglo-French source (*Livre*, 178), a *moult beal chemin* ('a very pretty route') is described, *par plainz et par bois et moult delitable* ('through plains and through woods and very delightful'). Somehow, probably through a scribe's eye-skip or a wandering mind, *moult beal* became 'perilous'.

'Behold we have heard of it in Ephrata': Psalms 131[132]: 6; also Ruth 4: 11; Micah 5: 2, describing Efrat as Bethlehem.

a pretty church . . . beautiful marble pillars: a description of the Church and Cave of the Nativity at Bethlehem, a crenellated basilica and major Crusader and pilgrimage site (see *CCKJ* 1. 137–46). The thirty-four nave columns of the church were distinctively painted, in the twelfth century, with eastern and western saints (see *CCKJ* 1. 146).

Flowery Field: this *exemplum* reflects popular religious texts rather than Mandeville's 'geographical' sources. Stories of martyrs and virgins not consumed by flames (a strand of imagery ultimately based on the Burning Bush) are common in medieval popular religion, as seen in the legends of St Agatha, St Lucy, and St Thecla. In related stories, a child dropped in a fire is unharmed (*IE* 2035), a fire avoids a convent (*IE* 2034), a holy man passes unharmed through a fire (*IE* 2038), and so on. The rose was a symbol of female beauty, of the Virgin, and also of the blood of martyrdom. There was a field known, from the thirteenth century, by this name east of Jerusalem (*CCKJ* 3. 360), associated with Elijah's ascent and the site of Jesus' arrest, the Garden of Gethsemane.

38 *church*: i.e. the church of the Nativity, Bethlehem.

38 *Crib of the Ox and the Ass*: there is a crib relic at S Maria Maggiore in Rome, apparently brought there from Bethlehem in the seventh century by Pope Theodore; it is still there, exposed for veneration each year at Christmas. However, Guy de Blond, a twelfth-century French monk, also claimed to have crib relics from the Bishop of Bethlehem, which he distributed in France (*CCKJ* 1. 155). The Crusader period led to a proliferation of such relics of dubious authenticity.

Jasper . . . Saraphy: the Magi are unnamed in the biblical source (Matthew 2: 1–12), but were later given various names. *GL* 1. 79 explains, equally confusedly, 'In Greek their names were Apellius, Amerius, and Damascus; in Hebrew, Galgalat, Malgalat, and Sarachin; in Latin, Caspar, Balthasar, and Melchior'. The Magi, patrons of travellers, were venerated as saints in the Middle Ages, their relics enshrined at Cologne.

Holy Innocents: commemorating the Massacre of the Innocents (Matthew 2), in which Herod ordered that all young male children in Bethlehem be put to death to prevent the birth of a King of the Jews, as predicted by the Magi. Their story is from *GL* 1. 55–9, as later repeated by Mandeville (see p. 46); *CCKJ* 1. 155.

St Jerome: (d. 420), historian and doctor of the Church. Sainted as a holy author, Jerome's translation established the Latin Vulgate as the definitive and most widely read version of the Bible in medieval Europe.

Adjacent to that church . . . she had delivered her child: the church of St Nicholas and Milk Grotto (Cave-Church of St Mary) at Bethlehem. The distinctive white limestone of the 'milk grotto' was, and remains, associated with the Virgin's milk, and many medieval pilgrims claimed it as the site in which the Virgin suckled the infant Jesus. The Italian pilgrim Niccolò of Poggibonsi, writing in 1346–50 and therefore at around the same time as Mandeville, said that the Virgin rested here during the Massacre of the Innocents. See *CCKJ* 1. 156–7.

Massap . . . Harme: these words are versions of the Arabic 'book' (*mushaf*, also 'The Book', i.e. the Qur'an) and 'sacred, sanctified' (*haram*); for information on Islam, Mandeville is following William of Tripoli's *Tractatus de statu Saracenorum* (late thirteenth century) here, but the relevant injunction concerning wine can be found in sura 5: 90–1 (Qur'an, 76).

39 *'and his iniquity shall come down upon his crown'*: Psalm 7: 17[16].

Old Law: Leviticus 11: 7; sura 5: 4 (Qur'an, 68).

sixty wives . . . three hundred lovers: 1 Kings [1 Samuel] 18: 20–7; 2 Kings [2 Samuel] 3: 15.

a church where . . . the nativity of Christ: the 'Shepherds' Field' (*Kanisat al-Rawat*), now associated with the Palestinian town of Beit Sahour; the church of the Shepherds was documented from the fourth century, but seems to have been abandoned and ruined by *c.*1100. See *CCKJ* 2. 315.

Rachel's Tomb: a site sacred to Christians, Jews, and Muslims has stood at or near this site, on the road from Jerusalem to Bethlehem, from around the fourth century. On the late medieval structure here, which was controlled by Muslims, see *CCKJ* 2. 176.

she died straight after . . . twelve children: Genesis 35: 19–20, which states that Jacob erected 'a pillar over her sepulchre'; the 'twelve stones . . . engraved with the names of the twelve tribes of Israel' feature elsewhere (Exodus 39: 14; Joshua 4: 8; 3 Kings [1 Kings] 18: 31).

Jebusalem: the etymology of Jerusalem was frequently subject to this kind of interpretation; 'Jebusalem' is mentioned in various sources used by Mandeville, including Peter Comestor's *Historia scolastica*, Isidore's *Etymologies* (p. 301), and Gervase of Tilbury's *Otia Imperialia* (*Otia*, 202–3), based on the founding of Jebus (the precursor of Jerusalem) described in Judges 19: 10, 1 Paralipomenon [1 Chronicles] 11: 4.

Judas Maccabeus: Judas (or Judah) Maccabeus, Jewish warrior, described in the biblical books 1 and 2 Machabees. He is one of several of the Nine Worthies (a group of heroes, three pagan, three Jewish, and three Christian, who exemplified medieval ideas of virtue and chivalry) mentioned by Mandeville, together with Joshua (p. 50), David, Alexander the Great, and Godfrey of Bouillon (p. 41).

40 *There used to be a patriarch . . . the country*: a memory of the Crusader kingdom of Jerusalem, which had its own Latin patriarchate; the last mainland outpost of the Crusader kingdom, Acre (Akko, Israel), was lost in 1291 and the tiny Crusader island of Ruad (Arwad, Syria) fell in 1303, marking an end to the Crusader presence in the Holy Land.

Ramatha-in-Ephraim: unlike the other cities mentioned here, this is a biblical, not medieval, location; see 1 Kings [1Samuel] 1: 1.

church of St Chariton . . . an affecting thing to see: St Chariton, abbot and ascetic, lived in a cave near Bethlehem at Wadi Khuraitun (see *CCKJ* 3. 158); it was deserted by the twelfth century and the body translated to Jerusalem, where a church dedicated to St Chariton and located near the Holy Sepulchre became a pilgrimage site. Regarding the painting of Chariton's martyrdom, Seymour (*Defective*, 144–5) suggests that Mandeville misread *compaginati* ('skeletons') from Peter Comestor's *Historia scolastica* as *compincti* ('painting'), hence the moving artwork.

Medians: of Media, a former Persian kingdom.

a hundred and fifty years: the Anglo-French text (*Livre*, 188) gives 140 years, suggesting its earlier composition or circulation. Jerusalem fell to Saladin's forces in 1187.

church of the Holy Sepulchre: pre-eminent holy site of medieval Christendom and one of the main objects of the medieval Crusades, the site is venerated as the location of Calvary (Golgotha; Matthew 27: 33; Mark 15: 22; Luke 23: 33; John 19: 17), where Jesus was crucified, and the place of Jesus' burial and resurrection. The church was rebuilt in the eleventh century and largely retains that fabric and structure today (see *CCKJ*

3. 6–74). The church was the destination for Christian pilgrims throughout the Middle Ages. See map 3, no. 1.

40 *little house*: the aedicule, the monument containing the sepulchre, enclosed by a rotunda. See *CCKJ* 3. 23. Many pilgrims commented on its semicircular shape and its rich mosaic decoration.

a burning lamp . . . rose from death to life: the Middle English text suggests that this was a weekly occurrence, rather than an annual Easter miracle (*Defective*, ed. Seymour, p. 29)! See Andrew Jotischky, 'Holy Fire and Holy Sepulchre: Ritual and Space in Jerusalem, 9th–14th Centuries', in Frances Andrews (ed.), *Ritual and Space in the Middle Ages: Proceedings of the 2009 Harlaxton Symposium* (Donington, 2011), 44–60.

41 *Godfrey of Boulogne . . . kings of Jerusalem*: Godfrey of Boulogne or Bouillon (*c.*1060–1100) was the first ruler of the Latin kingdom and one of the Nine Worthies; Baldwin I of Edessa (d. 1118) was King of Jerusalem.

'But God is our king . . . in the midst of the earth': Psalm 73[74]: 12. The Greek is inaccurate.

'What you see is . . . of this faith': this phrase's source is unclear; *Livre*, 195 n. 11, speculates that this might have been the text on the mosaics, which partly survive, in the Franciscans' Calvary chapel; however, pilgrims' accounts of these mosaics do not record this text (see *CCKJ* 3. 28–9, also 3. 23–4). The Greek is inaccurate.

'Forty years long was I neighbour to that generation': misquoting Psalm 94[95]: 10.

Gaius Caesar: i.e. [Gaius] Julius Caesar (100–44 BCE) who reformed the Roman calendar.

42 *a bridle for his warhorse . . . won all these lands*: the legend of Constantine's horse (based on Zacharias 14: 20) often followed that of St Helena, Constantine's mother (as in *GL* 1. 283); see Barbara Baert, *A Heritage of Holy Wood: The Legend of the True Cross in Text and Image* (Leiden, 2004). There were various prestigious nail and bridle relics in medieval Europe, including the nail fashioned into the 'Iron Crown of Lombardy' at the Monza treasury (Italy), and other items at Carpentras (France), Trier (Germany), and Vienna (Austria).

The Lives of the Fathers: the *Vitae patrum*, biographies of the ascetics of the early church, compiled in the third and fourth centuries. A staple book of the medieval monastic library.

Joseph of Arimathea: see John 19: 38. This is a description of the 'compass' which can still be seen today in the church of the Holy Sepulchre.

place where Our Lord was put in prison . . . other places: the Prison of Christ has no scriptural authority, but became (and remains) a popular pilgrimage site. The Prison is a small medieval chapel in the northern side of the church of the Holy Sepulchre (map 3, no. 1a).

she thought that He was a gardener: John 20: 11–18.

Canons of the Benedictine order . . . Patriarch was their leader: by the time Mandeville was writing, the dominant Latin Christian order at the Holy Sepulchre was that of the Franciscans.

'Woman, behold thy son': John 19: 26.

'After that . . . Behold thy mother': John 19: 27, i.e. the words Jesus addressed to St John the Evangelist.

43 *St Stephen . . . stoned to death*: Acts 7.

Golden Gate that cannot be opened: this tradition derives, in both Jewish and Christian sources, from Ezekiel 44: 1–3. In the Middle Ages the gate was opened on Palm Sunday and on the Feast of the Exaltation of the Cross. The Byzantine gate was bricked up in 1541 by Sultan Suleiman I, to prevent the Messiah from entering.

where the Knights Hospitaller have their institution: the Muristan (map 3, no. 2). On the Hospital buildings see *CCKJ* 3. 192–201.

Nostre Dame le Graunt . . . Vatyns: the abbey church of St Mary the Great (*CCKJ* 3. 253) and the abbey church of St Mary Latin (*CCKJ* 3. 255); see map 3, nos. 3 and 4. The latter was reputed to be the first Latin church in Jerusalem.

Mary Cleophas and . . . Our Lord was put to death: for the two Marys see John 19: 25. In the gospels of Matthew (27: 56), Mark (15: 40), and John (19: 25) Mary Magdalene and Mary Cleophas are described as witnesses at the Resurrection. The association of these women with this place in Jerusalem first appears in the Crusade chronicles (*c.*1100) of Bartolf of Nangis; see *CCKJ* 3. 253.

Temple of Our Lord: the Dome of the Rock and Al-Aqsa complex on Jerusalem's Temple Mount, the most holy site in the city for Jews and Muslims, regarded as the site of the location of Abraham's binding of Isaac, and the First and Second Temples, and the location of Muhammad's ascent to heaven. In the period in which Mandeville was writing, following the Crusaders' defeat, the Dome of the Rock had been re-consecrated according to the Islamic rite. See map 3, nos. 5–8.

letters of introduction from the Sultan . . . his seal: the chief seal has more authority than the Sultan's seal, or 'signet'. The text emphasizes the narrator's proximity to, and intimacy with, the Sultan. The Anglo-French text makes this much more of a feature: 'I went in there, and other places I wanted to, thanks to the Sultan's letters, in which there was a special commandment to all his subjects to allow me to view all the places and to explain all the places and the secrets of each place, and to take me on a tour of the city if needed, and to receive me and my companions politely, and to bend to all my reasonable requests as long as they were not contrary to the royal dignity of the Sultan or of his law' (*Livre*, 198).

God's body: i.e. the Eucharist.

there used to be Canons Regular . . . obedient: i.e. a monastic community living under the Augustinian rule; the Canons Regular of the Templum

Domini were established here in the early twelfth century. *CCKJ* 3. 401–3.

44 *Holy Foreskin*: this *exemplum* of the granting of the foreskin to the Frankish King and Holy Roman Emperor Charlemagne (d. 814) was well known in medieval Europe; at least thirty-two different foreskins were claimed by medieval churches. The popular pilgrimage destination was, in fact, Charroux, which almost all scribes of the Anglo-French manuscripts mistook for Chartres. See Robert P. Palazzo, 'The Veneration of the Sacred Foreskin(s) of Baby Jesus: A Documented Analysis', in James P. Helfers (ed.), *Multicultural Europe and Cultural Exchange in the Middle Ages and Renaissance* (Turnhout, 2005), 155–76. The Anglo-French text (*Livre*, 199) says, according to different manuscripts, that King Charles took it to various places: Poitiers then Chartres; Aachen and seven places in Liège; Rome, to the church of San Giovanni in Laterano (Aachen and Rome had foreskin relics which rivalled that of Charroux).

thirty pence: Matthew 26: 15, the thirty pieces of silver paid to Judas to betray Jesus.

Julian the Apostate: (*c*.331–63), Roman Emperor and philosopher, who rejected Christianity in favour of Neoplatonic paganism. Julian ordered the Temple at Jerusalem to be rebuilt as part of a programme of encouraging religions other than Christianity. See Rowland Smith, *Julian's Gods: Religion and Philosophy in the Thought and Action of Julian the Apostate* (London, 1995).

Hadrian: Hadrian (d. 138), Roman Emperor. He suppressed the Jewish Bar Kokhba revolt of 132–6, the event which apparently informs Mandeville's biography. Hadrian long preceded Julian.

Helyam: in the tradition of the earlier story of the naming of Jebusalem (p. 39), Mandeville gestures to the Roman name for Jerusalem, *Aelia Capitolina*, converting *Aelia* into Helyam (which sounds more like Jerusalem), without apparently realizing that this was a Latin name.

Holy of Holies: the sacred inner sanctuary and 'most holy place', originally of the portable Tabernacle (Exodus 26) and then at the Temple, in which the Ark of the Covenant was said to have been kept.

'This is Jerusalem': Ezekiel 5: 5.

45 *'I saw water coming out of the Temple'*: echoing Ezekiel 47: 1, 'behold waters issued out from under the threshold of the house'.

Moriah: Mount Moriah, the traditional location of Abraham's sacrifice of Isaac (Genesis 22: 2).

Bethel: the location of Jacob's dream (Genesis 28).

Ark of God containing Jewish relics: Hebrews 9: 4.

With this staff . . . he performed many miracles: Exodus 14: 16, 9: 23, 10: 13.

Tabernacle of Aaron: Aaron entered the tabernacle with Moses (Leviticus 9: 23).

'Indeed the Lord is in this place, and I knew it not': Genesis 28: 16.

Israel: Genesis 32: 38–35: 10.

David saw the angel . . . the sheath: 2 Kings [2 Samuel] 24: 16.

St Simeon presented Our Lord to the Temple: Luke 2: 22–40.

Our Lord set Himself . . . provided Him with light: an apocryphal story that prefigures the rocks which were rent at Christ's Passion (Matthew 27: 51).

Our Lady sat and learned her psalter: a reference to the very widespread (non-biblical) story of the Virgin being taught to read by her mother, St Anne.

Christ was circumcised: Luke 2: 21.

angel first revealed the nativity of St John the Baptist: Luke 1: 13.

Melchizedek first made an offering . . . prefiguration of the sacrament: Genesis 14: 18.

46 *David fell in prayer to Our Lord . . . Help of God*: paraphrasing 1 Paralipomenon [1 Chronicles] 22: 7–19, 2 Paralipomenon [2 Chronicles] 6: 21–42. The Anglo-French text adds (*Livre*, 204) a description here of how outside the Temple door Jews would sacrifice pigeons and turtle-doves, and how the Saracens keep a sundial there; this sundial was mentioned in various medieval travellers' accounts.

Zacharias: a prophet, said in the New Testament (Matthew 23: 35; Luke 11: 51) to have been murdered by Jews in the Temple.

St James: St James 'the Great' (d. *c*.44), often described as the first apostle to die for the Christian faith; his relics were translated to Spain, probably in the ninth century, and his cult (based at Santiago di Compostela) was phenomenally popular in the later Middle Ages. His martyrdom was associated with the chapel of St Mary (*CCKJ* 3. 310), adjacent to Solomon's Stables (see next note); map 3, no. 23.

School of Solomon: Solomon's Stables, adjacent to the Temple Mount (*CCKJ* 3. 311–12) and Temple of Solomon (map 3, no. 8). It had been a mosque until the Crusader period, when the Templars are said to have used it as stables. The confusion likely comes in the conflation of the Anglo-French *estable* ('stable') with *escole* ('school').

Temple of Solomon: the al-Aqsa mosque, on the Temple Mount and adjacent to the traditional site of the Temple (map 3, no. 8). Islamic tradition holds that the mosque was restored by Solomon. From 1119 until the fall of Jerusalem the Knights Templar were based here. See Malcolm Barber, *The New Knighthood: A History of the Order of the Temple* (Cambridge, 1994), 90–2.

Bath of Our Lord . . . Our Lady's Bed is adjacent: the 'Bath of Our Lord' (referring to Jerusalem's cisterns) and 'Our Lady's Bed' were described by the German pilgrim Theodoric, travelling *c*.1170, whom Mandeville follows here. The bath, explains Theodoric, was in the form of 'a large stone shell . . . in which the infant [Christ] bathed', whilst the Virgin's bed is where 'she lay down when she suckled the child' (see *CCKJ* 3. 310). See map 3, no. 23.

46 *Joachim, Our Lady's father, in a stone tomb*: Mary's father Joachim is not named in the gospels, but was a popular saint in the medieval Christian tradition. The description here is of the abbey church of St Anne (*CCKJ* 3. 142–56); map 3, no. 11.

St Anne also used to . . . translated to Constantinople: it is doubtful that a church existed on this site prior to the First Crusade, although this area had long been associated with the house of Joachim and Anne. From the eighth century the Hagia Sophia at Constantinople claimed the body of St Anne.

Probatica Pissina: whilst it is not named, either here or in the Anglo-French source, Mandeville describes the biblical Pool of Bethesda, known to the Crusaders as the Sheep Pool (see map 3, no. 12); the miracle which follows is described in John 5: 9.

'Arise, take up thy bed, and walk': Mark 2: 9.

Pilate's house was next to this place: a Crusader-era pilgrimage site/sight with a chapel of the Flagellation (see *CCKJ* 3. 93–5); map 3, no. 19.

King Herod: Herod the Great (*c*.73 BCE–4 CE), Jewish client-king of the Roman provinces of Judea, Galilee, and Samaria. Map 3, no. 20 (the Crusader-era 'Condemnation' chapel).

47 *all the evil deeds that he could*: this account takes as its starting point the well-known story of the Massacre of the Innocents (Matthew 2) (see too p. 38). The non-scriptural story here of Herod's cruelty to his own wife and children is based on Josephus' account of Herod's prosecution for high treason of his wife Mariamne I and the children he had by her; the main medieval Christian source for this story is *GL* 1. 58–9.

Herod the Ashkelonite: Herod the Great, see note above.

Herod Antipas: Herod Antipas (before 20 BCE–after 39 CE), son of Herod the Great, described in the gospels (Luke 9: 9; Mark 6: 16) for his role in the death of John the Baptist and, in Luke 23 for his role in the execution of Jesus.

Herod Agrippa: Herod Agrippa or Agrippa I (10 BCE–44 CE), grandson of Herod the Great and nephew of Herod Antipas, and early persecutor of the followers of Jesus (as described in Acts 25).

church of St Saviour . . . St Stephen's head is there too: the church of St Saviour was outside the city walls (map 3, no. 21), and Mandeville's report describes the church of St Saba (map 3, no. 13; see *CCKJ* 3. 356); the confusion in names is no doubt due St Saba (or Sabbas) being an Eastern Orthodox saint, his cult unfamiliar in the West. Mandeville could be describing one of several relics of Chrysostom; his bones had largely been translated to Constantinople and then looted by Crusaders in 1204 and brought to the West.

beautiful church dedicated to St James: apparently referring to the church of St James the Great (*CCKJ* 3. 168–82); map 3, no. 14.

a pretty church . . . Augustinian abbey there: the abbey church of St Mary of Mount Zion; *CCKJ* 3. 261–87; map 3, no. 15.

the stone the angel carried . . . St Catherine's monastery: the red stone, a popular attraction, served as the church's altar (*CCKJ* 3. 268–9).

the gate: the Zion Gate, from which one could take the road to Bethlehem, with an accompanying apocryphal pilgrimage narrative.

the great big stone . . . life: Matthew 28: 1–3. This paragraph reveals the proliferation of pseudo-biblical pilgrimage places in later medieval Jerusalem, sites which flourished both during the Crusader era and the subsequent era of Christian pilgrimage under the auspices of the Franciscans.

Annas: Jewish high-priest and interrogator of Jesus (John 18: 13–27). The 'house of Annas', a twelfth-century chapel, can still be visited in Jerusalem, although Mandeville seemed to have mixed up the houses of Annas and Caiaphas (see map 3, no. 21; *CCKJ* 3. 112).

St Peter committed . . . cock crowed: John 18: 13–27. The church of St Peter of the Cock Crow (*ad gallicantu*) was founded beside Mount Zion by the fourth century. Map 3, no. 16; *CCKJ* 3. 346–8.

48 *'Peace to you'*: John 20: 19–26.

'My lord and my God': John 20: 28.

in the form of a flame: John 20: 19–23; Acts 2: 1–13.

Our Lord's knee: the Anglo-French source states that John slept at Christ's chest (*peitrine*), suggesting a maternal gesture; the Middle English version, 'in oure lordis kne', suggests the childlike gesture of sitting on a parent's knee, perhaps making John more a recipient of Christ's care rather than parental, Marian love. The iconography is based on John 13: 23, describing how 'there was leaning on Jesus' bosom one of his disciples'.

Mount Zion: the Anglo-French source adds that 'this is the place where the Jews violently threw the body of Our Lady when the apostles carried it to be buried in the Valley of Jehoshaphat' (*Livre*, 209), one of several moments at which the Middle English version downplays the Anglo-French text's violently anti-Jewish invective.

St Peter wept . . . denied Christ: John 18: 27.

Christ resurrected the young virgin from death to life: the story of Christ's raising of Jairus' daughter (Mark 5: 21–43; Matthew 9: 18–26; Luke 8: 40–56), a popular scene in medieval ecclesiastical art. Mandeville's account here seems to conflate this incident with the story of Jesus giving sight to the blind man, which was marked at the Pool of Siloam in the location described by Mandeville (map 3, no. 9).

Natatoire Siloam: the Pool of Siloam, described in John 9. Map 3, no. 9.

48 *tree on which Judas hanged himself . . . still there*: the biblical account merely says that Judas hanged himself (Matthew 27: 5), but this tree, sometimes described as a fig tree, appears on numerous medieval maps and plans of Jerusalem and seems to have been a pilgrimage destination. Map 3, no. 18.

'I have sinned in betraying innocent blood': Matthew 27: 4.

a pretty church where the tree . . . made for Our Lord: the Monastery of the Cross, then a Georgian foundation, in which the tree relic can still be seen. See *CCKJ* 2. 33–40.

49 *Our Lady met St Elizabeth . . . his creator, Our Lord*: Luke 1: 39–56. The church of St John the Baptist at Ein Kerem (Israel). *CCKJ* 1. 30–8.

Emmaus: Luke 24: 13–27. There was a Crusader church (*CCKJ* 1. 52–9) of Emmaus Nicopolis ('Amwas) near Latrun (Israel), but, during the Middle Ages several other sites were associated with Emmaus.

Mount Joy: a village north of Jerusalem, known in Arabic as Nabi Samwil (Palestine), literally 'the prophet Samuel'; *CCKJ* 2. 85–94. There was a large Premonstratensian abbey church of St Samuel here.

church of Our Lady: the Crusader-era church of Our Lady of Jehoshaphat (*CCKJ* 3. 286–306). Map 3, no. 17.

seventy-two years old: the accepted age of the Virgin's death, as given in *GL* 2. 78.

Judas kissed Our Lord . . . arrested by the Jews here: Matthew 26: 47–50; Mark 14: 43–5.

'My Father, if it be possible, let this chalice pass from me': Matthew 26: 39.

a chapel where Our Lord sweated blood and water: there was a Byzantine basilica at Gethsemane (the church of St Saviour in Gethsemane, *CCKJ* 3. 358–65), in honour of His Agony, adjacent to the site at which it was believed Jesus was arrested. The church was probably destroyed shortly after 1187. See map 3, no. 10.

King Jehoshaphat: the Anglo-French source explains that Jehoshaphat was a local king who, converted by a hermit, became a worthy man who did many good deeds (*Livre*, 214). This account is ultimately based on 3 Kings [1 Kings] 22 and 2 Paralipomenon [2 Chronicles] 17, which praise Jehoshaphat as a devout, law-giving king who smashed the idols of Baal.

His left foot . . . imprinted in the rock: there was a Crusader church of the Ascension, at the centre of which was a small white marble tower imprinted with Christ's footprint, which had been venerated since at least the seventh century (*CCKJ* 3. 72–6); abandoned in 1187, by 1212 the building had been transformed into a mosque and the footprint taken to the al-Aqsa mosque where it became an Islamic icon; see Amikam Elad, *Medieval Jerusalem and Islamic Worship: Holy Places, Ceremonies, Pilgrimage* (Leiden, 1995), 171. However, by Mandeville's time the church seems to have been re-established, and various pilgrims reported not one but two footprints (*CCKJ* 3. 75)!

'Blessed are the poor in spirit: for theirs is the kingdom of Heaven': Matthew 5: 3.

Paternoster: the Lord's Prayer. The church of the Lord's Prayer is on a site identified in this way since the fourth century; *CCKJ* 3. 117–24.

St Mary the Egyptian: originating in the fourth century, she was famous for being a reformed prostitute who spent forty-seven years as an ascetic in the desert; *GL* 1. 227. Mandeville refers here to the cave chapel of St Pelagia, associated with St Mary in the later Middle Ages (*CCKJ* 3. 343–4).

Palm Sunday: Matthew 21: 1–2; Luke 19: 29–30.

Bethany: a popular pilgrimage site to the east of Jerusalem, which included sites related to Lazarus, Simon, Mary Magdalene, and Martha; part of the site was turned into a mosque, and its fate in the later Middle Ages is unclear, although Christian pilgrims certainly visited in the fourteenth and fifteenth centuries. See *CCKJ* 1. 124–5.

Simon the Leper . . . Julian: Matthew 26: 6–13 and Mark 4: 3–9. The conflation with the legend of St Julian 'the Hospitaller' is from *GL* 1. 126.

50 *she washed his feet . . . with her hair*: John 12: 3–8.

Lazarus: John 11.

Our Lady appeared . . . after her Assumption: the story of St Thomas' lack of belief in Mary's Assumption to heaven, a scene which mirrors his doubt at Christ's resurrection, was made popular by *GL* 2. 82.

the apostles gathered . . . about Christ's resurrection: Matthew 28: 1–8.

Between Mount Olivet . . . her death: referring to the abbey church of St Mary of the Mount of Olives, almost certainly destroyed in the twelfth century and long before Mandeville's time; *CCKJ* 3. 316–19.

Rahab the harlot: in the Christian tradition, Rahab was understood to have been a prostitute who helped the Israelites capture Jericho; her story is told in Joshua 2: 1–7.

'He that receiveth . . . reward of a prophet': Matthew 10: 41.

'command that these stones be made bread': Matthew 4: 3. Scripturally, this takes place in the desert, not, as Mandeville suggests, on 'a great mountain'.

a hermitage . . . because St George converted them: the description refers to the priory of Quarantine (*Quarantena*, *Jabal Quruntul*; *CCKJ* 1. 252–4; the word is a Latinate name for a period of forty days); by the fourteenth century the Crusader-era community of Latin hermits had given way to a Georgian or Greek community. The Georgians in fact especially revere St George, the patron saint of their country.

'Jesus, Son of David, have mercy on me!': Mark 10: 48.

Zoar: another name for Segor (Genesis 19), where Lot sought refuge after the destruction of Sodom. See *Livre*, 236.

50 *'asphalt'*: that is, Dead Sea native asphalt. A bituminous composition and used as a medicinal 'glew' for phlegmatics, this is the 'slime' described in the Old Testament (Genesis 11: 3) and known as 'Jew's pitch' and 'Jew's slime' in early English for this reason. See *Properties*, 2. 836–7.

51 *Sodom . . . Zoar*: Sodom and Gomorrah were well known through the account of their destruction in Genesis 13: 10; Adama and Seboim are mentioned as towns 'in the neighbourhood' of Sodom and Gomorrah in Hosea 11: 8; 'Zoar' is a corruption of 'Segor', the town mentioned with Sodom and Gomorrah in Genesis.

Alsiled: an 'Arabic'-like name, adding the Arabic article '*Al*' to the Middle English 'sile' (a boggy, filthy mire); likewise, the Anglo-French manuscripts call this 'Alfetide' ('*Al*' plus '*fetide*', 'the stinking place').

Lot's wife lingers . . . these cities were submerged: Genesis 19: 26.

They were both circumcised on the same day: Genesis 17: 23.

Jor and Dan . . . from them: a frequently repeated medieval etymology, e.g. *Etymologies*, 281.

region of Idumea and the region of Botron: Idumea is the biblical Edom, covering the area that is now south-east Israel and south-west Jordan, its main town at Petra and its port at Eilat. There was no medieval area named Idumea. Botron is perhaps a corruption of the biblical Bosra in Edom (Genesis 36: 33).

Maidan: the Anglo-French text adds a note that this means '"fair" or "market" in English'; this is then the Arabic, Persian, and southern Russian *maidan*, bazaar, market-square, or parade-ground; large bazaars appeared along the Islamic pilgrimage route to Mecca. See *OED*, 'maidan'.

Job's Temple is in that plain: a church of St Job, built in the twelfth century, was a pilgrimage site, located at Khirbat Bal'ama south of Jenin (Palestine). See *CCKJ* 1. 106–7.

52 *'This is my beloved Son . . . hear ye Him'*: Matthew 3: 17.

Naaman of Syria: the story of Naaman the Syrian leper is told in 2 Kings [2 Samuel] 5.

city of Hai, which Joshua attacked and took: Joshua 8: 14.

a sturdy castle . . . A French king, called Baldwin: the Crusader castle of Montreal, at Shoubak (Jordan). Built 1115 by Baldwin I of Jerusalem (*c.*1058–1118), a leader of the First Crusade.

Gabaon: Joshua 9: 3.

through Ramatha, through Sophim: Ramatha Sophim is one place (mentioned in 1 Kings [1 Samuel]).

mountain of Ephraim . . . the prophet was born: 1 Kings [1 Samuel] 1.

one reaches Sybola . . . the prophet Eli: the Ark was kept at Shiloh (1 Kings [1 Samuel] 4: 4–6), evidently an unfamiliar place-name to the scribe. Eli was not a prophet but rather a high-priest.

Our Lord first spoke . . . administered the sacrament: 1 Kings [1 Samuel] 3. 'The Lord revealed himself to Samuel in Shiloh' (1 Kings [1 Samuel] 3: 21).

Sabon and Rama Benjamin, about which Holy Writ speaks: 'Sabon' (given in Anglo-French as *Gabaon*) and Rama Benjamin seems to be a rendering of the Gabaa and Rama of Benjamin mentioned as place-names (literally 'hill' and 'height') in 1 Kings [1 Samuel] 15: 22.

53 *Our Lord spoke to the Samaritan woman*: John 4: 1–12.

Shechem . . . New City: an important biblical city (Shechem) and the Roman city of Flavia Neapolis, now Nablus (Palestine). It was captured by the Crusaders in 1099, who named it Naples; it was the seat of Queen Melisende of Jerusalem (1105–61) through the 1150s. The city was captured by Saladin in 1187.

Jacob's daughter was raped . . . slew many men: a reference to the rape of Dinah by Shechem and the vengeance of her brothers, Simeon and Levi (Genesis 34).

Garrison: 'Garrison' is Mandeville's rendering of Gerizim. The Samaritans regard it, rather than Jerusalem's Temple Mount, as the location chosen by God for a holy sanctuary.

Valley of Dothan: 2 Kings [2 Samuel] 6: 13.

pit is there . . . they sold him: Genesis 37: 20.

Sichar: John 4: 15 ('a city in Samaria').

St John the Baptist . . . beside the Dead Sea: there was an ornate cathedral church of St John the Baptist at Sebastiya (Palestine) near Nablus, and the tradition involving the tombs of Elisha and Obadiah was established by the sixth century (*CCKJ* 2. 283). Mandeville follows the biblical account in locating John the Baptist's execution at Machaerus, present-day Muqawir (Jordan).

the finger with which St John . . . the Lamb of God: John 1: 29, 1: 36; St John the Baptist's index finger was variously claimed, including at Lô and St-Jean-du-Doigt. A reliquary now in the Nelson-Atkins Museum in Kansas City was made for Cosimo de Medici's relic of this finger, which he was given by the Pope and which he bequeathed to the Florence baptistery in 1419.

St Thecla the Virgin . . . made to it: whilst not mentioned in the Vulgate Bible, St Thecla became widely venerated. Mandeville's account of Thecla's escape seems to refer to her journey into the Alps (*GL* 2. 139).

The head of St John the Baptist . . . St John the Bishop: the Cathedral of Our Lady at Amiens (France) continues to claim the relic, brought by a Crusader from Constantinople, of part of St John's skull, for which the cathedral was rebuilt in the early thirteenth century. Other traditions locate parts of the skull at Genoa (the Cappella del San Giovanni Battista in the Cattedrale di San Lorenzo), the relics of which were acquired around the time of the First Crusade, and Rome (San Silvestro in Capite), which claimed the head from the twelfth century. St John 'the Bishop' refers to John Chrysostom (347–407), the relics of whom were taken to Rome following the sack of Constantinople in 1204; Chrysostom's skull was also claimed by the Vatopedi monastery (Greece), and was later held at the Moscow Kremlin.

53 *I don't know, but God knows*: a comment in the Anglo-French source, 'wherever one worships it, the good St John willingly accepts it' (*Livre*, 234), was not translated into English, but characteristically makes clear that sincere devotion is more important than 'correct' dogma or ritual.

Jacob's Well: John 4: 5, and a Crusader pilgrimage site (*CCKJ* 1. 258–64). Now within the monastery of St Photina at Bir Ya'qub (Palestine), near Nablus.

54 *Jews' letters*: most of the names of the letters given by Mandeville are correct or almost correct and are largely in the order of the Hebrew alphabet, but the shapes of the letters bear no resemblance to Hebrew script. However, in Charles V of France's 1371 French manuscript of Mandeville a scribe familiar with correct Hebrew was employed. See Kupfer, '"letres . . . plus vrayes"'.

'A serpent shall come out of Babylon that will devour the whole world': this is not a biblical quotation. It may come from medieval Antichrist literature, based on the image of the serpent (*coluber*), which in Middle English manuscripts is transformed into a dove (*columba*)! The quotation employs the apocalyptic image of the beast of Babylon (Apocalypse [Revelation] 17). See e.g. Job 26: 13 ('His spirit hath adorned the heavens, and his obstetric hand brought forth the winding serpent'), Amos 5: 19 ('As if a man should flee from the face of a lion, and a bear should meet him: or enter into the house, and lean with his hand upon the wall, and a serpent should bite him'), Jeremias 51: 34 ('Nabuchodonosor king of Babylon hath eaten me up, he hath devoured me: he hath made me as an empty vessel: he hath swallowed me up like a dragon, he hath filled his belly with my delicate meats, and he hath cast me out').

'Woe to thee Corozain . . . Woe to thee Capharnaum': Matthew 11: 21.

Canaanite woman: Matthew 15: 21–8.

His first miracle . . . water into wine: John 2: 1–12.

fourteen years old: this age was frequently given, e.g. *GL* 1. 197.

'Hail, Mary, full of grace, the Lord is with thee': Luke 1: 28.

55 *'flower of the garden'*: not the correct Hebrew etymology but rather a medieval invention, here taken from John of Würzburg (see Deluz, *Jehan de Mandeville*, 458).

Our Lord's Blood: there was a medieval pilgrimage site near Nazareth called Our Lord's Leap, celebrating this non-biblical incident. Its medieval French name, *Saut Nostre Seignur* ('Our Lord's Leap'), is given in multiple manuscripts as *sang Nostre Seignur* ('Our Lord's Blood'), hence

Mandeville's place-name. Mandeville's place-name better reflects later medieval ideas of the passive, suffering Christ than the active agency of the earlier name.

'He passing through the midst of them, went His way': Luke 4: 30.

'Let fear and dread fall . . . which thou hast possessed': Exodus 15: 16 so not, in fact, from the psalter.

You need to be aware . . . she lived for twenty-four years: this paragraph reflects the medieval additions to the life of Mary; *GL* 2. 77–98.

'it is good for us to be here: and let us make three tabernacles': Mark 9: 4; Luke 9: 33.

Our Lord revived the widow's only son: one of Christ's miracles (Luke 7: 11–17). This site is now at the village of Na'in (Israel).

56 *Our Lord walked with dry feet*: John 6: 16–21.

'O thou of little faith, why didst thou doubt?': Matthew 14: 31.

'and they knew Him in the breaking of the bread': Luke 24: 35. Mandeville was one of several writers to locate Christ's post-Resurrection appearance in Tiberias; see *CCKJ* 2. 360. Mandeville is referring here to the Crusader-era church of St Nicholas (now the church of St Peter), which still stands in Tiberias (Israel).

Arabian Desert: the Anglo-French text here includes a note on measurements of distance, to the effect that the narrator is counting in 'our' miles, which are not the same as those of Gascony, Provence, or Germany, which are larger (*Livre*, 246).

Jacobites: a branch of the Syriac Orthodox Church (see note to p. 57), actually named after their founder Jacob Baradaeus (d. 578), Bishop of Edessa.

'I will give praise to thee, O Lord, with my whole heart': Psalms 9: 2[1].

'I have acknowledged my sin to thee': Psalms 31[32]: 5.

'Thou art my God, and I will praise thee': Psalms 117[118]: 28.

'For the thought of man shall give praise to thee': Psalms 75[76]: 11[10]. In this and two of the preceding three quotations Mandeville translates the verb *confiteor* (literally, 'to confess') as 'to shrive'; the Douay–Rheims translation uses the more ambiguous 'to praise', which I have retained here.

'Whosoever acknowledges his sins . . . to be forgiven': actually paraphrasing Proverbs 28: 13. As Deluz and Higgins have identified, Mandeville's source is the eighth-century *Liber scintillarum* (*Book of Sparks*) of Defensor de Ligugé (fl. *c.*700), a collection of moral sentences taken from biblical and patristic sources. See *Liber scintillarum/Livre d'Etincelles*, ed. and trans. Henri Rochais, Sources Chrétiennes 77 (Paris, 1961), 158–9. As Deluz points out (*Livre*, 252 n. 42), this section is animated by fourteenth-century English controversies about the sacrament of penance, as auricular confession to a priest had become firmly attached to the sacrament of the Eucharist.

56 *'Our Lord pays more heed to thoughts than to words'*: *Liber scintillarum*, ed. and trans. Rochais, 166–7.

57 *'Sins that were done . . . conceived in the heart'*: *Liber scintillarum*, ed. and trans. Rochais, 162–3.

Syrians: Maronite Christians who, since the twelfth-century Crusades, maintain an Eastern rite but are in communion with the Roman Church. The Anglo-French text adds that their faith is 'between ours and that of the Greeks' (*Livre*, 249).

Girdling Christians: the independent Syriac Orthodox Christians, whose vestments include girdles. In early medieval times some Islamic rulers had compelled Christians and Jews to wear distinctive leather girdles. Mandeville is apparently repeating earlier accounts of these girdled Christians.

others called Nestorians . . . land of Prester John: various Christian movements, often considered heretical in the West. Nestorianism (named after Nestorius of Constantinople, d. *c.*451) held that Christ had two separate natures, human and divine. Arianism (named after Arius, d. *c.*336) regarded the Christ as Son of God as subordinate to God. Both movements were therefore in conflict with Catholic teaching of the unity of the Trinity. On the Nubians, see Mandeville's description at p. 25. By the Gregorians Mandeville refers to the Armenian Apostolic Church, sometimes called after St Gregory the Enlightener (d. *c.*331), who converted Armenia to Christianity. On the Christian religion of Prester John see pp. 107–8.

Damascus: the major city of the region north of the Crusader kingdom, Damascus was never conquered by the Crusaders. At the time Mandeville was writing it was a provincial capital of the Mamluk empire.

58 *Eliezar of Damascus . . . founded this city*: Genesis 15: 2.

Cain slew his brother Abel: Genesis 4: 1–8.

Mount Seir: referred to several times in the Old Testament (Genesis 36: 8; Joshua 24: 4; Deuteronomy 2: 12; 1 Paralipomenon [1 Chronicles] 4: 42–3; Ezekiel 35: 10), to the south of Jerusalem rather than the north as Mandeville suggests.

Nostre Dame de Gardemarche: the monastery church of Our Lady of Saidnaiya (Syria). Mandeville's account, including the miraculous panel, closely follows that given by Burchard of Strasbourg, visiting in 1175, which was repeated in many other accounts. The monastery endured long after the Crusader kingdom, with various travellers (James of Verona, Nicolas of Poggibonsi, Ludolph of Sudheim, Niccolò Frescobaldi) visiting in the fourteenth century. See *CCKJ* 2. 220.

Arqa: a biblical site (Genesis 10: 17), and the site of the Crusader fortress; now Tel Arqa (Lebanon).

59 *Corfu*: ruled by various western powers in the Middle Ages, including the Angevins, the Genoese, and, for the most part, the Venetians.

Port Myroch or Vlorë or Durrës: Port Myroch may be a corruption of the Slavonic or Turkish names, respectively Drač or Dıraç, for the port of Durrës (Albania). Durrës (Durazzo) passed between many different rulers in the thirteenth and fourteenth centuries, including the Venetians, the Hohenstaufen kings of Sicily, the Serbs, and the Angevins. Between 1346 and 1417 Vlorë (Albania) was a Christian principality ('Valona'), a wealthy trading-post en route to Venice. It was taken by the Ottomans in 1417.

At Mount Modein rests the Machabee prophet: from the twelfth century, Latrun, where there was a large Crusader castle, became identified with the Machabee city of Modein ('Modin', 1 Machabees 2: 1); Mandeville follows Niccolò of Poggibonsi (writing in the 1340s) in locating Machabee tombs there. See *CCKJ* 2. 6.

Tekoa . . . Amos came from: Amos 1: 1.

Constantinople: now Istanbul (Turkey). The great capital of the Byzantine empire; from 1259 until its fall to the Ottomans in 1453 ruled by the Orthodox Christian Palaiologan dynasty.

St George's Arm: i.e. the Bosphorus, the strait at Istanbul from the Mediterranean Sea into the Black Sea.

Pulverale . . . Sinop: Pulverale was apparently a port on the Bosphorus or Black Sea; Sinop (Turkey) is a town on the Black Sea coast that was, from 1261 to 1458, an independent emirate. The error-strewn itinerary in the following paragraphs is taken from Albert of Aix's twelfth-century description of Heraclea and Konya given in *History of the First Crusade* (*Livre*, 270 n. 20); the names of the towns, rivers, and valleys have become confused and bear little relation to actual geography.

60 *the Lake*: Iznik stands not on a river but on the Sea of Nicaea (Lake Iznik); the Middle English word Mandeville uses here, 'Lay', simply means 'lake'.

Mornaunt Alps: a corruption of the Anglo-French *Noire Mont*, possibly referring to Kara Dağ ('Black Mountain'), a volcanic mountain in Turkey.

Edessa: called *Rages* by the Crusaders (*Ruha* in Arabic), now Şanlıurfa (Turkey). The capital of a twelfth-century Crusader county.

Roman Plain on the coast of the Roman Sea: conventional terminology for Asia Minor.

Maraş and Artah: Maraş (or Kahramanmaraş, Turkey) is the ancient town of Germanica Caesarea and was briefly a Crusader possession; Artah (Syria) is a small settlement on the River Orontes, the site of a Crusader fort.

River Ferne, which is also called Pharphar: a description of the River Orontes; Pharphar is a biblical river (4 Kings [2 Kings] 5: 12).

Abana: a biblical river: 2 Kings [2 Samuel] 5: 12, identified with the River Barada (Syria).

60 *St Eustace (sometimes called Placidus)*: a popular medieval saint, Eustace's Roman name was Placidus prior to his conversion. *GL* 2. 266–9.

Antioch: an important ancient city and centre of early Christianity, near present-day Antakya (Turkey). The city was taken by the Crusaders in 1098 and fell to Sultan Baibars in 1268.

River Ferne flows into the sea: located at the mouth of the River Orontes, St Symeon, now Samandağ (Turkey), was the main port for Antioch.

Baalbek: a town in the Bekaa Valley (Lebanon) with extensive Roman remains, repeatedly fought over in the Middle Ages. The Crusaders never managed to take it.

Pilgrim Castle: the Crusader fortress at 'Atlit (Israel), a few miles south of Haifa, was known in the Middle Ages as Chastiau Pélerin, literally Pilgrim Castle. See also p. 19.

61 *Tartary*: Tartary describes a large region in the central Asian steppes to the east of the Caspian Sea. The account of Tartary is largely derived from Vincent of Beauvais's *Speculum historiale*, itself based on the account by John of Plano Carpini (d. 1252), who visited the Great Khan; see G. Guzman, 'The Encyclopedist Vincent of Beauvais and his Mongol Extracts from John of Plano Carpini and Simon of Saint-Quentin', *Speculum*, 49 (1974), 287–397.

The prince of this region . . . a city called Orda: Batu Khan (*c.*1207–55) was a Mongol ruler and founder of the Golden Horde ('Orda'), the sub-khanate of the Mongol Empire. Batu was a grandson of Genghis Khan (1162–1227). 'Batu' derives from the Mongolian word for 'firm'; horde comes from the Turkic word *ordu*, for army camp. The 'capital' of the Golden Horde was at Old Sarai (probably on the Volga river, near Astrakhan (Russia)) then, from *c.*1300, New Sarai (today Kolobovka), near Volgograd (Russia).

Russia and Nevelond and the kingdoms of Krakow and Lithuania: reflecting the main powers in the fourteenth-century Baltic, of Russia (vassal states of the Mongol Horde, and the Novgorod republic), Nevelond/Livonia (see p. 7), and the kingdoms of Poland and Lithuania.

Gasten: Deluz (*Livre*, 271) identifies this with Arasten, an eastern land mentioned in *chansons de geste*.

62 *'Kera! Kera! Kera!'*: various theories have been put forward for the origins of this war-cry. Deluz (*Livre*, 271 n. 36) suggests a Russian war-cry *houra* (presumably from the interjection *ura*, analogous to the English 'hurrah', and later used as a Cossack shout of attack), Seymour (*Defective*, 150) the Persian *khar* ('trouble'). See *OED*, 'hurrah, hurray'.

Massap . . . Harme: see p. 38.

those who are good . . . still remains virgins: whilst the Qur'an was available in Latin translation in the medieval West, Mandeville's material on the Qur'an in these paragraphs is taken from William of Tripoli's *Treatise on the State of the Saracens*, with material from Vincent of Beauvais and

Jacques de Vitry. See Higgins, *Writing East*, 113–18; John V. Tolan, *Saracens: Islam in the Medieval European Imagination* (New York, 2002).

63 *Takina*: the story of Takina, taken from William of Tripoli, is adapted from the spirit of God which appeared at the birth of Jesus according to Islamic writings (sura 19: 16–33, Qur'an, 191–2); Takina's name is, according to Deluz (*Livre*, 284 n. 5), from the word Arabic *taki* ('fear of god').

'Don't be afraid, Mary': Luke 1: 30.

Missus est angelus Gabriel: Luke 1: 26.

fast for one entire month: the Islamic festival of Ramadan, commemorating the month in which the first verses of the Qur'an were revealed to Muhammad.

65 *'For the letter killeth, but the spirit quickeneth'*: 2 Corinthians 3: 6.

66 *They spoke French . . . so did the Sultan*: here, the narrative's language of his 'own country' is implicitly French, in contrast to statements elsewhere (especially p. 68) that the narrator's native tongue is English.

67 *Khadija*: Mohammed's first wife, Khadijah al-Kubra (Khadija the Great), *c.*555–619 CE.

620: as with most of Mandeville's dates, there is considerable scribal variation here. In Anglo-French manuscripts the date appears often as 610. Historically, Muhammad's journey to Medina, the *hijra*, is dated to 622.

tribe of Ishmael . . . his handmaiden Hagar: Genesis 16: 15.

Saracens, after Sarah: following *Etymologies*, 195. The story of Sarah and Hagar is in Genesis 16.

68 *chief imam*: the Anglo-French and Middle English words used (*'archiflamins'*, 'archesleven') suggest Roman pagan priests, thus describing Islam in terms of paganism.

'There is no God but one alone and Muhammad is his messenger': Mandeville's Latinized version of the Islamic creed, the Arabic *shahada*.

we have in England . . . thorn and yogh: these two letters were normal features of fourteenth-century English. Thorn, runic in origin, was used where we now use 'th' (so 'þe' for 'the'). Yogh could represent several sounds, often where a Modern English word has a 'y' or 'gh' (so 'ȝit' for 'yet', 'niȝt' for 'night'). This is one of Mandeville's statements suggesting an English, rather than Continental, origin of his text. The Saracen letter-names given by Mandeville are also inaccurate, much more so than his Hebrew alphabet (p. 54).

four rivers, which come from the Earthly Paradise: this information, frequently reproduced on medieval world-maps, describes the four rivers—Euphrates, Tigris, Nile (Gehon), and Ganges (Phison)—described in Genesis 2: 10–14: 'And a river went out of the place of pleasure to water paradise, which from thence is divided into four heads. The name of the one is Phison: that is it which compasseth all the land of Hevilath, where gold groweth. And the gold of that land is very good: there is found bdellium, and the onyx stone. And the name of the second river is Gehon: the same is it that compasseth all the land of Ethiopia. And the name of the third river is Tigris: the same passeth along by the Assyrians. And the fourth river is Euphrates.' On the Ganges/Phison, see p. 120. See Alessandro Scafi, *Mapping Paradise: A History of Heaven on Earth* (London, 2006).

69 *le Port de Pounce*: i.e. the Port on the Pontus or the Gate to the Pontus; *Pontus Euxinus* ('the Hospitable Sea') was the Classical name for the Black Sea.

Quicumque uult: the Athanasian Creed, beginning with the words 'Whoever will be saved'. This Creed is not a psalm but rather a Christian statement of belief in the Trinity.

Emperor of Trebizond: there was a medieval Empire of Trebizond (1204–1461), a Byzantine successor state; see Anthony Bryer, *The Empire of Trebizond and the Pontos* (London, 1980).

Le Castel d'Épervier: i.e. Castle Sparrowhawk. This detour knits 'historical' and 'romance' elements, its setting describing the castle at Kızkalesi (Turkey), an ancestral seat of the author of Mandeville's ultimate source, Haiton of Armenia's *Flor des estoires de la terre d'Orient* (*c.*1305) which had been translated by Jan de Langhe.

70 *Erzerum*: Erzerum (Turkey), the ancient city of Theodosiopolis, was sacked by the Mongols in 1242.

mountain called Ararat; the Jews call this Thano: in the Hebrew Bible the place where the Ark came to rest is called *Harei Ararat* ('the Ararat mountains', Genesis 8: 4, or 'Armenian mountains' in the Vulgate). *Thano* is possibly a corruption of the Persian name *kuh-i-nuh* ('Noah's hill').

Noah said Benedicite: this refers to a late but apparently popular and distinctly Anglo-French addition to the legend of Noah, first found in the Anglo-Norman glosses of *Queen Mary's Psalter* (a deluxe manuscript dating from around 1300) and later in Mystery plays. See Anna Jean Mill, 'Noah's Wife Again', *PMLA* 5 (1941), 613–26, at 620–2.

71 *Cardabago*: apparently a reference to the palace gardens at Isfahan (Iran); 'Cardabago' comes from the Persian *chau bagh*, 'royal gardens' or *chahar bagh*, 'four gardens'. The Anglo-French text supplies some fanciful information here on *char Dabago* (literally 'Dabago meat') and the Persian word for meat (*Livre*, 298 n. 18).

Kenarah: Mandeville is describing the ancient ruins of the deserted city of Persepolis (Iran), dating from the third to fifth centuries BCE; Kenarah is the Persian town nearby. Mandeville's account is a condensed version of that given by Odoric of Pordenone.

Job, Zara's son, was a pagan: Genesis 36: 33. As Deluz notes, this story is useful in showing God's charitable view of pagans (*Livre*, 310 n. 3).

manna: sweet, medicinal plant preparations—of manna gum (*Eucalyptus viminalis*) and manna ash (*Fraxinus ornus*)—were described in medieval herbals; here they are conflated with the biblical, miraculous manna (Exodus 16: 14).

72 *Amazonia*: described since Herodotus, the female warriors of Amazonia (or 'Femenye') were frequently mentioned in medieval literature, including Alexander romances, Chaucer's 'Knight's Tale', Lydgate's *Troy Book*, and Ariosto's *Orlando Furioso*. See John Block Friedman, *The Monstrous Races in Medieval Art and Thought*, 2nd edn. (Syracuse, NY, 2007), 129–35. The Spanish explorer Francisco de Orellana (d. 1546) named the river in South America after the Amazons on account of a group of bellicose women he encountered there.

they killed all the men left in their country: the Anglo-French text explains that these women wanted all the other women in the country to be widows as they were.

Alexandria: Alexander the Great (356–323 BCE) did found multiple cities called Alexandria; the city suggested here is Merv (Turkmenistan), indicated by Mandeville's naming of the region as Turmagut. This is a corrupt version of the name Terra Margine, or Margiana, the region's Latin name.

In Ethiopia there are . . . body from the sun: like many of Mandeville's monstrous peoples, the description of the 'sciapod', the monster with the podiatric sunshade, is from Pliny (*Natural History*, ed. and trans. Healy, 78) via Vincent of Beauvais's *Speculum historiale*.

73 *city of Saba . . . Bethlehem reigned there*: in later medieval art it was common to represent one magus as black; see Paul Kaplan, *The Rise of the Black Magus in Western Art* (Ann Arbor, Mich., 1995), 1–69. Saba (Sheba) is mentioned in 3 Kings [1 Kings] 10.

multiply and grow through the years: many medieval accounts of rocks and minerals suggest that they are alive. On medieval descriptions of the liveliness and expressiveness of stone, see Jeffrey Jerome Cohen, 'Stories of Stone', *Postmedieval*, 1 (2010), 56–63.

May-dew: dew gathered on May Day or during May was held to have medicinal qualities on account of it being impregnated with the 'vegetative' forces of spring.

75 *Hormuz*: a small island (now part of Iran) in the Persian Gulf.

men's bollocks hang . . . physical degeneracy: the Anglo-French version is more polite here: where the Middle English records 'men ballokez', the Anglo-French describes *ly perpendicles de homme, videlicit testiculi*—'male hangers, that is to say, testicles'—hanging down to the knee (*Livre*, 313).

the adamantine rocks . . . pull the ships towards them: Bartholomew's encyclopedia describes adamantine as an Indian stone which draws iron 'by a maner of violence' towards it (*Properties*, 2. 833). See also p. 107.

Thana: now a suburb of Mumbai (India), this ancient coastal city on Salsette Island was visited by Mandeville's source, Odoric of Pordenone, after Hormuz.

75 *a great difference between an effigy and an idol*: the correct form of mimetic representation was evidently an abiding, if confused, concern of Mandeville's, returned to several times: see pp. 75–7, 78, 86, 95, 121, 123. In the Anglo-French source, the suggestion is clearer that simulacra represent a known thing, whereas idols represent unnatural imaginings. The Middle English word used for 'effigy' is 'symylacris', from the Latin *simulacrum* via Old French *simulacre*, a representation. 'Symylacris' also described 'idols' in fourteenth-century English: for example, the Wycliffite Bible renders the line, 'Keep yourselves from idols' (1 John 5: 21) as both 'kepe ȝe fro simulacris' and 'kepe ye you fro maumetis' (a 'maumet' is a pagan idol or deity, the word being derived from 'Muhammad').

76 *Kollam*: also known as Quilon (India), a city on the Malabar coast.

Archiprotapapaton: this invented word comprises three European words to describe a senior cleric (*arch* (Latin 'chief'), *proto* (Greek 'foremost'), *papa* (Latin, Italian, 'pope' and 'father')). The word is used in the *Letter of Prester John* (see Michael Uebel, *Ecstatic Transformation: On the Uses of Alterity in the Middle Ages* (Basingstoke, 2005), 159).

'gall': i.e. cattle gall or bile, used as paint and for medicinal purposes.

77 *Ma'bar*: a sultanate province, based on the city of Madurai (India).

Calamy: medieval traditions held that St Thomas's body was buried in the city of Mylapore, near Chennai (India). The body was translated to Edessa/Şanlıurfa in the third century.

'be not faithless, but believing': John 20: 27.

St James: the shrine of St James at Santiago di Compostela (Spain); see note to p. 46.

78 *Lamuri*: this name refers to Sumatra (Indonesia), in Middle English 'Lamory', from its medieval Arabic name *Lamri* or *Lamuri*, where Arab traders were based.

79 *'Increase and multiply, and fill the earth'*: Genesis 1: 28.

Tramontana: i.e. the North, Pole or Tramontane Star. The names of this star, and the Antarctic or Anteryk star mentioned subsequently, are taken from the *De sphaera* of the Irish-Norman scholar John of Holywood [Sacrobosco], *c.*1195–1256, who taught at the University of Paris. On the importance of this text, which was widely read in fourteenth-century England, see W. B. Veazie, 'Chaucer's Textbook of Astronomy: Johannes de Sacrobosco', *University of Colorado Studies in the Humanities (B)*, 1 (1940), 169–82.

Antarctic: the Middle English text uses the word 'Anteryk' (Anglo-French *Antartik*). The southern hemisphere has, for the last two millennia, lacked an easily recognizable pole star.

above and below: one of several clear indications in this text that, contrary to popular belief, medieval people did not believe the Earth was flat but knew full well that it was round. For a witty and clear discussion see Umberto Eco, *Serendipities: Language and Lunacy*, trans. William Weaver (London, 1999), 5–13. The scribe of Queen's College MS 383 glossed this passage 'Roundenesse of the erthe' (f. 86v), showing unequivocally how medieval readers understood this. Mandeville's assertion of the reachable, habitable Antipodes rejects Augustine's position, set out in *The City of God against the Pagans* (ed. and trans. R. W. Dyson (Cambridge, 1998), 710–11), that humanity descending from Adam could not have reached the southern hemisphere; 'there is no reason to believe such men exist', says Augustine. See also Nicholás Wey Gómez, *The Tropics of Empire: Why Columbus Travelled South to the Indies* (Cambridge, Mass., 2008), 122–5.

what I've seen: despite the eyewitness suasions, the account of the astrolabe largely follows Holywood's *De sphaera*, although the measurements given are different.

minutes: i.e. the angular measurement (minute of arc).

80 *Those people who live . . . facing them*: this is a rather unclear exposition of the medieval idea that the world was divided into four equal quarters facing each other. It is perhaps significant that the anticlimax of Mandeville's journey, as our narrator fails to reach Paradise, happens in a place precisely parallel to, or opposite, England.

one travelling from Scotland . . . keeps climbing: both medieval geography and spirituality held that the journey to Jerusalem was an ascent; Jerusalem is depicted as a mount, with Calvary as a final ascent, a small hill or flight of stairs.

'God hath wrought salvation in the midst of the earth': Psalm 73[74]: 12. Whilst there are, of course, shadows in Jerusalem, this belief was frequently repeated in the Middle Ages; see e.g. *Otia*, 864–5.

81 *the island he had visited before*: a similar story about a sailor from Bristol can be found in *Otia*, 82–3.

just as we think . . . we are underneath them!: the English account conflates a longer passage in the Anglo-French text which describes how one cannot fall off the Earth and restates that the Earth is round, circumnavigable, and firmly attached.

'Do not be afraid of me, who hung the earth from nothing': echoing Job 26: 7.

20,425 miles, according to the opinions of ancient wise men: Mandeville reiterates the standard Ptolemaic measurements here, found in a number of his known sources (Brunetto Latini, John of Holywood); Deluz (*Livre*, 342) notes how this measurement would be responsible for Christopher Columbus' momentous 'error' in travelling south and west to India.

82 *'climates'*: i.e. the celestial zone above one of the terrestrial climates.

so low in the east: the Ptolemaic climates extend only to about 51 degrees, so England, at about 51.5 degrees north, is just beyond its scope.

Sumatra: translating the Middle English 'Somober' (Anglo-French *Sumobor*) and given as 'Sinohora' by Odoric, this is likely to be Sumatra (in the fourteenth century, the Islamic kingdom of Samudera or Pasai). See also on Lamuri, note to p. 78.

82 *Java*: a large island, now part of Indonesia. At the time Mandeville was writing, Java was part of the Majapahit empire (the religions of which were Hinduism, Buddhism, and animism). Its wealth was partly based on trade between Arabia and China, especially, as Mandeville suggests, through spices. See Robert Cribb and Audrey Kahin, *Historical Dictionary of Indonesia* (Lanham, Md., 2004), 250.

You should be aware that nutmeg yields mace: perplexingly, the English text omits the reasons, given in the Anglo-French text (*Livre*, 344), of why one needs to know this: namely, that nutmeg has a covering (the mace) that is only ready once the nutmeg is mature.

83 *defeated in battle the Great Khan of Cathay*: Kubla Khan attacked Java in 1292–3, which led to a period of conflict with the Mongols. See Cribb and Kahin, *Historical Dictionary of Indonesia*, 250.

leaves: the original antidote seems to have been faeces (*fiens*, *Livre*, 345), but in most Anglo-French and Middle English manuscripts this is changed to leaves (*foilles*, 'leeuys').

no antidote or medicine can help: the Anglo-French source adds that a Jew told Mandeville that the Jews once planned to poison Christendom using this deadly venom (*Livre*, 345–6), possibly a reference to similar anti-Jewish allegations which surfaced in 1348–9 during the catastrophic outbreak of the Black Death in Europe.

four hundred . . . elephants: a more conservative rendering of the Anglo-French's 14,000 elephants (*Livre*, 347), itself taken from Odoric! On medieval ideas of the elephant see the description in the *Bestiary* (http://www.abdn.ac.uk/bestiary/translat/10r.hti).

a castle placed on the elephants . . . in this land: the elephant with a 'castle' on its back was a staple of the medieval bestiary; 'The Persians and Indians, carried in wooden towers on [elephants'] backs, fight with javelins as from a wall' (http://www.abdn.ac.uk/bestiary/translat/10r.hti).

85 *Tracota*: the land of troglodytes (Middle English 'trogodite', Latin *troglodyta*), from which the island's name derives. Similar troglodytes, but living in Ethiopia, are described in *Properties*, 2. 755.

dogs' heads: the Anglo-French text calls these people *Canapholez* (i.e. 'dog-head'), the Cynocephali of Classical lore. Pliny describes 'men with dogs' heads who are covered with wild beasts' skins; they bark instead of speaking' (*Natural History*, ed. and trans. Healy, 78), and Augustine asks in *The City of God* (ed. and trans. Dyson, 708), 'what am I to say of those dog-headed men whose dogs' heads and actual barking show that they are more beasts than men?'

If they capture . . . send him to their king: the Anglo-French text (*Livre*, 351), on the other hand, says that the Natumeranites eat those they capture. Evidently, Mandeville's references to cannibalism were not to all tastes.

amber Paternoster: a set of rosary beads. The beads would indicate when to say the *Paternoster*, the Lord's Prayer.

Ceylon: translating the Middle English name 'Sylha', now Sri Lanka, as described by Odoric of Pordenone. An important stop on the medieval silk and spice routes, at the time Mandeville was writing the island was divided into several small kingdoms.

86 *ointment*: the Anglo-French text describes this as a kind of lemon juice but, as lemons were largely unknown in England, this evidently meant little to medieval readers and scribes made this a more generic ointment. Other English versions of Mandeville describe the lemon as 'a kind of fruit, like a small peach'.

'Wonderful are the surges of the sea': Psalm 92[93]: 4.

fifty-four islands: at this point, the travel narrative becomes more of a list. The kinds of peoples described, often depicted in manuscripts of Mandeville's *Book*, mostly come from Odoric of Pordenone, supplemented by material from Vincent of Beauvais's *Speculum naturale* and *Speculum historiale* and Brunetto Latini's *Livres dou Trésor*.

87 *Manzi*: derived from an ancient China name for southern China, literally 'southern barbarians'.

88 *crowns*: the Anglo-French text (*Livre*, 367 n. 9) gives *corne* ('horn'), transformed by many scribes into *couronne* ('crown').

loires: otters. Mandeville, or the scribes of his *Book*, retained this French name and did not use the familiar Anglo-French or Middle English words for otter (*loutre*, 'oter'), and seem not to have recognized this as the animal they were describing.

bygoun: this name likely comes from the Chinese words *bai-jiu*, a distilled beverage, or *bai-gan*, a fine, white alcoholic drink.

Religious men, Christian friars, devout men, live there: friars had been established in missionary communities in Khan-Balic (Beijing) since before 1307, when the bull *Rex regum* appointed an archbishop of Khan-Balic and appointed seven Franciscans as his suffragans. Mandeville's source, Odoric of Pordenone, arrived in China *c.*1326. See Richard Foltz, *Religions of the Silk Road* (Basingstoke, 1999); Jackson, *Mongols and the West*, 256–68.

89 *Pygmieland*: the land of little people, frequently described; see too Pliny (*Natural History*, ed. and trans. Healy, 79), Isidore (*Etymologies*, 244), and Bartholomew (*Properties*, 2. 797).

Cadom: the description is of the Mongol imperial court of Khan-Balic or Tatu (now Beijing); Mandeville's name for it, 'Cadom', is possibly derived from the Anglo-French name *Caydo*, itself a rendering of 'Tatu'.

91 *irachite*: it is unclear which gem Mandeville refers to here. The Middle English words used ('garant', 'gerand') translate the Anglo-French *geracite*; this seems to be the 'irachite'—a stone which protects its owner from being bitten by flies—described in lapidaries (*Properties*, 2. 880).

war: the thirteenth-century wars referred to here come from Odoric's account.

92 *Ham was the one . . . father up again*: Genesis 9: 21–3.

On account of this Ham, the Emperor calls himself Khan: the etymologies of the two nouns are unrelated, Ham being a Semitic proper noun, possibly an Egyptian or Ethiopian toponym, the Turkic (via Arabic and Persian) *khan* meaning lord or prince.

eight years ago: the manuscripts give various dates here. Genghis Khan's elevation to the head of the Mongol tribes took place in 1206.

the first was called Tartary . . . the seventh Tibet: Mandeville's list of peoples is derived from Haiton of Armenia's *Flor des estoires* via Odoric, as is the section on Genghis Khan which follows. Deluz, *Jehan de Mandeville*, 478–80.

Chaungwise: Mandeville's rendering of Genghis or Chingis Khan (d. 1227); in France and England the honorific 'Khan' was elided with 'Chingis' to make *Chan-guys* (Anglo-French) or 'Chaungwise' (Middle English).

93 *Isakan*: the *Yassa* of Genghis Khan, a secret collection of wisdom and regulations, no copies of which survive, which was current throughout the Mongol empire.

94 *Chito Khan*: Genghis Khan was succeeded by his third son, Ögedei Khan (1189–1241). His oldest son was Jochi (1185–1226).

95 *camacas*: apparently a kind of fine, brocaded satin; its name may come from Camoca (Spain).

97 *Xanadu . . . Khan-Balic*: Shang-du and Khan-Balic (see note to p. 89), the Khan's summer and winter capitals. Although the text doesn't make us aware of it, Mandeville has already described this city earlier.

98 *lignum aloes*: literally 'aloe wood'; see p. 31.

Four elephants and four stallions go inside: the Anglo-French text (*Livre*, 398) makes clear that the chariot is pulled by these animals!

Veni creator spiritus: 'Come creator Spirit', a Latin Pentecost hymn sung at solemn events, including coronations and ordinations.

'neither shalt thou appear before me empty': Exodus 34: 20, mistranslated in the Middle English text.

99 *the Emperor's name was Kuyuk . . . third Charauk Khan*: these names can be traced back, via Vincent of Beauvais, to John of Plano Carpini's account of the Khanate in the 1240s. Mandeville's names here are, apart from that of Kuyuk or Güyük Khan (*c.*1206–48), awry.

100 *cuir-bouilli*: hardened leather which has been boiled in water and then moulded into shape. Cuir-bouilli was used for leather book-bindings in medieval Europe.

small eyes and little beards: understood, according to medieval physiognomical theory, as a sign of falseness and treachery; the Anglo-French text glosses this with the phrase *forme de visage faulx* (*Livre*, 410).

Next they say . . . do as I say: the Middle English Khan is rather more authoritarian than the version given in Anglo-French, in which the Khan gives his tribesmen the opportunity to *demoerer ou aler*, 'demur or leave' (*Livre*, 411).

101 *Tars*: the place-name here seems to be based on Tartary rather than Tarsus (the birthplace of St Paul) or Tarshish/Tharsis, a biblical seaport (3 Kings [1 Kings] 10: 22; Psalm 71[72]: 10; Jonah 1: 3). The Middle English romance *The King of Tars* (see http://auchinleck.nls.uk/mss/tars.html) features a Christian king and his daughter of Tars and the Saracen Sultan of Damascus.

Chorasmia: Chorasmia, or Khwarezm (today divided between Uzbekistan and Turkmenistan), home of an Indo-Iranian people, a medieval empire (1077–1231) and a vassal nation of the Mongol Khanate. Its capital, Gurganj/Urganch, was sacked by Genghis Khan in 1221 and destroyed by Timur the Great (1336–1405) in 1388.

Cumania: see p. 7; an area stretching from present-day Hungary through Ukraine.

River Ethel: understood to be the Volga, called the *Itil* or *Atil* in Turkic languages.

Maure, that is, the Black Sea: from its Greek name, Μαύρη Θάλασσα.

Port de Fer: now Derbent (Russia). This French name—literally Iron Gate—is connected to the Persian-derived name Derbent, from *Dar-band* ('closed gate'), and the city was long famous for its walls.

Sarai: simply 'palace' in Persian. See also notes to pp. 61, 102.

102 *Bukhara and Samarkand*: two major cities (now in Uzbekistan).

Sarmasse: this city is mentioned in the *Chanson d'Antioch* as being famous for its orchards (*Livre*, 425), but is not identified with any modern place. The place-name (given in Anglo-French as *Sarmasane*) is possibly a garbled version of the name Shiraz, one of the most important cities of later medieval Persia, but, as elsewhere in his book, Mandeville freely combines 'geographical' and romance topographies.

Tabriz: an important city, capital of a Mongol khanate stretching through what is now Iran, Iraq, and eastern Turkey.

Sarai and Karmanâ: perhaps Shiraz (Iran) and Karmanâ or Kermanshah (Iran).

103 *Shapur*: Shapur II (d. 379), Sassanian king of Persia, famous for persecuting Christians, founder of Nishapur (see p. 109).

'This is the Lord's doing: and it is wonderful in our eyes': Psalm 117[118]: 23.

104 *Mauretania*: a province of the Roman empire and a Classical kingdom with its capital at Tangier (formerly Mauretania Tingitana), Mauretania encompassed parts of modern-day Morocco and Algeria.

barnacles: Mandeville's account of the barnacle goose is common in medieval literature (e.g. *Otia*, 819–21, which says that this uniquely happens on the sea-shore near Faversham in Kent!). See Maaike van der Lugt, 'Animal légendaire et discours savant médiéval: la barnacle dans tous ses états', *Micrologus*, 8 (2000), 351–93.

104 *Caspian Mountains, which some people call Uber*: by 'Caspian' mountains Mandeville describes the Caucasus; the name 'Uber' comes from *ubera aquilonis*, the Breasts of the North, and appears in Alexander romances connected to Gog and Magog (see next note) as well as Classical sources.

Ten Tribes . . . Gog and Magog: the 'lost' tribes of Israel, the fate of which is not clearly described in the Bible. The name Gog and Magog comes from Ezekiel 38: 2. Medieval Christian traditions frequently connected the tribes with Prester John. The legend connecting Alexander to Gog and Magog is found in almost all versions of the Alexander romances, but the imprisoned peoples are sometimes Scythians, though in the later medieval period more usually Jews (D. J. A. Ross, *Alexander Historiatus* (London, 1963), 34–5). See further Andrew Gow, *The Red Jews: Antisemitism in an Apocalyptic Age, 1200–1600* (Leiden, 1994).

105 *lock . . . labour*: see pp. 101–2, for the related account of Alexander's Iron Gate at Derbent.

Queen of Armenia: given as the Queen of Amazonia in the Anglo-French text (*Livre*, 429).

106 *Bactria*: a Classical kingdom, at the eastern edge of the Persian region, south of present-day Samarkand (Uzbekistan).

trees here that bear wool . . . they make textiles: clearly a description of cotton, still known in several European languages, such as Danish, German and Swedish, as 'tree-wool'. See also p. 115.

Nisa: Seymour (*Defective*, 166) suggests the royal Indian city of Nishapur (Iran); Mandeville's form of the name may recall Nisa (Turkmenistan), the ancient Parthian capital and necropolis, described in many Greek texts.

107 *the adamantine stone would pull it towards him*: as in his account of the generation of diamonds, Mandeville regards stones as gendered entities.

Hormuz . . . it: another medieval invented etymology, here taken from Haiton of Armenia via Odoric (Deluz, *Jehan de Mandeville*, 484).

108 *pistake*: from the Latin *pistacia*, *psittacus*.

109 *irachite*: see p. 91.

Shush: Shush or Susa (Iran), an ancient Persian and Parthian city, destroyed in the early thirteenth century by invading Mongols. This description combines the *Letter of Prester John* with the account of the king's palace in the *Romance of Alexander* (Deluz, *Jehan de Mandeville*, 485).

sardonyx: a striped vermilion-and-white stone, thought to promote chastity; *Properties*, 2. 873.

His bed is fashioned out of sapphires . . . to conceive children: amongst the many qualities attributed to the sapphire was its power of chastity; *Properties*, 2. 871.

110 *Nearby Prester John's island . . . plenty of good things*: this paragraph is inserted from the Anglo-French text. In the Middle English text the scribe repeated an earlier line, about Shush's more temperate weather than Nisa's, in an example of the 'eye-skip' which was a professional hazard for medieval scribes.

Catolonabes: Seymour (*Defective*, 167) and Deluz (*Livre*, 485) suggest that Odoric was the source of Mandeville's story, ultimately a description of the breakaway Ismaili Assassin sect; Catolonabes is understood to be the Assassins' leader, Hassan i Sabbah, also known as *Sheikh al-Gebel* or 'The Old Man of the Mountain'. See too Higgins, *Writing East*, 193–5; Dorothee Metlitzki, *The Matter of Araby in Mediaeval England* (New Haven, 1977), 222–3. Catolonabes is here presented as a kind of Christian, and the story has much in common with medieval preachers' tales of false paradises: for example, that of the heretic who had a false vision of paradise but was converted by St Peter Martyr showing him the Host (*IE* 2544). As Metlitzki (*Matter of Araby*, 222) notes, 'The Old Man of the Mountain' and his brotherhood appear as a figure of speech in troubadour poetry, and the word *assassino* was used by Dante. Mandeville does not associate Catolonabes with Islam.

111 *'I will give you . . . a land flowing with milk and honey'*: Exodus 33: 3; Leviticus 20: 24.

made them drunk: the hashish described in the sources, from which the Assassins took their name, becomes an alcoholic beverage here.

River Phison: the Ganges; see p. 120.

112 *hazarding our bodies to pass through it*: translating the Middle English 'put oure bodyes in auenture', a phrase used in courtly literature at pivotal moments of danger.

113 *Beyond that valley*: here, and in the following list of marvels, Mandeville returns to Vincent of Beauvais's *Speculum historiale*, an extremely widely read encyclopedia.

basilisk: a legendary reptile in the medieval bestiary, it could kill with its glance; see the *Aberdeen Bestiary* account at http://www.abdn.ac.uk/bestiary/translat/66r.hti.

gadlibiriens: the name is Mandeville's (possibly derived from the Middle English noun 'gade', a fool, or 'gadeling', a rascal), but similar people are described in various authorities, back to Herodotus. The Anglo-French text translates this name as *fol desesperez*, 'hopeless fools' (*Livre*, 449).

114 *In this region*: in the following section Mandeville moves from 'ethnographic' information to natural history.

115 *girsant*: a kind of giraffe. The word seems to derive from the Arabic word *zarafah* (French *giraffe*; giraffe) assimilated to the Middle English 'elefaunt', 'elevaunt'.

115 *Island of Brahmins . . . Land of Faith*: the Brahmins were the priestly caste in Hinduism in the Indian subcontinent. Higgins, *Writing East*, 227–31, traces the source of Mandeville's interventions here to thirteenth-century Alexander romances.

116 *Synophe*: as Seymour (*Defective*, 182) suggests, this place-name derives from the 'naked philosophers'—gymnosophists—Alexander is said to have encountered in the East.

117 *'I shall write to him my manifold laws'*: Hosea 8: 12.

'And other sheep I have, that are not of this fold': John 10: 16.

'That which God hath cleansed, do not thou call common': Acts 10: 11–15.

Tree of the Sun . . . death to him: cf. *Otia*, 82–5; these trees 'supply answers to any who questions them. Alexander received oracles there concerning his wife and family, and also concerning his own death which was to occur when he went back to Babylon' (*Otia*, 85).

118 *Prester John*: this account is original to Mandeville, *Prester* simply meaning priest in Anglo-French (*prestre, prestir*).

Tabrobane: the ancient Greek name for Sri Lanka ('Trapobactane' in *Properties*, 2. 814–15).

119 *Orelle . . . Argete*: the mythical gold and silver islands of Greek mythology, details of which Mandeville probably took from Brunetto Latini's *Livres dou Trésor* but were anciently described by Pliny as 'Chryse' (derived from the Greek χρυσός, golden) and 'Argyre' (from ἄργυρος, silver). Orelle is a Frenchified name, replacing 'Chryse' with the French *or*, gold. Argete derives from the Anglo-French *Argite*, from *argent*, silver.

Canopus: the brightest star in the southern constellation.

120 *I can't really describe Paradise properly*: this paragraph on Paradise repeats some of the commonly held beliefs about Paradise, describing a garden at the 'top' of the Earth, close to the lunar sphere. See Scafi, *Mapping Paradise*, 163–76.

sphere of the moon: what Mandeville calls the moon's 'cercle', describing the concentric spheres believed to surround the Earth and carry with them in revolution the moon, sun, planets, and stars.

'gathering': *Etymologies*, 280.

'turbulent': *Etymologies*, 280; *Properties*, 1. 655.

tiger: *Etymologies*, 280–1; *Properties*, 1. 656.

'growing well': *Etymologies*, 281; *Properties*, 1. 656.

122 *'Come to aid, saints of God'*: from the Latin service for the commendation of a soul to God.

123 *'and all the ends of the earth fear him'*: Psalms 66[67]: 8[7].

'all nations shall serve him': Psalm 71[72]: 11.

book of Moses: i.e. the Pentateuch (Genesis, Exodus, Leviticus, Numbers, Deuteronomy), 'the Five Books of Moses'.

Chaco and Calo: from the Greek κακός, bad, and καλός, beautiful.

124 *come to rest*: the Anglo-French text adds that this rest has been imposed by gout (*Livre*, 479).

1332 . . . 1366 . . . thirty-four years: as above (p. 6), the dates vary in manuscripts, with Anglo-French texts tending to a departure date of 1322 and a return date of 1356.

the Pope: the pope at the time was John XXII (pope 1316–34), but he was at Avignon, where the papacy was based until 1377/8.

Mappa mundi: see Introduction, p. xv.

INDEX OF PLACES

Where clearly identifiable, places mentioned by Mandeville are listed here by their modern or English name, cross-referenced with the name given by Mandeville. Mountains and rivers are listed under their identifying name (e.g. 'Olympus, Mount').

GENERAL INDEX

The Oxford World's Classics Website

www.worldsclassics.co.uk

- Browse the full range of Oxford World's Classics online
- Sign up for our monthly e-alert to receive information on new titles
- Read extracts from the Introductions
- Listen to our editors and translators talk about the world's greatest literature with our Oxford World's Classics audio guides
- Join the conversation, follow us on Twitter at OWC_Oxford
- Teachers and lecturers can order inspection copies quickly and simply via our website

www.worldsclassics.co.uk

MORE ABOUT **OXFORD WORLD'S CLASSICS**

American Literature
British and Irish Literature
Children's Literature
Classics and Ancient Literature
Colonial Literature
Eastern Literature
European Literature
Gothic Literature
History
Medieval Literature
Oxford English Drama
Poetry
Philosophy
Politics
Religion
The Oxford Shakespeare

A SELECTION OF **OXFORD WORLD'S CLASSICS**

	The Anglo-Saxon World
	Beowulf
	Lancelot of the Lake
	The Paston Letters
	Sir Gawain and the Green Knight
	Tales of the Elders of Ireland
	York Mystery Plays
Geoffrey Chaucer	The Canterbury Tales Troilus and Criseyde
Henry of Huntingdon	The History of the English People 1000–1154
Jocelin of Brakelond	Chronicle of the Abbey of Bury St Edmunds
Guillaume de Lorris and Jean de Meun	The Romance of the Rose
William Langland	Piers Plowman
Sir Thomas Malory	Le Morte Darthur

A SELECTION OF OXFORD WORLD'S CLASSICS

	Bhagavad Gita
	The Bible Authorized King James Version *With Apocrypha*
	Dhammapada
	Dharmasūtras
	The Koran
	The Pañcatantra
	The Sauptikaparvan (from the Mahabharata)
	The Tale of Sinuhe and Other Ancient Egyptian Poems
	The Qur'an
	Upaniṣads
ANSELM OF CANTERBURY	**The Major Works**
THOMAS AQUINAS	**Selected Philosophical Writings**
AUGUSTINE	**The Confessions** **On Christian Teaching**
BEDE	**The Ecclesiastical History**
HEMACANDRA	**The Lives of the Jain Elders**
KĀLIDĀSA	**The Recognition of Śakuntalā**
MANJHAN	**Madhumalati**
ŚĀNTIDEVA	**The Bodhicaryāvatāra**